The Ritual of Forgetting

After Ever After

BOOK I : The Ritual of Forgetting

Mindi Meltz

LOGOSOPHIA BOOKS, LLC • ASHEVILLE, NC

AFTER EVER AFTER
BOOK ONE: THE RITUAL OF FORGETTING
By MINDI MELTZ

LOGOSOPHIA, LLC

Logosophia, LLC
90 Oteen Church Road
Asheville, NC 28805
Logosophiabooks.com
Logosophiabooks@gmail.com

This book is a work of fiction, and thus of the author's imagination. None of the characters, places or incidents represented within have any real connection to any actual persons, places or events, alive or deceased, beyond the coincidental. The main protagonists are based on well-known literary characters: Snow White ("Schneewittchen" *Grimms' Fairy Tales*, 1812); Cinderella (earliest version *Rhodopis* told in Strabo, 7 BCE; "Ashenputtel" *Grimms' Fairy Tales*, 1812); Sleeping Beauty (earliest version in *Perceforest* 14th century; "Little Briar Rose" *Grimms' Fairy Tales*, 1812); and Beauty and the Beast (*La Belle et la Bête* by Gabrielle-Suzanne Barbot de Villeneuve, 1740).

Second Edition

Library of Congress-in-Publication Data is available upon request.

Meltz, Mindi
After Ever After, Book One: The Ritual of Forgetting

ISBN 978-1-7350432-0-3

Original cover illustration by Heidi Herzberger
Cover design and interior layout by Susan Yost
Interior art by Chiwa

for the birds—
thank you for giving love language
(boundary, beauty,
longing, belonging)
and for binding the worlds by those songs

North
Moors

Leo's
Castle

River Golden

Glass Mountains

Temple

Council
of
Waterfalls

South
Forest

Welcome Beach

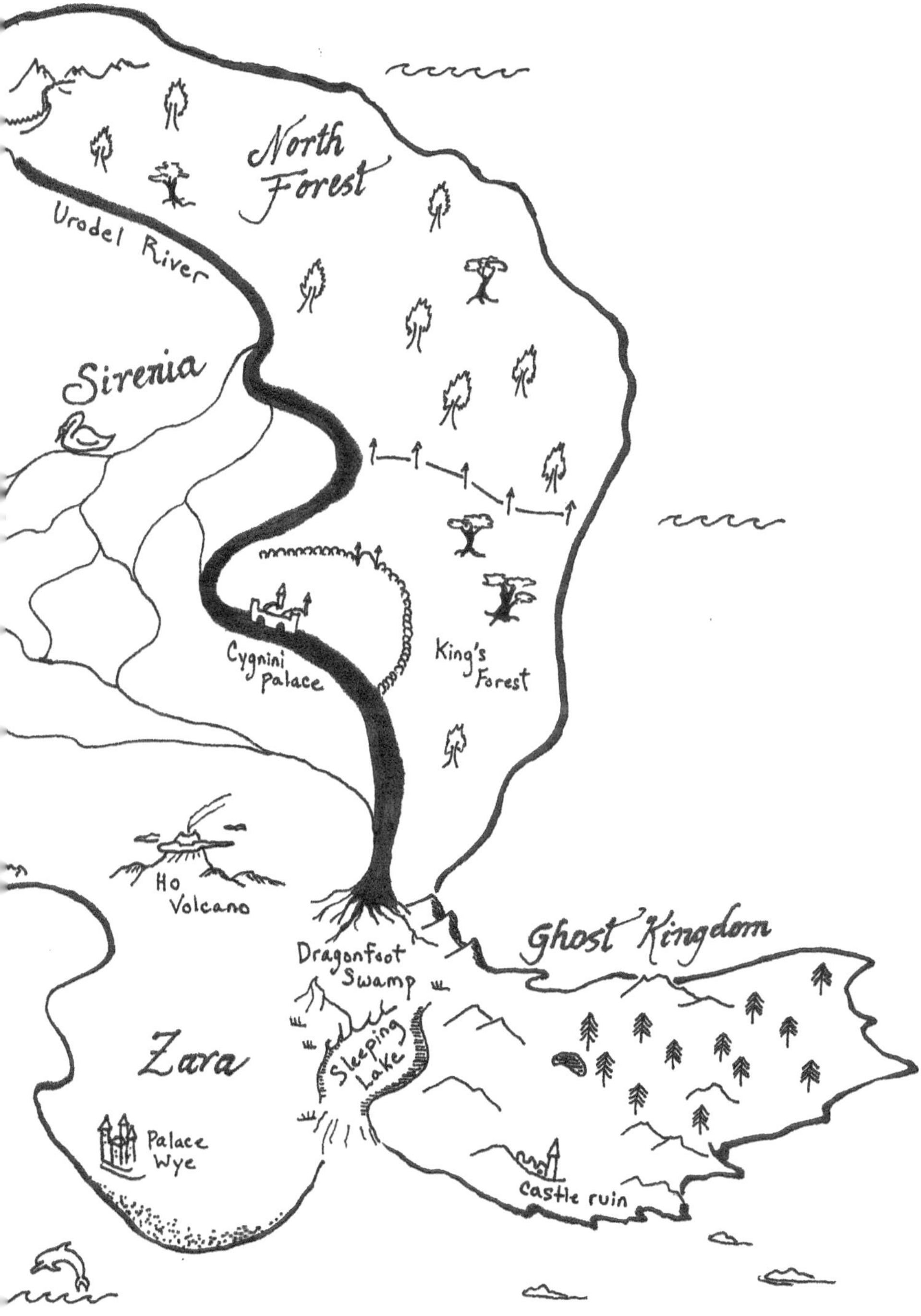
North Forest
Urodel River
Sirenia
Cygnini palace
King's Forest
Ho Volcano
Dragonfoot Swamp
Ghost Kingdom
Sleeping Lake
Zara
Palace Wye
Castle ruin

Characters

Northlands, kingdom of the Barbarians

- **Princess Rowan**, half-fœrie
- **Prince Leo**, aspiring ruler of the Barbarians, bastard son of the current Sirenian king, who claims Rowan for his wife
- **King William Anai of Sirenia**, previous and temporary ruler of the Northlands, father of Rowan
- **Rhiannon**, Dark Fœrie of all the worlds, mother of Rowan
- **Queen Mona**, King William's Barbarian wife
- **Jade**, Rowan and Leo's son
- **Rufus James**, the huntsman

Sirenia, kingdom of the Sirenians

- **Princess/Queen Ella**, daughter of a nobleman and his unwed mistress
- **Prince Solon Cygnini**, second royal son, her husband
- **Anna**, their daughter
- **Jonah**, their first-born son
- **Alden**, Solon's older brother and heir to the throne
- **Narsa**, Alden's wife
- **Kiera**, Solon's younger sister
- **Queen and King of Sirenia**, parents of Solon, Alden and Kiera
- **Leyla**, Ella's lady in waiting
- **Loren**, a knight and friend of Solon
- **Aurora**, Solon's horse
- **Rufus James** (see Northlands)

South Forest, land of the Hummingbird People, and Zara, kingdom of the Wyes

- **Lemara**, Priestess of Hummingbirds
- **Micah Wye**, king of the Wyes, her husband
- **Uriah (Uri)**, their son
- **Ruya (Rue)**, their daughter
- **Tiras**, Lemara's first beloved in the South Forest
- **Esha**, Lemara's friend in the South Forest
- **Rhiannon**, the Dark Færie who cursed Lemara to sleep for a hundred years

Ghost Kingdom, kingdom of the Ghost People
(descended from Hummingbird People and Wyes)

- **Princess/Queen Mina Fox**, daughter of a merchant from Sirenia
- **Prince/King Nicolai Wolf**, the "beast" who became a man and married her
- **Rhee and Ona**, elders in the Ghost Kingdom
- **Macha**, their granddaughter
- **Linny**, Mina's friend in the Ghost Kingdom
- **Addie and Lara**, Mina's sisters in Sirenia
- **Amos**, Addie's husband
- **Rhiannon**, the Dark Færie who cursed Nicolai to be a beast

The prince carried her away with him, causing the cursed apple to pop from her throat and wake her. Then he married her, and they lived happily ever after.

Rowan
(the castle)

You remember. My north walls rounded by buffeting storm, my south walls shapeless with ivy. My whistling tunnels between the gates, where the wind came in with you and panicked for a moment, tangling, before finding its way out. My copper veins, my wooden bones, my tapestried skin, my muscle of stone. The curves of my inner arms wrapping in stair and passageway round to the hearth, the arches of longing, the banners that meant something, the covered bridges leading inward to untouchable ideal and outward to glory. The ramparts, the barracks and the armor, the palisades pointed on top as if to bloody the very sky, because castles are violent.

You remember.

Prince Leo will say he rules me. But I cannot be ruled; I am rule.

He will say he owns me. But I am that old battle between ownership and nothing. I am a built thing in the wilderness. I am the castle you remember, when you hunger after history like the taste of blood.

I have no name, for no one has ever dared to name me. I was built by Dwarves, the ancients of the North, almost three hundred years ago. They built me like the inside of the earth. They built me like a law, at a time when the first law had been broken—a bulwark against the collapse of reality.

I press upon the earth; I grow up from the earth, more rooted in its darkness than the trees, and my shape reflects the sky, the dead-old grid of the stars. The Dwarves gave me voice that way, by anchoring me to these rhythms: the spinning, ever-returning universe above me, the eternal dying beneath me, the dissolution of things into particles, into liquid, into fire. The people living within me do not think of such things. But they are happening anyway. They are why you remember.

A castle is never afraid. A castle never reacts or trembles. A castle is slow in living, and slow in dying, and tempers the rash hearts of men. It retains forever the whispers of women. Wrens and swallows nest in its eaves. It crumbles, but never falls.

When I die, I will die layer by layer, sanctum within sanctum, spiral stair within spiral stair, each pattern exposed in beauty to the forgiveness of wind and the desolation of sun. I will become new castles of ruin upon the tumultuous, crow-pecked earth.

♜　♜　♜　♜　♜

Here, a room of voices. Once upon a time, the insults of ten or twenty or a hundred warlords crossed quickly here and were done, and their bones strengthened my floors. Once upon another time, this happened again. Agreements were made and broken, rules were formed and challenged, tales were sung and secretly revised, victories were celebrated and drowned in drink. And the fire of this hearth, in the center of their eating, was my heart; and the fire never went out. Until it did. And then one hundred years passed.

Once upon a time, here were only echoes digesting in space. I kept quiet. I listened to the crickets and phoebes and, once every day or two, the streak of a hawk's cry between clouds. I felt the ants describing grand sketches of hunger and decay with their immortal feet, I dreamed of beetles etching trees and one more stand of moss unfurling one more frond as an eon ended and began. And then, only yesterday perhaps, the court of King William and Queen Mona Anai from Sirenia murmured through in rustling silk, their voices first nervously triumphant and then tight with fear, as the winds drummed my sides with rising Barbarian threats.

Queen Mona saw the Dark Faerie Queen Rhiannon from her ebony window, and that Dark Queen held something she wanted.

Rhiannon said, I offer you this gift, and in exchange I will take whatever I wish from you.

I don't care, said the young queen. I hate my life, all alone in this dreary place. There is nothing I have that I want.

I warn you, I will take what I wish, repeated Rhiannon, and you will not even know I have taken it until it is too late.

I don't care. Take anything, repeated Mona.

And in the end, warned Rhiannon, this gift that I offer you will be all you have left, and it will ruin you.

Give it to me, said Mona.

It was a mirror.

☖   ☖   ☖   ☖   ☖

Later, they were gone. And today: Prince Leo, just arrived. He says the castle belongs to him—names me Leo's Castle, the first name ever given to a thing the Barbarians feared to name. His small band of warriors-in-training, sleeping in their heaving, stinking, snoring splendor, fills my heart-room of voices tonight, and he owns this small brotherhood who now calls him Prince, an achievement equal to the conquest of a thousand-man army in any other land, because the Barbarians have heretofore bowed to no one.

So that is something, he thinks.

To own a castle is to own power. The deep protection in layers of walls. The stronghold on high. And perhaps most of all, the view from the towers, for my windows are eyes. They frame it like a painting: the wide, serpentine moor-valleys full of hidden Barbarian clans, bastions of unused might—to Leo's eyes. To King William Anai of Sirenia, of course, my tower eyes framed a different painting: a wilderness of unrest, simmering shadow-lands of unruly animal-people, whose restless weapons called into question all the Sirenian priests held dear. And peaks rising higher behind me, with heights impossible to see, from which could and would come anything.

To the warlords who came before, for hundreds of years, from a hundred foreign lands, there was no time to look at paintings. No time to stand on high. And thus they never owned me. For to own a castle is to own vision.

Queen Mona, in her madness, looked here. She looked out of the eye and into it. Once upon a time she saw—from above where the Rivers begin—a Dark Faerie coming for her husband. Yes, and once she saw a Dark Faerie coming for her soul. And once she looked into the mirror and saw herself, at last, and that was the end of her.

For what happens in my round, high rooms? Down in my belly, the servants are busy with the magic of life: turning death into food, turning wine into spirit, making order of chaos, channeling the waters, blocking out the winds, feeding animals that they will soon kill, and all that humans do. But up above in my mind, in the towers ringed by so many eyes, the lords and ladies must consider all this. Separated by yet another drawbridge—arched almost delicately, so dangerously lovely, like the glide of a woman's long train—they own the privacy of their special rooms. They dream the light dreams and the dark. They make love or they don't, and then they sit awake and alone, long into the night, when the view out those windows is nothing but distance—and lights so far away in the sky you can hardly believe in them.

Does Prince Leo pace in my mind tonight? After all, he channels the smoke of my hearth with a dragon's head, a louvre he ordered made despite frightened protests, and from whose flaring nostrils smoke signals a warning to all who attend: Prince Leo rules here, and he fears not even the dragons who lurk in the mountains above him. Leo, the new Barbarian prince.

Does this prince who boasts a determination beyond normal human strength, which drew him from near-starvation in the Northern Primeval Forest to the life of a warrior, because his mother was a Barbarian (at least he thought she must be) and in his veins ran the blood of people who always chose death before surrender, combined for the first time with the blood of Sirenian royalty, and because he had fought every challenger and won, and because of all the feuding warlords he was the most cunning, the most handsome, the most convincing, and the most intuitively equipped to recognize weakness in any situation and slice cleanly to its heart—does he pace alone on this night, and does he ever tremble?

Only I know.

I remember when he carried in the princess. And so does he.

The inhuman paleness of her face, the unrippled liquid of her black hair, her crafty smallness and bird-wing bones, and most of all her blood-red mouth. Leo has slain more men than he can count; he has watched men die in every gruesome manner imaginable without flinching; but to him the violence of that hot red brushstroke across that white face is more than he can bear to gaze upon without a cold flame passing through him. To gaze upon that mouth makes him convulse in dark parts of his body; when she parts her lips, he feels that he is witnessing something more obscene than nudity. When he closes his eyes, he sees...

The Dwarves live beneath the northern rivers, the rivers that run screeching from the source of all rivers, the source of dragons, over long slates of black stone into craters tended by these, the oldest gods. Where Barbarians never go. What looked at first to be rows of cairns piled in river after river in the rocky distance transformed into small horrid men as he came closer. Sentinels. As if they had been waiting for him. Not moving but merely watching him as he came on, and as he passed them didn't they seem like hundreds? Until he realized only the same ones repeated over and over—and finally they came closer together, and then they parted, revealing what lay there in the water among them—

"Take her to the castle," they said to him, parting perhaps in deference to his sword, in words so barking, wild, and strange that he could not tell afterwards how he had understood them, "for it needs its rightful ruler." (He assumed that meant him. Only seventeen years old. Prince of the Barbarians.)

He and his men carried her in her glass box, up the long stairs, up to my mouth.

You remember, too. How when you enter a castle, you enter refuge or terror. You enter the grandeur of the sacred. Through gateway after fortified gateway, I swallow you in.

And on that day, upon my lip, upon the threshold where the "prince" entered again this house of sovereignty which he claims to own, he tripped. He did! Forever he will deny it, as will his men, so that they may live, but I know it. I felt it. He tripped upon my lip, and they collapsed against one another behind him. Dropped the glass case. Shattered her to waking.

Ask the Dwarves. It was for this purpose I was made, after all. The shattering.

Princess Rowan Anai. Born of Faerie and raised by Dwarves, abandoned by her father King William and sentenced to death by her stepmother Queen Mona, she was cursed to sleep and woke as she broke—but was the curse still on her? They all stopped and stared, bracing themselves against fear as if it were a mighty wind.

She wasn't cut too badly, though that little bit of blood looked very fierce upon her bright white skin. And it reminded them of something. Those colors, red and white—and the blackness of her hair as she cried out like an animal in the cold and snapped her body into a ball, her tresses enclosing her knees—were familiar to them. As they would be to you.

"Seize her," said Prince Leo to his men, as if she were running.

And I swallowed her up.

♖   ♖   ♖   ♖   ♖

Behind the throne of command, the voice of the mind, sits God.

Or so William Anai, cousin to the Sirenian queen, believed. And so there he set his little altar, and called the space a chapel. There in that floating space behind the throne, where my eyes turn inward, the light of the sun crosses from two opposing windows to confuse and transform a space of shadow. Through a crescent crack in the ceiling above that neither Leo nor William before him ever noticed, the midwinter moon imprints its silver stamp.

But the Dwarves didn't built it for God. They built it for something older.

Leo's twenty-three warriors—every one—have been woken from sleep and stand ready with their arms. The hall is heavy with their breathing, like an army in ambush; my dark glass flickers with the possibility of their power.

Leo is here before them: he woke to a nightmare he immediately forgot but which kept him from breathing. I know that nightmare. I have preserved it within my walls, building upon the fears of each monarch or lord or petty thief, for all the years I have stood here. The Dwarves, perhaps, planted its seed, but they did not make it a nightmare. It is the mind of man that did that.

"Light a lamp," he commands in the chapel, and it is done, though there is no need, because of the moon. "And get that priest." He means the one he has been keeping for this purpose, imprisoned and tortured and passed over to him at last by one of the clans less partial to priests, after the Anai monarchy fell. He was King William's priest, before King William died here of a wasting sickness or whatever it was that killed him.

Prince Leo, of course, is no follower of the Sirenian god or his blessed Savior. But since the fall of King William, Barbarian sentiment toward this god and his followers has swung wildly. Prince Leo wants all the gods on his side, and has particular, personal reasons for craving an alliance with this one. He is playing it safe. He wants this marriage—to a ghost-woman whose very humanness Barbarians doubt—to be legal. Especially in the eyes of those distant judges who sit so high and far on their civilized thrones, who think they judge all, and who once judged him.

The priest is brought before him. From his knees, he raises his head to Leo and exposes hollow, reddened eyes, a sparse, grease-needle beard, bleeding lips. "No," he groans with a madman's sudden sense of integrity. "I will not perform a wedding in the dead of night."

Leo snorts, as a strong horse snorts who is pulled too roughly by an inexperienced rider; his mouth falling open in a small, languid smile within the blonde curls of his beard. "You will," he says, not bothering to raise his voice, "or you will be dead before the light of day." He speaks to the priest in the Sirenian language, which was his own mother tongue until he was ten years old.

"My lord," comes a tremulous female voice from behind him, and Prince Leo turns to see the maidservant (a girl he has bedded once or twice) who has been caring for Rowan, holding her by the shoulders and nudging her forward like a little girl. Rowan's eyes glow in the dark. Her pupils flit toward the mass of men just below her, so quickly that he hardly catches it. He feels a rush of protectiveness and power.

"Can't you speak?" he demands.

"Yes," whispers Rowan. And the red lips close.

Prince Leo isn't deaf to the whispers, more among his own men than among the people, that he should have killed the princess. Whispers only, because the last man who doubted out loud that Leo could tame her lost his tongue. Fear is their downfall—these people. These people who carry talismans past the caves of forest lions, and never cross certain lines under the moon, and kill any child that resembles a Dwarf.

Rowan wears a white nightgown, and he can see the shape of her small breasts through the thin sheen of it, just as he can see the flush of her human blood beneath her snow-white skin. But she does not seem to realize that he can see these things, or care. Her white form is like a hole in space that keeps every man in the room frozen. It is like a shard of ice that, until removed, will keep every other object in the room so tensely pressed together that nothing can shift. He can see the swath of white her reflection makes in the dark windows behind her, and he secretly misses a heartbeat, to think that the reflection moves.

But then suddenly she draws her breath in, and he can see that all of this was an illusion—a foolish superstition that held him. She turns her face, her daringly beautiful profile cutting the darkness, and in that instant he sees her seeking some escape. Suddenly he can sense the desire of every man in the room. He has no idea how much time has passed.

"Begin!" he shouts, grabbing her, and the priest, pinned closely between the hulking forms of Leo's attendants, is dragged to his feet.

"We call on the Holy Father," mutters the priest, "to bless the union of this, our lord Prince Leo the Barbarian, with Princess Rowan Anai on this... on this night. We ask your blessing, oh Lord, oh Savior and Merciful One, to guide these two forth from the darkness into the light, and may their matrimony be dutiful and virtuous, and may it shine as a beacon to the people. Bless this man and this woman on this night, and lead them forth from the darkness—"

"You said that already," snaps Leo.

The priest gives a small hiccup, like a sob. "I cannot do it, my lord. I cannot marry you to a demon, a woman of darkness."

Prince Leo sighs.

The priest falls to his knees again, slithering from the grasp of the soldiers. "My Savior," he mumbles in a rush to someone unseen, "I am true to You, as You were true to my people. Forgive me my weakness. I shall never betray You again. I belong to You and am Yours for—"

He stops as his head rolls to the floor, and Leo, still holding the princess with his other hand, lets his bloody sword drop to his side. He will not hand it to one of his men to be cleaned. Leo never lets go of his sword, even in sleep.

Feeling relief, already, from some of the tension that held him, he looks across the man's gushing body to the rows of his small army, who stand obediently at attention and betray not a tremor of emotion. "No matter," he says to them. "From this day forward, we renounce all connection with priests and all the brainwashing of Sirenia. The Sirenians have no power over us. It is the old gods who gave me the princess, and she belongs to me as this castle belongs to me."

He waits. He checks the expressions on the faces before him. His sword hangs loosely at his side, dripping. Perhaps the princess trembles a little in his grip, perhaps she is gasping. He cannot afford to notice. "You have witnessed this marriage. By my sword it is done."

The men, who deep in their hard, steely (but very young) hearts were won by such outlandish words when first they heard Leo speak many moons ago, drop in unison, each to one knee, and bow their heads. This is their hero. This is the man who emerged alone from the Northern Primeval Forest which hates all men, nothing but a boy and without even a weapon, without a scratch upon his face or the slightest wisp of fear in his eyes—and now, surviving still, owns this Castle built by Dwarves.

Before they can look up again, Leo and his princess have gone.

They have passed through the tapestry, behind the throne, behind the god-space. Into the rooms of the most interior, most protected chamber. The tapestry, woven by Barbarian women, depicts Leo slaying several dragons at once, his arms spinning as if they number more than two.

"You belong to me, Princess Rowan," he hisses, guiding her with a will so certain it does not feel to him like force. They sweep past the attendants, within and within, through door within door. Now his whole body slackens, like a starving man's jaw within reach of food. Rowan backs up against the bed, but he snatches her. He encloses her in one arm and turns her fast against the wall. He leans his weight into her, enjoying the feel of her smallness. He reaches around to the terrible face—white, red, black—that he cannot see, and presses his thumb to her mouth. Her lower lip is dry and hot, so he dips his thumb into her mouth to feel the wetness there. He feels her little, perfect teeth. He spreads his fingers over her face, gripping her sharp chin, fingering her palpitating throat. And now he feels the fear, and it excites him almost beyond bearing.

Her breath absolutely silent, but desperate against his palm. Her shoulders shrinking her smaller. Her mouth—whispering something he cannot understand.

He mistakes the fluttering of her body as proof of her captivity. He feels virginity in her fear. He reaches down to tear apart his own robes, his other hand lifting her dress. All the emergency of his seventeen-year-old lust rises forth, and he heaves himself between her legs and catches her hair between his teeth in dizzy anticipation. She turns in his arms, and his last impression is of softness and needles at once, like the crushing of feathers against a struggling bird.

She's gone.

An empty hole of night blows open between him and the window. The moonlight yawns. The tapestry of battle shakes slightly in the breeze and mocks him with its barren, womanless tableau.

Listen—an owl's blank cry somewhere in the night. And Prince Leo is a little boy again, cast into the Northern Primeval Forest beyond the Sirenian palace on pain of death, huddled in the cold corners of giant oak roots, listening to mythical beasts tiptoe toward him through shadows that even Barbarians fear to tread. The darkness wails, and his loneliness grows wings. There is no one and nothing that loves him. His existence denied.

The men at arms shift position outside his door, a quiet bending of cloth and metal, and Prince Leo tastes hatred on his own breath.

He will say he owns me.

But the Dwarves did not build me for him.

I am a dream dreamed long ago, that you will dream for a thousand years after. Every stone in a castle knows where it comes from. My structure—the precision with which my pillars share their weight and the equality of my beams and the mathematics of my triangular trusses—contains more integrity than any story you could tell, or any human mind. And him—this angry boy-prince of a brief, passing age—you will not remember at all.

I am dark. I am damp with rain, breath, tears, the earth's condensation, and everyday fog. My walls echo the rivers' moan. I am cold. I give no comfort, for I have none. I have only the everlasting fire, which sometimes goes out.

But my floor is made of everything you are. Bones, spit, blood, ashes, animal excrement from all the ages. I am the darkness from which civilizations rise up again. And Leo will not win. No one will win. There is no system that will work. The rulers will change, and change again. And yet the throne is sacred.

And she is not gone.

Maybe hers is the only face capable of shocking a Barbarian, her body the only body that can make a Barbarian tremble. But she is also a woman, and a woman escapes inward, not outward.

I have channels of water running beneath me into earth, in patterns that the mind of such a warrior as Leo—molded like metal by fire—cannot perceive. The rivulets that run north and south and in all directions from the sacred Source just above me, whose birth dragons midwife, which will descend, later on, into the nameable passages of the Rivers Golden and Urodel into bright-day living kingdoms—oh, these secret, secret veins of water run under me, too, ever scattering and coalescing, without meaning, the water always moving yet in each place always shaped the same, like a storm that forever gathers and forever breaks. I am built upon water, and water changes reality in slow, downward ways you cannot see, only feel. I have passages between my walls, as soft and pliable as my walls are hard. My alcoves, my cellars—all have invisible, trickling doorways into darkness that can take her in, in an instant.

All along, it was I who swallowed her. And now I swallow her even deeper, deeper than he knows. For moments, for hours, for days and nights—I can keep her until it is time for her to emerge.

For the Dwarves built me. I contain all of history, a history the Dwarves traced in their ancient language at the moment when it seemed first in danger of being forgotten. And through the night while Leo sleeps in despair, Rowan moves through the mazes of that history. She will know, now, what patterns unite to form the Urodel and the Golden. What all the worlds are made of, and where they will come together, in love or in war. She trusts me as easily as she trusted the huntsman, the Dwarves, the mad queen in her disguise. Innocence doesn't even begin to describe what she is.

White—the unbreakable perfection that imprisons you.

Black—as unselfconscious as the frame of a window.

Red—your own destruction, the only violence that could free you.

Rowan, you are called princess. Rowan, you are called woman. You were born in a mirror, and you will die in one.

I feel her brushing lightly along my innards with her fingertips, her lips. I hear her whispering back the sounds she hears, of the wind playing through my shapes like muffled organ pipes. I feel her bowing her face to the deep waters, a shadow drinking. And she knows now, as I do, where she comes from.

But you would never know that she knows it. She knows it in the way the animals know it, in a way that guides her every movement but that she could never explain.

*The slipper fit perfectly, revealing her true identity,
so the prince married her,
and they lived happily ever after.*

Ella

Dear my people,

Whatever happens, I want you to know that I forgive you.

Just as our priests tell us, these days, that our holy Savior took our sins upon Himself to save us, it is the burden of a king and queen to bear both the blame and the worship of their people. Sol, my beloved, knew that. It was the one thing he understood perfectly about ruling. We are here for you to dream about. We are responsible for everything.

Dear my people—but who are you, after all? Do I know you, any more than you know me? Sometimes I think of you en masse, an advancing tide of consciousness swelling with rage or shrinking in fear. Sometimes you are a single beggar whose unheard voice nags at my sleep, or a single family who greets me in the Hall on your knees, unaccountably weeping—not for poverty and not for despair, not for joy and not for gratitude, but only for the emotion of being in my presence, an emotion I have not felt for so long, sometimes it bewilders me to witness. But it's true—I stood once in your shoes, and I, too, longed to kneel, though I was forbidden to.

Once, you were a mist of lanterns upon the Urodel River, cheering my wedding. And once, not long after, you were a child calling out to me from the plaza at the cathedral. Did I lie to you then, when you strained forth with such lovely, brazen curiosity, pulled just as strongly backward into the crowd—by those urgent hands of propriety—as my prince tugged at my own waist, to pull me back into the relief of the carriage? Did I lie to you, when you cried out to me, ignoring Prince Solon's gentle, dismissive remonstrance, "Please, Princess Ella! What is it like? What was it like to be one of us, and then become—?"

The cathedral's construction was only just beginning then, and I was exhausted by the wonder of presiding over it with Solon at my side, greeting the best masons, carpenters, sculptors and artists of Sirenia, who would spend their lives in the exquisite work of creating this colossal altar to our Savior and God. I was trying to mimic Sol's regal gaze, his gracious interest, pretending an attitude of inspired grace I did not feel, avoiding the wondering, admiring, scrutinizing gaze of hundreds, outside and beyond and all around me.

"It is like a fairy tale"—that was my answer. Your question frightened me. But I wanted you to believe whatever you needed to. I wanted you to grow up determined and brave—a woman, a queen of your own. I still want that. Have you done it, I wonder?

And I understand now, what you need me for. There are peoples who refuse monarchy—the Hums, the Ghost People before Mina Fox came to them, even the Barbarians perhaps—who find safety in councils, votes, consensus. But think: the kings you loved, the queens that moved you, that changed this world for good—they will live in your legends (much longer than the tyrants will), and you cannot make a legend from a council of many. Power brings risk, that is sure. But so does following your heart without fear when you love. Sometimes the heart makes mistakes, or is fickle, or cruel. But to live in its glow and shadow is to live.

So I take your blame with your love. But I am not guilty. And I do not say I am one of the great ones, one you will remember. I am old, now, and I no longer live for your opinions; instead, I live for you. But if I would teach you one thing, my people, I would teach you empathy, as a mirror through which you will better know yourself. I write my story here for that reason, because I must, though I cannot imagine what will become of it. I know that as your queen, it is my duty not to tell you all the little details of my humanity that I yearn to confess. Yet time changes that responsibility. What you need to know now, in order to be inspired, is different from what you will need to know a thousand years from now, in order to feel whole, in order to forgive.

♛　♛　♛　♛　♛

Most of you, perhaps, are able to imagine quite clearly what you would do if you had riches. If you had influence in decisions that affect the world. At eighteen years old, I could not imagine either of those things. When I was seventeen, the glassblower's son once asked me to run away with him. When I thought about that, I thought, "If I run away with him, then tomorrow night I will sleep in the arms of someone who likes me, and perhaps not be cold, and have no chores to do, and no soot on my face." That was as far as I was able to imagine.

When they first brought me into the palace, into the courtyard to bathe and purify me from my former life, I found myself trembling between the hands of royal servants like a ghost ensnared for the first time by a body. I was intolerably embarrassed. I had not thought yet about the life before me, or marriage to the Prince, or the responsibilities of royalty, or how much money was spent just to make the curtains that surrounded the tub. I had no practice in thinking of such things. I only thought of the dress they were removing from my body—the best dress I had ever owned, the one it had taken such courage for me to secretly don the moment I knew who waited at my stepmother's door, despite how my stepsisters would mock me and how I might be punished for it later.

"Wait!" I cried, but then held my tongue. Oh my people, it was the only fine and flattering dress I owned, with silk ribbons clustered at the breast and beads hissing in loops from the sleeves when I lifted my arms! It means more to me still than any of the bejeweled cloths I've worn since. I'd made and remade it three times since I was thirteen, when to my astonishment a mysterious tradesman from Zara gave me a bolt of the most exotic green fabric I had ever seen in exchange for a single kiss. It was my running-away-from-home dress, a thing of hope I had made with my own hands that had kept me alive. But it was nothing to the ladies in waiting who stripped it from me with soft-fingered disdain.

I needn't have cared what the ladies thought, of course. I was to be a princess in but a few days, and I could have ordered them to keep that silly gown for me and never given a reason. But I had never commanded anyone, and the thought hardly occurred to me. And they knew that. And even though they should have heeded my little cry of "wait!"—and not the meek sigh that followed—they did not. I regretted that weakness for the rest of my life. I did not know then that my past had any worth. I did not understand that I was giving it up forever.

I remember particularly the sun that day—a different sun that I'd never seen before, one that seemed especially designed for royalty, a lace of light inlaid with gold—which oversaw the sweeping of clouds across its worshipful populace of sunflowers. The ladies left me alone for the first time within palace walls. The tub sat like a magic cauldron in a tent of beige satin curtains, partially open to the breeze from the gardens. I felt foolish reclining in water, for even at my father's house, which was finer than many, we had bathed in a barrel. I thought I wouldn't know how to arrange my body, but the warm embrace of that water claimed me instantly. It was the first time I could ever remember bathing in water that no one had bathed in before me. I touched the rim, scalloped with the last unicorn ivory from the Ghost Kingdom. I leaned forward and bit my own knees, because I thought I would laugh, and that might prove that I really was losing my mind. I clutched my own feet in that fur-lined tub in that shiny water in the royal garden, and I told myself sternly, "I am going to be married to the prince. Ella Gladstone, you are going to be married to Prince Solon Cygnini. Princess Ella." And then fast, my practical nature took hold of my thoughts to keep them steady. I began to size myself up the way I might size up my family's food caches in a time of drought. Was I enough? Would he still want me, when he saw me denuded of whatever magical something had clothed me on those nights? I examined my skin, my thighs, the texture of my wet hair, my fingernails. I swept my face with my thumbs.

My new lady in waiting found me weeping—I don't know why. Her name was Leyla. She knelt with a dancer's grace, like a swooping bird with a secret message to deliver, and it was her sole purpose to serve my every desire, but as I stared at the sleekly parted black hair upon her bent head, her perfectly trained beauty, I could not summon a single command.

♛　♛　♛　♛　♛

To me, as it was to you, the Cygnini palace was the heart of Sirenia, and Sirenia the heart of our world—this fertile valley answering the dreams that had guided us two hundred years before across the sea from the east; an anchor of civilization amidst yet stormy wilds; the center of all possible trade routes and futures to come. It did not bother us terribly then, being the only kingdom with no access to the sea—for we had come from the sea, and found security in being landlocked at last, awaiting our Savior where His rebirth had been promised to us. In those days we considered ourselves the only real city.

Despite all that has happened, the shape of Sirenia looks not much different now than it did back then, being formed as it is more by the natural paths of branching waterways than by any urban plan we designed. We are still graciously nurtured by the arms of our two rivers—water that pours down from the north with ferocity at first, I am told, but by the time it divides to embrace Sirenia, turning tame. The palace still rises against the far, eastern bank of the Urodel, and beyond it the King's Forest still bleeds into mystery, beyond what we women can see—into the Northern Primeval Forest and on to the sea. To the west, the Golden River still divides our farmlands from the Barbarian moors to the north and the jungle of the Hums to the south—but back then, this river dragged a murkier train, more treacherous to our imaginations. While the outer farmlands became increasingly sparse and haunted places, sinking deeper into superstition, spooked by unpredictable Barbarian raids and all but forgotten by the city folk, Sirenia itself swelled bright and proud: it smelt richer than ever of butchering and dye, wax and sweat, oil and sewage, opportunity and despair, smothering wealth and proud, reckless poverty.

Remember how when our God found us this land when we were refugees, He taught us to build a city upon swamp—using tributaries of the Urodel instead of roads for passage, weaving ourselves into the land by way of water. We rechanneled our sparse knowledge of ships, which had carried us across the sea, into the making of river boats, and built our houses to float like rafts where the land wasn't solid. I will say here (since I am saying what I cannot say), when I look down upon the candlelit mazes, or close my eyes to imagine I am among you again and remember the echoing nudge of boats against ripple-lined doorsteps in the stillness of early dawn, I cannot help but believe that this city was built like a woman. It bent to fit this land, defined by curves of water.

To describe this place, our birthplace, the knowledge of whose shape our bodies and hearts share in common, comforts me now. Written words can do this, I have learned: just as the Holy Scriptures comfort us with the memories of our Beloved, or the numbered tallies comfort the rich man as tangibly as fingers caressing each coin, these foolish, fond words of praise for my city bring me closer to you now. Oh my people, the way the Cygnini palace extends out, arch after arch, along the far bank of the Urodel, so that a mirror image of the palace and all the activity within it reflects forever in its smooth waters—did it never seem to you like a dream of us, or a parallel life? Has every one of you, at some time in your life, made that heavenly crossing? I hope so. The poorest man, if he can get a boat, can legally paddle about in the shadows of those dove-nested arches—and when I was one of you, I myself often traded a suggestive smile for such a ride, to pass among the swans and look up at the royal windows, imagining I could see inside them.

But in the days before my wedding, which were numbered by the time it took for my dress to be made, I was cloistered away in a room far to the north. From the highest towers at the back, hidden from the city's view, I could see the great wall in the distance, defended by two ramparts and a palisade of spearheaded tree trunks, which separated the King's Forest from the Northern Primeval. No guards watched at those towers anymore, since Barbarians had largely abandoned the North Forest. So far from the bustle of the Great Hall, my ivory-rimmed windows invisible to the eyes of the populace, I could look to that bending grey horizon with nothing upon it but the occasional perching raven, imagining my unknown future like a great awakening that boiled suddenly over its brim. Of course, little did I know the violence that northern horizon truly held, so many years later—but that story, my dear people, you already know.

Leyla—I never knew where she came from, what gave her that bewitching hue, that thick night hair—was my only companion, for I wasn't allowed yet to the feasts or even to mingle among the royal populace. "I'm not a princess yet," I told her. "Don't bow before me, please!" Not knowing how to make a friend, I could never bring myself to ask her any question about her background, though I often practiced such questions in my mind. Instead I answered every one of hers, in order that she might find me agreeable. Without meaning to, I made her my confessor. Yet she learned little more than what apparently everyone knew—that my mother was not my father's wife, that she was accused of seducing him by sorcery and that he had not defended her, only taken me in after her hanging, out of pity. *Maybe she learned her magic from the Faeries across the Golden River*, Leyla speculated, and instead of hushing her, I went pale. Leyla, who missed nothing, backtracked quickly. *No, of course not*, she amended. *Witchcraft is always the accusation of one woman betrayed by another. Everyone knows that.*

After my first morning prayers in the palace chapel, Leyla took me to meet the king and queen. I begged her to wait for me outside, for fear I should be lost upon my return. Oh my people, you cannot imagine the maze of it—the glorious bridges between the archways and the walled courtyards on the shore, with their fish ponds and sunflowers and riches of animals, and in the palace above the arches each royal person has a private sitting room, and prayer chamber, and wardrobe, and these often occur in turrets that lift outward from other turrets, one upon the other, or connect to each other by little bridges in the sky, so that you feel one day you might ascend a few more steps and come accidentally into Heaven.

The queen required an elaborate series of rituals for the approach of all persons, including her own children, into her royal presence. Leyla had me practice that morning: curtsey upon entering the room, walk forward to the chapel in the east wing of the throne room beside her, kneel, make the sign of the Savior, kiss the Savior's image, then kneel before the king, then the queen, then kiss the royal rings on the hand of each, then stand and curtsey again to each, then stand with head lowered until spoken to. The king, already in his third cup of wine this morning, in contrast to the queen's statuesque posture, did nothing to alter the slouching, leonine repose of his body against the arm of his throne, and watched my trembling genuflections with a kind of greedy amusement that flushed my heart with shame.

I'd been too frightened to admire the beauty around me, but now that I must turn my humble gaze to the stones beneath my feet, everything I could not see seemed to watch me with eyes as indecently mocking as the king's. The buttresses above me yawned open spaces the likes and height of which I had never seen but could feel now, like the wings of a hawk spreading over its tiny prey. In the awesome silence that settled upon us—a silence like church, like wasted fields after a drought, like the sky that veils our view of Heaven—broken only once by a clinking of glass from the buttery behind the Hall, I dared not move or breathe.

The queen spoke. "I don't believe in this idea of marriage for love," she said.

I looked up, forgetting to veil my face with any kind of appropriate expression.

You may have seen the thrones of Cygnini, or you may not have. Of all the things that were destroyed later, besides the cathedral, they were the thing most precious to me. The Cygnini palace was built more for loveliness than for protection, and that was to be our downfall. Yes, those thrones were made all of glass. They hung from the ceiling, attached together as one, dangling with crystal bells, and the king and queen sat there with their toes just touching the royal carpet, and the sun shone down through the rose-tinted skylights high above them in a thunder of beauty that regularly brought supplicants to their knees. If you came there with a petty request, you would quickly forget it. If you came with an unjust accusation, it would disintegrate around the bare bones of your own conscience. Or so I thought then.

The king, looking heavy in his glass seat and yet entirely at ease, still watched me with that same awful gaze, as if he awaited the beginning of his favorite theatre performance. He had Solon's eyes, nakedly blue, but they were also hard beneath heavy brows, in a face lined permanently from some perpetual expression of cynical constriction. His dull gold hair fell disturbingly loose and long, hanging nearly halfway down his broad, bejeweled chest. When he grinned at me, I looked back fast at the queen, horrified to realize I'd been staring back at him.

"Young people choosing their mates, as if you could know what a marriage is," continued the queen, speaking as if to herself.

"My wife will be the expert on marriage here," growled the king with weary sarcasm. The queen ignored him. They had yielded to the pressures of the modern only to this extent: their second son (the one not destined to be king) had been allowed to choose his own bride, so long as she was of noble birth—which I half was, though I'd never felt it.

"I know what you think you see in each other, the two of you, mesmerized by a handsome face," the queen continued quietly. "But it's an illusion. A kind of magic. A trick. Can you maintain it, I wonder?"

And now my heart sank into a base, cold darkness, for she spoke the words so slowly and with eyes so intent upon mine that I felt certain she referenced the magic I had used on those nights, as if somehow she could know. The king's dry laughter broke over me. "Let her be, woman. She deserves a second chance at life, living under the shadow of that wretched mother of hers, that witch"—and he grunted these last words, drowning them in another gulp of wine. "It isn't her fault."

When I looked at the queen, I wanted to weep for my own willowy, fragile youth. Here was a woman whom the wind could not chill, whose mighty stone face did not waver in its certainty beneath any number of wrinkles, whose beauty was something she had earned over time and tended proudly with each perfected gesture. I saw her take a breath: the royal bosom filling with royal air to which she felt utterly entitled.

"Come with me," she commanded. "We have things we will speak of in private, you and I."

Astonished, I followed her out of the Great Hall, our steps losing themselves in the muffled field of the floor's tapestry. The palace is narrow running east to west, and we passed through only two doors before emerging onto one of the little open bridges overlooking the shaded back river. She turned to face me, and I bowed my head.

"You must learn to carry yourself differently." She lifted my chin with two fingers. "Shoulders back. Head back. No, not like that. Your head floats upon your shoulders. You are royalty now. You model the divine."

Then she sighed, as if the impossibility of my ever understanding tired her extremely. I struggled to harden my jaw.

"Yes, Your Highness." It was the first time I had spoken, and I was almost surprised to remember that I could.

"Now," she said, and turned her gaze upon the swans below us, as if in some gentle, feather-light play-acting of royal awkwardness, "we must speak briefly of something unpleasant to us both. Your stepmother and stepsisters." And she turned the full force of her eyes back upon me. "Normally the penalty for lying to the royal family, or to any of our agents, is death. But I give it to you to decide their fate, for you are soon to be princess, and it is you who have suffered them the most."

Not knowing what was required of me, I curtseyed again and looked down. It was my only fallback. She raised my chin again with the tips of two fingers.

"Float," she commanded. "You are in a position to decide someone's fate. Be worthy of it."

"Your Grace," I said, but could not go on.

"Ella," said the queen, and I teared up at the sound of my name and—did I imagine it?—the hint of kindness in it. "My husband will froth at the mouth about all of this, so I took you aside, but I want you to know that I do not believe in witches. This whole business of hanging poor women who, though they may have strayed regrettably from the Lord, cannot possibly possess the kind of powers that men blame them for, is abominable to me—and would have been abominable to our Savior as well, I feel certain. Unfortunately, my husband refuses to lift a finger to prevent such murders."

She did not say that she was sorry for my mother's death; she would never apologize for anything. What I felt for her, I did not yet recognize, because I had never felt this kind of respect for anyone. I was accustomed to authority, and to cringing beneath it, but after eighteen years of life I had finally learned that my stepmother's authority was not true power, but rather a reaction to some bitter weakness inside. Though I had continued to wordlessly obey her, I had ceased to believe that true power existed. It was all a front, I had thought, an excuse for cruelty. I accepted it because I saw so little of worth in myself, and the god-fearing values that kept me submissive were all that protected me from my mother's fate. But in the easy grace of my new mother-in-law's every motion, a grace immune to ugliness or mortal fear, I learned that true power can give those beneath it space to breathe.

"Look at me."

I looked.

"It is well to be proud, but not stubborn. Let us tarry no more. What will be their fate?"

"Please, Your Grace," I said finally, speaking only because she wanted me to, and I needed so much to please her. "I do not wish them to be killed. I wish them to be content with all they need in life. Only—I wish them to be far away from me, never to see me again."

The queen nodded. She watched me for a moment, and probably she thought me righteous and good for my forgiveness, but it was not forgiveness. It was fear. "Good," she said. "It is done. Now, do you have any questions for me?"

I dared not turn away from that face, but I felt the haughty beauty of everything, the casual brush of wind through the only ancient trees left in the kingdom whose tops shivered just above the courtyard wall, the demure murmurs of the royal doves in conversation. *Why?* was the only question that came to me. I thought of the terror of mortal men when visited by angels of the Lord. *Why me? How will I survive this gift? How will I deserve it?*

I must have parted my lips.

"Go on."

"Do you wish that I weren't—that it wasn't so?"

The queen scowled, then, but it was an elegant scowl. "Did I, or did I not," she asked in a tone of level ice, "ordain that my son the prince should choose his own bride?"

"Yes. I mean yes, you did, Your Grace."

"And do you have reason to suppose that I, the queen of Sirenia, should ever doubt my own command?"

"I—no! Of course not."

"Do you imagine that I make decisions based on some personal whim of the moment, some selfish preference?"

"N—no—"

"What?"

"No, Your Grace."

"You are a princess, Ella. You are not playing dress-up, this is not a game."

I shook my head, tears rolling freely now.

"Never forget that." She laid her hand upon the wall, and I heard the clink of her rings against the stone. It is a gesture I still remember today, because she did not notice it, and yet I feel now that she needed something to support her, just for a moment, as she stood beneath the weight of her own command.

Then she turned her face back to the interior door, indicating by her cold gaze where my feet should take me.

"You may go."

♛   ♛   ♛   ♛   ♛

I ate my fill every day. I can still remember when that surprised me more than anything.

Sometimes I cried while I ate, grateful to Leyla who averted her eyes every time. Sometimes I overate and was sick. Sometimes I felt nauseated and afraid and joyful all at once, merely from the visual feast that extended so far around me. Instead of spending much of my day amid grease and soot, focusing on my hands as they stirred and kneaded and tended, or gazing in unconscious desolation at some crumbling plaster wall, I now looked regularly, without even trying, upon vast orchards, fields of flowers and colorful vegetables enough to feed hundreds, and the best views that river, mountain, and proud jutting outline of stone tower wall had to offer. Until my marriage day, I was not allowed into the Great Hall. Yet sometimes at night when I couldn't sleep, I walked out and peered down into its giant well of shadows, imagined the feasts at that masterful, ship-sized table, felt the sacred silence hovering around the sleepy guards as they creaked and ached in their armor, and tried to know that soon I would be a part of all this. It was the last time in my life I would ever be invisible.

As the wedding neared and my dress unfolded its expensive artistry under the guidance of the seamstress whose life goal was to make every dress I would wear forever after, I wandered freely, with no duties whatsoever. I never heard anyone speak a harsh word to me, and the sweet, low voice that spoke to me most regularly remained unwaveringly servile. My body, used to hard labor, must now accustom itself to hours of rest. Yet hardly a moment passed in which I did not feel guilty, as if there were some duty I had neglected. I felt too ignorant to use such luxury properly. I felt so jittery with stillness and comfort, I had to sit down alone and calm myself, remind myself where I was and why, for I could not breathe. I felt certain that at any moment my stepmother would come screeching from some hidden room behind me, accosting me for pretending to be a princess and neglecting my duties.

Sometimes I let Leyla guide me through those shaded acres enclosed within the palace grounds, but only at such times when we were told that Solon was sure to be occupied elsewhere, for he and I were under strict orders not to meet again before the wedding. During these times I was unable to relax in the fluid shadows and musical garlands of birdsong that fell over me, for I thought of him constantly. I couldn't believe in any of this. I couldn't believe in the magic, in the palace, in me as princess with Leyla as my servant, but I believed that Solon had desired me once. I'd felt the tremor in his hand, seen the question in his eyes, felt the comfort of knowing for an instant (when he caught me and kissed me at last) that I was real and not a ghost in this world—and all of that was almost, almost familiar. For men had fallen for me that way before. I just hadn't known it could happen to a prince.

♕   ♕   ♕   ♕   ♕

The day of my wedding was the bravest day of my life, though of course I didn't know that then, and I know that you, envying my good fortune, cannot believe me. I cannot blame you for that. What courage, you wonder, does it take to accept a life of ultimate ease, privilege, and abundance?

Leyla stood beside me in a little recessed alcove behind the balcony that overlooked the Urodel, where I would emerge and take Solon's hands before a crowd of thousands. I remember standing in my wedding gown, a bubbling cascade of scratchy lace that was meant to look ethereal and cloudy but which to me felt the way a prisoner's chains might feel as they held him before his interrogator. The dress made me visible. It made me the most important person in Sirenia at that moment.

"Oh Leyla," I said. "I don't know how to be a princess. And I have needed your help, and you have been so good to me—"

"Hush," she interrupted, and captured my hands for an instant in her own, and we looked into each other's eyes—how clearly eyes reflect one another, so much more clearly than these mirrors everyone was raving about then! It was her eyes that told me I was enough, I was beautiful enough. To this day, I still believe she meant it, in that moment.

So I turned from her in a swirl of cumbersome fabric, tripping a little as I turned, for I was unused to such large and important clothing. My dear people, whom after many eras of life I did finally learn to love as a ruler should love, if only you could know the abyss over which my unworthy soul wavered that day. You waited in your boats in the river, holding your lanterns aloft in celebration, waiting to cheer on the miracle of common girl turned princess. You were so beautiful, far more beautiful and magnificent than I. My people, I was raised in shadows and cinders, the daughter of a ghost. My only comfort was a forgotten grave. The only times I ever felt free from inner and outer torment, judgment, and threat were when I disappeared: when I became invisible in fallow fields or uncultivated marshlands, or in my own home by learning to blend into walls and developing the craft of silence. And now you asked me to appear before you in the finery of the royal family. You, the entire city, demanded that I—myself, my body, my face—be the entertainment of the day. Every hour, every moment, I had dreaded this performance. The years that stretched before me in luxury and splendor, the life of a princess, did not seem reachable to me beyond it. To hold myself steady, I tried to focus on the keystone at the center of the archway, its leadership and its sturdiness and the way the other stones held fast around it. I thought of our Savior, and tried to hold fast to the thought of Him as the stones held to that keystone, and I didn't realize what I was actually thinking—that my whole mind was filled with such an awe for the beauty of such a thing, the archway of a palace entrance, and such a tormented desire for this to be my life—until I heard my elder stepsister's gloating, lofty voice chanting in my head, "Not for you, Ella. Not for you."

Then I woke in Leyla's arms. Was it a dream? The palace, the wedding, the dress like chains and the deadly light of the archway? No. I had fainted.

Leyla looked a little frightened as she helped stand me upright again, but her arms were so gentle. And maybe she was only doing her job, even then, as perfectly as she did any part of it; maybe she was as practiced in sympathy as she was in the management of lower servants or the braiding of hair. But did that make it any less real? We are all doing a job, every one of us—the servants, the priests, the farmers, the queen, the cattle and the birds of the field—and the more truly we do it, the more utterly it becomes who we are, until there is nothing more real than the doing of it.

"Are you alright, my lady?"

"Ella Gladstone," came the command of the chaplain. It was time.

"Leyla," I said. "I can't do this."

"You have to, my lady."

For some reason, this calmed me. At least I was doing what I was commanded to do. Fast, before I could lose my nerve, I whirled toward the light and entered it.

Then it all happened—I stood before you—and for a moment I could not actually be afraid, for all the world lay below me, and you lifted your hopeful little lamps over the water, and we looked upon each other dazzled, and fell in love—remember?—and I knew what the queen had meant. And I didn't mind if I died of terror, for the world was so beautiful: the river was the deep surrender of God's blessing, and the city beyond it, my city, my people that, like me, had survived and arisen from persecution and dared toss their lights out into the night—the most beautiful city in the world.

And then I heard the words that would free me, whispered in my ear so close I could feel them, in a sudden intimacy at once carefree and forbidden.

"I couldn't wait to see you again."

When I looked at the prince, this boy appointed to be the love of my life, I smiled so wide that my own smile broke me, and the stern voice of the queen speaking his name and calling him to attention made me laugh with joy, and all the formal words of the marriage ceremony were as nothing to me—I did not even hear them—so relieved was I at the sight of this one face.

♕   ♕   ♕   ♕   ♕

Dear my people,

Prince Solon Cygnini was the prettiest male creature in this world. I still believe it to this day, and I know I am not alone in that belief. His face was slim and smooth enough to be a boy's, but hard enough in the right places to be a man's, his jaw at once muscular and tensely tender as if it forever held a mouthful of sweet liquid, his lips full and forceful even to look at, let alone to kiss. His smiles and his motions came fast, his turquoise eyes held to women with fierce delight, and to be caught in the current between his lithe, playful hands was to be made delicious— melted and crystallized as perfectly and helplessly as a ready cake.

If you were chosen by such a prince, would it be easier for you than it was for me to believe it? "Why?" I asked him at the wedding feast. I couldn't help myself. I didn't even know who I was anymore. Subsequent to uncountable dishes of partridge, goose, eel, lamb cooked in figs and spices too expensive for even my family ever to have tasted (saffron, maybe, from Zara), custards and breads of chestnuts and dates, served with bowls of honey, eternally refilled jugs of wine, and a larger dish of salt at every other elbow than most families in Sirenia saw in a month, we were now licking from our lips the remnants of sugared ginger from the South Forest and bride-and-groom-shaped marzipan. The wine had blurred in my mind the many speeches mingling Solon's name and mine, the rude theatrics of the jesters concerning our after-dinner plans, and even the token religious performance enacting the chaste love affair between the Savior and His Bride, which the king jeered, if it is possible for a person to jeer under his breath. Everyone who looked at me smiled, and everyone who spoke to me shared some eager, mischievous gossip or laughing warning about palace life or the Cygnini family, and ne- glected—to my relief—to ask me anything about myself. A hundred years ago, it seemed, I had sat here nervous and alone in a crowd, a young girl mistakenly stranded in a forest of giants, as the high, haunting prance of pipe music supported by the stately beat of drums opened the evening to a mythical level of abundance ordained by invisible spirits.

Now, as quiet strains of dulcimer melted the voices of the night into drunken watercolor, Prince Solon woke me from my delirium with a hand whispering over my thigh. I must have looked at him with such childish surprise, for he laughed a little before overtaking me with a kiss that blinded me. "Why?" I cried out, when his lips had barely parted from mine. For I had seen him long before he'd first seen me. I had seen him riding through the city when I was a child without hope. I had seen him when I first became a maiden, when the mere idea of the Savior's friendship was not enough for my loneliness and I longed for Him to sit beside me warm and solid—and Prince Solon Cygnini, even from a distance, with those same luminous eyes and rich human lips, that same wise boyish face I'd seen all my life in statues and carvings of the Savior (call it a child's confusion), became—I admit it—like an image of Him, to me.

Tonight I was his bride, yet unlike the Savior's Bride, I would not remain chaste, nor did I want to now. And what did that mean? Prince Solon's hot fingertips flickered under the table, so lightly I could barely feel them. My lips sizzled, as if sunburned, and I could not close my mouth. Oh my people, when our Savior came to live among us, it was the first time in the history of the world that God came to us in human form. Our Savior taught us to love God intimately, as if He were one of us. When He died, His apostles' hearts broke, as they would break for a lover. And ever after, haven't we been seeking to feel this love again? Haven't we loved, since then, with a different kind of love—not a functional love, not a familial love, not the simple linking of one human heart to another, but a love we call romantic, a love we call love but which is really a seeking forever after, a seeking to be reunited in Heaven?

"Why?"

"You mean why did I choose you?" he said, very low and very sweet—his mouth crimped a little to the side in that way it did, that way I would learn to love, with a mock coyness that begged forgiveness of boyish sin. His skin baked golden from the sun of his daily adventures, his eyes full of candlelight—I closed my eyes. And it was unbearable to me that he should answer my question. Modesty is not the word for what I felt. I knew I was pretty, despite all the taunts from my family over the years—though my prettiness was another thing I wasn't sure belonged to me, for I was certainly never allowed to take pride in it. My breasts were big, and men like that. I was taller than the ideal, my face made of plain, sharp bones, my hair straight and darkly blonde, and I'd always thought mine an everyday kind of prettiness, an up-close, alleyway kind of prettiness—not the finely wrought kind to command the attention of thousands, to be chosen from thousands. Yet that wasn't the reason, in and of itself—no, it was only that anything Solon answered to my question, any words he might speak that could touch me where I had never been touched, I thought, would hurt.

"I told Rufus James," he said, "that he would know you by the way you moved. The kindness in it. Like you're comfortable in your own form—not waiting for anyone's admiration." He surrounded my hips with both palms under the table, dropped his voice to a whisper. "Even the way you look at me now. Soft. Everything you do is honest."

"Who—but who *is* Rufus?" I stammered, to change the subject, for the shame of what I felt inside his touch, inside his blazing attention. "I mean, he seems so gruff and—and strange."

"Don't you like him?" asked Sol, his gaze unwavering, his voice teasing.

"No. At least, I don't think so."

"But we must be grateful to him," said Sol, "for he is the most renowned tracker in this kingdom—and only he could have found you, or so I believe." He watched my reaction. "He is a Barbarian," he added, and waited for my little gasp, which I helplessly gave him.

"Are they all like that?" I asked. "So ugly?"

But now my beloved was kissing me again, and inside that kiss I was able to forget effortlessly what conversation tried and failed to erase: the words I could not believe and yet needed to believe in order to survive, the way my own wanting would break me, my instability upon this unexpected threshold, where the way forward and the way back seem equally impossible.

But the scene we made was too much for the table, and even Solon, with a natural sense of decorum but without any sense of guilt for having breached it, restrained himself for the time being. I glanced at the family members I had been so briefly introduced to, trying to calculate the level of shock our behavior had inflicted on them. To my relief, most seemed too drunk and giddy with wedding cheer to notice, though I sensed an eerie, underlying watchfulness, a constant awareness of me, the stranger at the table. Solon's sister-in-law, Narsa, was the only one who met my gaze, for an instant, and I felt that she disapproved, but it seemed to me she disapproved of everything, and perhaps in this moment her irritation arose principally from the sleepy, drunken state of her husband, Solon's older brother Alden. Kiera, Solon's thirteen-year-old sister, waxed only brighter as the night waned. One of my easiest luxuries was simply to watch her. She was the most beautiful girl I had ever seen, the prize of the kingdom. She knew it, but the knowledge didn't hurt her charm. She had greeted me as if it were she who should be awed and privileged by my presence, her great grey eyes unabashedly wide beneath heavy lashes, her cheeks flushed in such pretty spots just beneath them. I was too naive to notice the effects that careful makeup and pruning had wrought—the way her eyes winged up at the edges, or the mathematically perfect arches of her thin, plucked eyebrows—but I know she would have been dazzling even without those touches, though I never saw her without them. Now she flirted with a gaggle of dukes while the sleepy actors and musicians looked on with smiling hunger. Her hair was exceedingly pale, and fell so finely, like a spill of flour down her back. She had a way of tilting her face at constantly different angles as she laughed, like a small bird about to dart away, and the perfect, rather prominent little lines between her nose and her expressive lips were damp with excitement, making her look girlish and sweetly touchable.

Solon squeezed my hand, still gazing at the crowd. "It's a good story that brought us together," he murmured. "A fairy tale." Even with all his charm and confidence, there was a kind of pleading in his voice when he said it.

"Yes," I cried in an earnest whisper, "it is."

Everyone began to clap in rhythm as the pipes started up again and Kiera danced solo on top of the table, twitching her perfect shoulders and balancing her arms on the air like feathers tilting on the wind. She swung her wrists and twirled her ankles, her rippled skirts blossoming around silken feet that had never touched the earth. And I was exhaling, as I realized that Solon would never ask me any hard questions. He would never wonder how I, for example—a girl turned slave in her own house-hold—could have appeared at his ball in those three dresses so fine, or those earrings made of glass and silver, or those slippers made of gold. In his world, everyone had those things, and it would never occur to him to wonder how someone without them could ever have obtained them. I'd stuffed those enchanted garments beneath my bed on the last night of the ball, telling myself for the final time that I wouldn't return to the garden of my mother's grave, and by the morning they'd disappeared. I'd waited breathlessly to be apprehended, certain that someone had discovered them, but I never was, and I never saw them again.

After a hundred years the prince woke her with a kiss, and they married, and lived happily ever after.

Lemara

I woke in Roses. Flushed and scared, their faces nodding in the breeze all wet with color, petals scented milk-pink and their shadows violet inside. Then he threw the grey blanket over, and it shut me.

Oh, and itching with the blanket's tiny claws! His lips cold kissing, and the kissing woke me, tore open the Dream—Oh of Tiras, who waited and warned me of something desperate to know—what? There was fear in that kiss that woke me, and not my beloved's.

Roses the color of my sleep, and the scent and the sound of it—a sound only heard in Dreams—of petals falling endlessly into death, sweeping over each other like a Rain without Sky to begin it or Earth to end it. Even now I feel them growing, never stopping, from Sprouts to Vines, from Vines to Trees, from Trees to thickets, then becoming a great castle of Roses—and because they grew, I did not have to grow. I am still that age I was then, the age of initiation, the age of the Sacred Marriage. Yet I know I have slept far longer than day and night, longer than the Moon swelling and forgetting, longer than a season or more.

Enchanted Roses. One of my fathers bought the seeds from Sirenian traders, in exchange for my first Priestess gown. Made of Egret feather and the white peeling skin-bark of young Nuba Trees, but he did not return it to the Trees, no. He sold it to the Sirenians, for the Roses. They've held me like a seed in a dormant pod, these Roses, while I Dreamed.

They fight the Wye prince as he carries me, they mean to protect me. Each time he cries the raw cry that sickens me, I duck my head, the thorns comb my hair. Each time he cries out, as the Roses tear him, I remember a Dream like a body torn to pieces, I remember it in flashes that cover my eyes, I remember it like dark, speechless Birds passing over, I remember the Dream I Dreamed while I slept, but no. I can't remember it now. Tiras, my beloved, cried out in that Dream as if by some violence, but I cannot, I cannot remember!

By the Wye prince's sword, the Roses shatter into light. We emerge from atop the Temple of Women and I know where I am—that I Dreamed here, where my people planted the Roses all around me to protect me. He woke me, and my Tiras is gone. This face coarse with beard and rough of eye, not like our sweet Hummingbird boys—oh, I woke weeping, and could not tell why.

Never before have I seen a Wye-man, the color of driest dust. And never have the women I love not come running. And never—oh Faeries that bind and light and tend, what has happened? On I am carried, through the Sun and into His falling, and no one cries for Him but me, and terror seizes me lest He never return. I cannot see nor feel the Moon. On and on now within this thing called Carriage, a cavern drawn by Horses, sad creatures imprisoned by reins, moving as if in place forever.

Where my La-deer friends, my best girl Esha? Where my Mama, and her lovers and sister-friends? And where Tiras, Tiras, Tiralas... I have come into a world that does not love itself. The Earth smells too faint, as if She doesn't want the Sky, and the Sky far away, smelling like no Rain forever. No Mist moves between them; the lone Trees strangle and weep, the Sun is not tender but lashes us, never sweetening. The Air formless, the portals to Dreams not singing, not alive. My body imprisoned and I cannot feel the land, I am broken from the land of my Ancestors and will die—a twig broken off—and the things—I cannot really touch them with my eyes, I cannot reach them—they say, *This is all.*

And the people out there beyond the carriage— I do not know them. They look, almost, like my people with their wild River eyes, but their hair is yellower like the people who came from Sirenia and tried to change us. They smell a hissing, angry, sour smell like dying bodies with no Earth to welcome them in and receive them; they sit alone atop the hard, hard soil, squatting alone around the dirty things they live in. Awful, dead-flesh people.

We are not for sale, said the woman who was old, the woman inside the dark of the Tree. I remember her long-sighing wheel that spun life into thread, telling me I could have what I'd never seen... And she would weave from this thread my marriage gown...

We splash through a Stream whose shape I seem to know—the Stream speaks the name of the *River Golden*—but it's like a skeleton with the flesh of green all gone around it. These people watch me and I wonder if they have heard some tale of me. I wonder do they know I am Lemara Hummingbird, Priestess of Hummingbirds, of the Southern Primeval

Forest? Where are we, Faerie of the River Golden? Where are we, Deep Forest folk with your castles made of shadow? No Animals, not anywhere. Forest muted, no Flowers and no wings. Only the poor Horses that drag us on, bound.

What is it pulls me backward; what is it breaks my heart? The Temple, pulsing still beneath and now behind me as if the women sung below me while I slept, Dreamed a Dream through me. I squeeze the ropes of my hair, run the light through my fingers, and I hug myself, my shoulders, breasts, heart in my arms. The blanket falls to my hips, Air flirts along my spine almost recognizing me and I sigh, *oh*. I feel the Wye-prince beside me, and the two other men. My heart heats and bleeds, *what is this?* I clutch the blanket over my bare breasts. *Shame,* says my heart. *It is called shame.*

Why?

I don't know, says my heart, and begins to cry.

I move my knees, my toes. Am I here? Can I flee? Ancestors, I cannot find myself. The carriage bumps and throws me side to side—can I leap out of it, or will I be lost between worlds?

Now here stands a high church—I recognize the shape—like the one they tried to build in the South Forest, but we drove them off with Dancing. How we used to laugh at their backwards stories, like their story of how the world began, of how woman was created out of man—from some part of him—instead of the other way around. It was like a jokester story, the kind we tell to make the Faeries laugh on midsummer's eve. Like telling that the Deer eats the Jaguar, or that the old one grows smaller year by year and dies a babe—this funny story of woman being born out of the body of a man.

I hunger, but I will not eat the dead meat Prince Micah offers me.

He speaks, but I turn away. I know some of this Wye prince's broken half-words, for long ago our languages were the same, our people were one. But they took our language and dried it out—only a husk now with no hands to give it spirit, no breath to give it song: clipped words without tails. His mouth moving, and no other part of him. I turn away, and perhaps he believes I do not understand him.

My last meal I remember—Dewberry wine, Flame Mushrooms, a bowl of Snails that Awhee gathered and brought for Esha and me, for Awhee is the best at gathering Snails. A slow, sweet day, Esha shivering her fingertips on the inside of my arm, and I sighed for the froth it made in my body, saying I'm restless, Sha-sha, I will go out and find Tiras. Our marriage day only seven days away, and every night we would meet to taste each other's mouth-nectar with our lips, cheek sliding to cheek and thigh shaking to thigh the way the leaves of the Rain Tree shudder before a Rain. Each night I loosed a single strand of his braid, only to feel his muscles loosen against mine, his voice silenced by desire... And Esha whispered no, you are to stay here in this Nuba Tree-palace today, for your Mama bid me watch you. But Esha didn't mean it. She would do anything for me. Kissing my shoulder, her lips always wet, eyeing my lavender nipples I'd ringed with white shell gloss. Watch me what? I teased. For a whole moon before the Priestess's day of marriage, no one made love, and we all trembled together with the pent-up, delicious Fire.

And then we heard the Humming sigh.

Like the Hummingbirds would sound all around the Tree-palace we made this season, if you stepped outside on a limb, for it was built in basket-nests and lithe little bridges into the great Nuba Tree itself. The way they would hum all around you, a loving little roaring, beating their tiny star-hearts. But not this sound. This sound sighed deeper, and on and on.

A darker sound from down below, it seemed, and deeper, darker in. I'll go, I said, and see what that sound is. And Esha called No—don't go, my Priestess, for your Mama bid me watch you. The curse is near in these days, she told me. The curse of the Dark Faerie, that waits for you at the count of fifteen years.

But it was a new thing, this counting of years, making a number for each time the season came again. They only did it for me, because of the curse. I shook it off me, I did not like it. I laughed at Esha—for how could I believe her, when my body rocked in joy? I could not hold myself.

I remember now—how I went forth to that sound.

Breathless, I spiraled around the great Nuba trunk, my hands and feet all skittery over the Tree's peely skin, not knowing what I longed for with my faster and faster heart, only that it reminded me of the wings of the lusty Hummingbirds in the Rain, and I thought I would find that something that pulsed in my Dreams all year now... *Oh Tiras*, I thought.

At the base of the Tree, a cave among its roots, tall as my tallest father once and a half over. *Never seen an old woman before, ha*, said the old, old woman inside it—her skin pale as her hair, like the old Sirenians—where the Humming led me. No one had gotten so old in the South Forest for a long time, the forest so wet and hot with Jaguars and sickness. But this woman who was old felt irresistible to me, her with her humming, sighing wheel, the infinity of it. I had never seen infinity moving before, except in the River. What is it? I asked, and she said, *That is the Animal fur becoming a thread; that is the mortal thing becoming immortal.* And I did not understand.

She said, *I will make you a dress, Priestess, a dress of Silver and Gold, for your wedding day. See?*

Without stopping the turning of the endless Wheel, she nodded so that my vision fell upon the Silver and then upon the Gold. Such colors we did not have, there in the Southern Primeval Forest. They are not colors at all, but something else altogether. Like times of day. I fingered them—the Silver made of Moon, the Gold made of Sun; the one like desire, the other like satisfaction. How Tiras will tremble, I thought, when he feels it.

I will make you a dress, she said, *if you invite me to the ceremony. If you let me see the Sacred Marriage.*

We do not show that, I told her. It is a secret of our people.

But you have shown other Dances, said she. *Show me this one.*

Mara! called Esha to me from up above. She was afraid.

But I called to her, Don't be silly. It is not the Dark Faerie. It is a Sirenian woman, come to see the Dances.

Do you agree? asked the old woman, looking suddenly at me, and I stepped back just one step, at the greed in her eyes. But I could not look away. *Do you agree to invite me to the ceremony?*

I nodded. I wanted the Gold and the Silver. I had never seen such a thing. I thought of how Tiras would sigh for me. It seemed such a little thing to give—to let one old woman see the ceremony.

Then this is a magic wheel, said the woman, and she laughed a laugh like leaves in the dry season rubbing one on the other and lifted her hands in the Air, offering me the spiral of thread upon the spike of wood, from where the story unwound. *Spin the wheel once,* she said, *to put your spirit in the thread, and then your dress will be made to suit you.*

So I reached out, and felt pain...

"Give them something," Prince Micah is saying now, his voice halting and gruff. I watch his face and see that he is sorry for the people here, begging and reaching at the carriage—my people, or are they? But there is nothing he could give them: they are lost, like me, from their home of color and song! What does his man hand them—some Silver and some Gold? But what could my people want with money? I am ashamed for them, taking money and bowing like stupid Sirenian slaves to this man who knows nothing of our ways. *It is dangerous,* I want to tell them. *Do not take the Silver, do not take the Gold!* For it will steal your life from you! It will make you sleep, and if ever you wake, you will not know yourself. Like the pale people. But I am silent, I cannot find my voice.

I know now. Oh Tiras, my love, I have made some terrible mistake, and I am frightened.

We are not for sale, said the woman who was old, when I pricked my finger on the spindle and cried out. And her hair no longer white, and her skin no longer pale. *You did not invite me to your birth, but you invite these strangers to the Sacred Marriage. Who gave you your story? Where did you come from, if not darkness?*

Ah, Rhiannon, I remember you, Dark One. You tricked me, after all. What has happened to me? To what awful, nowhere place have You cursed me?

"We are to be married," speaks Prince Micah Wye to me now. I turn toward him, forgetting to pretend I don't understand. Looking into my eyes now, at least, and with a bare bit of reddening on his cheeks. What does it signify? What could he possibly mean by such words?

And now a desolate stretch that hurts my bones to see, the Trees murdered and fallen, the ground starving, the sap crying into it. Oh what are these nowhere places, each so much uglier than the last? I am Priestess of Hummingbirds: I die without beauty. If Zara, city of Wyes, looks like this, I will run away. I will find the River Golden and follow her back through Rain-heaving leaves, into scented Mountains, into Trees bigger than castles. Though I've never traveled so far away as this, I will find my way back home. I will follow the invisible singing of the Bats, the sigh of the Serpents. I will sleep in Nuba Flowers when I'm tired, and eat the fruits that are everywhere, where I come from. No one ever hungers, where I come from. No one ever kills. The Rains come now, and I will hear them Dancing to bring them down, and the Rains will come over them as their hands over their bodies, singing, and then—then I will truly wake! And my Tiras will be waiting...

When I can no longer bear it, I ask the prince. I betray my knowledge of his language, pleading. "Where are we? Where do you take me?"

So strange the looks of this man, and yet deep the warmth of his hands as he takes mine between them. What does he think, behind those eyes? What does he feel, behind that voice which is a wall? His Eagle nose, his heavy brow—barbaric, to my eyes.

He doesn't answer me, and I explode from his grasp in a flight of fury. "You will answer me," I command. "Where is the Southern Primeval Forest, where I come from? Take me back."

Again he takes my hand in his, and again I struggle, panicked by his silence. But "Priestess!" he cries softly, and reaches for my cheek. And this gesture, more human, more Animal, quiets me long enough to understand the look in his eyes, at last. It is kindness. No, it is pity. Something I have never seen before. It frightens me, and I look away.

"Priestess Lemara," he says, slowly, and so softly that even the Horses don't turn back their ears. "We haven't yet left your country's borders. These *are* your people. This *is* the Southern Primeval Forest—what's left of it. Where you come from—all has been changed."

But I cannot hear him, because before me now rises a bridge that I have never seen. Bigger than I ever knew a bridge could be, crossing over. Crossing over—*Oh Hummingbirds*—the River Golden. In a place where she has never been crossed. The last traces of Dream flee from me, I think forever, and I panic. *I am Lemara Hummingbird. I am chosen Priestess of Hummingbirds. My Ancestors have blessed me. I am daughter to the Faerie of Ocean, daughter to the Faerie of River. Daughter to the Faeries of Meadow, Swamp, Deep Forest, Young Forest, Edge. If I cannot Dance my Ancestors, if the land does not sing under me, at least I will say their names inside me...*

"Priestess. Priestess, you must listen to me."

I shake my head. His tongue stumbles over the word *Priestess*. He does not even know how to say it. And I cannot hear him, because before me now rises—beyond the River, beyond where I have never been, a story I have never seen with my eyes but only heard with my ears. The Volcano. The Volcano Ho. I know it, from the stories of childhood. I know what happened in there. I know what happened to the Wyes, why they turned pale—not as pale as Sirenians, no, but missing something.

I turn and look behind me. I see nothing I know, in any direction.

"Priestess. You have been sleeping for one hundred years."

When she wept tears of love upon him,
the beast transformed into the handsome prince he
truly was, and so they married,
and lived happily ever after.

Mina

My dear sisters,

How can I tell you? I am not coming home.

How this letter will reach you, I cannot yet imagine. But more impossible things have happened to me than this, and I'll find a way.

I need to tell you why I've left you, why I've chosen this. Please understand—you know me. Please hear what I have to say, and tell Father what you can. In some way he already does understand, but it is not for him to understand everything that I will tell you now. The beast you feared had enslaved me—he is not a beast. He is a man. I have married him.

Just now he is hunting, in his old embroidered hunting gear from long ago, not with teeth and claws but with a bow. Just this morning I watched him flex and test it with his own hands, for it remained to him from boyhood, and then I watched him sit on the edge of our bed and stare, as he often does now, at those very hands—with amazement. And then seize my hand—not with savagery but with love—and entwine it with his, grinning like a happy fool, still amazed. His face no longer clothed in hair—he even shaved his beard.

How can I begin to tell you? You know, I have all my old diaries here, and at times I've had nothing else to read but them. I'm only sixteen, as you're fond of reminding me, but I've written so many pages. You used to wonder (idly, I think) what was in them—how I could be so silent, but have so much to say. It's only recently, reading them over, that I understand myself. How perfectly everything led to this moment. The parts of me that fell away, and then returned to me. How I never knew what I was seeking, until it began to hunt me.

Dear, restless Lara. Dear, sweet Addie. How many times, after lying awake for hours, discussing the fine points of how various suitors perceived you and how their wealth should be measured and compared, did you finally turn to me saying, "Let's ask our Mina, she always has something to say about it"—? And I had held myself awake for so long each time, knowing that you always would ask. And that you would wait respectfully while I considered, with that silence so unusual to you. Though you never took my advice, I think it mattered to you even so. Why? Not because I, the youngest and least worldly, am in any way wise. But I think because I looked deeper. Always. Into everything. If there is anything you ever respected about me, your shy, dreamy little Mina, wasn't it this? You used to tease me, but how fiercely you defended me, Lara, if any one of your suitors made some careless comment about my lack of social graces—and "Mina knows what you are thinking, and can surely see inside your very heart," you said once, Addie, adding your easy laugh to your words so the poor boy wouldn't be frightened.

Perhaps if you—or anyone—had seen my beast as he was, a beast is all you would have seen. Perhaps I was delirious when Father and I first arrived here, guided as if by magic across Sleeping Lake, for I'd slept the whole way, with a sleep that felt forced upon me. But I was not afraid when I first saw him. You made me describe him to you when I came home, but I never could do him justice. His primordial eyes, the size of my fists. The scents of his fur changing with the weather and the season and what he'd been hunting. His playful tail—always moving, knocking valuables off the old castle shelves on purpose to break them, once he saw how it made me laugh. I knew him when I first saw him, as I know him now. His rugged brows, his strong chest and thighs, his brambled hair like an unkempt mountaintop still as white as the beast's was, though he stands before me a young, healthy man—he is not so different, now. If an innocent maiden met him alone in a dark forest, she would run. But an innocent maiden would never enter such a forest, and perhaps I've never been as innocent as you thought me.

There are things I could never tell you—not so you would understand. The sound of his howl, night after night, every night, for a year, and what it did to me, what it woke in me, how it beat me down with compassion until I could barely rise each morning. I do not think you could feel anything unkind toward my husband if you had heard such a wail—stretching so far into the night, longer than a river stretches from mountain to sea, gouging an emptiness in the sky, and quieting, finally, upon a hushed, panting breath of hopeless isolation. In the sound of that howl, I almost lost hope, too, realizing that all the little tasks of care I took upon myself in the castle each day—the cleaning and ordering, the pruning of the roses—were for no one's good but my own and mattered not at all. They could not matter to a beast.

You used to ask what I wrote about, what I thought about so long, wandering through my silent childhood—oh, I hardly knew. I could hardly have explained why I hunted the things I hunted, with my huge and quiet senses.

The images I saw in the streets of Sirenia, the muffled echo of wood against wood underwater as the boat hulls struck the house landings in the evening, the songs of the doves pouring over each other, the sylphs and griffins that played in the carvings on the columns of the palace dock—how I wondered at the way time could be stopped that way, by art, and how I knew that the lives of those mythical beings continued on into the past and the future, but on some other layer of reality we could not see. I wrote of the pigs' foolish antics as they jostled each other for scraps in the empty town square after market day—one of the few things that made me laugh. I made up stories for the faces I could not see beneath the hoods of the peasants, as they passed with their parcels and donkeys over the little bridges that crossed the canals—the beautiful arc of the bridge capturing them for an instant in time, making a painting of them before they moved on and were lost again in their own unknown stories. I loved to watch the way, after a rainstorm, the garbage of both rich and poor all mixed together. I loved to watch how the glass-blower's hands trembled but the glass unicorns still came out perfectly, and how the bee-keeper looked a monster in his bee-keeping suit, and how the music of a wandering minstrel changed the shape of the sky and the pace of everyone who passed, and how everyone distrusted the miller and talked behind his back and accused him of cheating, but his face never changed and his hands never shook as he poured the grain like sand onto those ancient scales, measuring out the food of the world, and how sometimes when I had been watching for a long time and least expected it, I saw shadows pass in the windows of the Cygnini palace, and I wondered about the people inside, and if they were happy or sad, and if watching the swans that sailed below them made them feel peaceful and tender toward the world as it did for me.

Living in the castle with the beast, it was the same for me—the same beauty overwhelming, in the great stained-glass mermaids and the up-side-down snowflakes of glass in the silent Great Hall, the empty, ruined rooms now open to the wind, and the jagged shapes of sky framed by the upper balconies all fallen to rubble. I never wanted to own the beautiful things you did, but I loved to watch beauty. And now, you see, here in the Ghost Kingdom, for the first time it was watching me.

As far as I knew, I was the only human creature alive here. There is a madness in that kind of solitude, already, but it was intensified by the ever-shifting reality of this land, a slippery uncertainty in the very air that I took a very long time getting used to. Night winds carry illusory voices, and mists hide the day. The moon shines brighter than back home, as if it is closer to the earth, or more desperate somehow, and it changes familiar shapes with more daring. When I lived here with the beast, every room, every step, seemed haunted by some living, awful history whose meaning and intention I could not tell.

It took me many moons to realize that the invisible presence that hunted me was not a ghost in the castle or in one of the sculptures but rather the beast himself. He followed me. He followed me through the garden of roses, as I lifted them upon fingertips he did not have and shivered from their thorns with a bareness of skin he could not feel. He watched me while I ate the meals I'd cooked from the meat he left me and the overgrown weeds. I found his moon-colored hairs on the diaries I had lain down the night before. He glimpsed me when I bathed, when my eyes were hidden by my wet hair.

What did he want? You might think him perverse, but he was an animal—can an animal be perverse? To tell the truth, it thrilled me, secretly, with a subtle, dream-fragrant whisper-bite of rapture. I have not truly explained to you what his eyes were like, how they understood things about me I had not understood myself. Not only my loneliness, but my desire for something so beautiful, I had never seen it. On the night of my sixteenth birthday, I caught his eyes in mine, kneeling suddenly before him at the foot of the tower stair, when he descended in exhaustion from his long, desolate howl. "Dear Beast," I said to him, "I beg of you, do not howl in the night anymore. Let us comfort each other, somehow." They were the most intimate words I had ever spoken to anyone—but I supposed I was half out of my mind with loneliness, too, and could not help it. When he came to me, he smelled like the trees' breath at night, the hidden sweat of prey before it succumbs. He knelt as an animal kneels, with his knees bending backward, and lay his head in my lap. I felt his throat against my thighs, his brutal fur scratching my skin through my nightgown, and a gulping ache within me that I do not know if you have ever felt before, my sisters—I have never asked you. For years, I wanted to, but was ashamed.

I told you once of a cave I found in the forests here, a womb of crystal among glassy springs, with a darkness breathing cold from its mouth like the breath of the night sky. But I did not tell you it was he who brought me there. I did not tell you of his presence beside me, exploding over and over with emotion that only I could feel.

I never knew what God was—I still don't know. I don't hold in my mind such a clear idea of Him as you do, when you blame Him for the pirates that took Father's fortune, for the collapse of your dreams and the disappearance of all your rich suitors—I know I didn't lose what you did, and it was easier for me, but it never surprised me. I can't define why exactly, except that maybe I knew that what we had owned we had not really owned, for our life had always seemed to me as great a mystery as everything else in this world—the glassblower's trembling hands or the minstrel's songs which were always sad but which made people happy. I will always feel nostalgic for those evenings we spent in the country, once we left everything behind for the little cottage out there by the Golden River—when I'd finished my work and sat alone by the creek and looked at the stars and the invisible light behind them. Addie, you were weeping in your bed, and Lara, you were disappearing half the night, wandering in hungry rage we knew not where—and I was so sad for you both, I loved you with all the love I knew, and yet I was not afraid. God was a question I could never answer, and I loved the not knowing. I love it still.

You may laugh at all of this, my dear elders, my savvy sisters. I don't write it in the language you are accustomed to hear me in—I who never use more than a few words to answer your questions. When I read my old diaries back to myself, I find that I hardly exist in them. They are first my childhood impressions of the world, and then later my retellings of your love stories and adventures—when I was yet too young to imagine such things for myself. Oh Lara, you were always the talk of the town, with your elegant bones and sharp, wistful face framed by layers of dark red wings. And Addie, darling "Adeline" upon so many fervent lips—how languid your walk, your shoulders drenched in freckles, your face always laughing. If I walked with you, I only did it to help your cause—to increase the dazzling spectacle of our hair, that fever of red, red hair which you both wore loose but I always kept in braids. You used to tell us, Lara, when we were children, that in the old days before the Savior, on the old continent, our people believed red-heads were touched by the fire of gods. I don't know if it's true, but unlike other aberrations, red hair did always seem to dazzle our peers, inspiring wistfulness instead of suspicion. I enjoyed sharing that magic halo with you, in my quiet way. But the truth is my hair is darker, duller, a shadow of your own. I hid my boyish, narrow body behind your curves. I never looked at myself in the mirror if I could help it—my face too severe, and dusky like our Wye mother's, not fair like yours. I never wanted a separate identity from the one we shared. If someone had told me, two years ago, that I would ever part from you for more than a day, how it would have wounded and bewildered my heart just to think of it.

It still does. I cannot bear that I shall not see you again until some unknown time. It is the only thing that mars my happiness—that, and the fear that you will not forgive me. I adore you, both of you. I was perfectly content doing most of the housework, even when poor Father scolded you for your neglect of it—I understood that you suffered as I did not, that you had lost more, and I loved to work for my family, I loved to know that I could be there for you in any small way. To be honest—I think you know this—I always tried harder than you did to replace our mother, who after all died giving birth to me, so I felt a certain responsibility. Perhaps, I think now, I was not actually born to be a merchant's daughter, though of course I will always be grateful and admiring of Father's hard work and the esteem in which he was once held. What I mean is that working with my hands, taking care of home, of family, of animals, of vegetables—of anything—I felt at home in myself for the first time. But now Lara, now I have seen you married well enough, though I don't think you realize how well, and your good husband will take care of Father in his declining years, I know. Addie, I know you will soon be well cared for, too—I saw it in your prospects during that brief time when I was home.

Now it is my husband who needs me. And I, Mina, rejoice to be needed by him.

His name is Nicolai—Nicolai Wolf, I call him, for he was cursed to be one for fifty years. Everything I wrote just now about God, and the dreams I dreamed when I was young—perhaps I have been trying to prepare you for a kind of magic you will not believe. And yet you believed well enough in unicorns, when Father came here hunting their ivory—the very last of it, they said, that could be found in the world. Well he found none, because the unicorns were all destroyed or disappeared all those many years ago. Nor are there real wolves here any longer. Those, too, were massacred long ago. It was for these crimes, and more, that Nicolai—and all his people—were cursed by the Dark Faerie Rhiannon. I suppose she wanted him to experience the desolate loneliness of an animal who cannot bear to live without his pack, in a land where he was the only one, so that he would understand the devastation his people had wrought upon this place. They are called the Ghost People now. But once they called themselves the Unicorn Riders. It is a long story, one I hope to tell you in person one day when we see each other again. But for now I imagine you have enough to take in, if you are reading this—and as I write it I am distracted by a nervous anxiety, as dusk falls so gently, too gently, over the castle stones and my love has not yet come home.

I only want you to understand, by mentioning his history, the sense of responsibility he carries—as a prince, as a sovereign, and especially for me. In his mind, it is I who woke him from the curse. He cherishes me as the one who brought him salvation. When he first held me again, after the transformation, I remember he felt light—lighter than I expected, and I wished he would let himself go completely and accept my embrace with all his being, but I knew also that he felt it incumbent upon him to act with caution. He doesn't ever want to treat me as a beast might treat a woman. And yet I love all of him—the beast, the prince, the man.

And he loves me. My sisters, I know in your hearts you will want what's best for me. He is the only creature I have ever known who feels this life as deeply as I do. If only you could see how sweetly he honors me. If only you could have seen how—even as the beast—he used to sleep outside my door to guard against the nightmares, or sit beside me at my times of deepest sorrow in missing you. Did you never wonder how I made it home to visit you? Has Father not told you of that treacherous passage, which killed all of the men on his expedition, and only spared us on our journey because (I believe now) Rhiannon's magic swept us on toward my destiny? The inlets of Sleeping Lake, the seas full of serpents, the trio of mountains that separates the bog from the sea, too steep on one side and cascading with constant avalanches on the other through flesh-thick fog? How did I make my way across the windless Dragonfoot Swamp—why didn't you ask me? Did you think I escaped my beast? No, for it was he who carried me all the way there. I was too desperate for you, too desperate to let myself think of the impossibility of such a journey. I was going to do it alone, and I would have died. But he met me on the dark road the night I tried to leave without telling him. I thought he might kill me for my betrayal, but instead he faced me with glowing eyes, growled with impatience for me to mount him, ride him. He protected me from ghosts and mists. He hunted for the both of us, as he always had. He galloped so light of foot over those screes and canyons, I felt I was flying, and he knew the paths that no human could ever know or remember, from one solid island to another, through the long Swamp, and I knew (without knowing how I knew) that it was his ancestral wolf memory which guided him—memory of hunting beavers long ago, memory of their abandoned lodges, memory of where they hemmed the water in and where it flowed out again. I held to his warmth as he swam us through sad, milky waters, where all you can hear are occasional loons. He slept by my side, his warm, breathing presence holding me as the night sky holds the stars.

At home, you thought I wasn't myself. Distracted, jumpy, not the quiet, self-assured little sage you had once depended on. Sometimes Father had to ask me a question twice before I heard. I could not promise to stay with you. The smallest decisions of my day—whether or not to join you in an outing to the fair, whether or not to continue the daily prayers I had practiced before I'd left, whether or not to start in on the project of taming the flower garden now completely overgrown—felt difficult to me. You thought he must have terrorized me, subdued me. I spoke so little of him, you could only assume the worst. How could I tell you?

How could I tell you of my dreams, in which I tasted the world in the air? In which the night-white map of the forest cascaded past my body as I ran, but even more vividly than it came to me in vision, it came to me in scent—up my nostrils, over my tongue, down my throat, through the fur of my face, in a wind. And in scent, it came not as a map but as a fountain, an upwelling of life. My paws sunk into the wet leaves as I ran like teeth into tender flesh. The forest cleaved to my running like a body to a soul. In this dream, I felt perfectly clear for the first time in so long. I knew exactly what I wanted, and I was hunting it. There was no pain in this longing, no confusion—only a need so powerful it was like a heart, pumping blood into all my seamlessly coordinated muscles. I never stopped running, leaping when I must leap, crouching when I must crouch, twisting when I must turn, and my running was a rhythm my hunger fit to.

How could I tell you, Addie, that when you shook me awake, murmuring words of comfort to my cries, assuming they arose from a nightmare, I had been crying out in passion—for I felt him hunting me, and I wanted that hunting—how I stumbled with anticipation, already bleeding before he'd bitten me, already growling inside, tasting mud like hot pudding.

And then I chose. I must have been more than just a part of you, a shadow to your red-maned glory, I must have wanted something of my own. I must have felt so certain, to be able to resist your pleas. You were afraid for me. And I am sorry. But I knew he would be waiting for me when I left the villages behind at night, let my hair down loose at the edge of the trees.

Back at the castle, we passed under the familiar strands of ivy, and I touched his thick mantle of silver hair. I felt bold, bolder than you've ever seen me, when I took him to the garden of roses I had tended so lovingly and so long—for their breath is freshest in the night. I was afraid, after all, when I knelt there before him, but the earth comforted me, and I closed my eyes. He did nothing to me; I undressed myself. When I lay down in the scented, petaled darkness, when I felt the lips of a man against my own, it didn't surprise me—the feeling was no less unfamiliar to me than the mouth of a beast. And now there seemed to be some other Mina in my place, one you would not know—nor did I—who would do anything for what she felt. I asked for this, my sisters.

We married the next morning, at dawn.

"There are no rules, now, Mina," he said to me, in his new, sonorous voice. "There is no kingdom. There are no people. There is no king. We are re-making the world, you and me."

We stood together, he wrapped in a blanket and I in my cloak with nothing underneath, and we looked out from the windows of the tower where we'd climbed, where once he'd howled alone but now he whispered into my hair, while I opened my lips against the salt skin of his shoulder. He grabbed my face and kissed me. It's winter now, the season of wind. The air sweeps the sky clean, and it's the only time of the year when you can see everything. At night, I could see the needled trees studding the dry slopes down to the stony sheen of the sea, in a river of darkness, and giant, mica-flecked boulders leering up with mustaches of dripping lichen. The wind pounced among them, grasping scents of loam, pine resin, tangled seaweed waiting for the tide—and then the roses, always the roses, heavy as the heat of our own bodies finally so close. There was no sound but the wind. I realized how much I'd missed this place, while back in my own kingdom with you. I think it is the mystery itself that has begun to feel like home to me.

"There is no one to marry us," said Nicolai, "so let us marry ourselves."

Then he took both my hands, his clumsy in their new power and twice the size of mine, and looked into my eyes for so long. His eyes were the only part of him that had not changed. And it's true I thought of many things while I gazed into them—the life I might live here, and if we would always be alone here or if any of his people remained, and if truly the curse was lifted now and we might explore the kingdom both by day and by night, and most of all if you would be alright without me, and I without you—but we gazed so long that these thoughts, for a time, fell away, and the dawn came, and I saw it beyond him with my wider vision, that unearthly light reflecting off fields of innocent green, as innocent as the first unicorns before they were enslaved and destroyed, and I heard maybe ten kinds of birds singing, all distinct and yet somehow blending in harmony, the way birdsong always does.

"Do you think, now, that we know each other?" Nicolai asked. "We have known each other a long time."

And I do. I think we have known each other, in these past four seasons, more intimately than some couples might do in a lifetime.

"Then I think, Mina, we are married now," he said. "Because we are certain. Because the dawn has blessed us. What more can we ask for? Are you mine forever, Mina, as I am yours?"

I am, and I said so.

He said he must never hurt me, that I am like the unicorns to him. He said, touching me, that I remind him what it is to be human again—that I bring him back, every day. I found out I am beautiful, at least to him. I never felt beautiful before. Of course, he has never seen you. But he likes the firm grace of me, he says, how there is no wasted flesh, the way I respond to him. He says he never knew a woman could be so hungry as a man, could weaken for touch the way he does—and I do. I always knew this about myself, but I was always afraid of such feelings, until now. So you see we are matched, he and I. If it is darkness, something in me called it to me. Please forgive him. It wasn't his fault.

And I see him at last, now, oh sisters— still far away, but winding up the path from the forest, backed by the great expanse of stars and the cliff edges to nowhere, the wind blowing his long, white curls: I can see them glowing faintly against the grey. He carries the body of an animal slung over one shoulder, and his pack of arrows over the other. I think he looks up toward me now, but it is too dark to see, and I do not know if he can see me yet from this distance. How relieved I am! I laugh at myself now, but I realize that for the past hour or so of writing, I have been straining against a burning anxiety in my belly—to think that he might never return, that something might have happened to him. I never in my life wanted or loved something so much that I felt such terror at losing it. It seems to me, almost, that something so good cannot last, that I will not be able to keep it. But no, for now he is coming, coming over the hills, and his face rises to meet me, and I will lay down this lonely pen and all the silent words of my childhood—you must forgive me, I beg of you—and I will stand upon my human feet, and call out to my husband his human name.

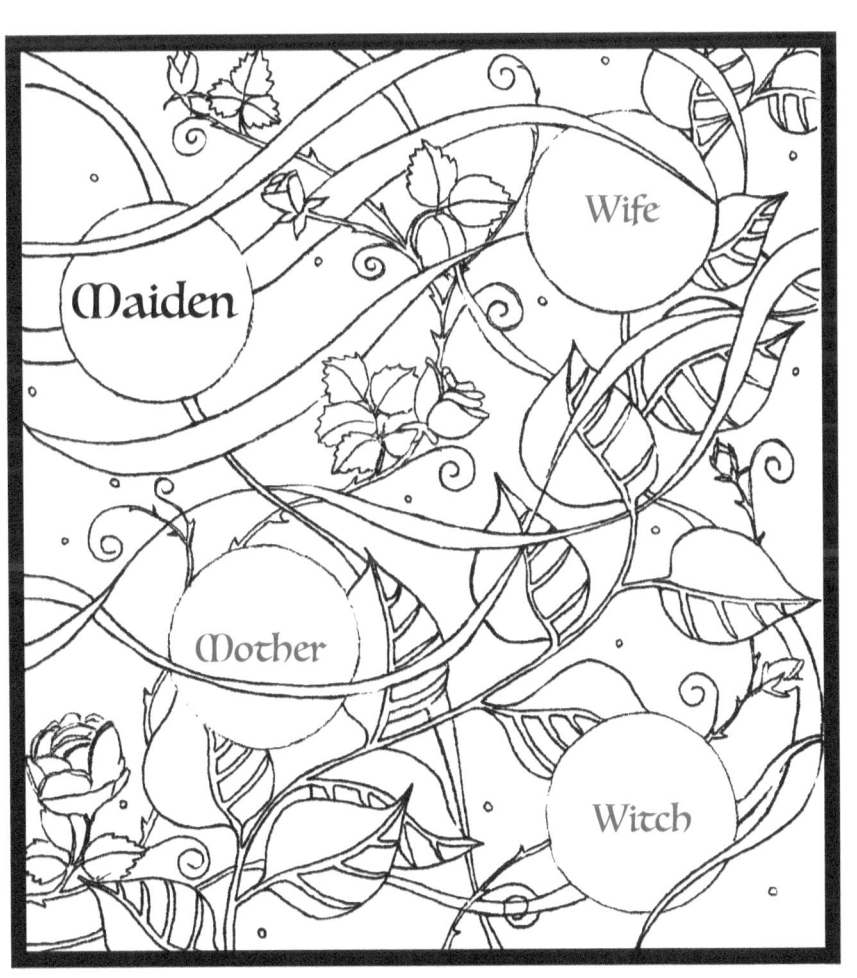

Lemara

The Sirenian god made his world with his hands, like a ball of clay.
The Wye god made his world by speaking holy words.
The Barbarian gods made their world from the chaos of destruction.
The Earth and Sky made love, and from love our world was born.

In the beginning lived the virgin Goddess, the Earth Herself, the original Ancestress. She woke laughing and Dancing one day from the Sea of Her Dreams, full of passion and Life to give. She wiggled her toes and they were Fishes. She tossed Her hair and it swirled into the flight of Birds. She rolled Her hips to make Snakes, Her buttocks and breasts were pungent brown Mountains, from Her singing mouth came Dragonflies and from Her vagina foamed the Rivers. Her laughter was the Wind. Her thoughts were the Faeries who tended each element and She was perfect.

And all the Plants that grew were all the same height, shivering in the Sea Wind, and all the Animals and People were sleeping; they were Her sensations, Her Dreams, the questions yet unasked. And no thing had any color. And there was no need, and all the Trees looked the same.

But once She birthed Herself from the Sea, She was a Self now and beautiful, and because She existed there was space beyond Her, there was all that was not Her, there was distance and Other. She wondered how and why She had woken. She looked out into the darkness and saw His eyes, which are the Stars, watching Her. He was watching Her with His thousand eyes, and He was loving Her. So She blushed and heated, the color began in Her, She swelled and deepened in peaks and pools, She misted for Him and He laid His dew upon Her. Their longing for each other became the colors of the World—Her joy and Her aching, Her trepidation and Her lust, Her jealousy and Her tenderness, for all emotions are shades of Love. The Sky, too, turned rose and peach and violet and cobalt, but though He wanted Her, He was afraid that if He came into Her, He would lose Himself and die. And the Earth was afraid that if She let Him in, He would break Her to pieces and destroy Her.

The Faeries were Her wisdom—they knew the story and how it needed to be done. They knew that the pieces of the world must come together, for otherwise they would come apart. The tension would fade, the Sky would drift away, and the Earth would turn to dust—already She was beginning to dissolve. So the Faeries made themselves into tiny winged beings of heightened beauty, who could fly so fast and hard that their flying made a Hum that stopped time and opened a passage. These first Hummingbirds, these messengers of Love, crossed worlds between Earth and Sky, and from Sky back to Earth, drinking the nectar of longing from each, so that They were pollinated like two blossoms, closer and closer, until They overcame Their fear and gave in to one another at last.

But the Hummingbirds also were warriors, just as they are today, and so they made sure not to allow the male to come into the female in a violent way. No, for they taught Him the language of beauty; they taught Him how to honor the Goddess, in the way that is called making Love, in the same way that the Priestesses teach the boys today.

So the Sky gave forth His Rains, and the Earth received Him, and all things were born. Back then, the Rains were not only Water, but also Food: they contained all the nourishment we needed. And so the Jungle bloomed in Flowers, and all Creatures made Love and also devoured one another. For now there was longing in the world, and the longing bound the world together, so that it could never fall apart.

morning

I listen for the Birds.

The Birds begin singing at the beginning of the world. We know the Sun is coming when we hear them. Some of the Elders can hear so far, they can hear the Bird languages from faraway places—*Hoo-Hoooona, Feee Feee Feee* in the Ghost Kingdom, then *Swheeelt, swheelt, teet teet teetana* in the Wye Kingdom, then finally *Hoppa wheyla chana chana cha-cha-cha cawww* in our Southern Primeval Forest where the Hummingbirds *tstit tstit tstit* their little shouts. Birds pass the message from Tree to Tree, slow over Swamps and fast over Meadows, across the Edge of the Sea and into Deep Forest, until they have reached us wherever we are, and our ears have opened our hearts, and we can smell the Sun burning across all that distance, and we begin to call and bang upon our drums and bodies to awaken His passion, to celebrate the day He brings us. When the Sun comes up in the beginning, He is only a child, and needs encouragement. He is the Sky being born again out of the Earth, after the Earth receives Him in the night.

But I cannot hear any Birds from my balcony in the Wye palace. Only the ever-sleeping wash of the Sea. I see the Sun coming, all innocent and laughing, all shivery and afraid. I am the Priestess of Hummingbirds and I am responsible. The Birds will call Him up, and the Monkeys and the Insects. But Human voices, too, are necessary, to give Him the courage to rise again.

My Elders say the more people you love who have died, the stronger your connection to the Other Worlds. Your Dreams carry you more easily, your conversations with the Ancestors come clearer, the Sky talks to you. Everyone I love—almost all of me, almost all of what I am—has gone down into the Earth's belly. So why can't I Dream anymore? I wasn't there to sing and cry them into the Earth, into the embrace of Ancestors. Someone wailed for my Tiras. Not me. Perhaps they have forgotten me.

I cannot believe what the Wye-prince told me, no, I will not. Somewhere my people are Dancing, nestling together in the laps of Nuba Trees, helping the Fireflies find their beloveds... And yet he says, a hundred years have passed. Not one of them alive today would I know by name. I am their Ancestor.

And it is up to the Priestess to keep the rituals, to be beautiful when all else is lost. The Elders told me this, when first I watched a Sirenian priest baptize a child. *They will take everything from us. But you must not be taken.*

The palace behind me crouches in caverns of stone. I have never stood so high above anything, and it dizzies me, yet I have not left this balcony for all these days. There is a room behind me, what Prince Micah calls my room. But I do not understand rooms. I sleep out here, on the stone. I try not to think of the gaping mouth behind me. Yet the ones who bring me food go in and out from there.

How the Water froths below me against cliffs so severe, how it flies against the stone making towers that instantly fall! How restless. I watch it all day, trying to learn its language, the tension between things liquid and stone. The Wind here so dry and silent, it chills me. It speaks of space, such giant space—we do not have such space, where I come from!

The first time I saw the Sea, more than a hundred years ago, I was coming from the Cave inside the Temple of Women, from my initiation. People came from far away for my blessing, and my best girl Esha dressed me in fruits that the children gobbled from my skin, smearing me with juices. I was Priestess and I led the Dance, I Danced over the body of the land, greeting each of our Ancestors with my feet. I knew the way, in the memory of my body. I sang my own song to the shaded boulders of Old Forest Faerie, and I made love to myself beneath the Waterfall of River Faerie, and in the Flower ring of Meadow Faeries, the Hummingbirds slept in my hair. And in each place I met the community there—the people of Young Forest, who can speak best with Plants, and learn from them the state of all things; the people of Old Forest, who are the best Dreamers; the people of the Swamp, who are the most beautiful. At last our Sea people greeted me upriver with garlands of Seaweed and brought ten of their handsomest girls and boys to take me down to the Sea Cave. Around that Cave where the River Golden gushes into the Sea, she is thicketed so wildly, so deeply, so close, even many of my own people do not know where to step without tangling in Snakes or falling through invisible holes to be devoured. I myself did not know, then—so they taught me. The River birthed us from there right into the Sea, and then we crawled along that quiet, stone-cupped beach where a mermaid built of shells bared her breasts to the waves. *Don't touch her,* they giggled, *or you'll be cursed with ceaseless rapture...* And that night, that night I met Tiras...

Rhiannon, did You truly take everything? Even this?

For She was the other Faerie. The one I did not visit, in my thirteenth year, though I knew in my heart I should. My mama said, *Don't go to Her. She holds a curse for you. If She sees you, She will remember.* The elders shook their heads—they'd seen it all in Dreams. *She is the Dark One, the Guardian of Death. You think She would forget Her own promise?* Because my parents had failed to perform that original rite at my birth, because they had listened to the Sirenian priests when I was born and did not keep that ancient ceremony for fear of Her, I had never met the Jaguar. Never received Her blessing, but only the promise of a curse to come. And so I wouldn't know where to search for Her, even if I tried. I could Dream each night but I could not fully cross over, as a Priestess was supposed to do.

I never received the blessing of Darkness.

"Priestess Lemara?"

I turn. The sweet voice of a woman numbs my face with sudden longing.

"Will you come out today?" the woman asks. They ask me every day, when they bring me food, but they never look at me. And I am terrified of the mouth of dark warmth where she stands, the inside places, yet I cannot remain here any longer. I am a woman of the South Forest. All our lives we move from place to place, swinging high and low, following our hunger and a thirst for Rain. To be still like this, to wake each day in one container of stone, is killing me.

"You must put something on," the woman says. Sharp, tall bones and a hard nose, hair wonderfully sleek, bound in a rope behind her—the way men's hair is bound where I come from.

"What? What—on?"

Like an offering, she lifts to me on her palms a folded clump of fabric whose pretend softness I recognize—like her own dress.

"No!" I say, laughing.

Her smile fades, and I feel sorry for her as her hands falter, the dress escaping partway from her uncertain fingers.

"I cannot," I try to explain. "I am beautiful. I am Priestess. I cannot cover myself like that." I was the desire of every man and woman in the South Forest: I was blessed with beauty, grace, and all loveliness at my birth, by the seven Faeries. I wear today the same Grass and Cloud-Bird feather skirt I wore the day the Wye prince woke me, the same I have worn every day since I came here. I found a chip of white chalkstone in the wall and made arcs under my breasts and rays upon my chest, yet I felt sad when I did it. Without touch, how can I know I am still beautiful? A dress will not make me beautiful, but only hide me from myself.

The woman cannot look at me. "Please," she says more softly. "Only wrap this blanket around—please, like this." And she lifts it from the bed.

The Wind settles around my shoulders. *Trust her. You must go through, to get out.*

"Today is your wedding day, Princess Lemara," says the woman in the dress.

I step toward her, balancing. Perhaps I am Dreaming now, after all. If so, I had better pay attention.

Zara

White stone balconies trail into stairways winding round flowered cliffsides, tinkling with bells. Birds nest in alcoves curved around trickling water. We walk a pathway lined with giant statues of men they call Ancestors. I did not know people could do all these things. A storehouse full of grain—but I have never seen or eaten bread.

"You live in the jungle, where food and all materials are everywhere. Here we must grow our food, or catch it, and make sure it is shared equally. We must divide our work equally, to each the work that suits him. There are many of us here; bound by the sea to the south, your kingdom to the west, the volcano and the Sirenians to the north, and the marshes and Ghost Kingdom to the east, we have nowhere to expand to. We must make sure everyone is provided for in this small space."

It is hard for me to listen to their words, so separate from their bodies. I am always watching their bodies with mine, trying to understand. This woman who guides me uses words in all the wrong ways. It is like the way I recognized my people but did not recognize them at the same time. It was the same place, if place is nothing but location between one space and another, but the Nuba Trees were gone, the Ancestors were silent, and it was not a place at all.

All the people I meet now are women. At first I think they have no men in Zara, but no, it is because the men work in separate places, they do not work with the women, they do not even speak to the women unless they are married to them, and then only at meals, only in the night. Through houses of weaving, orchards, wash houses, kitchens, schools, we hear sounds of men in the distance only—shouts from the ships or the buildings of metal and Fire. Yet the women, never touching, never seeing the men, seem happy. Laughing about little troubles with cooking machines, laundry presses, creaking doors, so many objects of what meaningless function? So many people busy with so many things, all part of a grand structure they have built, a ritual I do not understand. Their laughter swallowed back gently and yet so bright, like Fireflies in a closed palm. And I know I frighten them.

the separation

"Did you see him?" they whisper, when we've passed the Temple door. "That was the prince who will now be king! The one who will be your husband!"

I saw him. I knew him. The man who tore open my Dream with his sword, so that I cannot find it, even in memory. I knew him by his broad back, where he knelt alone before a wooden stand in a great dark room, upon which unrolled a span of terrible pages. I know what they do upon those pages.

"He was all alone," I whisper, shivering.

"He was praying," they say, as if to answer me.

"Does he have no family? No lovers?" I ask. For his aloneness frightens me. But they shake their heads, tighten their mouths.

"He will be your husband!" they cry. "What do you mean, *lovers*?"

And I begin to weep, because I understand now that their language will destroy mine. Whole forests of emotion, pools of knowing and remembering, will starve and fall away, because I will never be able to communicate them unless I can somehow return to my homeland and speak with my own again.

"What is this?" This doorway in the wall—but no, not a doorway, some kind of portal? I look again—it is us, the Hummingbird People Dancing, or a Dream of us without scent or sound! I touch the image, and it feels like the wall. Not the likeness of faces that some of the Deep Forest folk carve into dead Tree trunks to help a spirit pass on, or the stories we make in the dust and later destroy—No, these are magic pictures, too real! Dangerous, to trick the worlds in this way!

"Your dances are very beautiful," says one of the girls. "I saw them once, when I was a child."

"What is this?"

"What do you mean? It is a painting—it is art."

"What is art?"

"Why...perhaps you have a different word for it. It is like your dances. It is making something beautiful. Something that represents something else."

I shake my head. "Our Dances are for speaking."

"But no, I mean—your dances are a creative act, and when we watch them, they feed our souls, they express what cannot be said in words. That is art! I am sure you have a word for it."

"No. No word." Dances are not watched. We dance for Healing, for renewal, for grief, for seducing the beloved. But the Sirenians began to pay us so they could witness the Dances. And whatever "art" is, it is something like the "writing" I know lies deadly upon those pages Prince Micah reads—it separates a thing from itself, as if a person could be separate from one's own body. Oh, a separation yawns between Worlds, that was never there before! Oh, the hundred years I slept! A space between past and present that should not be there. A space between Earth and Sky with no Trees in between to connect them, no Hummingbirds to carry the nectar of their love.

They find me later in a garden, sleeping with Cats, beneath a column of Water that runs upward. (Yes, Esha—you would not believe me, but I am not lying—it is called a fountain.) The little clumps of Shrub and Lily whisper their spice to me. Some of them hard and fleshy, holding Water tight. *All places are here,* says the Tree to me, the only Tree in the garden, a smooth copper-skinned Tree I do not know. *You are always home.* For the Tree has never been anywhere else, does not know there are different places, does not know that roots can ever be undone.

"Wake up, Princess Lemara. You must dress for your wedding. We could not find you," say the voices of the women.

I don't want to open my eyes. I sleep with kittens, and the mother Cat, trusting me, Purrs against my belly. In sleeping, I was safe. In sleeping, I was home. In sleeping, I knew I would wake to sing up the Sun with a sister or brother of my choosing, I would wake in the Grove of Dragon-flies, I would ask all my questions to the great, hunched Vulture Tree on the Green Hill, and I would know what to do.

We pass into a great dome, a room, filled with steaming Water! Sun-light mists down from windows in the ceiling like the fluff of Milkweed. These are the baths, the woman tells me—not a Hot Spring, but heated by Fires the people tend. Prince Micah has commanded that they be heated for me, that I may bathe and purify myself before the ceremony.

"Alone?" I ask her, as she turns away. And I weep as she leaves me, even in the beautiful cave where the Water instantly loves me. I weep as I touch my skin, my body without people, and I think of Esha, my best sister-friend, and the hidden Hot Spring in the folds of the Mountain that is the Temple of Women—now impenetrable with Roses. How we would go there when I wanted to please her, for I was the only one she wanted. Sometimes I forgot her constant, muck-black desire, kept absolutely still, until I happened to kiss her hair in affection, and then she would grip my hand just that much tighter. Her skin, hued like the heart of a Fire, tasted like Water. When I led her to the Hot Spring, she walked quietly beside me, but I could feel the oily ache of her walk, because she knew what was coming. Sometimes she tripped, which wasn't like her. When the Water caved around me, sucking and boiling, devouring me even as I devoured her fingers, her tongue, there was a madness in her that no one knew but me. She used her knees and her heels, her chin, her teeth. I'd lift her up above me and hold her hips over my head, and I'd shout my life into her, with all my joy, and she'd shout right back—a sound only I ever heard.

From a bower on a hill, I can see everything. I can see the dock extending out to where the men are, at the end of the black sand beach. I can see the spires of the towers echoing the Mountain peaks in the East, where lies the Ghost Kingdom. I never saw so far and wide, living in the Jungle. I must close my eyes to hear the voices of the Flowers that trail down the white columns near us.

They have not done with wrapping me in fabrics. They wrap me and wrap me, now touching me with Butterfly hands, now giggling. I begin to smile, for I feel my beauty again—I am a woman again, I am almost alive. I let them dress me, but they won't let me dress them. I let them dress me because I want them so badly to hold me. Because in the South Forest we always dressed each other—how could we spin our creations without other eyes to see them, hands to grasp and change them? We left some spaces open and kept some secret. We changed what was secret and what was shown, just to see the effect upon each other, and to understand that way what we were—as girls, as boys, as People, as Animals.

When these girls cry out with wonder and pride at their creation at last, beholding me, I laugh with them, and then begin to remove it all but they stop me—they grab my hands, *Wait! Don't take it off. This is your wedding gown.*

At first I feel swaddled, as if someone hugged me close. But later I feel constricted, as if my skin cannot breathe.

I remember what the Elders told me—*They will teach that the body isn't even real. They will teach you to disappear. Beware the bodiless God.* With our bodies invisible, our language dies. The heart cannot speak.

the king

Wye people have some of that Gold Rhiannon showed me, inside them, but it's quiet. Micah's limbs don't shine like Hummingbirds; they're like wood with the bark stripped away, or like Riverbeds in the South Forest where the Water is gone. He has hardly any smell. The Wyes aren't entirely colorless like the Sirenians, but they're missing their Animal nature, which is bad, because you cannot be really Human without the part of you that is Animal.

In the South Forest, the young virgin men grow their hair long, but they bind it back in braids to show their restraint, making themselves safe for a lover when she comes—and when she first accepts him, she unbinds his hair, strand by strand, as she welcomes him into her. And so I would tease Tiras, pulling a single strand from his braid with my teeth, one, and then one more, twirling it around my tongue as he sighed... But how could I ever play with a man like Micah, even if I wished to? All his hair is cut short.

He sits beside me for the supper, and I feel the silence in him, but to me it is a violent silence. It is the silence of this table, made of Trees felled by axes. He doesn't look at me. He doesn't show me that he feels me.

"God of our fathers, God of our ancestors, who has worked miracles and brought us to this sacred land... In Your name..."

Food is not everywhere for the picking and enjoying, here in Zara. We will eat *supper* in a great *room*, at a *table,* at a special appointed time. People called Prophets are chanting, before we can eat. At first I thought we would do deep magic here, for the room is all lit with fire—they are called candles—and they amaze me with their white columns and tiered flames, some higher and some lower, like the towers. The food, they say, will also be changed by Fire, and I will be afraid to touch it, but also I am very hungry, and I wait for it. Only the chanting, the prayers—how they go on and on! With so many words!

"On this holy day... In Your name we give thanks... In Your name we ask..."

The Prophets are older than any men I have ever seen. How can they inspire such listening, with their hooded eyes and stiff, grisly necks and greying skin? Droning such prayers, with no music and no passion! And everyone listening rapt, especially Micah. For Micah's father has died, and now Micah is king. That is what the crown means (ugly and metal) upon his head, that has been placed there today. This much I know and understand, from their words.

Only when he lifts his spoon, at last, can we all eat!

I have learned to use a spoon for the foods they brought to my balcony, but I haven't the patience for it now, so I eat what I can with my hands. I lean back my head, drop the food in, my whole body alive again with hunger and eating, and I forget all the hardness inside me. Beautiful tastes! So many spices I recognize (ones that are not found easily, beneath the bark of very young Passion Trees, or in the husks of certain seeds during dry season), and others I do not, and all mixed in ways I would never have imagined, for they do not mix naturally, where you find them. And bread—for the first time I taste it, and how I wish I could tell Esha, for we had heard of it and she used to long for it, though I would tease her *How can you long for something you have never tasted?* and she would sigh sorrowfully, *I just do!* And oh, Esha, it is like—like nothing! Like a flesh of nectar. As if Plants had breasts and gave milk.

But then I see Micah looking at me at last—and oh, what a terrible look! His brows hard and heavy—no one should look at someone like that while enjoying the bounty of food together! It is sacrilege, to look like that! And I see now that others at the table don't eat like me. They eat like they speak, like they do everything: without their bodies. How can the food ever reach them—how will the Plants (and the Fish, too, for they are eating Fish, though they knew I would not, so they gave me none) know they are honored, if the people do not eat with joy?

"Why do you look at me so?" I cry.

He doesn't answer me at first, but begins his slow, careful eating again. Then he says, "Priestess of the Hummingbirds, I know our ways are strange to you."

Still he looks away from me, out across the table. A hundred, two hundred people eating here with such restraint and quiet, the women to my side and the men to his side—I feel suddenly I cannot bear the stagnant air. It has been breathed too many times, without Plants to revive it. It cannot keep me alive.

"What we believe about royalty, and our duty as leaders, is very different from what people in other places believe. We, the leaders, are the most humble of our people, for our responsibility is the greatest." He pauses. His silences are like words. He uses them the way we Hummingbird People use our hands.

"Each thing we make, each part of our palace, is beautiful, for we believe in beauty as a tribute to God. And yet we have, and need, few things to survive. We never have more than our people do. We lead our people, and yet we are humble to them, for they are a manifestation and an instrument of God. In everything we do—even the way we eat—we set an example."

So smooth and solid he sits there, like the waxed table, and so smooth and solid his words, while I sit here like a Bird who has lost the Sky!

"What is that smell?" I ask. "Something is wrong—something is dying."

"What smell?" He doesn't look at me, but tilts his face toward me.

"Something—burning. Smoke. Something is wrong!"

He shakes his head. "I cannot smell it. But probably they are lighting the fires for the sacrifice."

Before I can ask him what this means, he continues—"Priestess, do you know why we are married tonight?"

I laugh. "What marry? I cannot marry you. I don't know what you mean."

"I know. Let me tell you. It was prophesied that on the day I was crowned king, I would marry you. It is for this reason that, immediately after my father's death, I rode to where you slept among the roses—my people had known about this place for a hundred years—and woke you."

"Prophesy—whose?"

"You will remember, perhaps, a time when our forefathers met with your family to speak of peace between our two peoples?"

"Yes—I know this." I remember the Elders were thinking of the Wyes in a new way. Before, we had laughed at them, or feared them like the Sirenians and the Barbarians. Those people seemed not like real people to me at all. But the Elders were Dreaming this. They said the Wyes were once a part of us, they abandoned us long ago and now they return to us. But they do not yet know us. We must be careful. There must be ritual around the return.

It used to be that the Wyes never came to the Jungle. They could not find their way through. But always they were expert with the boats upon the Sea—and we'd see them far off sometimes, fishing. I do not know when it first happened, that the first Wye-man stepped upon our shores for the first time in living memory. There is only one open beach on the shores of the South Forest, where the Jungle lands can be accessed by strangers from the Sea. We came to call it Welcome Beach. By the time I was born, everyone associated it with the Wyes. It is where the Wyes would come to meet us.

"There was one particular meeting, after you were—after you were sleeping, Priestess Lemara. They came again to your people and asked for an alliance between us. The Sirenians were exerting too much pressure on your land and people, and neither of our peoples wanted that. Your people sought to free themselves from Sirenian oppression, which we well understood, having suffered it ourselves. We wished to help you, because if the Sirenians took over the South Forest, they would surround us on too many sides, making our small kingdom vulnerable. Here in our ancient homeland of Zara, we had finally returned and found safety. We will never relinquish it again.

"So in this meeting, my father's forefather four generations back, the king of Zara at that time, met with the leaders of your people—or those who were willing to speak as leaders, for you were sleeping. Your mother was among them. They told us that the elders of your people had prophesied that you were to marry a distant descendant of this king, when it was time for you to wake, and that man, Lemara, is me.

"Our forefathers had never heard of such magic before, but they knew that God's wisdom is infinite and things are not always as they seem. So they spoke with our Prophets, who hand down all Law directly from God, and these Prophets also said the same: that this marriage was destined, both for your people and mine. And so our people promised to protect yours from the Sirenians, and an alliance was formed by marriage—a marriage of the future, a marriage that will only now come to fruition."

"It is not what we do!" I cry.

"But it was prophesied by both your people and mine," he insists. "It was prophesied by your elders, also, that the marriage between your people and ours would heal an ancient rift. And it was prophesied by the Prophets of our own people that a child would be born of this marriage who would save our kingdom from ruin. Throughout our history, only the prophesies of our God have saved us."

How he goes on! This is why we do not let men lead where I come from! They cannot feel the way women can—their empathy runs not as deep, for they cannot carry life inside them! They cannot even listen to know if another is listening, or how another responds to what they say! "You should know, Lemara, that my people have already accepted this marriage, long ago. You will not have to prove yourself worthy."

"Prove...?"

"It may be different where you come from. Here, the people must approve the woman whom the king marries. She will be their queen, and so the marriage must be wise and correct: it must meet the needs of the people. A king serves his people first, and their needs are always first with him."

"But I do not love you!"

"Of course you do not love me. You have only just met me."

"My Mama would never arrange my life in secret! I am the Priestess of Hummingbirds. The choice I make in marriage is the most sacred choice in our world." And yet somehow I know that she could have done it. For all her kindness, my Mama was foolish, and her will weak. She frightened easily. She succumbed to the wishes of the Sirenian priests, when she chose not to submit my infant life to the Dark Faerie Jaguar according to the ancient rite. She welcomed the Sirenians easily, and taught me not to defend our ceremonies from their greedy eyes. But we Hummingbird People don't need an alliance with any other people. We have been raped by too many. All we need now is to heal ourselves whole again.

"No one could wake you for a hundred years," Micah is saying. "Other men tried, though it was forbidden according to the prophesy, and they died amongst the Roses. Those were destructive, magical roses, whose thorns ensnared men and bled them to death. They only opened for me, because it was time."

"They were not," I say. "They protected me. We traded for them..."

"From the Sirenians, yes. But do you know they did not originate with the Sirenians? They come from the Ghost Kingdom, and in that kingdom, perhaps, those roses were kept in check by the harsh conditions there.

But in your kingdom of abundance and warmth and constant rain, they grow without bounds."

"Well, I am not going to be bound," I say to him, leaning close and breathing hot into his face. "Do not speak to me of binding. Where I come from, we are not bound by this kind of marriage."

He doesn't pull away, nor will he look at me. "No? What do you mean?"

How can I answer him? He presses. "Have you no such thing as real marriage? No sacred commitment between two people, that lasts for their lives? No real fathers for your children?" Pain in his voice, as if it is he who has lost something.

"What is this 'real'? Yes, we marry, we unite. We have many fathers, like the Hummingbirds! The Ritual is sacred! The union between two, God and Goddess, like the union of Rain and Earth or Hummingbird and Flower! Does the Hummingbird commit to live with the Flower forever? No, but the Hummingbird still marries the Flower, all Hummingbirds marry the Flowers!"

I rise up, letting their hundreds of gazes turn like a wheel upon me. I don't care. "I will go now," I say, to him or to anyone. "I must sing to the Sun, for He is dying."

My voice isn't loud, but everyone hears me. I watch him sit very still; I watch him not raise his eyes to mine; I watch his stillness and it terrifies me, but I breathe and call upon my Ancestors. I know my duty to the Sun. Nothing will stop me.

But he doesn't try to stop me. I watch him control his breath, for a long time, as if he has never breathed before. I see again his aloneness, without sisters or brothers, without family, the lone king—and how this is the way here, this is how a man sits, this is how a man stands proud—and I want to pity him, but he is grotesque to me, like some swollen outsized part of the body...

"Where will you go?" he asks me at last.

I look around me. I see the people's strong-boned faces, so sharp that shadows fall around their eyes, terrible in their mystery.

"I—I will go high," I say, thinking of my balcony, where I have sung every night since I came here, though I don't remember how to get back there.

"Will you return when you are finished, at the commence of darkness?"

I look down at the back of his neck, the bare skin of it.

"Yes," I say, so that he will let me go.

"Very well," he tells the people, who listen. "The marriage ceremony will begin a little later than planned. We will wait. We will wait until after the Priestess has completed the ceremony that is... The ceremony that is sacred to her."

And so the Sun falls weary and bittersweet, at the end of the day, into the embrace of the Earth, who will care for Him through the night and Dream the story of their love-making in Moon-song across the Sky.

But on my way back down through veils of purple darkness, I smell again the smell I smelled, a rusting-sweet death smell of Animal flesh decomposing into Fire, and I know a body is burning—a Lamb, or a Goat—I know. I know at last what he meant by "sacrifice" and how our wedding will begin.

And I am gone, running, and I will never stop.

Up stairs and down, running, for no beauty can equal my horror.

Only I do stop—oh, I stop where every journey ends, where every River ends. I stop at forever. I am stopped by the Sea.

the Dolphins choose

Tiras. Tiralas. I listen to the Air take shape around his name.

My heart could not yearn so deeply and not receive a reply. He must return to me—be reborn in anything, in Rain or a leaf I eat or a Bird's egg. He would, for me—I know he would. I cup my hands around the shape of his face in the wind, until I can almost feel its warmth.

And yet nothing.

Not even Dreams.

Faeries who blessed me at birth and all my life tongued luxurious secrets into my ears, who Dreamed with me at night in steaming, musical darkness, who tranced my veins like wine—where are you now? For I have not felt you near since I came here—no, not even when I woke, among the Roses back home, do I remember you there. Surely in a hundred years, you who are immortal have not gone? Why do you not comfort me in my grief?

I unbind the lacings of the dress so that it lets me breathe. With the Moon's blessing, my body open to the Sea, for the first time I am able to feel—and what relief, to feel my own emotions like friends in the darkness! I run to the Sea edge, I fall to my knees and am kissed by cold salt, I cry while the roaring waves cradle my voice the way the great Waters cradle the bodies of Whales. No feeling is too big for the Sea to hold. So I rise up, finally Dancing. I reach for the emptiness with my arms, I swing my hair and shake my neck to feel the pain snake up and down me. I pound my feet into the waves, I spray out my hands, I Dance the fury in me, the fury that my own mother betrayed me to this man, to this people, to this killing marriage, I Dance my bewilderment, I Dance the swirls I would swirl around my lover in that other life I am never living, caresses he would give me—oh, I Dance the shapes of those who are gone, I Dance with the Air-bodies of absence.

Deep into the night I Dance, and then fall back against the sand and open my mouth to the Moon and swallow. At least I am not numb anymore. Now Hummingbirds may drink from my heart again.

Now you are bigger, Priestess of Hummingbirds. Big with tears, like the Sea.

The tide is coming up, reaching for my fingertips breath by breath, like a shy lover. *Is this how you speak to me now, Ocean Faerie? Through sorrow?*

Perhaps.

I thought you had gone.

It is you who come and go, child, not I.

And I weep afresh. The Faerie of Ocean is my very own special keeper. It is she who changed the Dark Faerie's curse of death and made it only a curse of sleep, so that I might wake again. She is my Faerie of Compassion.

And yet I feel that I would know, if Tiras were alive somewhere, in any form. If he were anywhere at all.

I rise up. I shake the sodden rumple of my dress, my skin scarred with sand.

For Micah is walking up the beach, slowly, following his own Moon-shadow. I stand exposed in the Moon's light, wanting to run, but I will not run. I am Priestess. Yet I am wary. I draw the dress back around me, for I understand now that it is my only protection here.

He is close upon me much faster than I expected, close enough for me to see his eyes glowing. Distances on a dark beach are tricky. I tense, expecting his anger, for I know I have escaped him here.

"I can see, now, Priestess," he says, his voice low and careful, easy to hear below the breathing of the waves, "how difficult our life will be for you."

I don't know what to say. If I speak, I might sing or howl.

"I saw you dancing." For the first time, I see desire in his eyes, helpless and silent and as familiar to me as the sound of my own name. I relax a little. I step forward, for him to see me better. His gaze falls over me, but he merely lifts his hand, palm up.

"Will you walk with me, Priestess Lemara?" he asks, and I see that he wishes me to place my hand in his. I will not. But experimentally, in my anger and my loneliness, I run my fingertips up the side of his arm. I want to see that desire light up again. But he cringes and pulls away, as if my touch stings. What does it mean? I hate him for it!

He catches up to my fast walk. It seems to me that nothing shakes him.

"Forgive me," he says. "There is a wound there, where you touched me."

I say nothing. What more good are words here? I walk and walk, with nothing to stop me, I walk hard—but he keeps up beside me.

"I always like to walk by the sea," he says after a while. "It opens my mind, and helps me to see things more clearly."

And all at once my heart rises up. "Nothing that is real to me is real to you!" I cry out.

He does not startle. "Priestess, I have woken a girl who slept for a hundred years. Sometimes I don't know what is real to me."

"We do not have laws where I come from," I tell him. "And we do not—" I am sobbing without tears, and yet my sobs do not stop me, they give me breath—"We do not kill for love." I will not look at him but I hear him listening, so I go on. "Our rituals we make for life—our rituals breathe life into all that is, throughout all you call time. Without us, you would forget the Sun, and He would forget you, and where would you be, in your nowhere place? And we rejoice when we eat our food, which we take in love and not violence—we do not stare it down in silence like you do—and you may stare at me in scorn while I eat and while I love, but you cannot frighten me, for our people, though we do not fight and kill as you do, are not frightened of anything, not of passion or feeling, not of sickness or death, not of anybody's god. You cannot keep me, and I will never marry you!"

Micah says, without the prelude of *Priestess,* "You are walking very fast."

I slow down, and when I do, I am cold. I am wet all over, chilled by wet sand in the small of my back. I wrap my arms around myself. Everyone I love is dead. I will never see them again. If I return to my homeland, I will not find them there; they will be gone.

"I am not keeping you," he says. "Do you think I have captured you? You are free to go."

Free to go? Free to go? I look at him in despair, my hair blowing all around me and in my mouth, and he sees and he knows, he knows I have nowhere to go. And I hate him for that—oh! But very softly, he clasps my elbow in his hand, stopping me and turning me all at once by the sheer force of surprise—toward the Sea.

"Look, Lemara," he says, leaning toward me and pointing out into the layered darkness. "There are the dolphins. Do you see them?"

They are flipping in and out of the white and the black, silver over silver.

"When my people first came here," he says, "they saw the dolphins, and they knew that this place was blessed."

"Can you speak with them?"

"I don't know. I have never tried. It is enough for me to watch them. But it may be that the fishermen speak to them. Everyone honors them. We make sure to keep the harbor safe for them, and we help them if they are ever in trouble or beach themselves, just as they, in turn, have been known to help us when we are lost out at sea."

And he goes on again, speaking. And I measure his voice by the pattern of Dolphins in the clapping hands of the waves. Can I find any music in it? Can they?

"Our great-great-great grandfather built our palace here because it is the furthest from the volcano, and so it is safest. But also because we feel that God is here. I have always felt there is some old wisdom in the sea. Our Prophets go alone upon the sea when they wish to find answers."

Each time the Dolphins rise, they choose life. For each breath, they must act, they must rise above or they will die. And so must I.

"What is your god?" I whisper at last. "Is it the same god the Sirenians talk about?" I don't know if he will hear me.

"No. We have our own God, with whom we have made a sacred covenant. He has given us all our laws—about marriage, for example, and how one shall marry one, and they shall only have two children, so that we do not tax the resources of this small, precious land. We do not waste, we do not fight amongst ourselves like the Sirenians. Our laws are based in kindness and respect, but we are strict in keeping them. They are what have allowed our people to survive through times of great leanness and danger, and they are our covenant with God, who has preserved and protected us throughout the ages."

"But who is he? Is he an Ancestor?"

"No. He is not a person who died. He is the God of all things."

"But I don't understand." I never understood it. All the desperation of the pale people. All their greed and their sorrow. The danger of it all, and the lure of it—I never understood.

"He made the world," says Micah. "He is the Truth, the light, the holiness of everything. He takes care of our people. He caused the Ho Volcano to cease its eruptions, so that we could cross over into the land He promised us here—a land no one else had been able to occupy. He is our guide, our father, our teacher."

"Where is he?"

"He is everywhere. But we cannot see Him with our mortal eyes."

"He is not in Earth, in Trees, in Sea?"

"No, for He is beyond those things. He is beyond what we can see and feel with our senses. We must perceive Him with our spirits—"

"And this is the world now? This is the world we live in?"

He smiles his terrible, sad smile at me, and he will never, ever Dance with me. "I know," he murmurs, seeing my tears. "It is all so strange to you. You are far from home."

"But aren't you lonely?" I beseech him.

"Because we long for our God? Yes, there is a divine kind of longing, that we all feel. But that is what makes life beautiful—this longing, this reaching of our souls toward God. When we die, we will wholly belong to Him again."

I hug myself a little tighter. "Priestess, you are cold," he says. He is so near that I can smell him, and he smells much different, much stronger than before. Like beetle nests beneath Rain Tree bark, or no, like ash and wet leaves.

"Why are you crying?" he asks, with that same tenderness that overcomes me.

"Because I am alone," I sob, "and I do not want to be here, and I want to go home. And you are ugly, and I have to marry you to survive, and I do not love you and never will."

Then he takes me in his arms, which are warm, unlike the Sea wind, unlike the voice of the Ocean Faerie. His body is grand and still—yet now I perceive that within all that stillness, there is trembling, the way the Sky trembles before a storm. I open my eyes just as desire darkens his again. He kisses me.

At first it's only a cold touching of his lips to mine, like something he has been told to do. Then it widens, and it makes the Sea blossom between my legs, a swift wave lifting me toward him—but then he stops, afraid.

That kiss told me something he didn't mean to say.

I don't stop. I open his robes and slide my hand down his chest. Something tells me not to touch him where he wants me to touch him—the fear is greater than the desire, and already he almost resents me for it. I think he has never before touched a woman, this grotesquely lonely man who does not know he is lonely. Whose God is what the Sirenians call a Ghost—a man who was separated from his body but did not die properly, who never returned to the Other Worlds, never met with his Ancestors, and floats somewhere that no one can see or find, and in all the land of Zara, the land is dead. For a moment, I feel so sorry for Micah, I forgive him everything.

I uncover my breasts. He looks and looks, and then he drops his lips to them, releasing his breath. I drag him down into the cold sand like a Jaguar—for the fury of what we feel makes him weak, and me strong.

"Lemara," he murmurs, and he is really afraid. "Not here. Not now— we are not—"

"Yes," I say. "Here, or never."

"No—we must be married first. This isn't how it's done. We *must* not—"

"What *must*? Will you die?"

"Yes!"

I laugh. It feels good to laugh. "This is how I marry you," I say. "I am sorry if you die of it. But I have already died, coming here. So take me or no—this is the only way for me." I reach inside his clothing and touch him—and am surprised by the depth of sound that comes from him. I take off his clothes from underneath him, and he watches me do it, holding himself up, eyes darting. His body makes me sad, not because it has lost its deeper hues and its Water-flow—for a Wye body, I think he is almost beautiful, with riveting edges and tight, swooping lines, and dark rushing inward around the bulging outward, and all of that which makes a man—but because it is not Tiras's body, which was the body I first touched in all my Dreams. It will never be Tiras. So that each touch brings pain.

He is weak with the wanting but his eyes are certain. Their hardness makes my hands shake. I grab his hands, unwind myself. "Now do what I tell you," I say. And we roll into the waves, and are lost.

I teach him the way a Priestess teaches, even though I myself was never taught as I should have been. I tell him how and where to kiss me, trace me, mouth me. When I climb on top of him to take him in, I feel afraid. This is the time when my women should surround me, and say the

Blessings. But there is no one to witness us except the Dolphins. I grip his face in my hands and look into his eyes. I am a Priestess. I must be brave. I know that even if I have not chosen him, even if I do not love him nor he me, he must respect me on this night.

"Say something to me," I command.

"Lemara," he whispers. "Priestess of Hummingbirds."

So I take him in. And in that moment when everything feels wrong, when I feel with a sudden horror of pain that there is no room for him inside me after all—every way he pushes feels like knives—and woman was not made for man after all, not at all, no—and again in the moment after, when ecstasy surges so fast up into my throat it nearly chokes me, I remember the Dream. I remember it so fast, I have already forgotten it again. But for a moment, it was winging there, between my legs and at my throat like death, in the hot breath between us, and oh everywhere—all throughout the raging Sea. The Dream I Dreamed for a hundred years, while I slept.

I keep moving after he is still, pressing his arms into the sand.

"I will marry you," I say, "for now, but I am not bound, and no animal dies for me at the wedding."

But he rolls me over with a furious, sudden strength I didn't expect, and we sit up together, somehow tangled, he pressing into me and I pressing into him, our voices straining through the wind. What frightens me most is that suddenly I am bound, after all. I did not know it would feel like this. He's no longer inside me, and yet he is. I feel I will never get him out.

"Lemara, I will not break all the rules for you. You marry into my people and things are done a certain way. Already you have broken a sacred covenant."

"No—it is you—it is you who have broken me." I'm gasping, weeping, out of breath and I don't know why.

"I am sorry, but you—you tempted me. God, I am sorry. What have we done."

"We have married, in my way. I told you."

"Never tell anyone, Lemara."

I stare at him. I will kill him with my stare.

"Marry me now, in the ritual of our people, and never tell anyone what we have done. Do you understand?"

"I want a Garden," I say. "I want a Garden that is all my own. One of your gardens, the one where the Hummingbirds come. I will practice the rituals of my people there, and you will allow this."

And isn't he gasping, too, as we thrash inside ourselves, two Fish cast up helpless on the beach? "Alright," he breathes. "But you must respect me as your king. You may not believe in our God, but you must respect our laws."

Breathe. Breathe. The Dolphins.

"I will be kind to you, Lemara. I will honor you. Don't you know this?"

I nod. The Moon arches high, high over us, and yet so close, telling the Earth's memory of the love She once knew in the long-ago day, telling of the love She once felt, telling the story that is told ever and ever again, and will always be told, no matter how the night of forgetting washes over us.

It is a deal that we make, here in the wet sand. And I am not accustomed to love as a deal—like the trades we made with the Sirenians or the Wyes, jewels for metal, feathers for silk, spices for money, secrets for Gold and Silver—but this isn't love.

This is all I have, because I made one bad deal with a dark old woman, and it went so awfully wrong. But I'm still a Hummingbird. I'm still a warrior.

Ella

My prince won nearly every tournament, and in the beginning of our story, he won every one for me. When I watched him, even war looked beautiful: the hushed, invisible moment before the attack, when each man looked within himself in a way he would never do at any other time, and asked what God was, and would He help; the coiling of the muscles in the man and the horse as they tensed in unison to spring; the steely shouts equaled only by the cries of love-making in their eerie abandon; the delirious clash of weapons that were themselves works of art; the intimate tangle of two nobly-armored, fiercely-fleshed men. The medallions we women wore upon our breasts and the little perfumed scarfs our men took from us to tie around their wrists as they flew, the banners like schools of triumphant fish in the seared summer sky above us, and the announcing drums that thundered through our bodies while we waited for life to hurl itself against life even gave it all a sense of meaning, as if it were all necessary, as all rituals are necessary, even if we've forgotten why. No one else existed for me as I watched my prince go riding forth in metal, both looser and prouder in posture than all the rest—to seal our roles as knight and maiden, lover and beloved. Sometimes he even shouted my name.

Swordplay was Sol's favorite, and his battles were often the longest because he held back his best strategies in order to draw out the games, lulling his opponents into false ease or weary frustration. He maneuvered around them with theatrical gestures and a half-open, wondering smile, as if he were more interested in finding out the effect his moves had on his opponent than in actually winning, which he took for granted. My Sol loved to tease, and in swordplay he teased those men, toying with their arrogance and their fears, as adeptly as he teased women with his charm. And I loved to watch this theatre, but I loved perhaps more deeply to watch him in the sports that challenged him more. For when he jousted, he still knew his skill, and he knew he would win—but only by extreme focus, and he could not afford to smile. It was then that he no longer seemed a boyish rogue, but a man. That there was a drop of weakness somewhere within the great force of him pained him, and I could see him straining with that secret irony, throwing himself into streaks of recklessness at the last minute when he knew he would die rather than reveal it. I knew I would never tell him that I saw this, and that it formed the core of my love, as it does even now.

When he came to me after the first tournament, exhausted from his efforts, but even more aglow with the life and power that was in him, he tore off his helmet and engulfed me in a kiss that hundreds of people cheered. I lost my mind in that cheer—I could not imagine myself the center of it—and close up, as always, Sol surprised me with his fevered eyes and damp hair: the realness of him, as if I did not know him. I did not feel he could possibly be mine. Yet only moments later, it seemed, I let him make love to me in some abandoned room of the armory. And then I found myself weeping.

"What do you think of me?" I cried. "Look what we do."

He froze, then tore my hands from my eyes in a gesture so rough in its sincerity that I stopped crying and looked at him. "What? What do we do? Why do you resist me?"

"No," I said, sobering up instantly, swallowing my sobs. I feared what he would think of me, but revealing such insecurity, I thought, might even worsen the judgments I imagined. "No, not you. I don't resist you. It's only—" I tried to think what I could say, glancing inexplicably at the door. But he rolled me laughing back onto the floor.

"No," he stopped me. "I understand you. You don't want to be *that* kind of woman, is that it? All your life you've been good? Afraid some priest would call you a witch, or something else nasty?" And the words were nasty, and would have hurt me, but for the tenderness in his voice, the way his eyes reached into mine with such a hunger to let him comfort me. Still, my throat seized up at the reference to my mother, the dark rumors that had birthed me.

"Now listen to me, my love," he said, stroking my hair. "I don't listen to priests."

"But Sol—"

"Hush!" he whispered, pressing his cheek against mine. "I hate them!"

"But Sol, how could you say such a thing?"

"I don't mind saying it. I love our Savior, Ella, I do, but I hate the priests who claim to serve Him. Isn't our Savior a friend, a brother, to each and every one of us? Why then should priests claim to know Him more than I do, or to determine how I should behave in His presence?"

"Sol, that's blasphemy!"

"Why, I ask you?"

"Because," I said, incredulous that he could even ask. "Because the church is His body, and the priests are the descendants of His apostles!"

"Ridiculous. Who has said so? They have. What is this body? Does the body of the Savior condemn our bodies for experiencing the greatest pleasures of being human?"

"The Savior was chaste with His beloved..."

"Say they. But who can know for sure?"

I shook my head. I needed to hold to what the priests told me. It was holding to their teachings that kept me good, that had kept me—all my life—just barely safe from banishment. "Then why...?"

"Because the more they separate us from the source of our own fulfillment, the more they keep us from making ourselves happy with the simple joys that God has given us, the more we will depend on them for everything that God is. We give them all the power. And that is what they want. That is why they call everything good and sweet a sin—have you never noticed that?"

I looked at him, all serious in the shadows, the suits of armor hanging above him with all their ancestral weight, and nodded. For his hold on me, of course, was stronger than the hold of the priests. It was stronger than anything now. He was my rescuer.

"Promise me, Ella," he said, giving me a little shake. "Promise me you will think on what I've said, and not just listen blindly to what they tell you."

"I will." And then, before I could stop myself—"Do you believe that witches exist, Sol?"

Perhaps his eyes flickered away, uncertain, or perhaps I imagined that. "Not at all," he said. "Do you?"

What could I say? There was a grave I had tended throughout my childhood, the grave of a woman who was hung for magic. I had prayed over that grave. I had asked for things no God, I thought, could ever give or forgive—and they had been given. But in that moment, I made my decision.

"No." I said it with a shyness that made the grin splash wider across his face—endeared me to him instantly, without my even trying. This way he was looking at me, with the armor still clashing and the horses still dashing behind his eyes, and all the world still cheering beyond our safe chamber, cheering for us—I needed this now, to survive. I knew I was alone in the world, but for this.

♛   ♛   ♛   ♛   ♛

Yet in the palace, more often than not, I lived without him. My prince who had made all this possible, on whom I hung my only faith, and who could always rescue me from my fears with his hot eyes and limber embrace, was rarely part of my day. If he wasn't hunting, he was gone on adventures for weeks at a time, exploring every corner of our kingdom, inventing noble deeds for himself, playing tricks on Barbarian raiders, defending damsels from rabid dogs, sleeping in fields. Sometimes he paired up with that Barbarian tracker Rufus James, wherever he was to be found, or his favorite knight Loren, to set right some wrong through their combined forces of cunning and passion. He was the younger of the two sons, and since Alden would inherit everything, his only chance at fame and fortune lay in making a name for himself by feats of arms. That's how my sister-in-law Narsa told it to me when I first asked, condescendingly explaining the obvious, twirling her lips in delight at the tremulous pain his absence caused me. But I knew him as she never would, and I knew that wasn't the reason. I knew he simply could not bear to be still. Many years later, when the tracker Rufus James would tell me of the Northland moors of his childhood, the primal, wind-wailing nakedness of that place would remind me somehow of Sol's inner landscape, though I had never seen either place—only imagined it.

Sol never invited me to his chamber. Always he came to mine, his mouth dark against my face, his body moving hard but with relief, as if he returned home from some comfortless mountain that roared with lonely dragons. In my sleep, it seemed I was always waiting for him, restless and unmoored in the luxurious grandeur of my too-big bed. Sometimes he'd return from his adventures in the grey hour before dawn, informing no one of his arrival, and enter the palace like a cat, deposit his noisy armor outside, climb the stairs behind the Hall, enter my room, enter my bed. Or he'd play at breaking into his own palace, scaling the tower wall where the layered rooftops were close, stealing in through my window, ripping off my covers—growling, pulled me to him in a ravenous net, "You are too vulnerable here in your sleep, Princess—anyone could get you—" For the idea of an enemy surprising us was only a fairy tale to us then, something to excite our imaginations.

Then he rode away again at any time of day or night on a muscular white mare named Aurora, whom I envied more than anyone in the world for the hundreds of nights Sol's eager, rushing body pressed to hers. None of us ever knew when he would return.

♛   ♛   ♛   ♛   ♛

In the home of my father, I had almost never seen a mirror, let alone been confronted with one every single day. The ladies who bustled around me each morning seemed to take it for granted, as if this long bout of gazing at oneself, into one's very soul, were simply ordinary. At first I closed my eyes while they dressed me up, but I stopped when they began to laugh at me and ask me why. If I had been alone, perhaps, I could have looked, and allowed myself a moment of giddiness—*I am a princess!* But I was never alone.

Sometimes I missed my former solitude with something almost like homesickness. I did not wish to be attended, or to be stared down for so long by my own face. I hadn't slept well. Perhaps I had spent the night in Solon's arms, and it shamed me to have other women near me—as if they could smell my pleasure, or see the burns of his kisses on my neck. Or I had been up all night, awash with nameless terror. I remembered wandering abandoned fields around my mother's grave, where the open, higher flatlands of farming country allowed me to run in a way we cannot do in the marsh-bound city—aimless, unseen. This kind of freedom, in the palace of Cygnini, would never come to me again.

After a time, when I became confident enough to make a few commands, I asked that the mirror be removed. I told them to dress me as they pleased, and I would trust them. Of course no one understood the courage it took for me to ask this. Now I became the princess who allowed her servants to decide what she wore and how she looked. I would not understand until many years later that it was my duty to look in that mirror and make decisions based on what I saw there.

How should I walk? What expression should I wear? My gowns trailed to my feet, and I worried I would trip (often I did). My hands, once accustomed to working with arms bare, now lost themselves in drooping, wide-ended sleeves, weighted down by jeweled rings. Nearly on tiptoe—as if afraid to disturb the true inhabitants of the palace—I traveled down the long, spiral stair spangled gold here and there by morning light, then rose up another long stair to the chapel above the Hall, where together with the royal family, I said my morning prayers. These moments were the most peaceful for me. If I did not know how to carry a crown or command servants, I did know how to kneel and pray to God. This I had been doing all my life, and in this I found comfort. You know how the stillness in a chapel of old stone and stained glass clothes you in softness, as if you are a bird cradled in the downy nest of God, and the lights of the candles sway and brighten in the breath of the singing, and the sound of the singing, at once deeper than earth and vibrating the heavens, settles your mind. But then it was over, and on marched the day of a princess.

I sat at breakfast and conscientiously said nothing, lest I say the wrong thing, and then after breakfast came the difficult, awkward time, lasting much of the day, in which I was compelled to choose among the ladies' arts and undertake my schooling in these. Dance, watercolor, music—I never showed any particular talent at any of these, nor felt much interest in them. I would much rather have been wandering alone in the royal forest or talking with Leyla, or even helping in the kitchens or the gardens, but it seemed these freedoms were not allowed to me. The obligations of my job as princess were so unclear to me that I felt whatever I did, I was doing something wrong; wherever I was, there must be somewhere else I was supposed to be. I wanted the queen's approval more than almost anything. I constantly fantasized that I might do some small thing to gain her respect. Instead, I was always making mistakes. Attempting to demonstrate my royal confidence, I would command a steward who was much too high up for me to command and could only be commanded by the king, or I would give orders for a page to refill the wine when this was the job of the Keeper of the Cups—a duty in which he invested all the pride of his life, a duty which his forefathers had carried before him.

My crown was a delicate little thing, a vining lace of gold inlaid with small, pink and turquoise sapphires near the points, and though it was very light, it pulled me up tall in order to balance it, as if it were heavy. In my new dresses I must tread very carefully, in order not to sully or damage them. I had grown up accustomed to run wild in clothing no one cared about, frequently dirty with work or play. As a princess, you might think I had equal freedom—after all, who could admonish me if I ruined a dress? But in fact, I think there were several who could have, and would have. I was not yet the master of my royal position. It was the master of me. Never could I be natural. Unlike a common laborer or merchant who attends to his work during the day and leaves it in the evening, returning to his relaxed state of humanness with family or alone, I had to be a princess every hour: I never had a moment off from that job.

The day of the first royal ball—the first since I had become princess, I mean—I hadn't seen Sol for so many days, my confidence had nearly run out. I'd been dreading the event since I'd first heard of it, for without the benefit of my mother's magic, without even the comfort of its memory, I would go without glamour, without anything to qualify me above any other lady for his love. These were my thoughts as I hid in the stables that evening, missing dinner in order to weep alone. The humble scent of horses comforted me, and here I felt relief from the scrutiny I imagined from above me—from the watchtowers atop the silo and at the ends of the high bridges. All day I had observed with guilty longing the important bustle of grooms and chambermaids, laundresses and cooks, who had such clear, unquestionable tasks to complete for the big night and could feel, I thought, both pride in their own usefulness and the relief of remaining invisible. All day I had been watched by my sister-in-law Narsa, or so it seemed to me, with cold disapproval in everything I did—and been accused of many small offenses, including "gossiping" at the table with Kiera, when all I had whispered was some desperate question about the propriety of making a garden for myself. And when I had been told that I could have a lady's garden, nothing practical but some small plot for flowers and butterflies at least, I had spent all the afternoon wandering lost amidst the vast architecture of the palace gardens, the gorgeous trellises and woven fences and lily-studded ponds, trying to imagine what miniature space I could ever tend that could have meaning amidst all of this. And when I had asked the servants whom to ask—Where? And what tools and plants were available to me? And how?—I was sent to the kitchens and then back to the gardens, and then back to the kitchens, until I understood the game they played with me and so ended up here, in tears.

I envied the servants, and they knew it and secretly mocked me for it. They held their heads high, in the work that they did, luxuriating in a constant network of laughter, gossip, and camaraderie that their special winding passageways and sweet-smelling rooms of wine, food, herbs, and animals afforded them. Whereas I—I had no task of any meaning. In the garden of my memory, the only one I had ever tended, whatever I had done had felt worthwhile, because I tended the spirit of one forgotten by everyone but me.

I had never known myself to be fragile, in my former life. I had hardened myself to the abuses I received, and I knew how best to avoid them, and I knew where to go to revive myself after I was forced to bow beneath their blows. But that's because they were familiar to me, in a way that nothing now was.

I moved deeper into the shadows of the stables, and saw Sol's horse gorging with restful intensity from a feedbag.

"Aurora!" I whispered from the cool shadows of the doorway, but she didn't look up. She didn't know me. She had no idea that I meant anything to her rider, or to anyone. Yet I knew now that Sol must have returned, and only recently. I saw a groom turning the corner, with that swinging, assured gait of one whose labor is necessary, and ducked away before I could be seen. In doing so I nearly collided with Sol's knight Loren, who stood gently behind me, watching me, for he had seen me first. I looked past him for Sol, but saw no one else, and now to my horror, Loren dropped to one knee. I backed up in surprise—perhaps I cried out.

"Forgive me for startling you, my lady," he said, and then he looked up, his face like that of a sunflower facing the sun, only with that strange sadness specific to him, the sadness of a man who (I used to think) had lived years in other worlds, or watched unicorns die. Loren's behavior toward me had always baffled and embarrassed me so exceedingly that I avoided him whenever I could. With more solemnity than anyone, he bowed to me whenever I passed, to the point where I began to feel he must be mocking me, though he did not seem like one to mock. He was much older than me, nearly forty, with kind, weathered skin and faraway grey eyes, and he looked as if he'd just stepped out of some faded tapestry.

"I did not mean to frighten you. But I am glad to have met you here, for I have been meaning to give you this poem. I wrote it for you, to comfort your lonely hours when your lord is hunting." He stood and handed me this rolled-up thing. "I humbly beg you to receive it."

It seemed to me that he was gone almost before I could look at it, though it didn't occur to me then to feel grateful for the kindness of his discretion. The scroll had been tied with a ribbon of my favorite turquoise color, secured by a dainty hair-clip made just for fine hair like mine, curved in the shape of an otter holding a crescent moon. The clip was made of unicorn ivory, which I had never worn and associated with Sol's sister Kiera. My hands burning as if with a stolen thing, I hurried back to my sitting room, taking, as usual, the least frequented passages. In my room I turned about, confused. I moved into my dressing room and placed the scroll on top of my dresser, with hovering fingers, as if it were a weapon I had not been taught to handle—just as Leyla knocked and entered with my other attendants to dress me for the ball.

"Send them away, please," I told her. They had barely closed the door behind them when I seized her hand. "I will never learn this, Leyla. I will never know how to talk to servants, or to anyone. Everyone I meet, walking anywhere at all, I must stop and think, is this person above or below me, and if below me then how far below me, and how shall I treat them—with exactly what combination of humility or command—I cannot do it. I am always in the wrong."

Leyla looked confused. "But that's how it is, my lady. That is how we all must think."

"Yes, for you it is natural, I suppose! You have done this all your life, and your parents before you."

"Forgive me, my lady, but I think you must be careful how you speak to the servants. They do not wish you to speak to them the way you do—as if you are their friend. They won't respect you, and you will confuse and frighten them, if you don't speak always as a princess. They look to you for authority."

But I did not think they did. I did not think Leyla did. I must have stared at her, speechless, for she quickly bowed her head and bobbed a little curtsey. "Please excuse me, my lady. I shouldn't have said—"

"No," I sighed. "It's alright. I want you to help me."

She bowed her head while I continued to stare at her, working the tears back with my jaw, and then I sat down at my dressing table as I was expected to. But when she began to touch me, I stopped her.

"Leyla," I said. "Will you please—will you please unroll that thing on the top of my dresser and read it to me?" For it was no use. The damned thing hunted my mind.

I turned away from the mirror while she read it to me.

Princess Ella,

If ever you had your own coat of arms,
Only this image would capture your charms:
An otter at play in the hands of the sea,
Swaying a dance in the moon's jubilee.
Each soft move you make is a motion of giving,
Your eyes open wide with innocent living,
The hardship you suffered has turned you divine,
Now you're trembling, unfolding your slow, secret shine.

Your hair is like laughter, your smile is like tears,
The wind halts in awe when your beauty draws near.

You will not believe that these words are for you—
And there lies your sweetness, for they are all true.

Your faithful knight,
Loren

I heard myself laugh out loud, looking up with sudden recklessness into the sun at the window, and the sound was awful to me, grating at my own ears. I could not have told you then what I felt. Only a kind of frustration, that the fragile semblance of poise I had been working at all day, to bring with me to the ball, was hopelessly shredded now.

"What is this, Leyla?" I demanded, but I wanted no answer. I had asked Sol once why Loren looked at me so, bowed to me so—and Sol had laughed and told me that Loren was "one of the *old-fashioned* knights." That I was his lady, that he would devote himself to me.

"But I am *your* lady," I had protested.

"That you are, my love," he had answered, "but Loren would devote himself to you in a different way. He does it to honor me, too. His love is chaste—and he will enjoy his longing."

And I had asked if that were really possible, and then flushed in embarrassment at the question, as I did now, remembering it, and Sol had teased me, saying, "My father certainly doesn't think so. But he doesn't understand Loren."

Now Leyla handed me the scroll, with deference, as if I knew what to do with it. "I think it's lovely," she said.

With purposeful care, I retied the turquoise ribbon and replaced the hair clip, even though they perfectly matched the dress I had intended to wear that night, and even though I knew it would please Sol to know who had given them to me. And I stood and replaced the whole, terrible arrangement on the dresser top, tapped it away with my fingers so that I could not reach it again (though I would reach it again, somehow, on more than one occasion, over the course of a year or more—I would force myself to take those words in pieces, phrase by phrase, until I was inured to the pain they caused me). Of all the foolish hurts that weakened me that day, of all the blows of confusion that left me trembling within the immobile hoops of a gown that seemed not mine, entering the ballroom that night, Loren's poem of admiration was the hardest for me to bear. I knew it was written about someone else, and I knew she must be the one everyone expected tonight, but by some terrible mistake, I would come in her place.

I am sorry, my people. I am sorry that it took me so long, to become what you deserved. It was many years before I could allow myself the luxury of gratitude. I did not understand that Loren loved me as I had loved Sol before I'd ever met him, and as sweetly. I did not understand that by refusing his words entrance to my heart, I was refusing God.

Perhaps the only consolation was that my anger—the first I could remember feeling, perhaps, in my life—afforded me a little extra strength that night, which I sorely needed.

♕   ♕   ♕   ♕   ♕

At first the greatness of the event overwhelmed my feelings—I mean that I had no time to think of how I felt, but only fixated my attention on all there was to see and learn, and on living up to the expectation of each interaction. They came one upon the other so fast, I could hardly keep up with them. The various lords and heads of estates were invited, who were almost all siblings or cousins to the royal family, including the Duke of South, who was working to establish order and religious rule in the Southern Primeval Forest where the Hums lived, as well as those governing the borders of the North Forest and the mining projects there. But the most interesting guests at the Cygnini balls were the successful merchants and tradesmen, artists and architects, engineers and scribes. Inviting these people was the king and queen's way of keeping a personal tab on the functioning of their city, and their only method of assessing potential suitors for their daughter in a kingdom isolated among what seemed to them inferior peoples.

Sol spoke with anyone, everyone. Anyone who was an expert on a subject he knew little about, anyone who lived a life so different from his own that he could only imagine it, anyone who had experienced adventures—whether on the high seas or in the South Forest or in the realm of spirit and philosophy—that he had not experienced, he wanted to talk to and question. Listening to these conversations, that night, I was able to relax into the background of his charm, and avoid dancing some of the dances, and learn basic agreements about reality that I could file away to sound more confident—I hoped—at another time.

I learned about the progress we were making with the Hums in the South Forest, and about feuds between the artisan guilds, and about debates concerning the use of the royal forest. I also learned about the history of our continent, which before I'd only understood in pieces.

I learned that long ago, only the Wyes and the Hummingbird People lived here on this continent. Perhaps they had originated from the same people, since they still speak more or less the same language. Far in the haunted, predatory north country—the moors and the Northern Primeval Forest—no one lived at all, until marauders from various pagan countries across the north sea began arriving in little waves, between three and five hundred years ago. Sometimes different warlords held fragile power, but they could never form a stable culture because of continuous onslaughts from new invaders. They never became educated or developed past their simple, barbaric language, which consists mostly of gestures and is without verb tenses or written form. When our people arrived over two hundred years ago, from the east, we took for ourselves the heart of this land, the fertile valley. We took it upon ourselves to spread the word of love from our recently martyred Savior among all of these peoples, thinking that perhaps we would unite them under our one rule, and live peaceably together until the Savior rose again. But with the Barbarians it was hopeless, for they were too ignorant and dangerous, though thirty years ago, the queen's cousin William Anai had married one of the Barbarian princesses and attempted (unsuccessfully) to establish rule there. We had some success with the Hums, but the Wyes clung stubbornly to their old religion, and eventually we drove them from the valley. Some disappeared into that fog-shrouded peninsula to the southeast, later known as the Ghost Kingdom, while others crossed over the volcano to the land their ancestors had told them they came from long ago—now called Zara.

Solon included me, by implication, in all conversation—squeezing my waist and pulling me to him as he made some particularly daring point, as if for reassurance or emphasis, and then offering me his arm of a sudden to whirl me off toward some other guest. Sometimes while he spoke, I watched Kiera dance those dances which I have never really felt comfortable performing, all my life, but which royalty learn from childhood. Once or twice she pulled me aside with as much suddenness and passion as Solon did—only for the purpose of whispering to me about the various suitors her parents were considering for her, and which ones she preferred. She wasn't to be married for at least another two or three years, so the prospect of ending her happy youth in the arms of a man she might or might not love seemed less of a burden to her now, perhaps, and more of a breathless mystery. "Oh, to marry for love..." she sighed, not for the first time, gazing at me as if I represented some miraculous achievement, and I thought for the thousandth time how lucky I was, and fell silent, for fear that I might not deserve my good fortune.

Meanwhile the queen moved among her guests the way a cook moves in the larder, drawing one personage to another and mixing the ingredients with delicacy, swiftness, and easy discernment until the music of various conversations wafted over the ballroom like the scent of a finely crafted pudding. All deferred to her presence, and yet her power brought no awkwardness to any conversation. The king arrived late to almost every ball, causing dinner to be delayed until some would complain from hunger, and Sol confided to me that great crowds like this tired his father extremely, so that he tended to put them off.

When all the feasting was done and the wine drunk so deeply that it began to be spilled more often than drunk, and Kiera began to doze just a little on her mother's arm though the queen nudged her awake, and the king unabashedly held a lady-in-waiting upon each knee, grinning drunkenly and bouncing them as if they were children, and I began to grow dizzy and frail and long for the dream of Solon's arms, Sol was still talking, still fascinated by some guest he hadn't yet questioned, still full of some idea he hadn't yet explained.

He often surprised people with his questions. He didn't only want to hear about the practical progress of projects: he wanted to know what people were made of, what lit them from within. He wanted to know what moved the artist to work—was his inspiration divine, and if so, in what form did it strike him?—and he wanted to know what inner qualities made the merchant so successful while the poor farmer must struggle from birth until death to survive—were they different in nature, or simply born under different circumstances? He wanted to know what everyone's opinions were on women's rights. He was the only one who spoke extensively to the newly crowned Wye King, Micah Wye—a rather controversial guest at that ball, I remember—and who questioned him openly about the secret to his people's advanced education. King Micah replied with equal honesty that it rested upon the Wyes' insistence on arguing and questioning all things, even their own religion, even their own teachers, even their own God—instead of submitting blindly to God's will, as he said we did. With nothing but passionate interest, and without taking the least offense, my husband gave him a little bow of thanks at the close of the conversation, and lectured me, as he whisked me off to the next conversation, about the Wyes' sense of class. "The truth is, Ella," he said, "though we are all ashamed to admit it, our city was better off before we drove them out. It was wealthier and smarter. And if I were king, I would welcome them back."

Next he was arguing with a group of ladies who were all cousin or second cousin or cousin-in-law to the king. Ladies of rank intimidated me much more than the men, for the men were either indifferent to me or frankly attracted to me—and these were both reactions I was long accustomed to, since before I'd become a princess. But the women, of course, judged me down to the smallest detail, even if they did it gracefully, under the guise of friendliness, for this is what women do to entertain themselves while men pit their minds together in argument. Kiera, in her uncannily candid sweetness, was the exception, because she had nothing to fear from me. I would never supplant her or rise above her. But these ladies, with their concealed but acid scorn, must have felt they deserved Sol better than me—and perhaps they did. Even when they ignored me, I carried on their work for them by comparing myself with them and judging myself by their standards: standards which I was intelligent enough to learn quickly, but not quick enough to meet.

I remember watching the ladies with perverse fascination, the way they leaned when they laughed, and how these leanings were perfectly timed with the motions and words of my husband. I watched the fluid cupping and waving of hands, the charming upturning of eyes, the proud yet languid sway of the hips when a lady came to a halt at her destination. I watched the way she stretched her neck daintily and pointed her chin toward a friend as she listened to some gossip, keeping her eyes fixed upon the room and her shoulders centered and erect. Every move a noblewoman made was art, and she knew it, and she crafted it on purpose to look as spontaneous as possible; then she offered it up like a gracious gift to the man who requested her attention. Amidst such flawless grace, what could Sol possibly ever see in me? Once I allowed this question—which, in truth, I was always fighting back, like a wild beast I must sedate again and again—to surface, it was only a matter of time before it conquered me utterly.

"But I tell you there is not such a distinction between the criminal and the common man," Sol was saying, "for they are still the same species— the former with an equal capacity for reform and good nature, and the latter with an equal capacity for evil."

"And what can be your evidence for such a claim, young prince?" asked one of the older ladies, smiling serenely. These ladies' husbands and fathers managed estates on the northern outskirts of the kingdom, and living in such wild places, they felt themselves to be high authorities on the more criminal element of society they felt certain haunted them.

"Why, only observe what occurs when a common lady is accused of being a witch, and the people all swarm about her with bloodlust in their eyes, demanding her death!" answered Sol. "This begs two questions, albeit contradictory ones. The first is, can an ordinary, decent woman suddenly turn criminal—nay, worse than criminal, but actually a servant of Satan? The second is, if this is not possible, then can these ordinary, otherwise God-fearing citizens suddenly turn into bloodthirsty scoundrels, bent on the death of their kinswoman, with a ferociousness that would appall and disgust our Savior whom they purport to worship?"

I didn't blame Sol. I forgave him for his breach of kindness instantly, as I forgave him anything in those days. Sol was so incapable of feeling hurt or abashed himself, he did not necessarily remember that others could suffer in such ways, or be sensitive to his words. Yet I do not remember the rest of the conversation, such was my horror at his casual mention of such things. How I wished to disappear!— but I could not seem to turn on my disappearing magic, the way I could in my old life. I could not un-expose myself. How certainly I felt that every one of those ladies was staring at me, asking herself—as surely everyone asked themselves, all the time—what on earth a witch's pauper-child like myself was doing married to a prince in the first place. How quickly my mad thoughts spiraled into the lowest, most abject views of myself, and knowing these thoughts to be crazy made it all the worse, for wasn't *crazy* what I'd always been afraid of becoming, wandering endlessly alone in my own mind, as an abandoned, windswept child? In an instant, I could become that child again, and it made me tremble in awe to see how easily this transformation was effected.

"You're very quiet, Ella," said Sol when we were dancing again, and I could tell by his tone that he did not much like it. It did not anger him, but it irritated him just a little, and it irritated him because it was boring to him—a reaction much worse to me than anger would have been.

"I am always quiet," I protested. "I have not learned to converse as if I belong here."

I knew immediately it was the wrong thing to say—it did not please him. "You wrong yourself, Ella, by making such comments. There is no shame in your past. The only shame is what you attribute to it. If you show them you don't care, they won't either."

Had he been testing me, then, with his comment about witches? But what he asked of me I could not do. As the evening dragged interminably on, I became so entombed in my own self-judgment that I found myself tongue-tied at the simplest questions. And the more I retreated into my own mirror chamber of horrors, the more Solon seemed to implicitly disown his connection to me, no longer offering his arm, no longer squeezing my waist, no longer reminding me of our enduring partnership with his frequent smile. He did not ignore me; he was solicitous to my needs and even politely asked me if I felt tired and needed rest. But when at last he mentioned feeling tired himself, I was terrified that, for the first time since we'd been married, he would spend a night in the palace without coming to my room.

But it was worse. He entered swiftly, and without teasing, without caresses. He was awkwardly serious, asking me if I was alright when he accidentally leaned on my hair as he came down over me. He touched me habitually, and I could not respond. I found it difficult to sense my own body, so frozen was I in his cold, unfeeling embrace. I felt we were strangers. When he finished, I lay awake, my thoughts racing in terror, until he woke, and with a brief, polite kiss, left me for his own room.

I knew I wouldn't sleep. And what did it matter what anyone in the palace thought of me now, or whether or not a princess was allowed to go wandering alone through the palace in her nightdress? I didn't think to put shoes on, and my feet made no sound. Delirious, seeking air, I went out to the river, stood over the post-midnight silence of slow, black water, heard my own breath louder than the distant echoes from Sirenia, and felt my own foolishness bare upon my skin. I wondered if anybody on the opposite shore could see me, a princess billowing like a ghost in the breeze, faintly glowing above the river. When I was a girl, that would have been the kind of fantasy glimpse that kept my imagination going for days. But the houses on the other side were dark. I missed them. I missed being nothing among them.

"Sister!" cried a hushed, familiar voice, and another barefoot ghost came giggling suddenly out to greet me from a different doorway than the one from which I'd emerged.

"Kiera!"

"Oh, what fun! You couldn't sleep either?" She sidled up beside me and leaned upon the rail, taking up a pose of romantic gazing beside me that mirrored my own but more prettily. She always spoke as if she had a dollop of honey teasing the end of her tongue, that tickled her and made her delight to form words.

"Why are you awake?" I asked her.

"Oh, I can never sleep."

I think I smiled in spite of myself. "Never? That hardly seems possible, Kiera."

"No, but I mean, I often wake at this hour, and a restlessness takes hold of me."

She scrutinized my face. Hers was just slightly damp from sleep, especially in the girlish crease beneath her lower lip and upon the flushed lobes of her dainty nose. She wore a red cape over her nightdress, as if she wasn't worried at all about being seen. "You looked as if you were longing for something, or someone, out there across the water."

"Did I?" I shook my head.

"Do you know what I do sometimes, when I can't sleep?"

"What?" I realized I didn't have the energy for listening to another wave of her breathless secrets, as much as I loved her. The very openness of her expression seemed to close me up tighter.

"You must promise not to tell."

I nodded. "Yes, alright."

"I get one of the boatmen to take me out on the river."

That startled me. "In the middle of the night?"

Kiera nodded. When she smiled, her mouth looked too big for her face, which was surprising since everything about her seemed otherwise so perfectly proportioned. But people fell into that smile. "It's beautiful, in the moonlight. And so quiet. At dawn, you can watch the fishermen come out and cast their nets, and they look like—like magicians."

I stared at her.

"It's quite wonderful," Kiera assured me again.

"But how— but surely the boatman isn't allowed to take you—?"

She interrupted me, now in a bright whisper. "Perhaps tonight we might go together!"

I shook my head. "Kiera, I'm sorry, I'm not feeling well…" I could not imagine, just then, having fun. It felt like so much effort, to pretend.

"Oh, you must!" She clasped my hand, pulled it toward her breast with such excitement that I began to see there was no refusing her. After all, no one could refuse her anything. "I am *begging* you, sister!"

She always won me that way, by calling me *sister*. Perhaps she knew it, though she could not understand exactly why. She could not understand what it was like to haunt the outskirts of a family all your life, watching two lovely girls who were supposed to be your sisters call out to each other in shared laughter while you slept in ashes for fear of being seen.

"Alright, Kiera, but only for a short time. Really, I—"

Kiera fairly bounced. "Wait here!" she cried, and ran off into the night.

I stood and looked upon the river, waiting for her, and it felt like a long time. *She doesn't know,* my fickle thoughts taunted me. *She doesn't really know you—how crazy you think. Where you come from. What you are. What you've—*

Kiera came running back, and I stopped myself thinking. What was I even thinking? What darkness did I think I was hiding? To this day, I cannot explain it. I only knew I could not bear her perfection tonight, her being Sol's sister and calling me "sister," the way she always reminded me of the best of his love. She took my hand and, without a word, led me back into the palace, past the Hall, down a side stair by the entrance, and to the dock beneath the arches where the boats were tied. At night, without clear images, the smells were stronger. I remember the smell of the water, almost heady with its willowy freshness, like how I imagine God might smell, if one were close up to Him.

"We get our own boat," Kiera whispered, as the dark form of the boatman crouched by the water, tying one boat to another. "He's going to tow us. I told him we want privacy."

I smiled absently. "Do we want privacy?"

"Of course we do."

"Why?"

"So you can tell me why you're sad."

I turned away. But Kiera clasped my hand again, and I had to stumble behind her into the boat.

"We must speak in whispers, though," she told me, leaning across the benches where we faced each other, "because he isn't that far, and voices carry on the water so well."

"Where are we going?" I asked. In the darkness of the archway, I could see only the whites of Kiera's eyes and the glow of her skin beneath the red cape, but I could tell we were drifting beneath towering oaks and mossy stone walls.

"Just around the palace," said Kiera vaguely.

"Kiera," I said, still struggling to master my emotion, and wanting to avoid whatever conversation she was planning, "how is it that the boatman allowed you to do this? I hardly think your parents would approve, and surely he is under orders..."

Kiera looked away and shrugged. "He always does," she said with intentional carelessness, "if I let him kiss me, or touch my breasts."

"Kiera!"

"Oh don't, Ella," she said, turning back to me. "Don't be harsh with me. Haven't you ever done it?"

"Done what?" I was too shocked to understand the question. Not shocked by what she'd done, I suppose, but shocked that she, Kiera, thirteen and a princess, had done it.

"Made a trade like that," she whispered sincerely.

"Well, yes," I admitted. "I made almost exactly the same trade, more than once, in my old life. To go on the river, too—for the very same purpose!" Kiera smiled, a happy, melting smile. "But that was in my old life, when I had no money, nothing else to offer. I would never have imagined that anyone in your position—"

"But it doesn't matter, does it?" said Kiera sagely. "Whether you're a princess or a pauper, there are still so many things you can't do otherwise, as a woman."

And I saw, with perhaps a little chill, that somewhere in that pampered, light-hearted bosom she sheltered an awareness just as jaded, just as cold, as the awareness that had helped me survive for all the years of my adolescence: the knowledge that if I had to, I could always trade *that*. The knowledge that I had all the beauty that women longed for, and yet it was not sacred to any man; it was cheap to them and therefore cheap to me; it came easily, and I thought of giving it easily, with a lazy kind of bitterness which Kiera apparently shared.

"So now," said Kiera, "why were *you* awake? You must tell me."

I shook my head, glad that my face was hidden in the shadows, and that I had only to arrange my voice to sound level in order to feign calm.

"I am fine, Kiera," I said.

"No you are not, Ella," said Kiera, "and you must tell me about it, because I tell you everything, and it is only fair."

Despite Kiera's romantic descriptions, the moon was nearly new tonight, and did little to reveal our surroundings, or each other, or our place in the universe. All was liquid darkness, impossibly still and as silent as sorrow, but for the sound of the oar rippling the water far in the distance. I was not frightened of darkness back then (that came later), but that night I admit it disoriented me.

"I don't know. I don't know how to say it." *It is all over,* I thought. *You can never win this game—so give up. It will be easier.* "There is something wrong with me."

"No! There could not possibly be anything wrong with you. My brother loves you."

Her kindness cut me. My voice was tiny, like the echo of someone dying at the bottom of a well. Our boat emerged from an archway out under the stars, and I looked up at them and tried to focus on Heaven. "Please, Kiera."

"Is someone treating you badly?"

"No, no."

"Well, that is a lie, I know. Narsa treats you badly, because she is a mean old bitch."

"Kiera! Did you just say that?"

"Well, she is," said Kiera.

To my surprise, I laughed, and then we both laughed and couldn't stop. We tried to suppress the sound of our laughter, but this only caused us to snort like horses, which made us laugh harder. It was only Kiera who could have done that to me. There was never another like her, in my whole life. Her confidence was real: not the kind that scares you, but the kind that helps.

"I have never heard you talk like this before, Kiera," I said at last. "You are normally so sweet, but now I see you are also feisty."

"I am sweet, and I am feisty," agreed Kiera proudly. "I think it is important for a woman to be both."

Crudely, I smeared the tears away from my eyelashes with my sleeves. I bent over so that my chin rested on my arms, which rested on my knees, and I dared to trail a hand through the cool sheen of the water. I didn't want to think anymore, about what a woman should be. "I don't know," I murmured.

"You should know," said Kiera. "You were tough and street-savvy. Weren't you? In your old life?"

And I couldn't help myself. That made me laugh again. "Oh, Kiera." You know how it is, in the darkness. How distance disappears, between both bodies and hearts. When you speak to someone in that kind of darkness, with only the faint sound of liquid in the distance, it feels almost as if you are speaking within your own mind. It feels almost safe.

"Sometimes I wish," I said after a time, "that the servants would not dislike me so."

"Dislike you?" said Kiera, concerned.

"Well, I only mean... They don't seem to know how to treat me, I guess." I didn't want her to know how badly I did with them.

"What do you mean? How do they treat you?"

And I could see now that I'd begun, she would insist upon hearing the rest, so I blundered on. "They just don't really listen to me," I said, shrugging carelessly, as if I had given up bothering about it. "They tease me sometimes. Or they look at me a certain way... I don't know how to explain, really."

"Well," said Kiera huffily, "you don't have to explain! I know exactly what you mean. I have seen that kind of behavior, and I'm not surprised, because they think—some of them, I mean—that you're not true royalty, and that it's alright to disrespect you. But it's terrible! Haven't you told Mother?"

"Oh, no!" I cried.

"But why not?"

"I don't want her to think I'm not earning their respect," I admitted. I felt, to my bewilderment, a glorious sense of relief.

"Well, that is silly," said Kiera, with prim certainty, as if she herself were the mother. "She must hear of it. I will tell her. There is no excuse for them behaving that way, and they will get in mighty trouble for it, I can tell you."

"Oh no," I murmured. "They will hate me all the more."

"Ella," said Kiera, "you must listen to me. It does not matter what they think of you. They are the servants. They are there to serve you. They are not your friends. Do you not understand?"

"No, of course," I said, because I had already been told this so many times. "You are right."

"I am sorry," she said kindly, reaching across the boat to place her hand over mine. "You have had a hard time of it."

"Don't, Kiera. I shall weep again, and that is silly."

"It is not silly. It is lovely to weep."

"Lovely?"

"Why, yes! Doesn't it make you feel better, when you are sad?"

I nodded. I remembered, now, the few times I had seen Kiera in a melancholy mood, where no one could quite reach her—and she wouldn't tell anyone her secret thoughts, not even me. There was no honey on her tongue then. Sometimes she skipped meals, and stayed in bed half the day. "But I have never seen you weep, Kiera," I said.

She looked off into the caverns of darkness between the passing trees. "No," she said thoughtfully. "I cannot seem to do it. I don't know why. I don't weep. I can't remember the last time I did."

"But that is strange."

"I know. I wish I could! It is so beautiful when women weep. It makes a woman a real woman, I think, to let tears fall down her face, like a goddess in the rain!"

"Kiera!"

"What?"

I laughed softly and shook my head. "Who thinks like that?"

"Every woman thinks like that," said Kiera. "Except you."

♛ ♛ ♛ ♛ ♛

I know now that it was only the sin of pride which kept me silent until then. How did one live a royal life, I wondered, without being always tempted by it? I know now that one does not.

Kiera must have been true to her word, because within a few days, the servants' behavior toward me underwent a dramatic shift. I did not even have to think about what tone to use for commanding them, or what to do with my hands as I stood before them. And still I felt ashamed, for having the queen speak for me, for not being one of them and yet feeling that I was one of them, for having to command them at all and for knowing they did not really respect me but only the queen—and yet it also amazed me to see that, unlike at any former time in my life, I had the ability to ask for help, and that help would then be given.

The night after the ball, I went to Sol's room for the first time, with my hair hanging loose, in a seductive costume of my own making. I had remembered my own talent as a seamstress, honed throughout my childhood by the demands of my stepsisters' ever-evolving, luxurious wardrobes, which I had forgotten in the deluge of fantastical, overdone dresses that had rained down upon me since becoming princess. I altered the surcoat of one of my dresses, an outer layer that only covered certain parts of me, and I undid half the lacings. I came to Solon dressed in a style which he had likely never seen upon a woman—a style which was new and surprising to him, and that was the most important thing.

I don't know if any awkwardness remained between us from the previous night, but I knew he was leaving for no one knew how long, again, the next morning—and I couldn't bear not knowing. I smiled with joy as he looked up at me, just to see him. I had imagined him lying in bed, but he was sitting in a thoughtful state of half-undress, and had been examining something in his hands. At first I supposed it to be some manly thing, a weapon or a piece of knightly gear that needed repair, but as my eyes refocused after taking in the wonder of his hidden chamber—a thing I had never seen, and hardly ever imagined seeing—I saw that it was something of my own.

"My gold slipper!" I cried, without thinking.

But he had already dropped it on the bed. "What's this?" he said, grinning as he came to me and took my hips in his hands. I had let my cloak fall as soon as I entered the room. It pleased me that he not only showed by the tenor of his voice and breath, the motions of his hands, and the behavior of his body that he found me desirable dressed like this, but also took the time to finger my creation and kiss the parts of me that showed through, asking me as he did so how I had come upon such a strange costume. I told him I had made it, but could not tell if he heard, for he was kneeling now, and his eyes were closed.

"Wait," I laughed. "I want to see your room."

"You can see it," he murmured, but his mouth was busy.

"No, but I want you to show me," I said, letting myself enjoy the way pleasure interrupted my thoughts, and he lifted me and laid me down on the bed.

"This is the best angle to see it from," he said. "How do you remove this thing, anyway?"

"You must unlace it all the way. It will take you a while."

"Ah, perfect."

It was about the simplest room, I thought, that a prince could have. An ancient sword, apparently no longer in use, hung on one wall, along with what appeared to be a golden bridle. There was a plain green chair and a faded metal chest. The bed was gorgeously hung with the richest materials, green and violet, but there was no decoration whatsoever— no tassels, no fringes, no brocade. Discarded clothing and pieces of armor lay piled on the floor. When he finally unwrapped me and then rose over me in his splendor—a man with muscles like braided fire—I was still, in my ecstasy, gazing around me at his hidden world, and then I looked back at him as he dove into me. It was the room of some wild, orphaned boy, a place to crash into sleep between adventures. He had probably never invited me to his room, not because propriety decried such an act (for what cared my beloved for propriety?), but because he had never thought of it.

"You don't mind me coming in here?" I asked him afterward.

He turned to me and surrounded me with serpentine arms, smiling. "Not if you come dressed like that."

I laughed again. How easy laughter felt that night! Sol reached from the bed and replaced my golden slipper on the window ledge. "Its place of honor," he said. I wanted, almost, to reach for it, to touch it again, but it frightened me. I didn't know what had happened to any of the other clothes I'd worn on those three enchanted nights, but I often worried, in my most secret of thoughts, that I had known something important on those nights—that in those costumes I had been someone else, with some kind of confidence and clarity of vision which was later lost in the transition, yet was essential to my survival.

"Did you really make that dress," asked Solon, "or whatever it was?"

I panicked, and then realized he was speaking of the confection I had just entered his room in. "I did."

"I've never met a lady who could make her own dresses."

I laughed and tried to slip out of the compliment. "How do you know who makes every lady's dresses? Perhaps many of them make their own, and you'd never know!"

But he shook his head, turning over to face the ceiling. I traced his ribs with my fingers. "They don't," he said sadly. "I know."

I didn't know what to say. Even when he wasn't doing anything, I loved to watch him. I watched his eyelashes flutter; I watched the quiver in his slippery, angelic lips when he breathed, or when he thought about something without knowing he was thinking it.

We talked late into the night, though he planned to leave early in the morning, and though I had not slept the night before. He told me about the weapons and things scattered about his room, the people he'd met or helped on his quests who had given them to him in gratitude, or the ancestors who'd passed them down. Lying on his back seemed to allow the words to unravel from his throat, and I lay still beside him with my arm slung sleepily over him, pretending I owned this beautiful man whom I knew no one could own. I asked him questions just to keep him talking. I asked him things I'd always wanted to know, like how he felt about his brother's drinking. He grew serious, with a tender frown upon his face that surprised me, for he thought his brother all goodness and heart, and could not bear to see him losing himself to drink like their father. It seemed that despite his casual mockery of practically everyone in the palace during the day, Solon saw everyone who was closest to him as having a heart greater than his own. And this troubled him, not because he judged himself or felt anything like envy for anybody, but almost as if he felt that these hearts deserved to be protected somehow, and yet he could not see how to manage it, even with all his skills at arms.

"Loren is pure of heart—*pure*—and that is all you must know," he told me seemingly at random, though I had told him nothing of the poem. "He asks nothing of you, in his love, but perhaps a smile in return for his kindness, the grace of your glance, the honor of your presence a moment longer for him to gaze on. Be good to him, Ella. He is a dear friend."

When we had fallen so deeply between the soft layered coverlets of whispers and silence, kissing and murmuring, sleep and waking, that I no longer questioned myself for asking, I asked him why his father was so bitter. Before that, I had not realized I knew that bitterness was the name of the ghost that ruled the king.

"He is bitter with himself," Sol said. "His bitterness is at himself." It was strange to repeat himself like that. But I remember it. He did.

"Why?"

Sol let out a laugh—a broken, humorless laugh, the kind of laugh that is just a breath, sexy and intimate and sad with surrender. "Because he is no good at ruling. He sees what he isn't fixing in this world, or what he isn't fixing well enough. He's weak. People like him alright, but he keeps their lives only bearable. He's tired."

"Alden will be a good king," I said, for though he had never ventured more than a passing nod or greeting to me in all my time at the palace, each one of those greetings had glowed with kindness and presence.

"Yes," said Sol, with beautiful gravity. And he looked so pensive, I snuggled up to him and kissed his neck to comfort him. "Ours is not a bad family, Ella—not as royal families go."

"Oh, no!" I said. "It is wonderful."

"But you and I are lucky we will never be on the throne, Ella."

"Have you never wanted to be?"

"No. Well, perhaps, when I was a boy, I used to be jealous of Alden and his future. But not now, now that I understand what it means. It is too much responsibility for me. I am not cut out for it."

I took his hand and squeezed it. It was more than I'd ever thought he'd reveal, even to me. "What standard are we held to, then," I wondered, "if we are not to rule and to judge, if we don't have to make those great decisions?"

He smiled again and looked right at me. "Our job is to be beautiful, Ella. We are the prince and princess. We are what they look to when their lives become weary. Leave the great decisions to my parents, and to Alden. We are the people in the fairy tale."

You know how it is when your love is still new. It lasts perhaps a year at most, that time of being children together. And yet when you remember that time, it feels like forever, as opposed to the "forever after" of the many years that follow it, which, when you look back on them, seem to have passed all in a flash. In that early time together, each experience is new, so that each day seems to encompass a lifetime. And later in our years together, I was able to draw from that well of forever, even when the day-to-day land of our marriage became dangerously barren. Even when all I could draw up from that well were a few murky, nearly forgotten tears of memory, they kept me alive.

Sol didn't mention witches again that night. He never mentioned them again, and I swore I wouldn't either. I thought then that my mother would fade out of my memory, like a foolish superstition that had kept me alive when I needed her, but was irrelevant now. Perhaps I hadn't yet learned how to stand proud before a people, how to be royal, how to be divine, but I had found a way to stand proud before my own husband, with a dress made not by magic but by my own dexterity. I had found a use, however small, for my hands. For the rest of my days, I have walked light and easy in mermaid-sheaths of silk, without layers, without puffs, without cages of lace, without mountains of bustle, just flowing—dresses I make by hand, princess or not. Sol liked me like that, and so did I. In a few years, half the women in Sirenia would be dressing the same.

When I woke, later that morning, to my ladies fussing around me, I found myself in my own bed, tucked gently in. Sol had carried me there. He had caressed my hair away from my face and laid it out on the pillow behind me. He had kissed my earlobe and I had smiled. And before he had gone again, I knew not where and I knew not for how long, I remembered that he had spoken once more.

"I love you, Ella," he had said, for the first time, in a voice not charming or teasing or sweet, but quietly naked. And I had slept on those words: they were my pillow.

That's how I began, my people. That's all I was. But I was something—and that was more than I'd ever been before.

Rowan
(the Barbarians)

They said that one day, Prince Leo came home angry from a visit to the far western clans.

Not only had the furthest clan declined so far to join his army, but one of his best men had been gored by a boar they had tried to take down on their way home across the moors. Leo resented the man for letting himself be killed for reasons that had little to do with courage, and more to do with the nervousness that had plagued them all since they'd passed a ruin they claimed was a Dwarven well—and what inconsistent madness was this, for didn't they also claim that Dwarves lived beneath the drag-on-rivers to the north, and that their wells (which could suck a man out of this world, never to return) were only to be found in the North Forest?

But his remaining men, who trailed behind him, said that the real reason for his temper and his hurry was the terrible length of this journey, and his fear of leaving Princess Rowan unguarded for too long.

When she disappeared into air, Leo knew now that she would return sooner or later—she wasn't gone from the castle entirely—though he was never able to touch her. He vented his frustration with the castle maids and tried to keep her constant evasion a secret, for he knew the tight superstition of Barbarian laws around women—never could they be touched in the haunted hours of dusk and dawn, never could they touch a weapon—which bordered on silent hysteria, and he knew that his political standing anchored itself in no other feat more powerfully than in the feat of keeping this daughter of the Dark Fey under firm control.

He had ridden ahead as they neared the castle, brooding over how to convince the outlying Barbarian clans that the life they lived was not enough. He contemplated again the idea of raiding Sirenia with his band, not for women or simple loot, but for real treasure or even prisoners who would speak the truth about life there. But this idea ran contrary to his greater plan of all-out war. He wanted the Barbarians to leave all of Sirenia alone for a few years, to lure them into false trust and carelessness while he formed his army. He had already started a rumor leaking among the clans, through the women of the castle, that he was the true prince of Sirenia, bastard son to the high king (Leo knew how the mouths of women were the fastest and most effective vehicle for spreading information, for after all, his own mother had been found out that way). But the last thing he wanted was for the Cygninis to hear this rumor.

Now he became aware of the voices of his men behind him and, furious that he had allowed himself, in his exhaustion, to drop his guard, he began to hang back, so subtly that they did not notice until they were too close not to be heard. And then he heard. He could have killed them on the spot, but Leo gave his warriors a certain amount of respect so that they would trust him, and anyway he would rather not lose three more warriors today. But when they saw his face, they knew they would be punished—if only by demotion, or not being included in the next mission.

"I'll deal with you later," he growled, suppressing his fury so they would not sense defensiveness and suspect the truth of their own words.

They left him alone, and when the servants came to help him with the horses and mules, he also ordered them away, for he was in no mood to deal with any man, especially those simpering subordinates who sought to help him. "It seems I can trust no one today," he shouted at them, "so leave me. Do you think I am some pampered king like one in Sirenia, who cannot tend his own horses? I raised these horses from wild babes, and I need no help to handle them."

The servants bowed and scurried away, and Leo was left with not only his horses and all the provisions to unload but with two mules whom he had never liked, who stood stubbornly and absolutely refused to pass through the courtyard between the arch and the inner stables, because they were tired and it was raining, and because Leo's general attitude did not lead them to believe that they would be given grain if they even made it to the stables. There was a little bit of grass growing between the stone and the gravel at their feet, and they were nibbling at that while Leo began to shout at them.

He had begun to beat them by the time Princess Rowan's maidservant came hurrying with head bowed through the arch and knelt at his feet. The mules were moaning unhappily, shuffling toward and then away from the pouring rain. Leo was so surprised to see the maidservant, and so concerned to think what her arrival might portend concerning Rowan that he dropped the rod to his side immediately and said to her, without the harshness that he meant to accompany his voice, "What is it?"

"My lord, the princess is watching you from her tower window, and weeps terribly."

What this could possibly mean, Leo had no idea, but his relief that she was still captive in her room, and doing nothing less womanly than weeping, returned his confidence to him, and he demanded in his more usual voice, which made the servant tremble as it should, "And what of it? What do I care for a woman's weeping?"

"My lord, if only you would... Perhaps gentle your treatment of the animals, for it troubles the poor girl, and she weeps so, and pulls at her hair."

The boldness of the maidservant in requesting such a thing startled Leo, but she was too far beneath him to anger him. Her words intrigued him, and something more. "Get up," he told her. She stood. "Bring her to me," commanded Leo.

The maidservant made a show of great haste in obeying him, but once inside the castle walls, reluctance slowed her pace. It was unnatural to her, as a Barbarian, to question or regret her own decisions, but she worried at the look in Leo's eyes in response to what she'd told him. She knew that look. Pity made some men feel powerful, but she saw now that Leo wasn't one of those men. And eerie as the little white princess seemed to her, with her folded, forgotten hands and her ever-feverish cheeks and her hair black as emptiness and too slippery to ever tie, the maidservant loved her. Rowan looked so young, and the way she gazed out the window all day long, insensible to the presence of another person, broke the maidservant's heart. She wore clothing the way an animal would, like a thing that hung on her by mistake, no more relevant to her sense of herself than the movements of Leo's armies. She allowed the maidservant to change her each day, untying and tying, wrapping and unwrapping, and only refused, adamantly and without coherent words, to be laced. *What will you eat?* the maidservant had begged her more than once—*for I never see you eat, and surely you will die.* But Rowan had stared at her too long for the maidservant to bear, and said at last, without explanation or interest, in a voice full of breath but lower than one would expect from one so small, "No. I will not die."

Now the maidservant caught Rowan in both hands, her motions rougher than she meant because she didn't know how to handle the substance of such a creature, and also she felt sorry for what might happen. "Dry your tears," she barked, rubbing urgently at Rowan's face with her own apron. "And come. Now. I am going to take you to the mules. So there—you must stop."

Leo waited, and the mules trembled and suffered beside him, and after a while he began to beat them again, idly and then with more passion. When the maidservant came and held Rowan before him, she wore no mantle but only a dark blue linen gown, cinched girlishly just below her breasts, dropping smooth as glass to her hidden feet. Leo had found a woman who could make Rowan's dresses from scraps of Queen Mona's old wardrobe, in outdated Sirenian styles, so that one day Leo would be able to show off to his people the way civilized people looked. Rowan always smelt inexplicably of some fermented forest spice, something he remembered from the cold rain of childhood which filled him with loneliness. She wore her dress indifferently, as a stream wears a leaf that falls into it by the way. Furious weeping had brought the flush to her cheeks in points of flaming color, nearly as bright as her mouth, and her eyes looked crystalline with tears, red at the corners, and she did not appear to notice her own shivering as her breasts rose and fell in a charming panic of emotion.

"Go," he whispered to the maidservant, because he could not trust his voice. The whisper was enough to terrify her, and she left.

"What do you want?" he hissed at Rowan, and as he said it he knew it was true—she actually wanted something from him—and the knowing gave him a vulgar thrill. He gave the nearest mule another savage blow, making it stagger, and Rowan threw herself at his feet, in a gesture so sudden that even Leo started.

"Please," she said in her low, windy, girl voice, and it was the first time she had ever spoken to him. She did not call him by any title; he felt that she did not even recognize him. "Please don't hurt them," she said, and her head was bowed as close to the calf of his leg as possible without touching it.

"You will call me 'my lord,'" Leo told her, sucking in his breath, and when she did not immediately answer, he gave the same mule another blow. Rowan and the mule cried out at the same time, and Rowan's cry took the form of the words, "My lord!" but her voice wore the words the way her body wore the dress, without meaning.

Prince Leo dropped and crouched before her. They were hidden in the shadow of the arch, where none could see them. It had been a long time since Prince Leo had faced another human being so low down. "Why shouldn't I?" he whispered, breathing hard into her face because he could not yet touch her. And because her eyes threatened to drown him, he looked down at her little breasts, which bubbled up from her dress like newborn creatures.

But she only stared at him, and he saw that this question required far too many words from her, and he couldn't wait. "In a moment, Princess Rowan," he whispered, "I am going to touch you. I am going to do whatever I want with you, and you are going to let me. And if you resist me, if you disappear, I am going to beat these animals to death."

She did not shrink back at these words, nor cower in fear; her gasping did not cease its desperate rhythm. The pain of the animals seemed to consume her, and he could read nothing but animal pain in her eyes.

"I own all the beasts," Prince Leo continued, to make sure she understood. "I own all the horses, and I will beat all of them—nothing will stop me, if you disappear, if you refuse to obey my commands. Do you understand?"

Princess Rowan did not nod, but cried clearly, in the same tone of wind and loss, "Yes!"

And now Leo swept her into his arms and carried her into the nearest enclosed space, a gatehouse in which an open-mouthed guard greeted them.

"Vacate!" snapped Leo, and did not mind what the man saw or what he would tell the others—for now someone had seen proof that Prince Leo owned his princess, after all.

"Kneel," he said to her, and his voice sounded high and fragile to him, ringing in his ears. Already he had bared his body's weapon; he leaned into its force and grabbed her. But hesitation, a feeling normally unknown to him, restrained him momentarily. What was she, after all—what thing? He did not trust her mouth.

In the end he didn't undress her, and he didn't grip her nipples in his teeth, and he didn't overtake her naked body with his. With a grunt he pulled her around, shoved his hands up her skirt, wrapped it around her shoulders and neck, leaned forward to bite her hair in his teeth and keep from crying out as he entered her. He did not wish her to undress. Her pale, amphibious skin moved parts of his inner landscape that he did not wish to be moved. He wanted her clothed. He wanted the satisfaction of raping a woman dressed like a Cygnini princess.

♟   ♟   ♟   ♟   ♟

From Rowan's bedroom window, the maidservant watched her disappear, not into ethereal vapor but into a chamber of stone, stumbling by

Leo's hand. Somehow this forced clumsiness, so unnatural to Rowan, was the hardest offense for the maidservant to bear. She remembered Rowan saying, at last, with a girlish quaver to her chin, "With the Dwarves, I ate honey." And seeing the maidservant's expression of horror, she had turned back to the window, easily relinquishing the hope of being understood. But the maidservant, overcoming her horror for the sake of loving her, had brought the honey all the way from her home clan, which Rowan had licked from her servant's fingers with a long, rolling tongue, grabbing the woman's hand like a utensil. The maidservant had let her—she had stood frozen and staring wide, and even now she remembered Rowan swallowing, eyes closed, with the intense concentration of a butterfly.

♜   ♜   ♜   ♜   ♜

At first, the Barbarians used to say that Prince Leo must have created the castle louvre in the shape of a dragon, with the smoke streaming from its nostrils and eyes, out of stupidity. After all he wasn't born here—he had come from somewhere, out of the cursed North Forest. He'd claimed the Dwarf-built castle, the castle no one ever named for fear of lending it any power, and he'd raised the image of a dragon as his very own coat of arms, in a land where even the word "dragon" was never spoken, for fear of waking the wrath of those ancient devils.

For several moons, they dreamed of that stone dragon's smoky eye, and cursed Leo loudly at their campfires, and swore to kill him. They were not a people to make idle threats. And yet they did not kill him.

Word had it that Prince Leo and his band of warriors did not raise animals for meat. It was rumored that they hunted their meat from the Forest itself, from the forbidden hollows, from places where the bravest Barbarian men only entered on special quests to prove their place in the clan or to complete a rite of passage. It was rumored that not one of Leo's warriors ever lost his life to a bear or a forest lion or a dragon, because they were favored by the gods somehow. It was said that these warriors lived on that meat alone, and that they could survive on very little. The rumors came on the lips of women, whom Leo released to their home villages once the castle and its men had taken their fill of them—on purpose, to spread the information he wished to spread.

The women said that Prince Leo kept very few servants and needed hardly any comforts, unlike the Anai monarchy before him. He had replaced the fancy, God-worshipping tapestries with a few furs in the draftiest ends of the Great Hall. Most rooms were never used. The new princess was kept in one of them. They said that all his men both slept and ate in the Great Hall, around an open hearth below the dragon louvre, where a great wooden table was set on trestles at supper. They said that Prince Leo raised animals stolen from the Sirenian people, and that these animals could be trained to his army's command, carrying them great distances and doubling the reach of their hunting—animals called horses.

In seven moons, no curse had fallen upon the people in reprisal for the raising of the stone dragon above the Dwarf-built castle. In fact, there had only been one dragon attack during that time, and no one was killed. And the clan leaders no longer spoke of killing Prince Leo. For he'd brought each one of them a dragon's head.

At first, no one could believe such a thing. No one had killed a dragon in living memory.

Winter in the Northlands was dry but deadly. Snowfalls were rare, but when they came they were the final blow. The dragon heads arrived after solstice, when only six hours of light lay between dawn and dusk. A sheen of ice gripped the moors. Leo's men were not expected. No one was expected. In the dead of winter, even feuding stopped. Families hunkered down at their hearths and rarely ventured outside. Stealing food was punishable by death. Men who owned woollies guarded them day and night, for at times such as these all the grazing was gone, and the woollies wandered to the marshes and the tree-lined edges of the River Golden for bitter meals of bark and fir. It was not unusual to lose half one's herd to beasts in the winter, and one was grateful if at least the men came home alive at the end of their vigils. When a warrior of Leo's now mythical army rode across white space into each clan's field of vision, the men who had been warned by lookouts waited with spears and knives to see which clan he originated from. Leopard Clan members would always be killed on sight by Bear Clan members, and Harpy Clan members by Eagle Clan members. Everyone figured Leo was in over his head this time. They had their ancient feuds, the clans, but they shared a sense of pride in their mutual hatred. So they watched to see, by certain symbols and signs of dress, which clan the warrior represented.

But these warriors represented no clan. They wore Leo's armor, and cut their hair short. They came to every one of the twenty-eight clans on the same day. Each one thrust his stake into the ground, and delivered this message from his king while the people stared mesmerized at the twisted, grimacing head of the creature that most of them had never seen before:

I am the Barbarian King. I am your protector and your leader. Take this head as a token of my loyalty to this place and this people, and give me yours in return. Send the leader of your clan to pledge allegiance to me, and I will visit every clan in turn, in the order in which you were presented. It is time we unite, for we have a common enemy, and it is not dragons.

Then with a grunt that acknowledged much more than words—the unarguable power of his height upon the horse, a slight but respectful disgust at anyone who would doubt the man who sent such a gift, the ancient ties that bound him to his people, and the astounding strength of the new loyalty that, despite that bond, called him back to his leader—the warrior turned and rode away.

The people swore to die before ever uniting with their ancestral enemies. Yet most obeyed Prince Leo (for they would not call him King, yet, no matter what the message said, and no matter the grunt and the horse and the look in the warrior's eyes that they would always remember). They sent their leaders to the castle, one by one, not understanding the contradiction or the web they entered into by doing so. They obeyed because the one and only code was that the strongest rules. Only with the strongest man in power can the people survive against the forces of nature. And Prince Leo had proven himself beyond a doubt. They obeyed because the dragon heads were a gift, and it is bad luck to ignore a gift, especially from one stronger than oneself. They obeyed because of the cryptic last line in Prince Leo's message, which they did not understand. For the first time in the several hundred years that they had been defending their homes on this land, the Barbarians experienced curiosity. The dragon heads stood outside their lodge houses and withered in the sun, until at last they were almost beautiful, like talismans that guarded them. The impossible had occurred.

By promising to visit first those who pledged their allegiance to him first, Prince Leo turned inter-clan competition into a united stream of loyalty toward himself. Not always overtly, but in their hearts, many began to vie for his favor. After all, the clans had been fracturing internally for a long time, though no one would acknowledge this; it manifested only in increased violence and more frequent overhaul of the warlords in power. The Sirenian priests, with their teachings of gentleness and compassion and fellowship of man, who came here during the Anai reign, had injected a question into the hearts of many—particularly the voiceless, like the women, the weak, and the young. The question was this: *What if there is another way to live?* Or sometimes it was this: *What if it is possible for us to love and be loved, in a way we have never done before?* These questions led to nothing, were never answered or even spoken, but their existence created subterranean fissures in the structure of the clans, fissures that shook the ground the clan leaders stood upon. Their women imagined a god of compassion who was kind to them. Their men who never won enough fights to earn even one woman for their own, or any object, or even enough to eat, imagined a god who was above all other gods—above the Dwarves and the dragons and everything they had ever known, and whose gifts were intended *for the weak and the downtrodden*, more than for the high and the mighty. There was doubt where there had never been doubt.

Into this time of unconscious trembling, Prince Leo had entered with his silent, horse-riding warriors and his shocking gifts. When he came finally to speak to the people, he did not enter their fire-proof huts or accept offerings of ale. He stood at the central cooking pit of the village and demanded audience from all men. He came at the end of winter, during the starving time. He always brought food. He always brought his hardest warriors and invited all the young men of the village to test their strength against them. Any who could prove themselves had a chance at joining his band. And he always gave a speech, which was something that had never been done before. The idea of performance and audience, among this campfire-singing people, was unheard of. But Prince Leo demanded audience: he created the very idea of audience with his voice and his presence.

Prince Leo was impressively handsome. His features and movements boasted the intimidating grace of the civilized peoples to the south, and his fair hair marked him a descendent of those peoples—with not a trace of that Dwarf blood which showed vaguely in most Barbarians and which all Barbarians feared to acknowledge—while at the same time his hard eyes and muscles proved him equal in strength to any Barbarian lord. His intelligence far surpassed theirs, but he did not use it to talk above them. Instead, he had learned the dialect of every clan, and altered his speech with each one to gain their trust. He spoke like a Barbarian, with his voice thundering from the gut, but there was something more in his speech—a unity of body, intelligence, and spirit—that filled his tall, wide frame as he spoke and poured from his eyes like the smoke from the dragon louvre. His voice forbade you not to listen.

He said to them, *Our common enemy is the Cygninis and their people.*

At first they laughed. They had been making raids on outlying Sirenian farmers throughout the two hundred years that those people had been living there. The raids were fun dares for their young men, much easier and requiring less courage than hunting in the Forest. Their purpose was to inspire fear and sometimes to steal women. The idea of those people having any kind of power against them was a joke.

The Sirenians do not have the warrior strength and courage that the Barbarians live by, said Prince Leo, understanding their laughter, *but they have other powers, and with those powers they believe they can rule us.*

More laughter, mixed with outrage. *Rule us? No one has ever ruled us, nor ever will.*

And how do you know, asked Prince Leo, *that you are entirely free?*

What do you mean? cried one. *No laws bind us.*

Who is more powerful, the Barbarians or the Sirenian people?

Their own instant of silence before answering unnerved them. A hungry woollie bleated in the distance. Women pressed closer to each other and glanced nervously at their men. *We are stronger,* a clan lord growled, in a tone that was threateningly lazy, as if Prince Leo's words were hardly worth a reply, but might be worth a fight. You had to listen in a different way to the Barbarians than you listened in other places. Words came simple, and tone might be your only warning. Prince Leo knew this, but he and his men had killed twenty-eight dragons.

Who is more powerful? He pressed on. *Is it power to starve all winter like this? Is it power to wander in shadow all your lives, in terror of beasts who outnumber you? Is it power to avoid one half of your kingdom, the Forest which holds more meat than you can eat, if you would only brave it?*

An incoherent sucking in of breath, and the women tightened and pressed back, fearing the wrath of their men.

Leo continued.

Or is it power to own a walled city protected from beasts, invasions, and the elements, to live in houses with three floors worth of luxury—every house like a castle with a hearth in every room—and to have servants to bring your water? Is it power to know the medicine for treating any illness, to have your bath heated and fresh each day, to eat bread at every meal, to travel on stone roads on horses with carts full of wares that can be sold at market for money? Is it power to have at your command every kind of machinery for tilling fields of crops so vast that the storerooms are always full and famine never claims any lives, and to drink wine every day, and to send your sons to learn a trade so they can get rich just for carving wood or painting glass, if they wish? Your women have seen their beautiful cloths and smelt their fragrant soaps. They don't need to hunt or to toil in the fields: their servants do that for them.

At this, the crowd relaxed a little. Prince Leo had been speaking of such ideas to anyone who would listen for seven years. They grumbled to themselves, *What do we want with all that? Books and pretty clothes, churches and jewels—it's all that what makes them weak, makes them weep before us when we raid them! And all those stupid laws. A man can't even avenge a murdered brother, in that land. They can't even defend their women.* And they chuckled to themselves.

Prince Leo was patient. *Every protest you make, every word you speak in pride of your strength, is your weakness. Do you know why?*

They did not answer, and their eyes were mutinous, but their silence asked him. Fascination stayed their anger. The winter was too long. If they killed him, nothing this interesting might ever happen again.

Because that is how they want you to think, Prince Leo answered himself. *They want you to scorn their luxuries, to cling to your base, physical life. It is how they know you are nothing but animals. It is their justification for ruling you, for ignoring your right to their wealth.*

And in the furious but wavering silence that remained after his words, he turned away and paced back the way he came, turning his back to them in an unprecedented show of courage against their anger, walking as if he would walk all the way back to his castle and not care what they thought and not fear their revenge for his traitorous words—and then when he had almost reached the outskirts of the circle, he turned back.

I tell you, it angers me, he said, as if in the face of all their silent anger, which did not even frighten him enough to keep them in his line of vision, only his anger was real. *Fighting, in my opinion, is a better defense than stubborn pride. They consider us as belonging to them.*

And who cares what they consider or don't consider? demanded the people.

And Prince Leo would enlighten them. He would tell them how some of the Sirenian wealth had been mined from these very mountains that belonged to the Barbarians, how the Sirenians had had their way with this land without ever bearing its hardships or compensating its people. He asked them why they, the Barbarians, the people of the Northlands, could no longer enter their own Forest—was it because the spirits there were angry and would not brook trespass? And if so, what had angered them? Was it the Barbarians' fault? Or was it the invasion of the Sirenians, those foreigners who had, once upon a time, somehow turned the order of things upside down?

The creatures, they grumbled, meaning (but not daring to say) the dragons—*they've been there since before all that. Before the Sirenians.*

Nae, but it was different once, said another. *Before the Wall. Before the King's Forest.*

What do you know?

You were only a babe when my father was killed for hunting the deer—

But swiftly, Leo gathered their anger into his hands—before it could divide them, before it could dissipate into some foolish little raid—like a sorcerer.

We are Barbarians, he said. *We fear nothing. The Forest is ours.*

He let these truths lie. Who could argue with them? He let them think. He let them remember the Wall now unguarded. He let them begin to feel unsatisfied with those little farmland raids across the sleepy River Golden.

I do not speak here of attacking a few peasants on the outskirts of Sirenia, with a small band of men from one or two clans, to steal a few women or trophies. I speak of our nation against theirs. I speak of our entire people claiming our birthright.

And when they said stubbornly, hoisting up their pride and expanding their chests to hide their confusion, *We have no nation,* he answered:

You are mistaken. And in that mistake lies your weakness. Do you know how many able-bodied warriors live in this realm called the Northlands?

They looked at each other. They'd never thought of their numbers en masse that way.

About two thousand, Prince Leo said. *And do you know how many able-bodied warriors the Cygninis have at their command?*

How many?

Perhaps a thousand. Half.

He waited for them to put words to their disbelief.

There's surely a hundred thousand in that kingdom—!

But those people are not warriors, Prince Leo interrupted, and he could not help, at this point, but break into a small, wicked smile, which he felt he'd earned. *The Sirenian people have lived for so long without fear of enemies, only barricading their furthest borders from small, insignificant raids, that their warriors have become like children playing at battle, testing each other only in foolish tournament games. No man ever meets another man in bloodshed.*

My friends (here he dropped his voice to nearly a whisper and changed his tone to one of conspiracy, so that the men all leaned ever so slightly closer, in spite of themselves), *most able-bodied men in that kingdom have never even touched a weapon.*

And he let that sink in.

Finally the clan leader would speak, and his voice expressed the absolute focus of the entire clan spirit, as it wavered on the edge of bowing to Leo's will. *They have only one god there,* he said. *That weak-willed, woman-minded god.*

Leo nodded slowly, still smiling, and waited.

Yea, said another, *there's no fight in that one.*

Imagine, said Leo, his voice low, constricted with passion. *What if our gods fought for us? What if we passed through the North Forest in secret, and they were on our side?*

The people were absolutely still. What he said contradicted every story. Yet everybody knew how Prince Leo had sought out the Dwarves among the river tributaries north of the Source, between the highest mountain and the sea, where dragons were born and the Forest loomed beyond. How he'd won the princess from them—from those monstrous deities of old, whom no one had ever seen, who filled their legends and thickened the darkness of the night around their fires like blood. Could he possibly mean what he seemed to mean?

What if I could resurrect them? asked Prince Leo of the Barbarians. *What if I convinced them to fight on our side, to fight the weak god of the Sirenians? Who would win?*

But when Rowan's maidservant, whom Leo returned to her home clan shortly after he claimed Rowan at last—for she knew enough now to spread the news he wanted, but would know too much if she stayed longer—told the men what she'd seen, their reactions were mixed. She and the other women listened behind the walls while the men spoke afterward, outside around the fire, and they made sure to keep silent, for they heard fear in the men's voices—not quite the kind that leads to beatings, but dangerous enough to keep an eye and an ear on.

Huh! said some, and figured it was settled. But others jabbed at the fire. For all his prowess at arms, that Prince Leo didn't know what he was about, they said, with such a woman. Every clan, no matter their lineage, kept stories about the Fey women, the ghost women of the Northern Primeval Forest. King William had not been the first to wither away in their power, seduced by Rhiannon the queen of them all. There was a reason every warlord before Leo had fallen, and civilization like Sirenia's could never be built here. There was a reason certain infants, if they didn't look quite right, must be left in the Red Fen, at the border between the moors and the Forest, to die. There was a reason for the Barbarians' wild loyalty to their own clans, without which, alone in the wilderness, they would not last one night. There was a reason men laughed so loudly at campfires in the evening, and never spoke of their dreams, and shut up their doors when the moon rose. It was possible to survive in this land, but only through careful appeasement of sinister forces and, if all else failed, brute courage.

The men didn't retell the old stories now—it was too late at night—of seal women who shed their skins and danced in naked splendor on twilit western shores stilled by mist and blurred by heather, of silent owl women who dulled a man's spear in the impossible softness of their feathers and drowned him in endless night, of the spider woman who wrapped men in spools of flaxen moonlight until they could not escape the caresses of her many hands, of fox women who spiraled around men's bodies as they slept in fields so that they woke in desperation, of salamander women in the shallow crossing where the river came down from the Source, with their tongues of fire, or of moth women who wailed around them like banshees if ever they stepped into the Red Fen alone on the first new moon of autumn.

But the women listening behind the walls knew their men feared such monsters more than dragons, more than death. For to die was to enter the land of eternal summer, the Other World of silken flowers and melting sun and warm sea, of giant canopied trees that would feed you luscious fruits all day and shelter you in sweet, fearless sleep all night. But the worlds were not meant to cross. And Princess Rowan, some men grumbled—whoever she was—should have been left where she was, in the realm of the dead.

The women listened, and heard.

And the maidservant remembered something that Rowan had said, Rowan who watched everything Leo did from her bedroom window— every way he interacted with his men, every command—the way a cat watches, missing nothing. Rowan knew what the Barbarians knew.

"His rule will not last," she'd said one day, though her voice still betrayed no interest, moving over the stillness of the room like a meandering breeze. "Humans cannot live here. Nothing belongs to them."

But the maidservant hadn't told that part to anyone. How the girl had called humans "them," as if she wasn't one of them. Maybe women seemed the best spreaders of gossip. But in secrets—only in secrets, and nothing else—they were far richer than the men.

Mina

Dear Sisters,

I haven't found a way to send you my letter, though I haven't yet given up hope. Today it occurred to me that continuing it—continuing to speak to you, through it—might ease the pain of missing you more effectively than keeping it locked away and trying to forget it (as I have been doing all this time). How is Father? Does he trust that he'll see me again one day—does he know how I love him? And Addie, whom did you choose, in the end, and how did you decide, and are you happy? And Lara, have you come to peace with your gentle stonemason? He has no wealth or prestige, I know, but he loves you as you are, in any mood or weather, and that's what matters.

What a strange world I have come into, without law or precedent! I never did pray to God the way you did—He always seemed to me more like a wind, or the sky, not someone to ask for help. And yet lately I have been rather wishing for some form of guidance, even beyond what Nicolai and I are able to offer each other. I feel so young.

The full moon that blessed our marriage had almost waned to a sliver in the cold winter sky before Nicolai set out in search of his people. I did not understand at first why he held back. I thought that after fifty years of starving loneliness, outcast not only from community but from the very form of his human body, living in a nightmare of wordless isolation, my prince would take me by the hand immediately and lead me rejoicing to the people he had long ago been torn from—and who perhaps missed him, after all these years. Would anyone he knew be still alive? Surely he wondered.

Yet what more could I ask for, then, but those days that belonged to just the two of us, days of wandering hand in hand over the stones overgrown with roses, around the southern cliffs where the sky pressed up so brightly, it seemed we could see the details of the air itself, cracked through with burning sunshine? This peninsula is made of such hard, flinty stuff—the only surface soil blown down over the eons into what is now the forest, and into the swamp to the west—that instead of sifting gently into beaches like any ordinary shore, these mountains are forever flaking into the waves, making sharper and sharper cliffs that not even time can soften. They used to say, Nicolai told me, that beneath the thin layer of soil that supports the hardy, stunted wilderness of these coasts, the land is pure crystal. I thought I could feel it, glowing along my spine where he lay me down, and he looked into my eyes as he made love to me, his hands turning my body to night, still shivering with the memory of teeth and claw and unruled breath that haunted us both with a kind of terror and amazement and made every stroke feel furred and wild. I wonder, my sisters, if you have been entered like this. So that a path is left inside you, through the fluff of tall grasses, and now winds blow ever through it, seeking him again—not a path that could be seen, by anyone outside of you, but a path that animals know, a path he knows. And knowing he will find it, just knowing that, makes your mouth water in the middle of the day, for no reason, in the middle of some ordinary task. The knowing that you might turn of a sudden, and find him there behind you.

I don't know how to explain it. But I belonged to him, and he to me—each day and night we gave ourselves again. "This is the first time in my life that I have truly loved," he told me. "Perhaps I need no people but you."

And yet we are sovereigns, I thought. And I wondered if somewhere out there, people needed us. People to whom we were responsible, beyond our own bliss. I sensed a subtle resistance every time I even tried to imagine asking Nicolai about them. But I was not impatient with him. I figured he would come to it in his own time. After all, I could not imagine what it would feel like to go through what he had been through, nor was I overly eager to begin a life of work which I so little understood and to which I might not be equal. Though he had poured out his history so openly to me that first night we stood in the tower, ever since then he had hardly spoken of it at all. I learned not to ask him any more about the unicorns, what they looked like or how they communicated with human beings in the days of innocence, for when I did his brow darkened, and he would grumble with some brooding unease normally invisible to me, "I would not know. I never really knew them."

It was during this time that we came closer to the sea than I had ever come before. You cannot imagine how it booms and clashes and grows and falls—not like a body of water at all but like an interminable landscape of motion stretching all the way to the horizon, and if you saw it, all would be changed in you. It is changed in me, though I can't say how. I can only say, I think you would believe in things you had not thought to believe in before. It's like a feeling so big, it makes all your little feelings small and unimportant. But it has a rhythm to it, you see—and you can feel that it's older than your heartbeat, older than time—and so that feeling is only an echo of some more ancient peace. There is no pain in it. And yet it frightens me. What it would be like, to touch it, I cannot imagine. I can't think that it would feel like the water of streams and lakes. I am not even certain that it is water at all.

The sea here can only be reached by certain narrow, hidden passageways made by ever-shifting avalanches along the cliffs, which I have never traveled. But Nicolai took me along the high cliff pathways, and a little further down to some places he knew would be protected from the wind, so we could watch the waves. Occasionally we passed old ruins that looked so like castles to me, but Nicolai said that was only the way everyone lived, long ago in the time of unicorns. These dwellings looked harmless and lovely in their ruin, abandoned to the growing earth—not one of them appeared to have been lived in any time recently, and I felt we were children stumbling upon a fantastic land left only for us. It's like a vision you might expect to see at birth or death. I know there is a holiness here still. Once, surrounded by gabbling seabirds, we came upon a little cave that Nicolai knew. To my joy, he told me that he'd played there as a boy. And I was surprised at the memories he shared with me there, since before when he'd told me his story, he'd spoken of his youth as such a blur of meaningless drunkenness. But it seems that in the days of his very early youth, life held wonder for him, very much like what I experienced in my own childhood. He used to frequent this cave, with friends and sometimes alone, and pretend he hid from a sea monster or escaped some evil, faraway king as a lost, shipwrecked sailor.

"It's strange," he said, caressing the figure of a warrior carved from unicorn horn, which had been his toy once and which he found there in a crevice. "We had everything; we lived in a world without pain or want. And yet it was as if we longed for the drama of suffering, or we needed something to fight for—and instead of pretending to live better lives, as I imagine children in hardship do, we pretended to be hunted or tormented, just to make things interesting. And I, who was a prince, who had all the power I could want, must pretend I was some refugee without a home or a single possession, struggling for my very life!" And his laugh had a bite of bitterness in it, as he tossed the little toy—to my sorrow—into the sea.

Those waves are good for devouring, it seems, whatever we wish to forget. Once I brought him a giant unicorn horn which I had discovered to be capable of music—I had not known that a unicorn horn is hollow inside, and tiny holes had been drilled in this one, for making notes. I had discovered it in the rubble of the castle's upper story long before, during the days when he was a beast, and now I was happy to be able to ask him, finally, if it were his, if he had once played upon it. But the moment I held it before him, I saw my mistake. He stood gazing at it for a long, difficult moment, his expression unreadable, and I realized that if he had wanted to be reminded of it—if he had wanted to play it again, or even think of it—he would have brought it out on his own.

"Mina," he said, in a low tone of secret pain, and I had never before trembled at his use of my name. "Do you not understand what I have told you, about the unicorns? Do you not understand what we have done? Never will I use any part of them again."

"Nicolai," I pressed—and I should not have pressed, I know. You would not think it of me! And yet you know how I am, how I could have stayed up all night listening to your stories, when we were girls. Perhaps curiosity is my one greedy flaw. "Was a unicorn killed for this horn?"

He didn't answer me for a long time. "No," he murmured finally. "For some things were given freely, long ago. That was given to my grandfather."

"Then perhaps," I began, for I felt sorry for it, and for the creature who had given it, whom I had never seen, "if it was made into something beautiful, and makes beautiful music, it cannot be wrong to—"

"Do not remind me of the past!" he half-roared at me, yet his voice broke. "It is all I ask of you. Is it so much?"

It frightened me, to feel his anger for the first time, so that I stepped back and tripped over some pile of debris behind me. He lunged forward and caught my hands to keep me from falling. I didn't begin to cry until he held me, babbling a desperate apology. I knew he was more frightened than I was—that he should become the beast again, unable to control his passions. And I learned my lesson. He didn't need to tell me again. I tossed that horn into the sea for him, so he would never more have to look upon it.

Then one evening at supper, Nicolai seemed quieter than usual, until—just as I had begun casting around for some conversation topic, wondering anxiously what could be wrong, since I had never had to try for one before—he spoke abruptly. He told me he had come upon a dwelling that day in the forest, while he was hunting. He had not made his presence known. And again I felt that subtle wall, so I asked no questions. But later as we lay in bed, I could feel him thinking about it, and I could feel the softness of his heart beside mine. Gathering my courage, I asked him, "Do you think your people loved you, my Nicolai?"

He seemed to think on this for a long time. Then he answered, "They celebrated me. I do not think they loved me. There was nothing that I did... I did not know how to be any kind of leader. There was nothing to love me for."

I waited some time, and then finally he spoke a few of his thoughts: "Will they want me now, Mina?" he asked. "Will they welcome me back, or will they condemn me for failing them? Do they know what has happened to me? Have they thought of me? What if they have sworn to kill me, should they ever see me again?"

And he tried to laugh, then, but the laughter came out hoarse.

"I will be with you," I told him. "I will stand by you, no matter what happens. You know that."

He looked into my eyes, and I saw the beast again—the beautiful beast, who could express more than most people can express in a thousand words with his eyes, because he had to. "I know you will," he said softly. "But it feels good to hear it." Then he held me, and after a moment he whispered, "You are stronger than I am, you know."

And I said, "Don't be foolish. I have not endured what you have endured. It is impossible to know—"

"I know," he said. "You cannot imagine how much I depend on you. You alone have saved me. You are all I have." And I knew all this, but it choked him up to say it, as if he realized it all over again by speaking it aloud. He clung to me hard that night.

In the morning, he rose early. He said we would go to the dwelling that he had seen. He was ready. And so I, too, tried to make myself ready—in my dress, in my bearing, and in my heart. We traveled most of the day, first descending through the valley between the mountains that separate us from Sleeping Lake and the hills that lean up briefly before cutting down into the sea—a delicious, open valley of silver grasses that look softer than froth as you come into them, and I always feel my body loosening with joy as if I must swim through such splendor, as if I must grow fins. And then past the old, sunken pond at the edge of the wood, and then finally in among the towering pines, further and deeper than

I had ever been except once with the beast long ago (it seemed), our footsteps silenced on their rust-colored carpets. Nicolai said the people have all moved inland now, into the deep forests.

Following a creek until we came to a path he remembered, we startled a heron to flight, and I thought it a good sign. I am from the city, where people take the sighting of a wild animal as a wondrous omen for the mere marvel of its rarity, as if nature were some carnival event, without realizing—as the people do here, and as they have since taught me—that to see an animal running or flying away is to know that you have disrupted something sacred. You have intruded, you have stumbled unbelonging and unaware into a world that people long ago betrayed, and it doesn't trust you.

We found the little hut nestled in the crotch of two damp, fern-thick hills, its low entrance threaded beneath the arched root of a massive tree that stood before it and all but hid it from the little path we traveled. The roof had been paneled with multi-shaded bark. Haphazard steps, overgrown with wild irises and small woodland flowers, wound down from the raised doorway in several directions, disappearing into wild-grown gardens, stacks of mushroom logs, a small circle of stone seats. In the doorway of the hut, framed with a weaving of willow branches that crossed over the top in a pointed arch uncannily reminiscent of a cathedral entrance, stood an old man.

Though he did not appear to me weak or malnourished, there was so little flesh on his bones, and so much light in his great, green eyes, that his twiggy, crooked frame seemed more spirit than body. His mossy white beard made his face look small and fragile. Behind him, an equally aged woman emerged from the shadows of the house's interior, and the two of them together were beautiful, their faces lined like bark, in a way that people from Sirenia almost never become beautiful, when they age. And the color of their skin, sisters—I can hardly describe it. Not like the oily prisms you see in the sunlit skin of Hummingbird People, from whom these people are supposed to be descended, nor like the dusky golden skin of the Wyes, from whom they are also descended—both of whom Nicolai resembles. Do they have a color at all? It is like the light the moon would cast, if the moon had an inner light all its own.

"Peace!" called Nicolai, who was holding my hand so tightly, it pained me. I could not read the expression on the couple's faces—neither frightened nor welcoming. As we drew closer, the man stepped down off the lower step and stood waiting to greet us. The woman folded her hands together, and only her slightly parted lips gave away her wonder at the sight of strangers.

We stopped before them, and the old man stood still and unafraid, looking into Nicolai's eyes. I realized I was staring at Nicolai in expectation, as he bowed his head before looking back up to face the man's gaze—and in that moment I truly understood that Prince Nicolai of older times had been nothing more than a boy, with no more than a boy's imperious command, if he had any command at all.

"Who are you, stranger?" asked the man. I liked his voice very much, and yet its compassion made me unaccountably sad.

"Sir," said my husband, "I am Prince Nicolai."

The man transfixed Nicolai with his gaze, beyond which I could not discern any emotion, and then replied at last, "So you are."

"This is my wife," continued Nicolai, his breath escaping him awkwardly. "Mina."

"Please come in," said the man, and, nodding to the woman, who smiled, we entered the house behind him.

The interior was dark and soft and tea-scented, with branching rooms and uneven walls, not unkempt but as complicated with living as the lines on the old ones' faces. An open stairway with rails of bent grapevine wound up into a hidden loft, from which soft reed curtains hung. The faces of two children, one female, one whose sex was difficult to differentiate but which later revealed itself to be male, peered with open awe from behind it. The couple sat down with us on simple woven mats before an earthen fireplace, offered us tea, and introduced us to their two grandchildren, and presently to their daughter, who came in from the gardens and moved without making any sound. All of them, even the children, had white hair like Nicolai's, and all of them glimmered like the moon, but otherwise they seemed ordinary enough.

"And so you are free from the castle now?" said the man at last—smiling faintly, almost as if to a child who played pretend.

Nicolai shook his head in confusion. "Do you know me?"

"Of course," said the man.

And we stumbled along that way. The old man, whose name was Rhee, and the old woman, whose name was Ona, showed no surprise that Nicolai had aged hardly at all since he disappeared fifty years ago. They had not known him personally. They, like everyone, had assumed that in the collapse of their world, the prince had taken flight to save himself. At first, Rhee explained, it was easy to blame him for everything—but as the tasks of survival took over their lives, people gradually began to forget him. When the unicorns disappeared, all the magical technologies of society collapsed. Many young people, unwilling to face such a crude life, took their chances with Sleeping Lake or the Swamp, in the hopes of escaping (but I doubt that many made it, for I don't remember ever hearing of any such survivors in Sirenia—or perhaps if they came and told their stories, no one believed them). Many who remained died of starvation or in violent feuds. There were men who invented plans for bringing the unicorns back (not believing they were really gone) or governing the resources of the new kingdom, but in the end all these men destroyed each other, as if the land were still cursed, long after Rhiannon came and left. The very few who remained and survived over the years were the hardiest, the ones with the most knowledge of how to reap their food and medicines from the earth. They lived in a quiet, secret way. They learned never to want too much, and they learned to mistrust power—or anyone who seeks it. There was never any attempt to form a new society. A kind of repentant spiritual discipline has formed over time, and though daily meditation draws the people together, when weather permits, into small, silent congregations—mainly in the sacred groves where long ago unicorns are said to have first held conference with human beings—there is no discussion or leadership at these gatherings. They are silent. There is no government at all, for no large-scale decisions need to be made, and no collective funds or properties need to be managed. People share the knowledge they need to survive, and do not strive for more than the most basic existence. When their loved ones die of disease, they accept it. There are no plans for expansion or prosperity, no greater hopes for civilization than this. I understood, without Rhee saying so, that if one were to strive higher, no law would stop him (for there are no laws), but his neighbors would look coldly upon it—and then he would be alone, which out here would be punishment enough.

Many who were alive to know Nicolai are dead now, and the blame died with them. As the fabric of a more careful world was rewoven, the new generation who made it were more thoughtful in their judgments. Their elders dreamed of a lone white wolf, terrible and unconscious, driven through the forest by need and suffering. They knew what he represented. They knew that to fear him or fight him or engage with him at all would enslave their minds once again to all they had worked to be free from. I began to understand that they never imagined Nicolai to be a real wolf—this kind of magic, even with all their history of unicorns, was beyond their interest or willingness to believe. Nicolai did not correct them.

"These dreams were reminders," Rhee explained, "of the baser instincts which had once led us astray. We knew that you were suffering, and that something kept you attached to that castle. Like you, it took us a long time to relinquish the objects of our old life."

I saw tears passing down Nicolai's face now, but he did not move, and I clasped my hands in my lap to keep from reaching for him. It seemed to me he was unaware of the tears, and if I touched him, I might hurt him.

As Rhee spoke, their daughter moved nearby, listening and playing quietly with the children at the same time. The rest of their family—the daughter's husband, the younger daughter, and another grandchild—had died in two waves of sickness that passed through during the last ten years. Hearing them speak of it without trouble in their voices, I no longer wondered that they did not show more passion or shock at Nicolai's arrival, for surely they had learned to be at peace with greater events than this.

"Those of us who survived," Rhee told us, "survived because we understood the wrong we had done. We understood the responsibility we all played in it, and that to look to a leader to blame or to save us was childish and useless. We have only ourselves."

"So you release me," said Nicolai, with irony.

Rhee smiled. But Ona seemed to hear more clearly the emotion in Nicolai's voice, and spoke at last.

"You have your own path, your own growth," she said, and I heard in her voice that she struggled somewhat with words, but out of kindness wished to speak these for my husband. "You will know it, in time." She nodded several times as she spoke, as if to urge along her own voice and imbue it with the heavier meaning she had meant to give it.

"My wife, Mina," said Nicolai, and I had fallen so silent I had almost forgotten myself, but when he spoke I felt a certain tension release within me, as if I had been holding my breath, "is the one who lifted my curse." At this, Ona took my hand and clumsily squeezed it, as if Nicolai had just complimented my cooking. I noticed that Nicolai never mentioned Rhiannon. Like his life as a wolf, she seemed beyond his power to explain—to anyone but me.

"It was foretold," he said, without saying the Dark Faerie's name, "that only a woman from another land could lift my curse, and that if she could find it in her heart to love me—" and his voice caught with shame, but now both Rhee and Ona smiled, and I felt they warmed to him for the first time. "That if she could love me," he continued, lifting his head, "I would become human again. It was also foretold... that this woman, who is Mina, would save our people—perhaps even bring back...the unicorns."

I could feel all eyes upon me, even Nicolai's. I bowed my head, terrified of their attention. What could they possibly expect of me?

"I really don't know," I found myself muttering childishly, my voice hoarse from lack of use. "I don't know how... I have no such expectations."

Ona patted my hand. "Good," she said.

"Memories, expectations, ideas of any grandeur or special role or revelation," said Rhee, "—none of these are yours to carry, child."

I felt relief.

"Where do you come from?" asked their daughter.

"From Sirenia," I answered, and then added hastily, "but my mother was a Wye." I wanted them to understand that I was like them, who were also half-Wye, though I felt foolish for saying it.

When we had finished our tea, we rose, and Rhee took Nicolai's big hand between his aged, wiry ones, which did not tremble. "Nicolai," he said, deliberately omitting any other title, "please give your attention to this one law we live by—the only agreed-upon law. It is that we have no rulers. All people counsel one another, but no man leads in any way. Do you understand? The world has changed. This is how we survive."

"Of course," said Nicolai—too easily, I thought. "But we still live in the castle, though the curse has lifted. It is our only home, for now."

"As you see fit," said Rhee, and the peace in his smile seemed sincere, I thought.

Their daughter brought us outside and showed us the gardens. They were neat and lush, but the amount of food that grew there seemed hardly enough to feed a family. It was never said directly—as if it were too obvious to be said—but they had led us to understand that none of the people ate meat now, that this was frowned upon. They were awfully thin, but they did not have the desperate, hollow look of hungry Sirenian beggars.

Before we left, she sat down with us in the little ring of stones that seemed to make a kind of council space.

"Is there no time or place where the community comes together?" asked Nicolai. "I would speak to the people. I would tell them how sorry I am..."

But at once he sensed his mistake, and his words trailed off, no matter how passionately he had intended them. The suggestion that he stand before a multitude, like one of those power-hungry leaders of old, must have alarmed her, for her face darkened suddenly and lost its grace in a quick, tight frown.

"We do not meet all together for speech," she said. "But we will mention to others that you have come."

When we rose, I wished suddenly that we had brought some gift for them. I felt ashamed. She asked with faltering concern, "Do you have a garden there, at the... at the castle?"

Nicolai hesitated, not wishing to tell her that he had been hunting for our food, so I answered, "We have a little garden, but we will have to expand, now, for the two of us. I have some experience—a little."

"We can surely help you," she said, and I sensed she meant more than just her family. "You must eat."

I drew my breath in slowly, for my heart was so full. "Thank you," I told her.

As we left, the whole family came to the doorstep to bid us farewell.

"Goodbye, Nicolai Wolf," said Rhee. "We will see you again." I felt Nicolai in pain beside me. Their kindness was painful, because it was a gift given in charity—handed down from those powerful in their belonging, to one alone and lost.

As we turned away, the little girl called after me, her bright voice startling after the morning of strained caution. "You can be Mina the Fox!" she cried. And then, "Mina Fox," as if to herself, grinning and tucking in her chin, enjoying words which seemed to taste delicious to her. "Because of your red hair," she added, when I turned to look back at her.

We left the cottage and began climbing up along the creek. Nicolai was brooding and silent. I understood what he was feeling, and I knew that nothing I could say would help it, so I stayed silent, too, and as we rose up into the wind in sight of the broken castle, I gave him my hand.

spring

Dear Sisters,

Spring in the Ghost Kingdom feels to me like the time most likely to beget miracles. Even now the rain falls lightly—it rains nearly all the time—but it isn't a dreary rain like we have in Sirenia, that rots our homes and floods sewage into the channels. Here, it makes the world bloom with colors so extravagant and fecund that it feels almost a forbidden pleasure to move among the flowering waterfalls. When spring happens here, I find it difficult to imagine that magic has abandoned this place, or that anything has been lost.

I think I can be happy here, my sisters, despite the always disorienting sorrow of my absence from you. Nicolai will adjust in time—I know he will. Community has a way of engaging us from so many directions, it's hard to lose ourselves too far in any personal drama. What sweet exhaustion last night, when we—and several other forest neighbors—finally finished repairing my new friend Linny's roof, and what sweet sustenance we shared, simple though it was, at her hearth in our shivering, soaking, laughing human bodies, together with people who help each other not for obligation, not for money, not for owing nor for trade, but because we all are all we have. These, our people!

The most beautiful thing about them, I think, is how grateful they are for everything. The Ghost People are dedicated to the solemnity of their ascetic lives and the rituals of gratitude that surround each task, and yet they are not without humor and fun—often clever and always surprising—and even mischief, in the form of tricks played by both young and old which, in Sirenia, would have seemed naive and childish, but here seem imbued with a special pleasure in the midst of this plain life. Some individuals have deep knowledge about particular herbs or creatures, and some are so quirky, so lacking in the usual social graces, that in Sirenia they might be called witches or even mad, but here they only make everyone smile. I've developed a companionable trust with Rhee's little granddaughter, Macha, who also worked with us on the roof yesterday—she'll happily work at anything, that child, and wherever I am working, it seems that's the job she wants, too. Her made-up surname for me, "Fox," has stuck—all the people call me by it. I can't explain how being with them makes me love being a human being in a way I never did before. I love the expectation of being a mother one day, of raising my children among them, of being part of this life on the simplest level.

One shining boy—a couple of years younger than me, I think—returned to the community last night from a "solo journey," to join our little group and partake in our stew of mushrooms and wild grains, his first meal in days. It is something men do here, often as a coming-of-age ritual but also at other times throughout life, based on the tradition of the unicorn. The lore tells that unicorns, who lived to be over a thousand years old, became more and more solitary in the later years of their lives, and so solitude is seen as the path to deepest wisdom. Thus the men go out on their own into the wilderness (I haven't heard of women doing this, for some reason, though I haven't heard a rule against it—there really are no rules here), sometimes for several days, sometimes for longer, and survive there with almost no food or water, until they feel they have reached some level of awareness and understanding. I know I'm being vague, but I don't know exactly what happens on these journeys. I only know that this boy, whom I'd met before, seemed more like a man when he came back. He moved without trying, without thinking of his own movements. His whole being seemed to radiate compassion and interest in others, yet at the same time he seemed more utterly at home in himself than before. Without any urgency for his food, he paused to give each of us a special greeting, resting his gaze like a world in each pair of eyes, as if he found God there. It seemed to me that he held Nicolai's hand a moment longer, as if sensitive to Nicolai's loneliness. A boy like him, I thought, could never exist in Sirenia. I think of your suitors, their cynical wit and scoffing boredom, their sophistication and self-conscious manners. I think of how they used to make fun of me for waking early and going early to sleep—always a natural rhythm for me. Here, in a place truly untamed, truly independent of every societal norm, all the people rise at dawn and meditate with the sun. It is light they seek, not darkness, and there is nothing they're trying to prove.

I watched this young man settle into the group again, saw Linny's younger sister gazing at him, and wondered if he had a sweetheart. I have taken a special interest in watching the couples, trying to understand what romantic love is made of here. Couples display such a beautiful ease with each other; the glances the young lovers give each other are sweetly modest, and the older lovers almost never need to glance at each other, so in tune are they with each other's every thought and intention. The brief and lawless marriage ceremony that Nicolai and I invented for ourselves, spontaneously upon our first human dawn together, seems after all completely appropriate for this place, where in fact there are no marriage ceremonies at all. In fact, there are not even marriages. Long-term commitment to relationship, like loyalty in friendship, is valued, but on a more practical level than the kind of romance we used to dream of. They almost never touch in public. There are no rules of modesty or decorum here in the wilderness, and yet something else contains and constrains these people: a subtle focus that pervades their every move.

You know how Father always told me I was more like Mother than any of us, that she had a kind of humility I would have admired. That is what I love most about these people and their religion—if one can call it that. Their humility is true humility, a humility that comes from gratitude and presence, not self-denial and holding back of secret greed. Have I mentioned how people bathe freely in the pond between the valley and the wood, together, whenever they wish, and are only sometimes concealed by fog or in some overgrown inlet? Nudity does not concern them at all, nor do they flaunt it. Even I am becoming easier with it. They have a way of bathing themselves with the simplest of motions, avoiding by unspoken agreement any direct gaze upon each other, and yet they move freely, with seemingly no embarrassment. It's because they don't think so much of their own bodies—their own persons—that they would bother feeling anxious about them.

You would laugh to see how relieved I am to finally live among people who don't value ambition so much (while I laugh to think of how little you would like it here, Addie—and you, Lara, would find it an interesting study for a day or two perhaps, and then be done!). The people like that it is easy for me to be solitary, to ask little of life—they have come to be that way through hardship and mistakes and loss, but they tell me I come to it naturally, and even Nicolai is proud of me, I know. He grins to himself when they give me their little praises, because he knows it makes me uncomfortable, and he will tease me about it later. Yet sometimes it does seem to me as if every kind gesture I make—even the smallest expression of compassion, a simple offer to sit by a sick child for half a day, a willingness to listen to another child's prattle for a single morning—is accepted with exaggerated smiles of eager good will, while all the help that Nicolai offers—whether helping a family to repair their home or helping an elderly couple to carry a load all the way home up a long, tiresome slope—is greeted with only the slightest nod of acknowledgment. Am I imagining this, because I know Nicolai does?

My sisters, they are so beautiful. I wonder if you would think them so! I want only to watch them—their faces, their motions. But it would embarrass them to even glimpse my admiration, so I keep my gaze to myself. The stark differences between the people they descend from have created such a variety in bone structure and expression. Lips can be sensual or thin, noses beaked or flaring, hips swinging or narrow. But all of their faces are strong in character, all of them move with an unknowingly regal grace. I asked Rhee once—I hoped he wouldn't be offended, but of course no one is ever offended here—why they are not the colors of the people they're descended from. I did not say, *You look like no human being I have ever seen, so eerily beautiful, I feel sometimes gross in your presence.* He only smiled enigmatically. "Our people have been through a transformation, Mina Fox," he said. "We hardly know ourselves as who we once were."

Nor does my Nicolai, whose body is big and rough, whose skin is richer than theirs, and his eyes darker.

I thought we'd walk home happy last night, in the bright, misted evening, for how useful we'd been, and how loved we were—and we carried in our arms five new fruit tree cuttings to plant, and all evening by the fire I'd watched him carving wooden creatures with two little boys who attended to his teachings with awe.

But he walked silent beside me all the way—my Nicolai who was once a prince, once a beast—and with such loneliness that I could feel it walking with us, a ghostly yet heavy companion. Does he yearn for his past, even as he hates himself for yearning? Who he was before, I will never know. When he told me his story on the morning of our marriage ceremony, a story that, to me, will always be remembered as part of that love ritual itself, he called himself selfish and ignorant—in the old days, before he was a wolf. He was raised in a land of gluttonous abundance I cannot imagine. His forefathers were the ones who had orchestrated the science of unicorn horns and the use of that power; they had helped to create the civilization that depended on it. He used to revel in his status and took a harem of mermaids when he was very young, refusing any human bride. He ordered the killing of the sea serpents, with the horns of unicorns. All the years of his youth, he told me, pass in his memory in a moment, without reality, without feeling. He cannot miss them.

And yet he released my hand as we entered the castle, and went to lay himself down without touching me. "I am no one, now, Mina," he said, in a dropping whisper that echoed behind him with his fading footsteps. "Look at me."

In his nightmares, he is the beast forever and can never break free. This morning he told me one in which I was present, for the first time, but I ran from him. And as he chased me, longing to tell me that he only wanted to talk to me, but of course could not speak, he was gradually consumed with a deeper terror, until at last he caught me at the top of the tower where he used to howl, and I was weeping, and he understood that he would devour me after all. He woke up crying out for real, and when I reached for him, for the first time he pulled away from me, shaking. And after he had told me the dream and let me calm him, and let me finally caress away his fears, and I teased him—in the hopes of lightening him—saying, "But I want you to devour me, my Nicolai! Come and devour me," and I opened myself to him, he turned away and stared up at the stone and would not touch me.

"What if I become the beast, again, Mina? The Dark Faerie never made any promises beyond the day you would wake me. What if I'm not good enough, at being human, and she turns me back again? How can I know? Sometimes I wake up in the night while you're still sleeping, and

I touch my body in a panic, fearing it has already happened. Sometimes I think you are the only thing holding me to my humanness."

I lay his own hand over his chest and pressed mine over top of his. I hushed him and told him to listen to the good heart that beat there—a heart I trust even more than my own. "Perhaps you will do a solo journey one day," I suggested, "like the young men do. Perhaps it will bring you peace, as it seems to bring them peace."

He let out a harsh breath that was almost a growl. "Haven't I already done the longest solo journey of all, Mina?" he said. "What more could I learn of loneliness in the wilderness?"

I do not think it is loneliness they learn there, but I didn't say so. There is something Nicolai knew, when he was a beast—something he is forgetting now. I want to remind him, but I have no words for it. About a moon ago, I asked him to take me again to that crystal cave, the one he took me to in those last days before he became a man. But he could not remember—or not at first. I pressed him, describing how we had climbed along a long, pine-shrouded ridge, come down slowly over the sea and then looped back inland, how we'd frightened a herd of mountain goats and he had looked at me then with longing, and I'd thought I understood him—how he was wishing to cease, forever, being a creature who frightened other creatures—and how he'd taken me down then by the most overgrown pathways into the inner soul of the forest, into the secret cavern of quartz, and because he'd bade me carry a candle in my hands, I'd lit it then, and he'd watched the fire also with longing. Finally he remembered, but not with the sudden, fond stroke of light upon his face that I'd hoped for—no, rather with a troubled expression, a vague nod, as if he'd rather not remember those days so well at all.

But he agreed to go back with me and try to find it again. We went back the way we thought we'd gone before. And we couldn't find it. We searched all day. It was as if we'd dreamed it all. I wept for the loss of it, but what hurt me the most was that he could not seem to understand my weeping.

Anyway, I must let go of such things, I know. Nicolai is undergoing an adjustment more painful than I can imagine, and he needs my light—only my light, and not my nostalgia or childish yearnings—to guide him clear of the past. And if there is anywhere I could ever learn to let go, it is here among the Ghost People.

I asked Macha once—for it is easier to ask the children such things—if the people hope for the unicorns' return still, or is it forgotten, or forbidden to speak of?

"They will come back," she said knowledgeably, and without fear, "but when they come back, we will die." I asked her why, and she said, "We must sacrifice ourselves for them, as they did for us."

I think of them sometimes—the unicorns. I wonder if anyone is alive here who remembers what they looked like, what they felt like, and if they gazed sideways into people's eyes the way horses do, or in some other way, like something more than animal. Sometimes when I think of them, the spring rains sound sadder after all, so that now there is heartbreak in the vivid watercolor all around me. I see how without the unicorns, this world is like a lavishly decorated palace, its tables piled high with rich feast, its beds draped in gold, its rooms adorned with the blessing of ritual music—all empty, with the prince and princess dead and gone. Or it is like a beautiful maiden, all fresh and brimming with youth and life, her heart open for love and her lips parted to taste it, all alone in an empty universe with no one to want her. Or like you, after we lost everything, and you were like expensive, exotic, hand-wrought wares in a forgotten shop that no one any more frequented.

midsummer

My Dear Sisters,

You remember how I told you of the sea—its greatness, the way it thrills and calms me all at once, just to look down upon it and breathe its breath. How can I explain it to you, who have never seen it? Even now, in the season of fog, when I can barely see it, it fills the air with its white, fresh presence. I think perhaps it's been changing me, little by little. Living near the edge of the world like this, and watching the nothingness beyond the world surge against it like a live thing, one is constantly aware of death, and of how life itself is merely a small island within it. Even the longing for you, for any news of you at all, becomes more bearable when I sit here and rest my mind in it.

I can no more describe to you, adequately, the form and effect of the meditations upon us than I can accurately describe the sea, yet it is the same. The Ghost People prefer to liken the mind's quieting (within the meditation) to the stillness of the pond, but I liken it also to the sea. Though the meditation is a practice of stillness and control, while the sea seems an expression of wildness and freedom, both the meditation and the sea have a similar effect—that of absorbing the dramas of life into the greater universe which is their proper place. Perhaps that's all God is, after all—only that which is bigger than ourselves, the sea which contains the earth, the stillness which contains the motion.

I think the meditation does Nicolai so much good. Those years as a beast—so many years, more than twice the length of my life—did humble him, and he does yearn now to submit himself to whatever makes him a better man. To sit with that intention, and even better, to sit with others of his people in the circle sanctioned by them, in the covered lodge where at least a few gather every morning, brings the breath deeper into his body—I can feel that—as if he finally feels deserving of it. I know it's still hard—the sympathetic attention they give him, that kind of gentleness you might use with a wounded animal, and I know he wishes they would treat him as they do me, as if I am already one of them. But though no one here knows how he actually lived as an animal (if he told them, it would mean nothing to them, except symbolically), when he struggles to speak to his fellow men some hint of the inexplicable devastation, loss, self-loathing, anxiety, and fury he feels sometimes inside, that rise up during the stillness, they always understand. As peaceful as they seem, they have come to this peace by days and days, years and years, and by similar losses. So then surely, he must not feel so alone.

We keep the practice together at home. I find it surprisingly easy to place my body in a posture of awake stillness and remain so until the sun passes the marking of an hour on one of our makeshift dials. The structure of the practice, like a firm marker at the beginning and end of each day, makes everything in between, no matter how chaotic, feel more manageable somehow. It helps with everything—with any little tensions we might feel over some miscommunication, or with anxiety about how deeply we owe our people and how much more we will need from them before the year is out, or with the constant hunger. Because it comes easily to me, I am able to help Nicolai in his struggles, so that he looks to me at the end of each sitting, telling me sometimes with excitement how connected he felt this time—with the subtlest things, the moss growing up the walls around us or the barely perceptible weight of fog upon our shoulders, and I know just what he means and how everything glitters and how the sudden song of a familiar bird just breaks your heart—and telling me at other times of what tortured him, like the envy he feels for the constant, humble kindness of all the people around him, how he wishes he could be that good.

autumn

Dear Sisters,

I'm not sure how I thought I would get this letter to you. I told myself that surely someone would journey to Sirenia one day—on some mission for certain supplies perhaps. It's not impossible. But that's me fooling myself, I guess. Excusing myself for the plain truth that I've not made a plan to visit you again myself. It's not for lack of missing you. It's not for fear of the hard journey. I just feel that Nicolai needs me, so badly, right now.

That little cave where Nicolai found and discarded his childhood toy, with the sea blowing and mixing below me, making a foamy lather on the rocks—I'm writing here now. It's called me more and more in this season, though there's so little time, anymore, to sit and dream. In autumn, as in spring, the veils seem to lift just a little. It is once more possible to imagine that all the magic hasn't been lost. It rains hard and desperately sometimes, but then also there are these evenings, and often days, too, of strange warmth. It's the only time in the year when one can feel really warm, and the sun feels really alive and intimate, like a god that remembers us. I was thinking about the sea just now, and the way the earth rises out of it so sudden and violent and strange—as if even the land is afraid of it. Have I said how no one here goes down to the sea? I suppose it's because of all the broken glass from the ruins, that they tell their children to stay away. And you know how no one travels from Sirenia to the Ghost Kingdom by sea, not only because the coasts are so steep that only a tiny boat could dock at one (and then where to go from there?), but because even in the civilized talk of Sirenia, the words "sea serpent" are still spoken in earnest, even today. But I thought Nicolai had told me they were all hunted to death, long ago, like the wolves?

I've never asked Nicolai about the mermaids. Before he was the beast, long ago, when he had every woman at his command, he chose instead the caresses of this other-worldly creature-woman of the sea. What must they have done to him, to lure him so? It frightens me to think of them. After all, I am so new to love. Before Nicolai, I knew not even the flirtatious games you were accustomed to playing with your lovers—and now I know a little more, but perhaps not much, after all.

I think it's their singing, in part, that draws me here. The mermaids, I mean. I can hear them.

Nicolai is sleeping now, and most days I would be, too. Some days we're so exhausted when we fall into bed, before the sun has even set, we forget even to hold each other before we fall asleep. And by the time the sun rises again, the problem of the day's nourishment immediately presents itself. I wish I could say that, after all this time, we have settled into this life with the ease and grace of the Ghost People, but we are usually hungry, and frustrated nearly every day by the question of how to create, grow, or obtain some basic necessity. Nicolai has lost the animal sensuality of his former fleshiness, and has waned lean and hard, though still broad. The people are always wary of the castle, and will not come inside even if invited, but they're often helping us in the garden, offering us the loan of tools or anything else. Not every day, but many days—it's a long walk to the castle, after all.

It is astonishing to think how much we have to learn. I am often at a loss to know how or where we should begin, and wonder how we can possibly understand all we need to survive in less than a lifetime. There were things I knew in our Sirenian peasant life, but I was still learning, and had so much left to learn by the time I left. We cannot buy anything at all here—not clothing, not tools, not a brush or a bar of soap. Everything must be made. And when you depend entirely on the land for your food, well, there is not only the growing and tending, of course, but the knowledge of so many intricate relationships, of seed-saving and weather and the characters of different soils and a kind of intuitive responsiveness to the constant shifting of elements that only many years of experience can provide. And the landscape is still new to me, the materials are different. And winter is coming, too soon, my sisters.

We, who called ourselves the sovereigns of a kingdom, feel sometimes like the objects of its charity, its needy, its poor. But of course, I know they don't think that way. I think there is no concept of debt. And—I don't know if you'll understand me, sisters—but isn't it always like this, in any kingdom? Isn't it always the case that people serve their sovereigns, without payment or reward—and without the people, the sovereigns could not survive? Only in most kingdoms, the sovereigns are not so aware of how much they depend on their people. They live in a bubble of luxury, like the Cygnini monarchy, and are hardly ever seen, and never known except at a distance. Here, our situation is more honest, though equally unbalanced. And here the people serve because they want to, not because they must; they serve because they are wiser than we, not because they are beneath us.

Anyway, life feels so different from how it was in the beginning, just the two of us—how often we used to make love, and how we were only for each other, back when Nicolai fed us by the skill of his bow. Now he would never touch that weapon, even if it were our only hope of survival (which of course it isn't, so that's a foolish way to think). We anchor ourselves steady by the meditations, and give ourselves wholly for the rest of the day to our survival and the needs of our community.

I suppose it's only my old tendency for dreaming that calls me out here this sunset to write to you, and to wonder. If only you could meet my Nicolai. If only you could hear the howl that's still inside him. How he haunts himself. I dream of it sometimes, and I dream of him appearing in the castle windows—in window after window, passing along the halls, while I stand alone outside, looking up, not knowing how to get in and comfort him. I dream he haunts his own castle, as if he's nothing but a ghost, appearing at each window—now a man, now a wolf, now a man again—and fading back from each one in despair, as if he hopes and longs to see me, and has been waiting forever that I might rescue him, and yet cannot see me, even though I stand there calling! I reach for him—I want to call out to him that he is not a ghost, but my beloved—but I have no voice.

Then during the day sometimes, while I'm scrubbing roots or laying walnuts out to dry or doing any old thing, I myself am haunted by some memory. The laughing eyes of a wolf—I swear, sometimes, they would laugh—from the bedroom doorway, as he swept the glass ornaments in a crash to the floor with his tail. A heaviness of heat against my back, as if an animal leaned there or breathed upon my neck—but it's only the sun, where I'm working on the rooftop. Once, when I was mending one of his shirts, I felt suddenly the touch of its fabric like his arms beneath mine—I remembered the shock of hunger, not for food but for each other's flesh, the taste of each other's sweat—the first time his paws became hands. And once—oh, we'd had some ridiculous argument, where I asked too much, like I always do (I wanted him to finish shoring up the crooked kitchen wall before winter, so we'd have one room at least that's warm, but also I wanted him to stop what he was doing sometimes and look at me, at least, like we are really together in love and not only working all day until we collapse), and he'd ended with *Why don't you make a list of your commands for me, then, Queen Mina Fox?* It angered me that he should use that name for me, the name the people call me by, in sarcasm—not because it hurt me but because I thought my husband was bigger than this. And I remembered lying down beneath him, it seemed so long ago, and giving myself up to the mouth of a beast, because I knew that he could change me into something I'd never imagined, and I wanted to be changed.

I meditated that day to calm myself, and it worked, mostly. Only it was wrong of me to meditate at the top of that tower—I thought I'd feel more peaceful there, high up with my favorite view of our land, that tumult of granite fields and deep cavern of distant flowers, but instead this memory kept nicking at my mind. How the beast had followed me one winter morning to the top of that single remaining tower. How the wind had beaten about the castle with such fury, from that height, that I'd clutched the stone frames of the window arches to steady myself against the sound. I remembered the scattered bones in the corners, and one that sat upon the window ledge, as if from a recent feast, attached to a chunk of hair. Before that, the tower was the one place in the castle I had never been. I had never gone there because I knew it was the place from which the beast howled. And perhaps also because I knew that to climb to this high endpoint of long, winding stairs was to come to a place from which there could be no escape, should he follow me. And yet that morning I had stood at the window of that tower and looked out at the wind, so clear and strong it was almost visible, and felt him coming. His footsteps were absolutely silent, and he took a long time. I knew that he was hunting me, and I did not know what he would do when he reached me. But there was a moment when I felt him arrive. I knew that he had rounded the last bend, and was standing there on the stair, his giant form filling the tunnel entirely, watching me. I felt as if the air behind me turned a different color. I felt it cleave to my body: my shoulders, my lower back, my buttocks, my calves. I could no longer see. I felt the blood of my life coursing through me, my head pulsing as if with terror, yet I was not afraid. I felt myself readying to turn around, because it was my only choice. And I did—and I remember. How it felt.

So these memories come, sometimes. Like when I stand at the top of the tower where he used to howl, and look out over the magical, sad, overflowing green world. I always go there alone. For Nicolai the man never comes there.

Anyway, I promise myself now, I won't add to this letter again, not until I am ready to complete it because I've found some sure and definite way of getting it to you. It's rambled on long enough, and I don't even know anymore if I've said what I mean to say. That I love you. What my new life is like, and how whatever it is, it is what I've chosen. It is what must be.

I suppose you will never hear a sound like this—the sound of the mermaids singing. It's a little like the howl of a wolf (though you've not heard that either), if a wolf could sing music and was far, far away. It's all folded in tight between the sheaths of the waves, so that at first I thought I was imagining it. It's pleasant, I think, but not the way birdsong is pleasant—it's hard to explain. Do you remember when we were children, and we met a man at the fair who was selling paintings from Zara, and I couldn't take my eyes off that painting of the Hummingbird lady dancing? They are such talented painters, the Wyes. The artist had been able to show, somehow, I don't know how, the way the spinning of her body and the wind around it had been going on forever and would never stop. You teased me all the way home, asking me if I had been trying to learn the dance by looking at it so hard, but that wasn't it—I was trying to imagine the music that could inspire an act of such terrible beauty. And now I think the song of the mermaids, though I can barely hear it—it sounds so far away, as far as the sea is wide—could be that music.

Anyway, I asked Nicolai if hearing this music could hurt me, because of the trickery he used to associate with these beings and the way they used to lure people (I think) into the sea—but he said no. They could hurt him, he said—and other men, perhaps—but never me, for I am innocent.

Lemara

dead language

First seed of a Woman, first child inside me, beginning of a being, where do you come from? Show me the way back.

Because someone from the Other World, where the dead go, has chosen to be born through me into this life again. That first time I made love to a Wye man, there was a reason for that, someone who wanted to come in. I speak to her, in my womb—she who comes from our Ancestors and still remembers, she who was sent by all the Priestesses before me, girl-child of my own body—*How do I get home?*

I know that the place Micah drove me in the carriage was not the South Forest. I cannot return back that way, even if I could remember or sense how we came here, because that was not the way. There is some other way back, some Dream-way, some way I am turning, and turning again in the Wind, in the Sea-mist, to find...

"Lemara. You cannot always live in this garden. You are my queen now."

Tiras is dead. He died while I slept. His long hair, so black it was blue, that I never got to fully unwind. Yet when I think of him, it is still only yesterday that I knew where in the Jungle to find him. I wear Wye clothing now, but I always find one thing, a strand of bristly seeds or a giant-fingered leaf, to bend round my hair or arms. I fill myself with the humming of Hummingbirds, from the inside out, and I almost feel him, Tiras, and my friends' laughter all over my skin, turning every little hair of my skin, my sisters and brothers, and they say *through the Dream, look through the Dream*, and I Dance up again through the honey-blue layers, and almost remember that Dream I Dreamed for a hundred years that knew everything, *everything*—

"Lemara. Come down from that tree and listen to me!"

I do not want him, this Wye prince, but I want. Oh, I want. And something binds me now. I cannot escape him. I have just come here to tune my body again, by the Hummingbirds' humming flight, but it gets stuck somewhere. I am thick with the food I eat here, I cannot hear my Ancestors so far away from the land that is made of them. I have come from the streets and rooms of Zara, from the good intentions of Wye women, from the suffocating details of their mechanical, busy lives. At Micah's instruction, they have shown me how to wash the clothes I don't believe in, how to cook food in a kitchen smelling of Animal flesh, how to sit and sit through half the journey of the Sun moving only the tips of my fingers weaving tiny designs for Wye children, how to walk with slack arms and cool eyes and motionless face on and on, turning ever away from the men—who are busy turning the Earth inside out, baring Her entrails, because they cannot trust the Earth to feed them as She has fed us forever, but must force Her on their own terms, hovering around their giant hordes of grain in fear of famine. I have come from all the chambers of work, I have sat in the touchless silence of women who do not understand me, cannot feel me, can hardly bear to look at me as I am, who fear me. And I have been directed by proud elders to observe the scratchings of students on paper, the pointed arguments they make between their minds, so that all things, every thought and every count, every rule and every alteration, every decision and every plan, can be recorded into history so that their people will live on forever in words— and yet everything that is captured dies. All these papers, scrolls upon scrolls, gathering like giant midden piles upon the Earth, leaving no room for breath. Don't they know?

"You are killing me," I say to Micah.

But he seems not to hear. "My mother died when I was young. I do not remember what it means to be queen, well enough to teach you. But there are women here who will teach you. The Prophets have said you will rule beside me as queen. You must be educated. You must learn, for example, to read and write."

"What do I care for your Prophets? I have never seen them. They do not speak to me."

"They are not meant to speak to you! That is not the role of Prophets. But you must learn. All Wyes are literate—women as well as men. You cannot be respected without this."

I'm scared, Tiras. Last night I Dreamed my friends and I were creeping through the Roses. Tika and AlaNAmana, smearing petals on their breasts, and Awhee, arching her lovely long neck, and Renny with her quick little fingers were crawling underneath the vines where the going was dark and easy, and Kar, too, with his delicate brows and hot-sand skin, grinning as he decorated his beautiful loins with berries, and Shulao with his arched nostrils and pudgy white-painted jowls, and Mescol with his low stubborn eyes, were swaggering and jiggling themselves, showing off for me the way they do, shattering the Roses as they went, in heavy, tinkling bursts of lavender. Esha glided beside me in her aching way, holding my hand, her thigh brushing mine. Tiras wasn't there. I wondered if maybe we would find him, when we arrived where we were going. They wanted to show me some secret, something that perhaps we weren't allowed to see. *Is it time?* I asked once, anxious, and Kar stroked my cheek and dipped his gaze into mine but did not answer. He kept close to me, as if to protect me. No thorns harmed us, yet once AlaNAmana pointed out the blood on some of the blossoms, and we knew it was the blood of the Wye-man who had been torn there. We were climbing the warm mound of the Temple of Women, and I was afraid. When Esha stopped, I stopped beside her. The others had disappeared ahead of us, and I could hear them laughing. But when I pressed through the petals, my face emerged into cold, thin breeze like the Air in Zara, and I was alone. All was silent, like the bottom of the Sea. I saw the bed I had lain in, for a hundred years. It was empty—I was gone.

Loneliness. We do not have it, in the South Forest.

"Even your people are learning to read now—we are teaching them," Micah is saying.

"We already know how to read. We read languages you have forgotten."

"They can still follow their traditions, Mara. But literacy gives them power—power to navigate the world of the Sirenians and the Wyes. It is necessary for them to learn the ways of the people in power, so that they are not overpowered *by* them. Don't you see? Literacy will allow you to think in a new way, to reflect on what you have said—and these abilities are part of what makes us human, part of what separates us from other creatures and makes us closer to God."

"I do not want separate! You are killing my people!" I crouch to roar down at him, he who will not listen, yet my voice sounds weaker to me now than it did. "I saw what you have done. Those people. They were not my people. That land. It was not a place."

"You blame me! You blame me, when I am the one who rescued you from thorns, who cares for you even in your ingratitude and your selfishness—"

"YOU HAVE MADE US HELPLESS. I have no world to return to!"

"It was not I, Lemara. Not we, the Wyes. So much—so much I have done for your people. I have dedicated so much of my life to helping your people survive what the Sirenians have done to them. You don't know what you say, Lemara—you are a child."

I stand up balanced upon the branch; I waver, I spread my arms; the new life in my belly holds me steady. "Where I come from, it is the children who know. It is the children we look to, for wisdom."

I try not to notice my dizziness, the places where the humming gets stuck. When he is gone, I will wash my face in the fountain, toss the Water up into the Air. *Tiras, Tiras, Tiralas.* I will run out the opposite door, the door that opens not into the palace but into the world. Because I smell the Rain. I smell Him coming.

the first death

In the beginning, the Ancestors tell us, the Hummingbird and Wye People were one. All were descended from the same Ancestress. Why did some People break away, and become another People apart from us, who could no longer understand the ancient languages? It happened during the time when the Sky abandoned us.

After the Hummingbirds bound the Earth and the Sky together by their threads of loving vibration, and each entered the other and They made love every Rain Season forever after, the Sky one day grew restless. The Earth was once everything to Him, but now She was broken by love, and He could not see Her wholeness so easily as before. He wanted to journey off into the beyond, to seek adventure beyond Time. So the Earth, because She loved Him, let Him go. He promised to return. But He did not.

In His absence, the Earth despaired and withered into dryness, She could no longer remember the touch of Rain. The Sun, only a pale memory of the love that once warmed Her, drifted off into white oblivion, and the Moon paled. All the world turned cold and barren.

These were times so bleak and desperate, Creatures for the first time since the awakening of the world began to Die. The first Creature to open the door of Death was Jaguar. *I will show you what to do,* she said, and she climbed down into the deepest nest of the mountains, curled up in the last moist soil, and died. At first no one understood what had happened. They called and called her to wake. Then her body gave off a new scent, and the Earth began to devour her. They saw that from this rich place where the Jaguar's body had turned to black Earth, new Trees and Vines were born.

Then all the Creatures and Plants understood that by dying, they would sacrifice themselves for the Earth. They would feed Her and give Her new life, and in this way She would be able to renew Herself forever, and feed them in turn. The Earth, in the voice of Jaguar, said *Take of my body as you have given me yours, take me in and be filled.* So the Creatures ate of the plants, and they ate each other, and this was a new kind of love-making, which kept the world alive. In this way we learned how to become Ancestors, to die and to pass into the deep realm, to pass then again into the bodies of Plants, then into the bodies of Animals and People, so that we would continually be reborn, and be always wiser from the journey.

At this time Rhiannon, the Faerie of Death who sometimes takes the form of Jaguar, was born. And all Creatures agreed to the sacrifice She demanded. Even the Birds, who spend their lives in the Air, still give themselves to the Earth in the end.

But not all of the people agreed. Some of the men left us. Perhaps there were women with them, too, or perhaps the women were born of them later—perhaps the Sirenian creation story in which woman is born of man, which we always laughed at in the Jungle, was true for them after all, by some twisted, inverted magic—but somehow when the Elders spoke of those who left us, they always spoke of men.

They left because they were bitter at the loss of their Father, the Sky, and they did not want to sacrifice themselves. They did not want to suffer with Sickness or feel the pain of the Jaguar's teeth or cramp with starvation and fall down into the Vines and turn to soil. They wanted to find a new world, better than this one, where such a surrender would not be necessary.

Where exactly they went, we do not know. Whether they climbed to the tops of the tallest Trees and tried to jump up into the Sky Realm, we do not know. Or whether they tried to walk upon the Sea away into the horizon, we do not know. But we know they refused to surrender. Because they could not bear to know that one day the Jaguar might devour them, or one year the Fruits might not ripen, and because they knew that predators must always eat and someone among them was always going to die, in order not to live in terror they decided they would take control of death. Each year, they would sacrifice one of their own, one that *they* chose—a man or a woman or a child—to Rhiannon. That way, they reasoned, She would eat her fill, and the rest would be safe.

But it is Rhiannon who decides who is taken, not men. Rhiannon was so angry at their arrogance, She wanted to destroy them, but the Earth, in Her compassion, swallowed them up instead.

Then these people became no longer like people. They lived inside the cave of the Earth's belly for hundreds of years, where no sound or scent or sight or touch ever reached them. They forgot how to feel. Their skin lost some of its pigment and faded to the color of dry leaves in drought. All that color and passion became lava that erupted far above them and made the Ho Volcano. For a long time after, the Earth continued to spew their lost richness and spread it over Herself, so that years later when they emerged, they would have to farm their sustenance by effort from Her flesh, to regain the strength and spirit that was once a part of them.

In that Dream of Darkness, they had only their memories and imaginations to guide them. And they were given one gift of magic to make up for all they had lost, though it was a terrible magic, not one that anyone would choose. It was the magic of the Written Word. It was a magic of describing things that could no longer be seen or felt or sensed in any way, a language that could only be read by the mind. They forgot all that came before. They forgot the Jungle, they forgot the Faerie realms, they forgot the name of Rhiannon, they forgot what they had been.

When the Earth finally tired of having them in her belly, she belched them up out of the Volcano, and they lived on in a new, dry world, taking their food from the soil by violence without feeling it. They were still ignorant, and they still made sacrifices to try to keep themselves safe from death, but now they sacrificed other Creatures instead of themselves, to keep death from touching them at all. Now instead of saying they were sacrificing to Rhiannon, or to the predators they feared—because they hated the Earth who had swallowed them—they said they were sacrificing to an angry, all-powerful Man-God. They worshipped that god. They thought they were making the sacrifices to appease him, so that they would live forever.

But they lived in sorrow: they lived the sorrow of the Earth's eternal yearning for the Sky who had left Her, and when they yearned for *God*, they yearned for Him—their Father who had abandoned them. They no longer spoke with their hands and their bodies, for these gestures could not be seen when they had lived in the darkness, and so they had forgotten how to read them. They spoke only by words, and they made their world by words.

The Wyes, of course, will tell of their origins differently. They will say that Writing was a gift given to them by their god, that they were chosen by him, that they are blessed. They will say that their people have been scattered by hardship and violence, living not only in Zara but in Sirenia, and across the Sea on island countries we have never seen, and that their

Word is all that ties them together, their book of sacred Words. They will speak of it with pride. But what People is still Human, whose identity is made not of place, not of green land and speaking leaves, not of singing Monkeys or flashing feathers or Owl Moon-stories, but of scratchings on paper?

They die anyway, like all people, and they forgot this: You cannot control the darkness of Rhiannon. But you must perform the sacred rites, for in the heart of the ritual, you are always safe. When the Birds are singing up the Sun in the morning, that is one time that Snakes and Jaguars never get them.

Rain

I taste His coming in the crackling of the orange skin where I lick it before biting it open. I see Him hastening the muscles in the broad fishermen's arms, who are folding up the Sea in their nets in the late afternoon, their backs a pretty bronze and their hair hot with salt—they are not supposed to see me, but I walk above them on the balconies, lift my arms and billow, let them look and love me as I eat my orange with the juice dripping down my neck.

I hear Him in the Wind the Sea lifts, the Wind that lifts my hair and my eyes over rooftop gardens, past all that is tame where I move wild, where the women stop their quiet work and watch my hips roll and the cloths I have made to shift around me opening and closing and the feathers fanning my smile. I hear Him whistling at the gates of the fields where women tend on one hill and men harvest on another; I hear Him in the bleating of the Sheep who have escaped their pens to wander the narrow roads between bumpy hillocks of moss and jump wooden railings—and the shouts of the boy-shepherds and girl-shepherds who run after them, intermingling by accident, for they can sense Him, too.

He will undo it all. They have cleared the Forests to make food they can control. They have chased away the wild things to raise Animals they control. They have locked reality into words to keep it under their control, but the Rain is coming, I can smell Him, and He will wash it all away.

I taste His wet scent overcoming the warm, treacherous, sinking scent of bread baking, the burning metal-work and even the crying blood-scent from the Butchers, the fetid overwhelm of waste from imprisoned Animals, the things I cannot bear. I imagine Him already, soaking the Gold and Silver coins that Wyes trade back and forth, back and forth, which (Micah says) keep everything equal in a city of many people, though I don't know what equal means (a thing with numbers)—greying them into mist. (I remember the Silver and the Gold that Rhiannon showed me beneath the Nuba Tree. They were not numbers. They were not even colors. They were times of day, Waking and Dreaming, male and female, the beginning and end of the world.)

He leads me to the fruits I know, to steal from the fields and orchards where no one will be, for where I come from, we do not eat meat and so must eat frequently, not like Wyes and Sirenians who stuff themselves like Snakes. He's in my tears when I cry now, for the strangeness of eating untouched and all alone. He leads me in a caress through a corridor beneath a bridge, where I know some Animals—maybe Foxes and Deer—pass through at night. I like to pass here, but today a young couple is kissing in the shadow of the bridge, under the Ivy, so passionate that they do not see me passing, and this brings me pain, but He feels my pain.

He is coming.

I smell Him. Dew-sweet and Swamp-sour, heavy as clay I smell Him. I smell the Sky taking bodily form, and in the Sky I smell my beloved, and I know He is going to Rain.

I forget Micah. Micah who cannot forgive me for not working dull all day long, my body decaying and my hands repeating, instead of Dancing beautiful doing the work of beauty, which is the work of a Priestess. For giving the gifts which are my joy—the only gifts that any of us have to give.

I kneel upon a wide path of bleached, wind-colored bricks, between statues of Wye ancestors (Micah's ancestors are made of stone), and no Trees, so alone without the great Trees I come from! A person should be small among Trees, through which our Ancestors rise up and speak. Where I come from, the world is all Trees, but here it is all people, with the Plants small and few—so I am like a child without family. But I kneel and look up, I look up at the Sky. I feel the people cringe from me, and I am alone. I am afraid. How afraid I have felt, these days and days with nothing hunting me, no forest, no Jaguar in the forest, no Trees above me, just humans all alone beneath the Sky and only the awful, lonely Wye-god leering lonely above us—oh, I want to be hunted again, I want to be soaked by my Rain-God beloved!

The wind caresses the orb of my breast, like Esha's hand that last day in the South Forest. Every day was potent, with waiting for the Rains. In our waiting, we were all walking loose, elemental in our longing. We slept wakefully, our bodies frothing, our wet places slurping over feverish skin, the skin whining and itching, our palms cavernous and calling, our tongues circling our lips. We woke hazily, pretending to bump accidentally, pausing in our restless wanderings to rest our faces in each other's hair, breathing and smelling, delirious. Oh, the rubbery, powdery scent of soft shoulders! The leaves tormented us; the sound of Water made us shudder; we wallowed in mud. The moon before the Sacred Marriage of the Priestess is the only time when everyone must restrain their lust for the purpose of magic. The life force of every single person in the community is necessary in order to call down the Rains.

When the time comes, we gather, not in the Temple of Women, where young girls and boys are initiated, but in the open Meadow, so that where the Earth first tastes the Rain, we taste Him with Her. I am Priestess; I lie upon the Earth, the oldest woman, the Great Ancestress of all beings, and surrender my life to Her. All around me the people Dance their longing up into the Sky, pleading for the Sky to remember His beloved, to caress Her once again, to feed Her giant thirst with his piercing touch. They Dance until their tension breaks them. They Dance until they fall upon the ground. When the Rains come, we are soft in our exhaustion, and the first drops are tender. I stand up, afraid, but my women surround me. They walk with me as I circle my people, and I breathe in their longing—their succulent pinkness and darkness. At last I take the hands of the one I have chosen, my Tiras. It is time. He smiles his deep smile, and I can feel the smiles of all the people around us. They say that at this time, the longing of all people is so great, the Rain makes steam when it touches us.

In the center of the circle, with my women around me, I unbind Tiras's hair, strand by strand. The touch of his own hair, each wisp floating down upon his shoulders, makes him tremble uncontrollably, and I kiss him softly where he trembles. His sigh goes on and on, and the people sigh with him, moving back and forth. As soon as we have begun to make love, they, too, will join us in their own love-making, even as the Rains explode upon us so thickly that we can no longer see—and their touch will encase us fully like another skin...

No seasons here in Zara, but Rains come when they come. Now. I open to silvered Sky, surrender to darkened Air, Rains simmering down—but can I catch them, when I am so divided? To imagine what "would have been" is not something our people have ever done. But I will live two lives now, forever. The one here; the one lost.

Drops of sudden Water slither down to me through the Air. Wye people are going into buildings, hiding from the Rain. I laugh! The Sky remembers me, recognizes me even in my loneliness!

I slacken my body and sling my hair.

But they do not come like Rains in the South Forest. They come slow and cold, as finely woven as the lace upon my tight, tight dresses. They hurt me like the prick of the spindle that sent me into sleep, a hundred years ago.

Yet even so, each drop wakes me, and wakes me again. Between and beneath these needles of ice, I am swarming—oh swarming, Tiras, with Fire.

I lift my face, and Rain enters my mouth, tasting like the molten, translucent colors of all the changing clouds.

When the Sirenian people first came to our land, boasting of their savior who was incarnation of the God, we were baffled by their obsession with this one man. Why remember only this certain man who embodied the God hundreds of years before? In our land, every Priestess is incarnation of the Goddess, and every man of the God.

words untouched by Rain

But I, Priestess of Hummingbirds, open my eyes and am all alone in a Stone world, white Stone rising before me, unmoved by Rain. I have never in my life seen anything unmoved, uncolored, unchanged by Rain. Unspeaking and solid. Yet it draws me in, this massive building raised upon columns and stacks of Stone, white in the thick darkness of Rain, and I pass beneath an arch, beneath levels of tall, rectangular windows, and all is made of white Stone and Air, like a skeleton. It smells of nothing, inside this covered entrance, for the Rain cannot touch it.

Yet the Rain has drawn me here. *Come,* the Sky has whispered, *for you have made love to this man, and here is where his Dreams are kept.*

Inside the Library in the heart of Zara, I hear my blood pounding in my ears, and the giant shadows swoop around me in a subterranean silence, the Rain muffled far away by walls of disembodied thought. Everything is written, in Zara. The law is written. The ways of people and the Earth are written. Only the special covenant written between the Wye people and the Wye god is not kept in the Library. This Book—the first Book, but they are making others now, with many pages of words tied together—is kept in the inner chamber of the sanctuary in the Temple Hall, inside the palace where the Wye rituals are made and the warriors train for war, the place where I first saw Micah kneeling.

I stand in the Library, passionate rivulets of Rain still joining and separating, separating and joining, all over my skin and in all the folds of this foolish clothing and beading in the hearts of the flowers I wear in my hair. Face dripping, Sky-tears on my eyelashes, I stand here, where all paths of Zara end.

Here is where the Dreams of Micah, and all the Wyes, are caged. I have let him come to me again, many times, for once desire woke in me, I couldn't stop it, and yet other times I have refused him, for I knew he couldn't fulfill it. When he touches me, he forgets what I taught him, he is hurried and nervous. A silence takes me, in his arms. I remember when I first rode proud upon him, gleaming for him and making my pleasure, he looked up at me with amazement. But now he likes to turn me over and lay me down.

And I am dizzy in this space that is big above me, roofed and yet somehow too large, ominously hanging. Cornered tunnels, in regular lines, the same thing again and again—a scroll, a scroll, a scroll, in piles, regular, the same. Whispers rising from them, voices of the dead, to be awoken only by the sorcery of reading—a magic I do not know. The man there in the corner, the guardian of this place—he walks toward me and I don't know how his neck can hold his head like that, all his life in front of his body, his shoulders deformed from forgetting, walking along bent over the paper, the paper in front of his eyes, not knowing where he is and not seeing me, listening only to the whispers, his body trailing along behind him like a forgotten thing. If he ever looks up, he will not recognize any face, any feeling! He will shrivel away into dust here, beneath the high, dry, hanging cavern, and never feel Rain!

But he does look up, now, and he sees me, Priestess of Hummingbirds dripping my colors on the floor.

"I want to speak to the Prophets," I tell him, breaking the silence of this world. "I want to speak to your god."

The man's eyes seize up with fright, he brings his fingers to his lips, he cannot touch me but he gestures me frantically to follow him back into the entryway.

"You cannot, Queen Lemara," he whispers. "This is not possible."

"Of course it is possible. I speak to my own God—Here are His words, here," I tell him, lifting the Raindrops upon my fingers, hovering them before his lips so that he draws back in horror, as if he's never seen Rain before.

"Queen Lemara," the man says again, trying the words out to steady himself—for always, they try to steady themselves by words—"I am sorry. This is the men's time. The women's time in the Library is later, in the evening—"

I laugh. "This is my time. The Rain called me here. See? I am here." I reach out to him, press the backs of my fingers with tenderness upon his chest. He caves inward, his mouth contracting, his tight hips twisting. I recognize the hard confusion in his eyes, the hot hang of his lips. He sees the beauty I give so easily, and it hurts him, because here people are not free to make love whenever they wish.

"I am sorry," I say, dropping my voice now to the whisper he asked of me, not out of obedience but from compassion. I must be gentler with Micah. I must be gentler—Goddess, I know—with all men. Where I come from, we do not let our men go hungry for lack of touch. We know that if men must fight for women, then they will fight, and if the life force is stopped from flowing, they will turn it to destruction. What a Priestess gives, she gives joyfully; she gives delighting in herself and the power of what she gives; her giving fulfills her, because of the gratitude she receives.

I step closer to the man, who trembles as Micah did, and I know the ways I would invite and then welcome him, and the way he would close his hard eyes and give in, and it makes me so happy to know this, there is a hotness in my ribs and jaw, a tickling all over in the places he longs to touch me! How I long for his longing! How I miss such longing.

But his eyes fix above and behind me, where suddenly Micah looms and grasps me with only fury, from behind. I jump in his grasp, scream—but he is dragging me by the arm from the building.

"Lemara," he growls. "You go out dressed like this, make a spectacle of yourself. Refuse education if you must, denigrate our ways and our language, but do you dare to defile our Library—"

"Defile?" I wrest myself free, and he looks down at his own hand, as if surprised to see that it still held me, that it still wanted my flesh in its grip. "I dress like a Priestess. I go where I will."

He shakes his head. "Like a whore," he mouths under his breath, but I hear him. I do not understand that word, but I've heard it, and I know it is an insult to life.

"You are only jealous," I say, crying, for I will never tell him now what I came here for. "Because I give what you cannot bear to receive."

"What are you talking about?" he says, his voice cold. The Raindrops trace his face, root themselves in the fur of his beard, catch between the strong, round, angry lips he uses only for speaking. "What do you give?"

"My beauty."

"Ah, that." He laughs a terrible laugh, one he does not mean. "No, Lemara, you do not anger me because I am jealous. You anger me because you never once behave like a queen."

"You regret it," I murmur. "You regret being married to me." I don't know why I say it. Only, we stand out here together, in the Rain, all the world making love, and yet we cannot touch each other, and it doesn't feel like I thought it would, like it always felt before. I thought I would feel Tiras again, when Rain touched me. I thought in the Rain he would find me. I thought I would understand, now, where I am, the way everything makes sense at the beginning of every Rainy season in the South Forest, when everything comes together—Sky and Earth, Rivers connecting, all things speaking to one another in the language of Water dripping, drumming, pooling and dropping level by level into the deep heart of all. But I have never heard Rain speak this language, the language it speaks upon dry Stone, with only the smallest of Trees to drink it. It speaks of loneliness. It travels, unfelt, down the face of a thinking man, and it speaks of sorrow. In Zara, Rain is the sound of sorrow.

I did not know.

"Sometimes," Micah admits, the anger gone from his voice, and he sounds as bewildered as I am. "Sometimes I do regret it. But God wills it."

The Rain ends, and I walk the long, white path without it, leaving Micah behind. When Water wants to go home, it goes down to the Sea. So I go on down that way again, having found no answer to my longing. Never before have I found so little energy to sing the Sun to His rest—not enough, I think, for Him to be comforted. I don't want to return to the palace. I want to sleep outside, with the Sheep or under the bridge, and let the wind caress me. But whenever I have done this before, Micah has been angry, and his anger frightens me. I know that Wye men fight, that they have weapons, that they are practiced in violence.

This Rain has left me cold, and I cry because the truth is I do not recognize it. I do not know the god of this place, and he does not love me. The Moon rises ripe and yellow over the Water. Between the strands of light, I can see the Dolphins rising and falling, and I remember how Micah showed them to me that first night, how he felt so open to me then. This year has passed without seasons, without purpose or meaning. I inspire no one; I lead no rituals; I give no gifts. My true consort is dead and gone. I don't have the energy now to feel rage, and yet I don't recognize myself without it. I think that at last, now, I will disappear, and perhaps that will be easier. I will go wherever my people have gone.

You are already home, says Mama Cat, pressing my legs, Purring. She leaps without sound upon the wall, and sits with me. I have learned a few comforts from Cat Dreams. The Cats are respected by Wyes, for many hundreds of years. The Wyes leave them be where they are sleeping. They share meat with them. The Cats keep the mice out of the grain, and keep track of imbalances—in bodies, in communities, in the network of sound and feeling. A Cat knows perfect balance. The Cats pity the Wye people a little, because they can only pray at special times in special ways, while Cats are praying with every move. Now Mama Cat, like a teaching, begins to lick her own body. I know she is showing me what "independence" means—something we do not know, as Hummingbird People, but something that is needed here. *You do not need another's touch,* she says. *Just lick your own body, and you will keep yourself real.*

But what kind of a world must I bring my child into?

return

In the middle of the night, while I sleep in my Wye room, she decides for herself and loosens.

I will become the Sea, Mama, she says, and collapses.

My heart in my womb, breaking. Pain grasps me from the darkest center of the world and squeezes me to pulp. *Take me, Faerie of Ocean.*

Eyes crossing, I tangle the vision of blood washing me to my knees— now stairs buckle me, and someone is yelling, a man's voice, the voice of a stranger, not Tiras.

No answer from the Faerie of Swamps, no answer from the Faerie of Deep Forests. Meadows are very, very far away. In blood she escapes down the stairs—escapes this life, just as I always knew that beneath and behind the complacent stone of this palace, I am in agony. Only so much loss can one person bear, even a Priestess.

Pain. *I let you go, I let you go, I love you—only please, please release me. Release me from this pain.*

For why be born to such a world? I cannot blame her. In this world, there are not enough Flowers, no women to raise you who know the songs, no Sunrise ceremony, no Dancing.

I suppose from somewhere, I hear this man called Micah moaning softly. I lean back against the withered stone and close my eyes, hot in a lake of blood. I was trying to get to my Hummingbird Garden, I understand now. As soon as the pain began, I tried to fly there. But I am only here, in between, in no safe place, in some empty hall, and there is no more life inside me. A Spider squats in the corner of the wall and watches me, patient and pitiless, Dreaming in the way I have forgotten. I look into her many eyes, and then close mine. They are the many eyes of my Elders, my Council of Elders in the Temple of Women. I am pleading to them with all my heart, all my blood, the blood of my child—pleading, please answer me this. If when people die they return to the Ancestors in the Earth, or into the Sky World, or into all the Plants and the Animals of the Jungle, what happens if the Earth and the Sky and the Plants and the

Animals—the Jungle, and all its beings—themselves die? What happens then? Where does the world go, when the world is gone?

girl

Among our people, the Moon-rising ceremony is performed each night by women. Crones at the new Moon, virgins at the waxing, mothers at the full. They do it in secret, their motions unknown to men, while the rest of the people bow their heads in keening sorrow over the disappearance of the Sun. At the night's finish, just before the dawn, it is the Elder-women, the women of Council, who call the Moon back down.

I am neither virgin nor crone. Nor lover nor mother.

But the Moon is the only witness to my grief, in this wave-lashed cove in my dress of seaweed and wind. I gift my unborn baby to the sand at the Sea's edge, where the Sea will take her back in her own time. Of course my body could not hold her. My body here in Zara is sick. It is made of different things. It is no longer the body of a Hummingbird, fed on nectar and beauty.

I have no drum (I was never good at making them, like AlaNAmana and Kar), so I use copper pots I stole from the kitchen. If they hear me, I do not care. Micah condemns me for my tears and wailing. In his religion, they hush themselves at Death. They say that if they make noise of lament and sorrow, the spirit will become lost, will not be able to let go of this world. So they tiptoe at Death, and speak in whispers, and murmur special words from the dead writing on the paper. Micah kneels on a hard floor, chanting with other men—always kneeling and bowing, these people—and talks all through the day and the night with his god, asking what we have done wrong to deserve the death of our child.

I do not speak to some god. I speak to my little girl. I lower my voice to a whisper, so that it will sneak beneath the roar of the Sea, and she will know I am speaking to her.

"I forgive you," I say. "It is a great choice, to come into this life as a woman. Sometimes it is too much."

The Wye people do not know how to grieve, but we Hummingbirds grieve every night, every time we lose the Sun. We are practiced in grief. Yet I have lost everyone, and have no one to help me mourn. When loss comes to me now, it comes harder. I do not know if I can survive it, Rhiannon.

Last night when I woke from my pain, Micah was there. His hand lay gentle on my side, though unfamiliar, as if he could not find where it fit.

He stroked my hair away from my face and looked into my eyes, trying to be kind.

"Lemara," he said to me. His beard was wet from the Rain, which began again in the night while I was sleeping, tightly curled against his face so I could see his wide, sculptured lips beneath his hooked nose more clearly. That hair on his face smelled like Animals, and it comforted me for just a moment. "I know we will make a child yet. You are young. Don't be afraid. We will try again, and I know we can."

I watched him for a long time, so long I thought he would look away, and when he didn't I asked finally, "Whose will it be?"

My voice surprised me, emerging so weak and faint that he couldn't hear me. He had to lean close and ask me to repeat what I had said. I breathed in the scent of his Animal beard, and my words came out on that breath, with tears in them that I didn't understand.

"What do you mean?" he asked me.

"Will she live in your way or in mine?"

I watched him think of his answer. I was so tired, it was easy for me simply to watch. I watched the sadness move in those eyes, like storm clouds joining and parting, never intending to Rain, only passing by. It was the only time I ever felt like I knew him, when I saw that sadness. The only time when I ever felt we were the same. But he did not speak it. He did not speak the longing behind such sadness. In the end, his eyes were only dark.

"If our child is a boy," he answered me, "then we shall train him in the ways of the Wye—our education, our holy laws, our path. He shall be the next king. But if our child is a girl, you shall train her in your own ways, the ways of the Hummingbird people. You are free to teach her as your people would teach her, and I will not force our education upon her, as long as neither she nor you disrupt my responsibilities as king."

And I wanted to be angry at his language, with its stony exactness and authoritative assumptions, but the idea of a daughter came into me so hot and desperate, I had no room for anger. I had not really thought, before, what it could mean to have a child. But now I imagined a daughter to welcome the Sun with me, to be my sole companion in the keeping of our ways—and my heart fired up so I could hardly speak. *Together,* I thought. *Together, we will find our way home.*

Then my husband, King Micah Wye, turned from me and left me, and he never sleeps beside me, but I sleep now with this promise. A son is the future. But a daughter cycles us home to the past, drawing up memory from the original spring of life.

For I am like other peoples now, broken off from the circle. Other peoples like the Wyes, who count time, must change and change again, and their cycles are long and not yet ended. They do not see where they have come from or where they are going, and it will be a long time before they come round again, and that time will be counted in years and centuries and eras.

Can we not change? I asked the Elders once, when they told me all this.

No, they said. *When the circle of the Hummingbird People is broken, reality itself is undone.*

Now I see that this has in fact happened. What could never happen has happened. Yet I am still alive. Yet I must have hope in this daughter to come. So I follow my bare feet up from the Sea now, returning to the palace of Wyes with my hungry womb, and the Moon walks close behind me.

Ella

"I have this nightmare all the time," Kiera told me on the open palace bridge above the Urodel, long past midnight, during one of our shared nights of insomnia. She was awake because the full moon always kept her so, and I was restless with early pregnancy. "Somewhere in the palace, right in the middle of things where you'd never expect it—I mean sometimes in the Great Hall during a crowded dinner, but it moves around, and it's never in the same place exactly—there's this black hole. Like a trap door into nothingness. Things are happening, people talking or dancing, and then suddenly I fall into that hole, and everything goes dark. The room disappears, the voices go silent, I'm all alone falling. I fall and fall, like I'll end up in the dungeon, or down deeper, in the river—where the dead lie. But I always wake up."

I didn't know what to say. What she told made me sad instead of frightened, as if it were familiar.

"Sometimes, I know it's going to happen. I get the most terrifying feeling. There are signs. Like my legs start to go all watery, or the light changes in a certain way, as if everyone becomes just a reflection of themselves, not flesh and blood anymore, and then I know. And I cry out in the dream—I cry out to my mother and father and brothers, it's going to happen, the hole is going to open! But this is the most terrifying part: they give me these cold looks, and they don't move. They never help me at all. It's so strange because in real life, of course, everyone is always spoiling me and loving me. But in the dream they just ignore me when I ask for help, and I'm all alone."

"Like they don't know what you're talking about?" I said.

"No, but the strangest part is, it's as if they do know. As if it's happened to them, too. And they don't want to talk about it because... I don't know, because there's nothing that can be done. It's just this thing no one talks about."

"Have you ever been down to the dungeon?" I asked her.

"No. But I don't think it's so terrible. My parents are not cruel. They don't torture people or imprison them longer than necessary. It's not like what you hear in the fairy tales."

"I know," I said, though I hadn't known. "And do you ever feel that way in real life, as if you're falling like that?"

She hesitated. We'd decided not to take the boat that night. I felt more cautious, now that I was pregnant, and hadn't wanted to. We lingered here in the in-between space, between the main palace and the courtyards, between the covered bridges to the east and west, where no one would look for us. We stood in the hidden pocket that escaped even the watchtowers' lines of sight. The stars were all ours, and the invisibly dark river kept quiet below us. "I don't know," she said.

"I thought, maybe," I said, "when you go inside like that, when you stay in your room and won't eat, and no one knows what's wrong..."

"Yes," she said. "I suppose so."

"Perhaps you're afraid of something?"

"I'm always afraid of something."

"Of what?"

"I don't know."

"Maybe the dream is only that. Some fear—maybe you're frightened of your marriage, and not knowing who it will be?"

Kiera shook her golden hair into her hands and stroked it, slowly, pressing it close to her lips. "It's just this nothingness," she said, "that swallows me up. But it's real. And it's something the others feel too. It's something in our family. Something no one talks about. It's almost as if, when you are royalty, when you have everything—such luxury, such *everything*—you can feel that nothingness on the other side of it. That emptiness. Oh, I can't explain it."

"Is that why Alden drinks?" I asked suddenly, because it came to me. We were friends, then, Kiera and I. That was a gentle time. I did not always have to think before I spoke.

"Yes," she said. "And why father drinks, and why he is so grumpy. And why mother never smiles. No matter how much luxury we have, nobody can have what they most long for."

"Like what? What do you long for?"

"Marriage for love. And the happiness of my family."

"Oh, Kiera. You don't know—maybe you can have those things."

She was silent.

"And the others? What do they long for?"

"My parents... I don't know. They don't even really believe in love, and yet they must long for it. And Alden... I think he longs for, I don't know, maybe faith."

"Faith?"

"I think the religion of the Savior doesn't satisfy him somehow. I think there are questions it doesn't answer for him. Sol scoffs at it too, sometimes, and so does Father, but for them it doesn't matter. They don't need that kind of faith to survive. But Alden does. I think it weighs on him, because he will have to rule one day, and the world is difficult and sad, and he knows it. Maybe he's afraid he can't fix it."

"Has he spoken to you about this?"

"Not exactly, but I see him thinking. I see him in the chapel, the way he thinks and thinks. I just know. I know the way I would feel, if I had to rule the world."

"You watch your family very carefully."

"Yes."

"What about Narsa?" I asked. "Why is she so mean?"

I thought Kiera would laugh, but she didn't. "She wants a son, an heir, of course."

"She has all kinds of ailments, Sol told me. I didn't realize. She gets sick a lot. Maybe that's what makes her mean."

Kiera sighed. "I know. I should be nicer to her. But sometimes, Ella... I honestly think she imagines most of them. She just likes to complain."

"And what about Sol?" I asked, feeling foolish because my voice caught in my throat and I realized I'd tried to keep the question casual, as if I were still a girl, breathless over a crush I hadn't yet claimed as my own. "What does he want, that he can't have?"

Kiera smiled at me. "Well, you would know better than me," she said. "Wouldn't you?"

And I know she meant it as a compliment.

♛   ♛   ♛   ♛   ♛

I remember I was happy, that day before I first caught Solon with another woman.

I was happy most days then, because I was six months pregnant with a possible heir to the kingdom, and Sol stayed home nearly all the time, adoring me and forgetting his adventures, and the family and all the highest attendants and even the rudest of servants honored me now as one of the family, and Narsa, still childless, envied me. Alden, to me always a paragon of kindness, never showed the slightest envy, but rather upgraded his compassionate smiles, when he passed me thoughtfully upon the balconies, to regular greetings which I somehow knew—though he never spoke of it directly—included respectful awe for the unborn life within me. Even the king, who previously had only noticed me with an occasional lewd grin, now sometimes patted my belly when he saw me, giggling to himself. I had learned how to joke with him, so that his looks no longer frightened me. I'd discovered that like the queen, what he wanted from me was simply confidence. Weakness made him suspicious. If I showed that I knew I was beautiful and tempting, if I teased him for those looks he gave me like a wayward boy, he would chuckle instead of leer, and then we would be like co-conspirators in a world of naughty boys and tempting women—a world I didn't exactly believe in, but at least could pretend my way into for the sake of his friendship.

I was happy every day, most of all, because of the little being that grew inside me, to whom I found myself speaking the way I'd once spoken to myself, long ago. Or I spoke to her the way I'd once spoken to my own mother's ghost, who had seemed just as imaginary and at once just as real to me as this invisible one within me. I tried not to notice that the way I spoke to her implied a wish—contrary to the wishes of my new family—that she would be a girl.

When it happened, I was in the Great Hall supervising the laying of the table, a small task which I had in the past year been deemed qualified to do. Kiera emerged suddenly from the stairway which spiraled up to each of our sitting rooms. She was smiling and blushing as if with gentle embarrassment at some girlish thing, and I remember thinking how lovely she looked and fantasizing suddenly that my daughter would take after her—remembering with a surge of joy that my child would be related to her after all, and would thus tie me even closer in kinship to this family.

But when Kiera saw me, the blood drained from her face, and the little smile passed away like a daydream crudely woken. Why should she be shocked at seeing me, her sister-in-law, simply standing in the Hall? It seemed to me that I did not know the answer to this question, and yet deep down below my thoughts, in my heart where I had always believed this new life to be nothing but a dream, I must have known. For I stared at her, and a knowing passed between us, a knowing she tried to withhold but could not, and then without thinking, without even pausing to ask, I went rushing past her even as she frantically shook her head, running up the stairs beyond her, beyond to those inviolate rooms in which we each kept our most private selves. I ran right to Sol's closed sitting room door, and I pressed my ear to it—I pressed my face to it, without even knowing myself, without thought, without hope—and heard what Kiera had just heard. I heard the cries she had listened to with her shy smiling, thinking, until she saw me, that they were mine.

What first struck me was how beautiful they were. This woman cried out her ecstasy in tones of velvet rapture I would never dare give voice to, even if I ever felt it. Her cries pulsed in their horribly vivid rhythm, each one curling upwards at the end like a *yes,* like an invitation, elegantly wordless, confidently quickening in tension, each breath sucking greedily inward and then gasping outward with a broken abandon that I never wanted to remember and would remember for the rest of my life because of the way it moved me against my will, so that my own heart disgusted me.

Even she can break. Even she, in her perfect grace, becomes helpless before my husband's glory. I was forced, now, forever, to know this.

A page was guarding the door, awkwardly horrified to see me. I seemed to be sleepwalking. I opened the door and saw Leyla's mystery-black hair overflowing onto the jaguar-skin rug, still unwinding from the clips that had held it, as it shook apart with each thrust of Solon's body, where he knelt behind her raised buttocks in a position he and I had never before taken together—a position I had never heard of, never thought of.

"Ella," choked Solon, and his voice as it spoke my name echoed in my mind for hours afterward, causing equal parts tenderness and agony for the sorrow I heard within it. He really was sorry, from the moment he saw me and probably, in some way, ever after. *But not before he saw me,* I would think later. Not before.

They scrambled up somehow and came apart, Leyla sitting up in front of him. She had the good grace not to pull her dress around herself defensively—a pathetic reflex I'd see in future lovers which always infuriated me—as if she knew that what she'd done could not be undone, disguised, or denied. Nor was she proud or defiant in her stance. No, she was just perfect, like she always was. Her mouth fell open in a perfect, neat little expression of surprise, and her breasts, falling out of the dress which he'd obviously torn from her body, were perfect: golden-brown with wide nipples flashing buoyantly upward. I never did know where her family came from, so smooth and feline, but today I believe she was partly descended from the Hums.

I could not seem to move at first. I kept staring at her beautiful breasts, like a dumbfounded child. She bowed her head when Sol stood up in all his stunning nakedness (had she asked him to undress? How had he come to be naked, when she was still half-clothed? Was there some secret fantasy in this arrangement?), and said my name again. We were both of us stupid with shock, I suppose. Even the page behind us was frozen in place. Only Leyla did not lose her grace, not once, not ever. All my life I would wish for such grace, and I would never have it.

It was his standing up that moved me. I ran again, back to my own room. I locked my door, remembering bitterly how he had not bothered to lock his. I sat in the window of my sometimes comforting, sometimes claustrophobic sitting room, and waited to weep. But I could not. I could not even tell what I felt. I watched the geese feeding in the field below, and I did not know that I was gasping for breath until I heard Sol pounding on the door.

"Ella, you must let me in," he said. I was surprised. *Someone will hear you,* I thought. He never spoke Leyla's name. "I love you," he said. "It is only you, Ella. You must understand that."

I looked at the door. I did not mean to be coy. I only could not think to move or speak. What could I say? I closed my eyes as if that would help me to shut out the sound of his voice, but all I could see in my mind's eye was the slow grace of Leyla's rising, her dress falling, the wide roses of her nipples, her impassive face.

"Ella, you must let me in. I will not leave until you do. Ella."

I don't know for how long I sat there. I kept thinking, *Where will I go now?* I kept thinking, *Of course. Of course. Finally.*

A deep cold set into my body. I'd felt it before, when I was very young. I'd heard my new stepmother outside my door—*I will not have her sleeping so near to my daughters. It is enough already that you have taken her in. There is an evil in her that can never be shaken out, and I won't let it taint them.* My father had asked, *Where will she sleep, then?* I had curled up very tight on my new bed in the dark, hoping she would go away, hoping that if I were very quiet, very still, very small, she would forget me. Perhaps I'd had some understanding—before she came in to snatch me away—that my father and I shared the same blood, that he might rescue me from orphanhood. But after that, I knew that no one was strong enough to protect me from that which hated me. I knew that no one was on my side.

Sometime in the night, I woke up in a princess's sitting room in the Cygnini palace, curled up by the window, with moonlight cast clumsily over my feet like a blanket thrown there haphazardly, without human care. I did not know at first where I was. I thought at first that I woke in ashes, as in the days of old. I felt hungry like I'd felt in those days of survival, when I knew I'd have to brave my sisters' taunts, pick through the ashes if I had to, do anything to get something in my belly. Then I opened my eyes wide and saw that I did not lie in ashes, that I was a princess still, and it was only the pregnancy which made me hunger so.

I had been so forlorn, I had forgotten to pray. So I prayed now. Though sometimes women are encouraged to call on the Savior's Bride for assistance, I did not call on Her now, for I felt ashamed before Her. Surely, in Her chastity, She would never have faced such a dilemma as this. How could She have compassion for my jealousy and self-pity? Instead I prayed the Savior's prayer, the one we pray when all else has failed us.

If it were not for the child within me, I would not have needed to eat, for my own need seemed nothing to me. But now I must calculate my daughter's survival. Instinctually wishing to remain hidden, I thought at first that I would ask Leyla to go and bring me some leftover supper. But then I remembered. I could never ask Leyla anything again. She was not my friend.

I went to the door, feeling almost strong. Survival and invisibility were two tricks I knew and had always known. I would be able to secure supper for myself without anyone seeing me or speaking to me, even here in the palace. But when I opened the door and saw Sol leap up from where he'd reclined on the floor, waiting, all my strength drained away. It was the look on his face that woke me from my childhood trance, a look of gruesome heartbreak, of which I had never before seen the like. He said my name. He had brought my supper in a little basket, though it was cold now.

♛   ♛   ♛   ♛   ♛

That first time, our hearts melted easily, with no violence needed to crack them apart. We believed in the best of each other; we wanted only to reclaim what we had momentarily lost, and would do anything—suppress anything, forget anything—to return to each other, as if we had seen God Himself beaten, and must rescue Him and soothe Him with kisses.

Sol carried me to my bed and covered me there, lay down behind me and curled around me. He had never held me this way before, without lust, without teasing, without sleepiness or passion, but with only a focused concern, like a child stupefied by loss, holding together pieces of a precious thing he has accidentally broken.

"I am sorry, Ella," he said. "You haven't been coming to the tournaments. I was afraid. I thought you didn't love me so much, anymore. I know it must be the pregnancy. But I'm foolish and weak, Ella, and I am afraid of what it will mean. I don't know if I will be a good father. Ella, whatever just happened, you mustn't ever think of it again. You are the center of my life. You are my ground, my... My everything. I love you terribly."

"Ella?" he said. "Please, my darling, say something."

I took a deep breath and made the effort. "Not enough," I murmured.

"What?"

"Not enough. But I am not enough. You don't love me enough to... to..." And I shook, so he held me tighter, and seemed also to sob, though I don't know, I couldn't see him.

"No, no," he said, whispering now. "It is that I am not enough, Ella. I am not enough for myself. That is why."

"Sol," I said.

"Yes. Yes, Ella."

"You don't understand, I..."

"What? What is it?"

"You don't understand—"

"I do, Ella. I do understand."

"I will do anything to keep this love, Sol. Anything."

"I know."

"Even if you hurt me. I will still love you. I cannot stop."

"I know, Ella. I know. And I won't. Ella, I'm sorry."

So we knew each other, then, or thought we did. We made up in a way that opened us, so that we fell deeper into each other, full of compassion for each others' secret pain, until, uplifted by wonder and shivering with hope, we rose up from the bed and ate our food and even laughed again, cautiously, wonderingly. Forever and forever, I will miss that first making up. It would never come again. Never again in my life could I afford such sweet helplessness. The pain would come again, but next time I might yell and plead, and he might turn cold, escape to the company of his wild horse Aurora, whom no one else could touch and who never judged him. Next time we would close instead of open. But that first time we went running with breathless gratitude back to the safe haven of each others' hearts. I will remember forever the way his body tensed in listening when I spoke, the way his whole being listened, expecting my perfection, the way I searched for his goodness, believing in it still, the way I took for granted that despite all my pain, I could still thrive within those arms, in a state of perpetual surrender.

I didn't know, then, what I was losing. I was so relieved, God, just to be able to keep him. But oh my people, do you remember that first breaking, that first forgiveness? Even more than the first love-making, I miss it to this day.

♛   ♛   ♛   ♛   ♛

What hurt me most, then, was realizing the next morning that Leyla had left the palace—left the kingdom, left the world, for all anyone knew—without saying goodbye to me. I was busy wondering if Sol had said anything to her before she left, if he cared about her, if he had tried to protect her in any way, when Narsa came directly to my room (so strong was her thrill in summoning me for a reprimand) to tell me that the queen wished to speak with me. *At once.*

Even as I stood before my judgment, my head bowed, not yet knowing why I stood there or why I was judged, and yet having felt accustomed to such bewilderment since early childhood, I caught myself thinking, *Whatever happens, I shall tell Leyla later—and she will comfort me, as she always does, with her perfect tact and grace.*

But no. Not today.

"It has come to my attention," said the queen without prelude, without saying my name, and even in my habitual fear of her, I started at the subtle fury in her voice, "that your closest lady in waiting has sinned against you. Is this true?"

I hesitated, baffled into torment, forgetting that with the queen and the queen only, the best answer was always the simplest.

"*Is this true?*"

"Yes, Madam."

"It has furthermore come to my attention that you did absolutely nothing to punish this sin, and that the lady in question has escaped from our palace and is not to be found. Is this true?"

"I—I don't know. Yes."

"You do not like to place yourself above others. You feel uncomfortable in regal attire. You even cringe beneath the decoration my son has given you to wear in your fair hair today, a gift from the man you claim to have married for love."

I could not help it—I glanced up at her, shaking my head in speechless denial. She could not have chosen a more terrifying way to address me than to lay out my deepest hypocrisy in this even tone—not that I didn't love him, but that I lacked faith.

"You must remember that these things are not for you. You wear them to act a part, to inspire the people with an image of royalty that gives them confidence. Your beauty is your gift to them, not a gift given to feed your pride. It is your duty to wear it, and wear it with grace. Whether or not you hold any respect for the dignity of your own person, I will not allow you to defile the dignity of this household. Do you understand me, Princess?"

I nodded, clenching my whole body. I felt a swoop of satin like the wings of a pouncing raptor, and she had risen and stood before me, no taller than I and yet towering over me.

"*I said, Do you understand me, Princess Ella?*"

I tried to speak—I tried. My eyes held hers tight.

"What is it?" she demanded. "Is it weakness? Is it a little fairy tale to you, to recline on golden cushions, to be served, to tiptoe about in a grown woman's dresses?"

I shook my head, even as the tears began to web my eyelashes together.

"Why, then? Answer me. I will turn you out of this house if I ever again see you behave so weakly."

Did she mean it? I will never know. Why did this mistake, which seemed to hurt me more than anyone else, anger her more than any other I had ever made? I did not know, at that time, and yet I answered. For she knew me then, as she always did. She knew how to force me to be stronger.

"Because I am myself," I said, breathless. "Because I do not punish the way you punish, and I never will. It is not in me to be angry like that."

She threw her shoulders back, looked at me. For one instant, I almost felt that we were equals. It was crazy even to imagine such a thing, and yet I felt it. I had spoken back to her, and I had not died.

"No?" she tested. "What is in you, then? Only love, I suppose?"

I did not answer, but my silence did not seem to anger her this time.

"Ella. You will never be great if you cannot punish even those closest to you for the sake of what is right."

"But I cannot act confidently, being what I am not, Madam."

I looked directly into her eyes, and saw the shifting landscapes there beneath the stone: ever-fading, wordless stories of a lifetime, a woman, a girlhood—stories I would never know. She lifted one hand and, without anger but with terrifying suddenness, ripped from my hair the ivory clip that Loren had given me, so that my hair came tumbling down in a thicket about my face and neck, and then she dropped the clip on the floor. It was one of the most precious objects in the world to me, but I dared not pick it up, and I never saw it again.

"If you do not wish to be what you are not, Princess Ella," she said at last, "then you had better know what you are. You have many tests ahead of you still, and neither of us knows what they will be."

♛   ♛   ♛   ♛   ♛

Anna, named after Sol's mother the queen, was born simply and swiftly, contrary to all expectations for a first birth. She had Solon's smile and hair like the wings of dandelion seeds. I gazed upon her joyful smile and blissful flesh with wonder, that she could bridge the gap between my past and my future, my world and Solon's, with such blithe acceptance. I thought it would be easy, for her sake, to be the mother I wanted to be—the mother I never got to have. And sometimes I woke with her in the afternoon, damp and warm in my arms, and she felt again like my secret, and I watched recognition flit over her brow and was afraid. I had wished for a girl, known she would be a girl—and had I created her by wanting her so much, just as I had magicked Sol into my arms two years ago by some force within myself that I still didn't know, but that my stepmother had seen in me when I was only a child? Then Anna would reach up and clutch my hair, and I would laugh. It was much easier to banish the nightmares, after Anna was born. Kiera, my closest friend after Leyla's loss, said that Anna banished hers, too. "It won't be so hard to be married," she used to murmur, playing with Anna's curious hands, "if I can have one of these."

When Sol sat down beside my bed to hold Anna in his arms for the first time, he moved his body slowly and carefully; he moved in a way I'd never seen him move before. In his smile I saw the apology and forgiveness of our first torment and making up together, three months before, and that memory to me seemed now to have nothing to do with Leyla or betrayal; it was only sweetness.

"I have been thinking, Ella," he whispered to me that day, "that it's time to hold a feast in honor of the tracker Rufus James."

"Rufus James? The Barbarian?"

"Yes, for finding you. I never thanked him properly. What would I have done, if I'd not found you? How would I live without you, Ella?"

My second child was born out of bitterness and heartbreak, for Sol cheated on me during that labor, though I never knew with whom, and so my boy grew up stormy and tormented inside. But I always thought of

Anna being born out of sweetness, that early-love innocence that could not last. Other couples love with innocence at first, I am sure, but not with the grandeur of ours. People loved Anna with a love so intense it baffled them. At two years old, she demonstrated more compassion for lost caterpillars and forlorn faces than our king demonstrated for his people. Just as Sol's and my first love was more than our human hearts could bear, so was Anna's sweetness more than this life could contain—and just as ephemeral, just as hopeless.

Yet when I married Sol, I married a family. I gained an elder I could respect, a mother figure who, though no warmer than my last one, finally cared for me, and in her fearsome power brought me confidence instead of misery. I came to love a father-in-law I had not known before, a man tired to the bone with ruling and with himself, a man I never fully understood but whose cheek I learned to kiss goodnight, who patted my hand when I gazed at him across the table, wondering what agitated his mind. And it was my new brother, Alden, who would comfort me after my son's difficult, lonely birth, when I refused to see or speak to my husband for seven days.

"Ah, it is good that I have found you," he said, giving his usual little nod as he swept toward me. I was sitting on a bench at the edge of a garden, trying to soothe Jonah, who sometimes cried ceaselessly and could only be soothed by fresh air. If it weren't for him, I wouldn't have felt the inspiration to ever leave my room. Not now. Not now that I understood what Sol could do to me and how helpless I was to stop it.

Alden smiled down upon Jonah. Narsa had by this time finally given birth to a son, too, so I no longer felt guilty holding mine before him. "He has Solon's mouth, like Anna," he observed, "but your eyes... And his hair—so dark!"

"They say my mother's hair was dark," I ventured, for I felt instinctively safe with Alden.

"Ah."

He gazed at me then, for longer than was normal, and though there was a teasing drunkenness in his smile, I felt his eyes were serious, and this intensity frightened me, though he himself did not frighten me.

"Ella," he said finally. "You are angry with my brother."

"Yes," I said, embarrassed that he should know, and know why.

"You must forgive him."

"And why?" I asked, startled.

"Because he is a child, Ella. Do you not know?"

I looked at him and felt an unutterable sadness. It fell through the anger and broke it all apart, and then I did not have the strength of the anger anymore, but only the sadness heaving in my bones like wet sand. For I did know.

"He is more a child than anyone else," said Alden, "more even than Kiera. To do what he did, you see... Well it is not uncommon, you must understand, especially in this family, but that is not the point... The point is that he did it because he was afraid of losing you."

"Afraid... ?"

"Yes, of course, because it was a hard birth, and you might have died. And it was terrible for him."

"That doesn't make any sense. If he cared for me, then why..." I teared up. I remembered begging the nurse to bring him to me, agony overcoming any fear for propriety, and I remembered what I knew—and the desolation of that knowing—when she returned, head bowed, without him.

"Because that is how he handles such emotions," Alden said. "You must see that, Ella. Surely you see that?"

I looked down at Jonah, mechanically smoothing his dark hair away from his brow, and he watched my tears emerge—watched my eyes like interesting animals, like curious, somewhat concerning apparitions in my face. He tracked them with his own.

"Poor Ella," said Alden softly, still gazing upon me like God, though I did not look at him. "I do not envy you, marrying for love. It is so much heartbreak, isn't it?"

I had thought I was the lucky one. I'd thought I was too lucky, more lucky than I deserved.

"Thank you, Alden," I said stiffly, unable to look at him.

"You will forgive him then? Please, Ella, forgive my little brother. Do it for me, at least, because I love him dearly, and you are the best thing that ever happened to him, and he knows that. He cannot stand without you."

Jonah clutched at my breast as he fell asleep, and I knew that he was Sol's son, and that the ties of family that bound me finally to this life, rescued my spirit from its past, nourished my confidence and sustained me, were all that mattered to me now. I nodded.

"Yes?" said Alden, leaning toward me with touching eagerness. "You will?"

"Of course," I murmured. "What else can I do?"

It was family that mattered. They became my own. They were a web woven and ever-weaving that repaired each one of the wounds Sol and I made in our childish love story—repaired them effortlessly, the way the body grows new flesh when a part of it is cut, because it must, because it knows in every cell what it is and what it is made for. In the web of our family, we were more than ourselves. When we fell down, they caught us. When we jabbed at each other, they cushioned us. When we yelled, our yells were lost in their history, their greater purpose.

To this day, I miss them no less than I did when I first lost them. For without them, Sol and I became orphans in a foreign world, not knowing what we were meant for, not even knowing what to say to one another. And after that, for a long time, we could trust nothing, least of all our own love.

Mina

spring, second year in the Ghost Kingdom

Mina, you little fool. You were only writing for yourself after all, weren't you? As if they could really understand. No, it's as if I'd forgotten who my sisters were. As if I were writing to different people entirely, who weren't real.

I never even gave them the letter. They were here with me, here in this broken room once clawed by a beast, and I never gave it to them—they're gone now. But I have my diaries. I've always kept them. Last night I dreamed Nicolai and I were both beasts, wandering lost in our castle, and I was looking for my sisters, because they were here with us but couldn't see us. I grew more and more afraid, while Nicolai just sat there on his haunches watching me, waiting for me to realize that we were unrecognizable to humans now, and there wasn't any point in trying.

It was my friend Linny and her mother who told me of their arrival, when we happened to bathe in the pond together one morning. "You have visitors," Linny said, grinning at me, anticipating my happiness. "They are looking for you. More foxes."

I had never seen Lara dirty before, or her hair half-undone. Addie was worse, and looked close to tears, though she leaned on the arm of a tall, capable-looking young man who gazed around unconcerned but a little bewildered—it was a rare moment of vulnerability for him, I found out, which would not be repeated. When I saw them, I forgot all about meditations and the slow, present way I'd learned to live this life—I screeched at them like a startled hen and went running into their arms, hysterical with joy. My sisters and I were never much for embraces, especially Lara, but they clutched me so tightly, as one, that when they let go and I could breathe again, I was crying. It was the most intimate moment I shared with them during the entire time they were here. I still miss it, with pain.

"We came to rescue you," murmured Addie, looking up at the castle with doubt rippling her sweet countenance, and then added in a breathless whisper, "The woman we met—she looked so strange! Are they even human, here?"

I laughed, kissing her face, and she drew back. I think I was bolder than she remembered me. "There's no need to rescue me," I said. "Come with me, and I'll tell you everything on the way home." I tried not to notice the way Lara narrowed her eyes at the word "home." And I did try to explain—only explaining was harder than I'd expected, harder even than convincing them to climb yet another hill, or convincing Addie's husband that I was strong enough these days to easily share the burdens he carried for them. What I mean is, it took only a few words for me to say what was necessary, but it was difficult—no, to be honest, impossible—to draw from them the reaction of wonder and support I had longed for all this time. They were exhausted, I told myself—they were lucky to have survived the journey, but still I told them what I could, because they kept asking, all the way home.

"Haven't you thought, Mina," Lara whispered as we stood in the shadow of the castle entrance, stern and doubtful, her eyes lowering, "that maybe it's a trick?"

"Maybe what's a trick?"

She sighed and shared a glance with Addie that made me feel ten years old again. "That maybe the *real* Nicolai *is* a beast, and the form of the *man* is just a spell," she said slowly.

I shook my head, bewildered. "They're both real," I said. "I know him—as well as I know you. Look, just come in, and you'll see." And when they hesitated, I hugged them both again, each one in turn. "Oh, I never knew you would do this for me," I sighed, overcome with sudden gratitude. "You came all this way, through such trials, to reach me."

"Of course," said Lara. "What do you think? That we would just leave you here? Father could never survive it."

Before I could reply, Nicolai was standing in the doorway. He didn't smile or say hello, and he left his big hands hanging loosely at his sides while he studied my sisters. I had never seen him before, the way I saw now that they would see him. Addie's new husband thrust out his hand at last, as if proving his courage.

"Amos Bardo," he said.

Nicolai hesitated a moment too long, then slowly cupped his hand around the one that was offered, and squeezed it, and let it go. "Nicolai

Wolf," he grumbled, and I heard—and I know they heard—the breath of thunder in the cavern of his voice. I had almost forgotten it was there.

"Nicolai, these are my sisters!" I cried with childish happiness, and he looked at me, as if he didn't understand, and then he looked at them and smiled, finally, for my sake, but I saw him retreat behind his eyes, and he didn't come out again until days later when they were gone.

"Oh. Good," he mumbled, and beckoned them in. They came. We all sat awkwardly in the room we use for a kitchen, the glassless windows open to the cold breeze, with the cloths that covered them pulled back. My sisters were strangely quiet, so Amos began heartily telling the story of their adventure, the days they spent fearing for their survival upon Sleeping Lake. Addie was quite dreamy in her admiration for her sailor-husband, who had seen them through it all using my father's castle maps as well as a special compass he invented and perfected himself, who had cheered them with pragmatic confidence each time their boat got stuck in the swampy shallows, and who had never complained—I couldn't blame her. I worried that something might have happened to Lara's husband, but he was mentioned in due time, along with her young son. Though I was bitterly disappointed not to be able to meet my nephew, I understood that a baby cannot be brought on such a journey, yet it seemed strange to me that Lara should abandon her new family to come so very far, even to visit her long-lost sister. I always admired her independent spirit, yet I worried about the poor stonemason who so clearly doted on her. I was full of questions for them, but once they found their voices, they kept interrupting me with questions for Nicolai—*Do the two of you live alone here? Is the castle yours? Who built it? Are those all unicorn horns?*—questions I could have answered just as easily, to save Nicolai from awkwardness; questions I could tell weren't their real questions, and Nicolai could tell, too. Finally Lara slunk a little forward, slipped Nicolai her most bewitching smile, and asked him just how, exactly, he had won the heart of "our Mina."

"Lara," I remonstrated, "how can he possibly answer such a question?" And Nicolai stood up, grumbled about gathering more roots for the stew, and went out.

Our home, of course, didn't seem like one to them. Addie got a little teary again when she found she would be bathing in cold water and forgoing meat. It seemed to me that because Amos pampered her sensually, she had become even more sensually demanding than I remembered. The life we live here was almost intolerable for her. And I thought about how marriage changes women—or at least, how it highlights certain aspects

of us and dims others—and wondered how my marriage has changed me.
How much Amos looked down upon our lifestyle, I don't know, exactly;
he was always gallant and jovial, but I could never quite tell the extent to
which he was casually mocking us.

That first night, I sat up late with my sisters in the makeshift beds we'd
made for them on the floor—sacks stuffed with old dresses I never use.
(Blankets, bedding, clothing—all these things are hard to come by here,
though we weave a little from nettle and other plant fibers. We're ever
reusing and remaking things from long ago, and one day they'll all wear
out, I know. But Ghost People don't think much of the future, beyond the
next season.) Amos wandered a bit outside, to give us time to talk alone.
They gave me a gift—one of the first books made in Sirenia, a blank ledger
I could use for a diary—and I thanked them so profusely they had to calm
me, I couldn't stop. Then they told me all about the news of Sirenia—and
about Prince Solon's new bride, Princess Ella, who was once a commoner
like us. And all the things they say of her—that she's pretty enough or that
she isn't (Addie thought yes, Lara thought no), that her mother was a witch
and that she cast some spell over the prince to make him love her, that she's
the soul of sweetness or that she's shy and meek or that she's aloof and
cold, that she's adored from afar but never goes out in public. Listening,
I felt at once sorry for her and quieted by admiration. I thought how
much harder it would be for her than it was for me, to become suddenly
a princess—for she truly has to play that role, and so much is expected
of her, and all the world's judgmental eyes upon her. I couldn't bear it, to
be watched so severely. And to live in that palace without a friend except
for the prince—whom I'd seen before, in his fancy carriages, and I always
thought him a proud fool, who thinks of nothing but his effect on pretty
ladies. What upholds her? I wondered, and felt almost pathetically grateful,
for the first time, that Nicolai and I have no true sovereign roles here. But I
said none of this to my sisters, and I think it was this very silence I noticed
myself keeping, on the subject of Sirenia's princess, that made me realize
for the first time how distant my life feels from theirs now.

"So you're telling us Nicolai is a prince?" Addie asked dubiously at
last, and when Lara returned her distracted glance with swift attention
to my face, I felt how long they'd been waiting to ask me.

"Yes," I said, and then wondered at my answer. "I mean well, no—not
anymore, not according to the people, and yet... And yet he was, and he
is, to me."

"But you live in a ruin," said Addie, with that same patient slowness
that Lara had used at the castle door. "And no one serves you. And you

don't make decisions for people, or rule over anything." And the way they both looked at me, I knew they were thinking I might have lost my hold on reality, just a little, living here.

I tried to laugh. "When you put it that way... But... Well, I think it's something we'll grow into over time. I think there's some reason we're here, some purpose for us. I just don't know what it is, yet. It's probably not up to me. Nicolai is still recovering—from his transformation."

And when they nodded without reply, I cried out at last, "Aren't you happy for me? I am married to a man I love, who loves me dearly."

"There's more to marriage than love, Mina," said Lara.

"And are you sure?" asked Addie.

"Sure of what?" I asked, heartbroken.

And they shared that look again, between them.

When I came to bed, Nicolai lay awake, waiting for me, but there was no warmth in his waiting, and he didn't reach for me. It was like that every night, while they stayed with us. "How long will they stay?" he asked me.

"I don't know. Are you worried about our supplies?"

"No, I'm worried about me."

"What do you mean?"

He'd gone cold like he does sometimes, when he's haunted by nightmares, and couldn't feel my touch when I lay my hand on his chest. "I don't know how to be with civilized people, Mina. What can I say to them?"

"You don't like them."

"No, I—" His lip curled in the shadow, with disgust or with pain or what I don't know, I couldn't see. The moon was waning, and the unicorn horns barely glowed.

"Aren't they beautiful?" I asked, proud of them as I'd always been.

"Yes," he said, his voice dull. "They're beautiful."

We took them walking over the mountains. I wanted to show them everything. But they complained of hunger and fatigue. When we returned to the castle to eat, we ate among the roses, which I have learned to tame and groom so that they bloom more profusely and grow in lovelier shapes, sometimes emerging in new colors which I cultivate, encourage, and occasionally transplant to open, sunlit places. I was proud of them, when I saw Addie wandering among them and lifting them to her face with delicate enjoyment. But then I saw how Lara and Amos were handling the unicorn horns that lay untouched around the old walls, in a way that felt so disrespectful—for no one here ever touches them, not for any reason—that I grabbed Lara's arm and made her drop one, so startled was she by my urgency. I wanted to hold them back before Nicolai flew into a rage. But then Amos banged one against a rock, and it was I who exploded.

"Stop!" I yelled.

He looked at me blandly.

"What are you doing?"

"I wanted to see how hard this thing is, if it would break."

"Look," I said, feeling Nicolai's anguish as he turned away and strode fast down the other side of the hill—to stop himself, I guess, from whatever he would do. I'd been speaking to them in our Wye-language before, so that Nicolai could understand, but Amos spoke it poorly, so I switched now to Sirenian. "Let me tell you what's happened here."

And all the while wondering where Nicolai went, and what he did, and what he felt and if he could ever forgive them, I told them of the people who once called themselves the Unicorn Riders. The people who came here, some Wyes and some Hums, all escaping persecution or trauma in their homelands—the ones who came from violence and could not believe in any kind of caring deity, the ones who came across swamp and sea without compasses and without faith, only hunger. I told them of what they found: a land more densely populated with magical creatures than Sirenia is with people. How the unicorns were everywhere then, grazing peacefully in herds, splashing about in the sea, their children's hooves ringing like bells over these crystal mountainsides, and how they were absolutely tame—for they'd never seen human beings before. How they let the people ride them, caress them like pets, and learn from them all their magical arts—the ability to psychically communicate with each other over great distances, heal sickness by focusing their minds, and experience other-worldly, psychedelic visions—through the channeling of power through their horns into people's minds. How giving they were, how curious and tender toward people, how unafraid. How innocence was simply part of their nature, the way greed is part of human nature.

"Then they were foolish," said Lara, "to let themselves be used." And I said no, they were not foolish; it was people who were the fools, who could not handle such an overflow of new awakening, power, and pleasure. The unicorns didn't know that. They didn't know how young humans were. They didn't know how to have such power all at once made mortal humans gluttonous, and then restless and fearful, and then bored. How they would begin to kill the unicorns, in order to take their horns and experience these magics even more directly, and cross to Sirenia (using the intuitive guidance of these horns to locate the solid crossings in the swamp that only beavers know) and then trade them there for more riches—for everyone wanted ivory in Sirenia, even though it mysteriously lost its magic once there. How they would enslave the unicorns, to make more beautiful materials like colored glass to build their palaces with. How they would shame their own souls this way, so that their children and their children's children, even now, remember how their forefathers forced something wild and beautiful and full of mystery to kneel, to bow, to make motions unnatural to it, like animals in a circus. How painful that shame was, and how desperate it made them.

I didn't tell about the Dark Faerie Queen, Rhiannon, and how she came to Prince Nicolai on a moonless midsummer night when he and all of his servants had passed out in the Great Hall after a night of revelry. How the glass lamps were still lit by magic, but when she swooped into the Hall, the lights all went out, and the darkness woke him. (Her voice, Nicolai said, like a quiet, pale scream.) How he had felt, at first, nothing, when she told him that all the unicorns were gone, that his people had wronged the land so deeply, the very fabric of the world was coming undone and could never be re-sewn. I know how it shames Nicolai, to remember that at the time, no one even noticed how long it had been since anyone had seen a real unicorn. They had become so proficient with the use of the disembodied horns. He had never known fear or sorrow. He had never known any of the difficult feelings that make one an adult. Rhiannon gave him one chance to make it right again, to free all the unicorn horns, to mourn what he had done, to give up his stolen pleasures, to regain his humanity. But he had never bowed down to anyone in his life, and he refused.

"The people were left in ruin," I told my sisters and Amos. "They lost everything—the magic of the land, all their wealth, all their powers; even the animals fled from them, as they do from other peoples of the world, and they starved because they had never learned how to hunt anything truly wild or forage for themselves. All this came to pass because of what they had done to the unicorns. We never touch a unicorn horn now. It is our penance, to leave them as they are."

"But it's not *our* penance," said Amos.

"What?" I said. I was too shocked even to feel angry.

He refused to be grave. "I only mean, these riches are going to waste here."

I thought about our walk along the cliffs and what I had tried to ignore. It was clear all along that more than anything—more than the mountainscapes like chiseled clouds, more than the cliffsides of mica that shattered into festivals of light every morning, or the great canopies of seabirds closing over the horizon or the lonely splendor of an owl's call over fathoms of plunging valley—my sisters and Amos were dizzied, riveted, by the jewels and riches left on the rocky shores to sift away into ocean and forgetting.

"Let us take some home with us," Addie pleaded. "No one has use for such things here. But think of the comfort your family could live in, back home, if we took even the little that we could carry."

"You don't live in discomfort now," I said, troubled. I didn't know of any particular rule against their taking these things, and it was true they weren't being used. But I was ashamed of my sisters, for their greed.

"Just because the people here have chosen to live without comforts, Mina," said Lara, turning her sudden, falcon's glance upon me, "doesn't mean the whole world has to live that way, in order to be good."

"But people will see what you have brought back from here, and they will send expeditions to hunt for riches."

"So?" said Lara. "Like Addie said, you aren't using them."

I shook my head. One thing would lead to another. Another wave of greed would follow that one, each one successively larger—this was how the original disaster with the unicorns had begun. But my voice was meek. I wasn't used to arguing with anyone, especially my sisters.

"Forget the jewels," said Amos then. "Three or four of those unicorn horns, and I'd never have to work again. Back in Sirenia, everyone thought you'd run out—we've been recycling the same ivory for years."

"If just one of these unicorn horns disappears from here," snarled Nicolai, who had appeared again without our noticing and stood looming behind us where we sat, not understanding Amos' words but seeing his intention, "you won't make it home."

Amos jumped up and stared him down. My sisters were staring at me, as if to say, *We told you.* "Is that a threat?" Amos barked in Sirenian.

Nicolai spoke back to him in Wye. "There are larger forces at work here than our own wills. But I am prince of this kingdom, however humble it may seem to you. I mean what I say."

I lay my hand on Nicolai's wrist. To this hour, I wonder if I did it to show my sisters that he wasn't to be feared. That he could be tamed. That I had tamed him.

"They can take a little something, can't they?" I asked my husband softly. "They are my family after all. I would like to make a gift to them, something to take home to my father, who once suffered so much for me.

Nothing of the unicorns, though," I added, forcing myself to face Amos' still-furious eyes. "We have told you they are sacred, and we will not tell you again."

So it was agreed, but I did not trust Amos, and I know Nicolai didn't either. It would have been easy for him to convince Addie that I didn't know what I was saying, that my mind was befuddled by my harsh living conditions and the fear of my beastly husband. Lara would stay out of it, as if she were above such sentimental arguments, but she wouldn't refuse what they offered to share with her. I wouldn't be surprised if our kingdom is missing a few more unicorn horns now.

"It hasn't occurred to you that this is the reason Amos was so willing to indulge Addie's whim—crossing a deadly lake that only the bravest adventurers have ever taken on? That maybe there was something he wanted here?" Nicolai asked me this question so gently, that night. Quietly, afraid to hurt me.

"Stop," I told him. "Don't."

And it was never mentioned again. But they couldn't stay long. How could they? Only a few days. It was too hard on all of us. I wanted Nicolai to share in the admiration I always felt for my sisters. Lara with her serpentine tresses and sharp, silky bones; Addie with her luscious freckles and curls the color of warm firelight. I know it sounds strange, but I almost wanted him to lust after them, like other men did. I wanted to show them off—what they had to offer, that I had none of. The Fox sisters. The people called them by the same name they'd given me, to tease them, and they enjoyed the attention. Adeline Fox. Lara Fox. "It suits us," Lara had laughed, even as the name ran off her like water. They were as dazzling as always. But Nicolai wasn't won. I could tell he was just barely kind to them, only for my sake.

They never said how they felt about the sea—seeing it for the first time. They never spoke of amazement. Although I admit, neither did I.

"Lara's only jealous of you, that's all," said Addie the night before they left. She was trying to cool the tension between us, when I flared up at Lara's suggestion—one more time, and I could not believe it—that I come away with them, that I leave my marriage behind as if it were nothing but a dangerous illusion.

"Jealous?"

"Sure, she's jealous that you won yourself a beast for a husband," she said, and she laughed, but I saw the mischief in her eyes, mischief that used to seem adorable to me but now seemed too crafty. "Even Lara has never been so wild as that."

Lara scowled, and I was surprised to wonder if there was truth in what Addie said. "Just think what he might be like," Addie continued, now ostensibly speaking to Lara but still looking at me. "You know—" And she inclined her head, nudged her plump shoulder in the direction of our bedroom, and I knew what she meant. I blushed.

"He's a man," I said, "just like Amos. Just like Father. There's nothing strange about him."

"Mina," Lara sighed. "You were always our little innocent." But she sat down behind me and began weaving and unweaving my hair, the way she'd done when I was a child. And the comfort ran so deep in me, that long drifting caress upon my scalp, like silent stars cascading very slowly through the sky of my mind, that I began to close my eyes and lean back into her, willing myself to let go of my defensiveness, to love our time together on this final night. It occurred to me that over the course of my growing up, my sisters had taken the place of a mother for me. They were different from me, but they never asked me to be different from what I was. They took care of me. They protected me.

"I missed this," I murmured.

Lara isn't one for expressing affection, but she said, "You always had the best hair, of the three of us. So slippery and fine, like mermaid hair."

And how could you know, I wondered sleepily, *what mermaid hair feels like?*

"Give my love a thousand times to Father," I said. "And tell him I'm alright. Really, I am. You believe me, don't you?"

"Visit us," said Lara quietly, "and tell him all about it yourself."

"I hope I will," I said, "one day. But I don't know when that will be."

Lara was silent for a moment, behind me, and her fingers repeated their motion in my hair. "You know how they always say the Sleeping Lake sinks deeper each year, widens. How the dragons' feet spread the swamp little by little with their spidery claws, and we never know. They say one day the peninsula will break off altogether and float away. Then we'll never see you again." There was a singsong lilt to her voice, as if she pretended to tell a fairy tale, as if she were playing—but she wasn't. She surprised me.

"Lara," I said. "What do you mean? Are you still afraid of losing me to this place?"

Her fingers pulled a little—without meaning to, I suppose. "But why not? Why not say you'll visit soon? Why not this summer?"

"But I'm needed here."

"By whom? Do your people need you?" she mocked.

"No," I said quickly, for I knew it was true. "But Nicolai does. He is my husband."

"Of course. And Mina will always be where she's most needed."

I turned around and faced her, my hair swinging free. "Of course?" I said. "Why do you say it like that?"

Lara pursed her lips and refused to answer. I looked at Addie, who looked down.

"Come on," said Lara. "Brush my hair."

I sniffed back tears as she came around to sit in front of me, feeling like the little girl she seemed to always think I was. "You hate anyone to brush your hair. You always say we pull."

Lara laughed. "Just do it."

And soon the night was over, and we slept. Will I ever see them again? And how? And where? With Nicolai or alone? When I wrote them that letter, season after season, did I write for love or for the fear of not loving enough? All I know is this: last night Nicolai and I made slow love on a crumbling rooftop, shrouded by warm rain. And it felt sweet to know we were once again alone together in this elemental, terrible-beautiful land that we could never explain to anyone. What a gift to know I have a purpose in this life, and to know I can fulfill it. That purpose is to love my prince, the man who suffered for fifty years as a beast and could only be awakened by my love. Sometimes I cannot help him, and I have to let go. Other times, if I am patient, if my love holds no expectation, I can.

And secretly (oh my diary, oh my words, I have you to myself at last)—the memory of the beast is so much of what I love in him! His skin murkier than mine, turning shades with the light, the way earth turns shades when water soaks it or wind dries it. His fierce, crooked, clumsy nose. He's like the Wyes and Hums from which he's descended, but he's also different from either of them, and different from his people. And it's because he was a beast—for fifty unconscious years. Nicolai the man aged only five years in that time, but the beast lived fifty. His cheek bristles against mine, his chest is furry, his flesh rolls me, broad and heavy. In the spring and fall, sometimes, when the warm days come, we leave everything behind and plunge in the cold creeks or the pond. I come out shivering in a moment or two, but Nicolai rolls around like a porpoise until I'm almost dry, whooping.

The truth is I'm proud of him for standing up to them about the unicorn horns. It was the beast in him that did it. If only he could see—it is the beast in him, as much as the man, that could make him a prince again one day, standing for his people.

Anyway, I admit to some strange and guilty relief in my sisters' going. There was so much I tried not to think about when they were here, and the trying tired me. How unhappy they were with so much that made me happy. Their awkwardness with Nicolai. Their unflinching greed. Their lack of engagement with any of the people here, as if their eerie, silvery looks frightened them—so childish it seems to me now, as if my sisters were just like any other Sirenians all along, frightened of anyone who looks different, and I never acknowledged it!

My life has changed so much since those days of my early youth when my daily chores, my interests and fascinations, all revolved so closely around the lives of my sisters. And it was rather trying, here in the Ghost Kingdom, to keep up with the responsibilities of our survival while entertaining them and meeting their needs at the same time. Nicolai and I have a rhythm we've worked out by now, by which we tend our home, take advantage of the gifts of each season, prepare for each season to come. How restful to have enough time again each morning for the meditations and then for greeting the garden in an intimate way! Time crystallizes once again, around our solitude. We walk into the forest, breathless with beauty, hardly speaking. The dark trees seem painted upon the air. Sails of mist fly ahead of us along the thin pathways we follow, on wayward breezes with mysterious beginnings and endings, like the tails of some gigantic creature. The composting needles smell so richly of sun and wetness at once, I want to touch my tongue to them, as if they are cake. Everything—every wild, broken bird echo, every pause in the breeze, every gush of cold green upon my skin as we pass close beneath the fog-drenched boughs—leans us into some other-world, some beyond there is no word for, beyond and beyond. We walk in awe. When we stop to eat our picnic, we remember that we are alive, and we are amazed.

Some days we are invited in for dinner, some days we help friends with their shelters, some days are about planting and tending while others are about harvesting and preparing for storage. There are no rules about whose home you can stop and eat at or who owes whom; no obligatory relationships; no mean-spirited jealousy. There is a kind of strange eternity infused into every moment, as if—paradoxically—the whole world could at any moment end, and we are filled with wonder. I suppose, in a way, the people feel as if the world already has ended, and they are living in Heaven. No one is ever in a hurry.

So I feel relief, yes, in being home in my home again, and in opening the book my sisters gave me—their one selfless gift—and writing, at last, only to myself. And justifying myself to no one.

summer solstice

It's time to prepare some kind of supper, but I'm too upset, so I'll write here for a moment and try to calm down. There isn't anything, really—just another of our little fights over nothing. But there have been so many lately. Maybe it's the anxiety that lies mostly unspoken between us, that we've been unable to conceive a child yet—though I know it is harder for some couples than for others, and there is still plenty of time.

How can you know, he demanded of me. *How can you possibly understand?*

I suppose we have different priorities, when there is so much to do. It's funny how when we first started out, we never thought to question whether this ruin of a castle could be enough for us—to me every rubbled nook, every broken tile, was beautiful the way every line of suffering memory on Nicolai's new human face was beautiful to me because it was him, it was his history, it was his soul I was loving into life again. And there was so much to learn, and everything was possible. But now it exhausts us—this place which is too big for us and forever falling down, forever needing our help, forever failing our basic needs for warmth, reliable food storage, dryness. So many walls, and yet so few of them protect us from the elements. So many rooms, and yet so few of them shelter us. We've been busy just surviving, just learning how to make food to eat every day and store enough of it for the winter months. Even with all the help we've received (which is less now, of course, since I suppose the community assumes we can get along well enough on our own now—and it's quite a walk for them, after all), we still barely make it. And I'll find myself wishing he would patch up the cracks in the bedroom before winter or find a way to insulate the kitchen, and I don't understand, if this castle was a prison to him, if the memory of that cursed life pains him, why not focus practically on the spaces we really need—why spend days cleaning the unused rooms, inspecting forgotten floors for broken glass, removing and replacing stones to channel sunlight in such and such a way upon the unicorn horns in the archways he'll never touch, reconstructing some old useless chimney for birds to nest in?

Yet it hurts me, for him to tell me I don't understand, because I do. I understand this befuddled longing to make right and beautiful those wrongs that can never be made right or beautiful. What is it, then? Whenever I am working and he is not, because some mood has taken him and he must lie in bed or brood upon the ledge, I blame him. And he blames me right back, saying I wander about by the sea at night and am just as moody. But it isn't the same—what he's really saying is not that I should work harder but that I don't care enough about him. And I feel guilty for that, for what if it's true? It bothers me that I don't always feel the same compassion that I used to. Are we too much together? How many days since we've seen anyone but each other?

I tell myself I must every day prioritize love more highly. I came here to love Nicolai. That was the reason I left my family and home and everything I knew, to return to this place, even after he let me go. I must never trade love for any other demands or desires. I must learn to handle my own stress and not take it out on him. It is possible to destroy the fragile, glowing spider-threads of tenderness that make a relationship brilliant; and then what would we have left? If something is wounded enough, I know, it will never heal right.

I looked in the cracked palace mirror just now, the one Nicolai threw away when he was a beast, but retrieved for me when he was a man. Most days I wear pants and don't bother to brush my hair. Nor do I enjoy contemplating my face for long, which never brought me any clear sense of satisfaction. But every now and then, I look in that glass when I need to be really honest with myself, when I really cannot figure myself out. *What do you want, Mina?* I asked. *Why does the idea of simply loving each day, learning the work of living, not feel like enough to you sometimes? Why do you still listen to mermaids? Why do you push and push, until something erupts?*

I only hate that he should say that. That I can't understand him. There is so little I can claim to depend on—not this land, not our ability, even, to feed ourselves each winter—but I depend upon our understanding of each other. I could not bear, ever, not to be the person he turns to. I couldn't bear that he should not speak to me in his depression, that he should lie in the dark like he does sometimes at night and refuse a candle—if he should not speak to me and tell me why. Like how he kissed my face that night, only a few days ago, when I finally coaxed him into tears, coaxed him into admitting why he's avoided the meditations for so long now (because inside of them he feels like he is dying, and worse, he feels that the people, in their colorless clothing and silence, want him to die—that he is a symbol, for them, of a past they wish to forget. How his own people, sometimes, fill him with dread—the way they continue on and survive, always in low voices as if afraid to awaken any feeling, as if living at the end of time, as if we really live in a land of ghosts). And I told him he can be anything, and we can go anywhere we wish—we can leave this kingdom, if we choose. He is not a symbol; he is a man; he is my beloved.

And when I'm good at loving, when I can help him most, I really see him healing—and that feels better than anything, better than being right in any argument, better than any kisses. Over and over, I awaken him anew from the nightmare of his past; I remind him where he is now, and who, and with whom, and surrounded by what love! I hold his hands and meditate with him, I remind him to be present right now, for the past is nothing. Ona taught me that all feelings are acceptable, and the point is not to fight them. *Look into my eyes,* I tell him. *This is the meditation. This is all we are. You feel what you feel and then it passes on, like a river, and cannot hurt you—do not think, do not judge it, just let it go.* And what I don't say is, *It is you who first taught me all this. You, who knew already the ultimate meditation, when you lived as a beast.*

I think sometimes, without meaning to, of what Addie said—or hinted at. What it must be like to make love to one so wild. I don't tell Nicolai how sometimes in the middle of the night, he takes me in his sleep, not gentle, but holding me down with his teeth, scratching me with his claws, overcoming me so that I yearn for days and days afterward to feel it again. And how rarely that happens now. I don't tell him because I know he only ravages me when caught up in a nightmare, and I don't want to wish upon him that nightmare. But oh, Rhiannon, it's not even the wildness I miss so much—it's the soul I miss. It's the raw presence of the animal I loved. The one to whom none of these mundane, bickering things mattered—but only the answer one pair of eyes could give to another, and the immediacy of a desire that could kill you, and the danger of not knowing whether I was hunted for food or for love, not knowing if anyone else existed in this world, not knowing if answering the question would destroy me.

He sat staring at that broken wall, watching the birds—and I know they bring him peace, but not happiness. Brooding over our loneliness here, a jewel from his long-ago broken crown sparkling jagged with beauty in his calloused palm. I asked him, *Do you think, my love, that maybe there was something you knew, once, back then? Something it would help you to remember? You were lonely for love, then, I know, but you didn't miss being a prince, the way you do now. You felt a different kind of longing. Do you remember?*

And he looked at me with a different kind of danger in his eyes—not one that hunted me, but one that left me shaking cold. *What do you mean,* he growled, *back then?*

When you were a beast, I whispered. It was the only time I'd ever said it. *When you were a wolf.*

And I know when you commit to someone, you commit to them for life, and you commit to them through everything that comes, even if it doesn't always make you happy or fulfill your private wishes—we are in it for our own learning, we are in it for what we have to give! I know that.

I handed him a rose, to appease him. It often helps him—when I bring the roses to his lips, to his nose, to let him know that this scent, now, at once sensual and ethereal, is his. No longer a reminder of all the luxury and tender caresses that are denied to him, no longer a cruel temptation left by Rhiannon, but an expression of love tended faithfully by his beloved, the one who believed in him and still believes in him and woke him to this good life.

But if he had cast the rose from my hand with violence, he could not have left me colder than his tone left me when turned upon me suddenly in anger.

How could you possibly understand? He said. *How could you possibly wish that of me—if you loved me, you could never wish me to be such a terrible thing.*

How can you say that? I begged. *You cannot say that—Nicolai, you are not yourself. Remember, it was I who saw you! It was I who loved you as the beast, exactly as you were, and still do.*

No. He shook his head and covered his face, so that I could hardly hear his next words. I crushed the rose in my hand. *You never saw me,* he said. *You never saw me kill.*

winter solstice

God. God of my people, Savior to whom I have forgotten to pray, for years now—would you call her a demon?

Sometimes the wind this time of year becomes unbearable—not the cold of it, nor the things it wrecks, nor even the bruising force of it, but its sheer relentlessness. It is more than sound, more than force. You cannot imagine it unless you have lived it. It seems, sometimes, to sweep away all sense and reason, all sense even of self. And I suppose this is a good emptiness, the kind of emptiness the Ghost People seek in their meditations, but sometimes it makes me feel lonely the way I did when I first came to the castle, and Nicolai was a beast, and I did not know that he could understand me, nor that he was secretly human, nor that he could love.

Oh God, she was like death. When I saw her the first time—the color of her face, the falling behind her eyes—it was the way death looks, those rare, rare times we think of it. Not Heaven, not the life beyond, not the idea of sweet release, not even the sea. But death itself, the wall of it, the inevitability.

No. Let me start again. She was cold. I never touched her, but when I looked at her, I felt it—like the bottom of a well. Loneliness blew like wind through her hair, and her hair was too long, awful because I could not ever see where it ended. I never looked directly into her eyes, because I knew that if I did, I would drown. I spent the whole time kneeling, with my head bowed.

And yet perhaps I lowered my eyes because I also felt such a longing, as if perhaps we long for death, after all. How easy it would be, I thought, to rest there in that darkness. And she was beautiful, too, though I only see that now. Just as you do not know, during a nightmare, that you are dreaming, I did not know then, in the midst of such horror, that it was beautiful.

It is a year since the day my Nicolai transformed into a man.

I was happy last night, at first, for we would join in the solstice celebration, something that had happened without us last year, for we did not know the people then—and had happened without Nicolai for fifty years. Nicolai was brooding again, but I thought he would come out of it after we did the communal meditation. The meditations always help him, but he doesn't have the motivation to do them on his own.

On Solstice eve, they gather in the valley with candles lit for the spirits of all who died in the famines and fighting during the downfall of the city. But it is not a sad time. The candles are so lovely, each one guarded by the shelter of a tender body leaning over its flame, lighting a beloved face. As we huddled together against the cold breeze, I imagined that those spirits were grateful, and that on this night we were closer to them than at any other time.

The ceremony was briefer than I expected, because the people consider this dark time to be a time for family, for circling close with our intimate familiars in our own homes. Only one person is chosen to remain out in the field through this longest of nights, guarding a single candle in honor of the unicorns and our promise to remember forever our mistakes and our gratitude.

When someone explained this to us, I could see that Nicolai immediately hoped this person might be him. It's as if he is always looking for a way to redeem himself with them, even though they ask no redemption, but the ways he seeks to redeem himself would also bring honor to himself, which I think is why they so often deny him. Watching him from a distance, for it pained me to hear the conversation I knew was happening, I saw him lean in to some of the elders. I could already feel a familiar constricting in my chest, a sense of anxiety that he should wound himself again, that I must help to tame his pain again tonight.

They did not choose him. They chose a boy who had recently completed his solo journey. I saw that the boy did not expect to be chosen, and yet immediately he bowed his consent.

Afterward, many people invited us to their homes for the night. "Tonight is a night to spend with family," they said. "You are so far from yours, Mina, and dear Nicolai, you have none but us. Come to us and we will warm you by our fires!"

But Nicolai, bundled up now in his darkness, as if he drew sustenance from his own bitterness, would have none of it.

"I understand," said Linny, who is newly coupled—though I've never found the courage to ask her about her own experience. "Enjoy this night together, then." And she smiled at us, assuming Nicolai wanted me all to himself in the intimacy of the longest night of the year. But I knew it wouldn't be like that.

"Go without me if you want," he grumbled, seeing my resentment. I refused, and was resentful anyway. He didn't ask much of me. He went to bed early and turned his back to me as I lay awake. I felt sorry, for I knew he hated himself for his behavior; I knew he saw his own childishness as clearly as I do, but could not find a way to banish his own feelings. I understand that, for I cannot find a way to banish mine.

Seeing that he slept one of those dead-heavy sleeps of depression, I left him sometime after midnight and walked out alone to the fields. I always love these lands in the moonlight. I seem to be wading through clouds, and sometimes I see something wonderful—an owl sailing like a slow secret down to its kill, or a shooting star that bursts up out of nothing and then disappears into infinite forgetting. I saw the beautiful boy sitting still beneath the stars, far away, his hands cupped tenderly around the flame he watched over, and smiled a little to myself. I wondered if he had a sweetheart, and who she was, and if he was satisfied by her side.

I admit I was feeling sorry for myself tonight, and did not even attempt to reign in my thoughts. Instead of thinking of all the things I had to be grateful for and the companionship of these good people who support us through all our trials, I thought of my unhappiness. I thought of my sisters, how I missed them in spite of everything, every day—I cannot bear to miss their lives, their children, their foolish talk about their neighbors or the princess of Sirenia. I thought about the happy families I saw tonight, the lineages they experienced in each other's company, the familiar embraces to which the touch of casual friendship can never compare, the knowing laughter, the cozy bliss I imagined when I saw the mother pressing her sleeping babe to her breast, rocking in the cold breeze, closing her eyes and smiling as if God Himself snuggled close to her skin. I thought about how Nicolai and I still had not conceived after a year of trying (and could that be why he refuses me even more often these days, I wondered, because he thinks it is his fault, and adds that to his heap of shame and sorrow?). I thought about how little I knew myself, compared to the person I once was—how lost I felt from the peaceful diligence of my childhood, how lost from my sense of purpose, how out of touch with the passion and certainty that had brought me here a year ago.

In the end I came home to the castle, for where else could I find myself?—but too restless to sleep, I climbed the long, sad stairs to the old tower. Once upon a time, I could not bear to hear the howl of my beloved, in his agony, arising from this place. Now I could not bear the silence. I could not bear the meaningless hiss of this old, bitter wind—and yet I climbed into the window to feel it blow against me, to feel the pain of its ruthless cold, to feel *something*. To cool, I suppose, the fury in me—the fury of missing the darting minnow of his tongue when he used to dip into me, everywhere, with such careless lust. In the beginning. When he was man and beast at once, when he did not yet know himself enough to be ashamed.

Rhiannon appeared to me in the air, like a mirror. Floating outside the tower window. I fell backward, startled out of a reverie so shameful, I felt as if she could see it. Rhiannon, the Dark Faerie Queen. She floated in the wind, the way a ghost might float but not like ghost at all—more like a dark, writhing, soaking piece of seaweed with a face like a monster's, or a faerie's, all at once.

She surged closer, leaning in to me, and I couldn't look at her but her skirts rustled in an old, empty way that horrified me, as if I heard the sound of millions of insect husks cascading from an open tomb, and I smelled the roses so suddenly up close, suffocating me.

"Mina Fox," she said. Her voice was impersonal at first, as if she'd come to deliver a message. It was full of air, like the sound of the sea.

"Who are you?" I gasped.

"I am Rhiannon. I made your husband a beast, and you turned him back again. Good work, my daughter."

"Why do you call me daughter?" I gasped, wrapping my arms around my body, huddled now on the floor and no longer hot. "You are not my mother."

I felt her smile, and her voice changed. "But you wish that I were."

I thought, *I wish no such thing,* but even as I thought it, I felt some vague yearning in my belly, I looked into the lapping layers of her robes, I wanted to lose myself there, I wanted to forget myself in that nurturing darkness, like a seed falling into the earth—knowing it could rest there all winter long, and nothing would be asked of it until spring.

"I wish only that Nicolai were happy," I said.

"Bah!" she barked, like a dog. "Nicolai, bah. It's you I'm interested in, Mina Fox. I did it all for you."

"Did—what do you mean? Did what?" I spoke into her rustling skirts, my throat so dry I kept coughing.

"Your troubles are only just beginning, Mina Fox," she said over me. "You will feel lonelier than you have ever felt. You will feel disconnected from your husband, your people, even from yourself! You will lose everything, and then you will be given hope again, only to have it taken away."

I think I actually cried out then, every part of my being rising up in protest. "But—why—" I began stupidly.

"And you will never bear children," she said.

"No," I murmured, weeping, for I believed her. It was the first time I knew that she was telling the truth. I felt, as soon as she said it, that I had always known this. And I wept for a long time. I felt so undone by the nightmare that enfolded me, that at one point I reached for the hem of her robes and held it against my eyes to absorb my tears. She did not move. She stood as solid in the air as a person stands on the ground.

"Why?" I asked at last. "What have I done? Why do you curse me thus?"

A wind came down upon my head then, and I did not know if it was her breath, only it was cold. "Fool!" she cried, and her cry held the high pain of a hawk's cry in a far, far sky, but it swirled in echoing crescendo around the little high tower room. "This is human, this talk of curses." Then she said, "I love you. I love by darkness. The darkness is necessary. It is half of the world's turning. Without it, nothing would transform. You know this."

"Then," I ventured, my desperation making me daring—for I already felt some of the loneliness she predicted, or so I thought—"will there be an end to it? Will this darkness, eventually, give way to light? Will there be some purpose for all—?"

But she interrupted me again in seeming fury. "I don't care!" she said. "That isn't my domain. I do not bring darkness in order for there to be light. I only bring darkness. If you are always thinking of the damned light, you will not be able to see in the dark, and it will get you—it will imprison you, it will eat you while you aren't looking!"

"But I need the hope," I cried. "I need it to keep me going!"

"No you do not," she said. "The darkness is a river. It goes down. Surrender, and you do not need anything. It is already going. You need do nothing."

"But is there no meaning in all of this? Why am I here? What is it for?"

I expected her fury again, but this time she only sighed. She was almost gentle. I almost wanted to look up into her eyes again, but I was too afraid. "I cannot answer you," she said. "If I answered you, I would transplant a flower into a pile of stones. Perhaps when your soil is black and rich, one day, in the darkness, the answer will grow there on its own."

Seeing I could not get the answer I wanted now, somehow I calmed myself and sat back, brushed the dirt off my clothes, and tried to regain some of my dignity.

"Good," she said.

"What is Nicolai's path, then?" I asked. "What is he meant to become?"

"Not your question to ask, Mina Fox."

"Will you come to him, too, then, and tell him his fate?"

"I already came to him fifty years ago. If being a beast for fifty years wasn't clear enough…" And she gave a kind of snort.

"What of my sisters?" I asked. I suppose I thought now that she might know anything.

"What of them?" she growled.

"Are they alright?"

"Of course they are alright. Everyone is alright."

"No, I mean, are they alive and well? Are they happy?"

"Yes, enough. They are well. They do not need you as much as you think."

I thought on this. I suppose I felt some relief. I had not realized how much of my missing them was guilt.

"And Nicolai? Does he need me as much as I think he does?"

"Not as much as you need yourself," was her cryptic answer.

An owl called from somewhere far. I wondered why she stood before me so long. I felt there was perhaps some kindness in her staying with me, though I probably imagined that, in my loneliness. I thought about the river she spoke of. For a moment it seemed I could feel the pull of that river, that flowing downward into infinite darkness, and the peace and release of it. I wanted to follow it. But I felt pulled back away from it, at the same time. It was as if Nicolai pulled me. My commitment to him. I thought, *If I ever died, he couldn't survive. I must make sure not to die before him.*

As if she could read my thoughts, Rhiannon said suddenly, "Do not tell Nicolai. Do not tell him of our talk. Never. He will not understand."

"Neither do I."

"Ah," she said, "but you do."

Then she was gone.

Why did she come to me? Why tell me all this? Did she lay that destiny upon me, or only warn me, so I should know?

I came back to our room, but did not return to bed. I have taken this journal out to a ledge to write. I have been writing all night. I could not sleep. I could hear the mermaids wailing, but now they have stopped.

You would think I would feel despair, hearing all that she said to me, but strangely I do not. Or if I do, I do not know it. I do not know what I feel.

Though she did not threaten any consequence, I know I will never tell Nicolai. I know she was right. He would lose his mind, to know I even saw her. She is his worst nightmare. Ah, but how can I keep it from him? How can I not tell him that we will never have children? How can I allow him to keep hoping?

I think how I have always loved the night. When I was a little girl, I used to say black was my favorite color—an idea my sisters teased me for and could not believe. I used to think of a shiny black, like the night sky.

I remember now, one more thing Rhiannon said. How strange that I should have forgotten it. Perhaps I forgot many other things she said, as well, and will only remember them years from now, if ever.

She said, "Every year on the winter solstice, you may call for me if you wish. If you have any question at that time, I will answer it."

Yet I can hardly imagine wishing to call upon such a deity as her. Her dark news of last night was enough to fill a lifetime.

Now the dawn comes bleak and unknown from across the water. Once I called this kingdom the end of the world, but really it is the beginning. It is the first place the sun rises. Everything is so fresh and clear and cold here, it almost hurts to live.

spring, year 3 in the Ghost Kingdom

Enough. I said it to Nicolai, and I say it, in secret, to myself. Enough of these memories. How can I speak to him of being present and contented in this moment, without longing for more from either future or past, when I refuse to practice this truth myself? It's time to move on from here.

We must give up this castle. We must give up everything it represents, the blood of unicorns and their stolen, now lifeless horns; for it is built on shame and denial. To return that which was stolen, to relinquish this blood wealth, was the first thing the Dark Faerie asked of Nicolai, and fifty years later, he has not done it. No wonder he haunts himself. No wonder such dreams. I have not fulfilled my duty to Nicolai. I have not finished awakening him from his nightmare—for this castle itself is a kind of sleep. I was called here to heal him from the curse of the past. And we must do more than give the castle up. We must destroy it.

Every able-bodied person came to help us, though we had not even told them what we planned. Men and women of all ages—even children—heaved the castle stones from the highest walls that had already begun to tumble, and soon enough we even laughed while we did it. The castle was made in a flimsy way—by people who, at the time, were gluttons for magic and had little or no experience, or interest, in the structural requirements of a building. Some parts of it seemed almost to long for their own unmaking—they had been tending that way anyway. Nicolai took an especially savage pleasure in rending the bedding, table cloths, and window dressing fabrics that had made it a place of luxury—until we reminded him to be careful, for we need all this material to replace some of the worn clothing people have lived in here for so long. We kept almost nothing—a few scrolls to read and read again over the years, since we may never have others, and some dishes and things of use which we could share. By the third day, our mood had become more serious, since we were at the point of breaking the unicorn horns from their places—or trying to. They are made of the hardest stuff in the world, held in place by some magic that no one anymore knew. They formed the columns in the Great Hall and the carvings in the walls (for crystal can carve them) and parts of the fountains and throne and bed frames and everything decorative. I suppose we had some idea of removing them from these vain structures and laying them in a pile, so that we might then decide how to symbolically release them. But we made very little headway in moving any of them from their places, and in the end we gave up.

Instead we lit a fire to burn the wooden elements of the castle and everything else flammable to the ground. The fire was extremely difficult to start and keep alive. Some people suggested we wait until a drier season to continue our work, but Nicolai would not hear of it, so eager was he to finish the wretched task and be done with it, once we had started. Privately, I thought he might fear to lose his conviction—no matter how easily he had forced himself to agree to this plan. Also, we did fear to loose a fire out of control once the dry weather came, and could not face the possibility of doing even more harm to the world in the midst of our attempt to make amends. So we labored on, and the result was a pitiful, smoky, gloomy process that did not help us to feel cleansed or satisfy our longing to make a great gesture of release. But then, the purpose was never our own satisfaction.

What we were left with, in the end, was a skeleton of unicorn horn, a silver-white ghost of the memory of things taken for granted, like an echo that asked us *What were these things, after all? Why were they so important?* But also, we were left with half-burned, charred posts and fallen beams, piles of incompletely destroyed debris, mildly disfigured stone walls that stood stubbornly in place. I thought, at least the roses will grow over the ruins and make them beautiful again.

After everyone had gone, Nicolai and I sat in the midst of it for a long time without speaking. *You can stay with us,* each family had told us, *for as long as you need, until you build a new home. You will be cared for. Do not be afraid.* I rubbed Nicolai's back as he quietly wept. It was a good ritual, that sitting there, that silence. It was a different kind of weeping, that I felt in him—the kind of weeping that contained and released something solid and now melted, the kind that would end. When he finally lifted his wet eyes to the sight again, I could see the emptiness there, and I knew he was wishing for some kind of sign that he had done right, some feeling in the wind that the spirits of old had accepted his gesture—even the smallest sense, in the patterns of ruin around us or the movement of nature beyond them or the slightest perceptions of his own heart, that he was forgiven. But there was nothing. The sky lay still and grey over our heads. The sun began to sink over the forest, without yielding any colors, for the clouds were too damp and thick.

I thought to myself then, perhaps I have really hoped, without admitting it to myself, that the unicorns still exist, at least in spirit, at least somewhere we cannot see. But I know now that they do not. The faded pieces of them that remained seemed to mean nothing. They were no longer imbued with any power. But we said a prayer anyway, so that just in case the Dark Faerie was listening, she would know our intention. I understood that I had been holding onto that hope, all this time—that there was something more to life, something more to love, than what I felt in every moment. Something more romantic, like the dream of a unicorn finally galloping home into our hearts from the long-ago and far-away, with all his brethren. But no.

We have only each other, warm and weeping, gazing at this smoldering ruin. And this is enough. I shall not think of Her again.

late autumn

My sisters would find my life here uneventful, perhaps, but no—there are births, of course, and the mild gossip of new partnerships, though without the drama of Sirenian life. Recently a few adventurous young men and women took jewels to Sirenia and, disguised as Sirenians, bought some much needed clothing and supplies for the whole community. We allowed ourselves some simple rejoicing when they returned, not only for these necessary riches but for the feat our friends had achieved, our relief that they had returned safe.

People, families, seasons, all seem to flow into each other. Peace weighs down each object. Sometimes when I am doing something undemanding—sewing patches on a pair of pants, cracking nuts, watering seedlings, cooking stew, clipping roses—I am so aware of the texture not only of each thing, but of the air itself, the shape of my hands around space, the careful firmness of flesh against nothingness. It is as if I exist inside a work of art. If I reach out my arms, I can touch with my fingertips all of the past, all of the future, all of possibility. But where I am right now, I am safe in the present, forever. Those other times are only the frame, a horizon that arbitrarily defines reality.

I've told Nicolai that I know I'm barren. I've told him it's just an intuition I have, something I know as a woman. At first he tried to reassure me, told me I was laying blame needlessly upon myself. Then, over time, we ceased to speak of it.

As soon as we began to wander through the forest together in search of the home we would make for ourselves, the home of our new life together grounded wholly in love and community and nothing more, a surge of fresh blood seemed to rise up in both of us—a youthfulness we hadn't felt in so long. In the intimacy of moss and fern and birdsong, feeling the presence of daily living all around us, I thought, I do not need to make another life in my womb. There is so much life around us. These are our people, whom we have too long lived apart from. We found our place here, and with their help, we built our little abode—simple, snug, hidden and human-sized, as unlike the castle as a thing could be—in barely a season.

I love how it is all one place, its chambers connected as one unit: a real house, an integrated being. The wind can't get in anywhere. We don't have to go out in the salty cold between broken-down rooms to get from our kitchen to our bedroom. Even the latrine is attached to the back, and is always at least a little warmer than the outside when we have a fire going. The floor is of earth, not stone, and the walls of branches stuffed with a leaf-clay mix we regularly patch, and the shape is round and lovely, and we have a tiny wood-slatted loft just big enough for sleeping, built around the great standing trees (one living, two dead) which we used for our main support. The roof is layered with bark, and because one can reach it by climbing the support trees that tower above it, we often wake to the happy surprise of shell and twiggy art that children have decorated with in their night mischief (back in Sirenia, children's mischief was usually meant to create disorder and harm; here is it meant to bring joy and surprise). It is pretty, really, like one of the little faerie cottages I have built with those same children at the bases of trees, demurely winking at me through its veils of fog when I come home in the dark and find Nicolai waiting for me by the fire he's made.

It seems strange to me, now, that I should have asked Nicolai—when we first left the ruin behind—if we could live by the sea. I was thinking of that cave where he played in his boyhood, and the renewing freshness of the sea wind, and the meditation of watching those waves as they rose up and devoured each other in ceaseless unity. It was strange of me to ask, though, because normally it falls to me to think practically—and true enough, Nicolai's response was laughing and gentle, at first, in his surprise. To sleep in the side of a cliff, struggling to keep fires going in the wind, endlessly gathering grasses to pad us against the stone, cooking somewhere else up above on the cliff and carrying food down, and growing food—where? I had answers to all these questions and concerns, but they weren't good ones. When Nicolai's eyes turned finally serious, and their darkness ran so deep that it silenced me, I kissed him—feeling a fullness in my heart, in my breasts, that I hadn't felt in so long, just to see that vulnerable universe inside him again: *I cannot,* said his eyes. *You know I cannot.*

And it makes ever more sense to live here in the forest, anyway, among our people. Now we truly belong. There is no trace of the distance we once felt. We are close enough to do for others as much as they do for us, and more. We know everything that happens—we know the daily news of all beings here as thoroughly as the crows do, though we are quieter about it.

I have come to terms with Nicolai's rhythms, for the most part. When he goes dark and inward, I can only stand by his side and love him, waiting for him to emerge. I understand it now as just an after-effect of what he went through, and I know that such phases always pass sooner or later, and we will make love again, and laugh together on the cliff-sides again, and go for picnics again and explore some place we've never been before—camp out in some far-off meadow. Nicolai and I understand each other as no one else understands us. He understands me sometimes better than I do myself. In the winter, he reminds me that I'm only irritable because the wind has gotten to me again, and he makes me come inside so he can do my chores for me and give me a rest. In the summer fog, he talks sense into me when I become again that dreamy girl I once was, and wander without paying attention. I even told him about the mermaids' song, the way it affects me. *I don't want to ever make you lonely, Mina,* he said. *I don't want you to ever be so lonely as I was, that you should have to follow their songs. We must take care of each other.*

I still come to tend the roses near the castle ruin, now and then. It seems to me that people avoid the ruin, though maybe that's only my imagination—it could be that they rarely have time to walk this far for pleasure. Yet for some reason, I'm wary of ever passing through those stone walls; I never go up close enough to touch any part of it. I told Rhee, the first man we met here and one of my best teachers, about my vision of Rhiannon. It was just an illusion, he said—something my mind made up to reflect my fears. Our lives are like a rainbow, he said—all the passion that we feel, all those beautiful colors, are only a reflection of the true light, arching above the earth (and continuing the circle beneath the earth when we die), and when we dissolve at last like the unicorns into light, we will no longer be tormented by such passions, but disappear into the center of the circle, watching the colors go round and round without any attachment to them.

There's a passage through thorns, below the ruin, that I think no one would know but me. It ends here on this little ledge, where I feel at once protected and wild, the stone of ages encasing my back and the wind of possibility pressing my face, freshening the skin of my throat where my breath comes. A fallen unicorn horn gleams in the sunlight, ever on the verge of being knocked (by the brush of a fox in the night, perhaps, or a strong winter wind) into the crashing waves below. I don't touch it, but I try to imagine what kind of music might emerge from such a thing—from such history, from the life of a thing that lived forever, but then disappeared—and if Nicolai played that music once, long ago, on the instrument I found in the castle and then threw away over the cliff edge when he got so angry about it. I wonder if it sounded, when played, at all like the mermaids' song, which drowns me in sensation, like too many colors, at once piercing and feminine, musical and cacophonous, more cry than melody, and yet—I don't know. Certainly it's for the best that we've nested ourselves so deep in the forest, among our friends. For the more I hear it, the more it draws me, and the more it draws me, the more it disturbs something in my mind.

Rhee told me once that the sea serpent is thought of as a symbol for the passions that cause suffering, the passions we subdue with meditation in order to be at peace. But it was his wife Ona, for some reason, whom I asked the question—*Are there still serpents in the sea? Real ones? For even the Sirenians still fear them, and will not cross our waters.*

Sometimes it's easier for me to ask Ona these childish questions. There's something stern in Rhee, that quiets me. But this time Ona only laughed her little laugh, soft and tickling like the crackle of a fire, and patted my knee. *A good thing they do!* She laughed. *A good thing they do fear them! Keeps them home, and leaves us in peace, nah?*

But she didn't answer my question.

Rowan
(the huntsman)

twenty-one years from now

- Rufus, when you were young, how did you know when you had
become a man? Do you remember when it was?
==
- Rufus, are you sleeping?
- Nae. I remember.
- When was it?
- I was fifteen.
==
==
- Rufus?
- She asked me for mercy.
- Who? What happened? Tell me.
- Why?
- Because there's something in you that reminds me of Sol. You are
gruff sometimes, but you have that flame Sol had, that I couldn't see, or
some call in the night that haunts you—and I feel it in my sons, too, that
unease. I want to know what they seek, when they seek to become men.
It frightens me, somehow.
- The call in the night. Rowan was that.
- Rowan? Who was she?
==
- You don't wish to speak of it. Why, Rufus, I think you loved once! I
never knew. There was a girl you loved, wasn't there?
==
- You say nothing. But I can see. You love her still! Who was she?
==

- Come, Rufus, I need some talk tonight, to keep me from madness in this place. You know everything of me. You found me in rags in the house of my father when I was eighteen years old—you alone have glimpsed my past. Tell me something of yours. Anything. You can trust me.

- I know it, Ella.

- Tell me about your youth, then. You don't have to speak of the woman. Tell me where you come from. You are such a mystery to everyone.

- Ha, and they like it that way.

- I don't. All my life, I've longed for closeness. I have only longed to make friends. You are a friend to me, Rufus, as I hope I am to you. What we share these nights in secret... Perhaps it is wrong of me, I don't know anymore... But I did it in friendship. Can you see that?

- Yea.

- So tell me, then, of the Northlands you come from.

- But I cannot.

- Why not?

- They are a different language. You do not speak it.

- What do you mean, a different language?

- The land.

- And do you have family there?

- Nae.

- Why not?

==

- Will you not tell me, dear friend?

- My clan cast me out, when I was a babe.

- But how horrible! And yet you say it calmly, as if it were nothing to you. I guess you have hardened your heart to it. Why did they do it?

- It is what they do to ones like me.

- Do you mean... ?

- With my twisted leg, my deformity, yea. And my face, like a Dwarf's it seemed to them.

- My God, you must hate them.

- Nae.

- But why not?

- It's what is done. Such a babe will die. He will bring a curse upon them. The anger of the beasts, the gods. The curse of a Dwarf-born child.

- What is a Dwarf?

- One of the old gods.

- And your people believe these are evil? The old gods?

- Not evil, perhaps. But you don't meddle in such things.

- But they are not real?

- Yea, they are real.

- But how could it be—do you say you were born of such creatures?

- I don't know. Maybe not. But my mother was rejected and forbidden from men forevermore, for fear she was cursed, or had relations with one of them.

- How terrible.

- Nae, for in some of the western clans, like the Dead Bear Clan, the mother is killed for such a thing.

- My God.

- But my sister wasn't like them. She was born to the wrong place. An angel, she was. And she cared for me.

- I thought your people didn't believe in angels.

- Nae, but she was one. She heard those teachings of your Savior, from the priests who came. The teachings of kindness. She loved those stories. She risked her life to save me, and so I live.

- Poor Rufus, you say it as if you regretted it. Do you regret it?

- Every day.

- Rufus. I am sorry if I have hurt you, bringing up such memories.

- You cannot hurt me.

- What was her name?

- I cannot tell it.

- Why not?

- Most don't give their women names.

- How awful!

- They are called 'the daughter' of someone, or 'the wife' of some other... But if someone loves her, he gives her a little name. Something to call her by.

- Did you give your sister a name?

- Yea, but I cannot say it, for we believe that names go with us when we die. To say it is to go there at the wrong time. It is dangerous.

- To go where the dead are, you mean? Your sister died?

- Yea.

- I am sorry.

- She came to the Red Fen that night, where they left me. She saw me when I came into this world. I was her only brother who was younger. The others were older and beat her.

- And is it common there, for men to beat women?

- Yea, but she was brave. They told her the forest would eat her, and she braved it for me. She became my mother. Raised me there, in the forest. Nursed me from some animal she found, but I cannot remember now. I only remember the warm, the fur.

- But that is amazing. I can hardly believe it.

- Nor I. I never knew a beast of the North Forest to love a human.

- And your sister lived with you in the forest?

- Nae, but she came near every day. Brought me food. Helped me learn to hunt though she didn't know how, brought me weapons to learn, though she wasn't allowed to touch them. Told me stories.

- She was brave indeed.

- Yea.

- And you learned to survive, then, in that forest, the most primitive, violent forest—where even Sirenian warriors almost never go?

- Yea.

- Isn't it full of dragons?

- Yea.

- And no clanspeople ever saw you?

- Nae, for if they saw me, they would kill her. For rescuing me.

- And you knew that, and kept yourself hidden.

- Yea. For eleven years.

- My God. But didn't you meet other hunters, in the forest?

- Nae, for they did not hunt in the forest.

- Not even the Barbarians?

- Nae, for the danger of it. The beasts make war on the people. And the dragons, too.

- But you were able to hunt there. And live.

- Yea.

- How?

- I learned to hunt the hunter-creatures, so I knew their lairs, and they could not hunt me.

- Did you hunt dragons?

- Yea. But not to fight them. Only to know where they would be. When you find where the dragons are, you come to know the forest, and nothing can harm you.

- And weren't you lonely, all those years?

- Yea.

- You never met another boy or girl?

- Nae. I went sometimes into the moors, where I should not go because the people lived there. But I loved the moors. I went at dusk, when the people kept close to their villages. And I watched them at their fires. I smelled the woolie-meat cooking. I saw the girls in their dresses. I saw the boys fighting. I followed their paths long and long into the night, touched their footprints. I wished, sometimes, that they would find me, even if they wanted to kill me.

- I have never seen another Barbarian, besides you. Do they—do they not look like you?

- They look all different ways. Different clans. Different dialects. Red hair and fair, big boned and small. Dark skin and light, all the colors of the earth. We come from so many places, over many times. We are not all one people. It is the Sirenians who call us one. It is the Sirenians who captured us all in one name—the name Barbarian.

- And Leo. Leo sees you as one.

- Yea. Leo does.

==

==

- But, it seems strange that no one ever saw you. In all those years.

- Nae. It is because you do not know the moors.

- Because it is so easy to hide there?

- Nae, because they are... Because they are vast. Like the sea.

- No tree grows there?

- Nae, for the Barbarians and the woolies keep it. Once the deer kept it so, but they are gone now.

==

==

- Tell me something else, about your sister.

- Her hands were soft. She was ugly like me, only not so much. She was kind.

- Did she give you your name?

- Yea, she named me Rufus, for it was a common name, then. Many of us in that clan had the red hair.

- But you are called Rufus James.

- James is the name I took, when I lived in Sirenia. So I would be like one of you.

- Are you proud of being a Barbarian, Rufus, even though they cast you out? You do not hate them.

- We are all proud. It is in our blood. I am one of them, more than any other thing. I am not animal, nor Sirenian.

==

==

- Well... I see now why you love that land. For the land raised you, did it not? You were all alone out there, except for your sister.

- Yea.

- You cannot tell me something of it?

- The moors I loved best. And the beautiful, dangerous places.

- What do you mean?

- The beautiful forest places, with the fern and lily and moss, where the dragons nest and play. The streambeds running off the river—they guard them. The dragons guard the beautiful places. And the Dwarven-built wells. Just a hole in the stone that led to darkness, but always clear, and always with a tree growing by it, white and stunted and older than anything. It is said they lead to other worlds from which we cannot return. But I feared nothing like that. When I found one, it held me. It held me close. They are everywhere. All over the forest.

- What are they? What are they for?

- That I don't know.

==

==

- What a strange, magical place. I wish I could understand it, without going there, for it frightens me, but it is haunting how you tell it.

- Where did your people come from?

- From a cold, northern country, too.

- That is why you are pale.

- But it was not like your country, I think. Not so wild and beautiful. There was a great city there. We were persecuted for what we believed. Because we would not make sacrifices to the gods they believed in. For us, there was only one God, and the Savior His messenger.

- And the people of your city were frightened. They thought if you didn't respect their gods, the gods would bring vengeance.

- How did you know?

- It's like that, with the Barbarians.

- But Rufus, you don't believe in gods, do you?

- I don't know. I don't believe or not believe. I am not clever, nor wise.

==

==

- Well, what happened, then, when you were eleven years old?

- I went in search of another clan, since mine would not have me.

- And your sister?

- I could not take her. A big man kept her now and would not let her go.

- A cruel man?

- A cruel man.

- In the end, then, it was her home that was most dangerous for her, not the forest.

- That is so.

- Could any woman survive such a life?

- Yea, if they were strong and lusty like men, or knew how to flirt and play in the way men like, so that their men would protect them.

- But your sister was not like that.

- Nae, and she could imagine things—worlds—that others could not. Her imagination hurt her. She used to dream we would go together to the kingdom of Sirenia.

- But why didn't you? Why didn't you take her there?

- We did not know how to find Sirenia, then. We knew nothing.

- But you knew something. She must have heard stories, to want to go there.

- Yea, she told stories.

- Like what?

- Like your people would be kind to her, and gentle. Your god was kind and would not let anyone hurt her. No beasts hunt you. You wear robes like apple trees wear blossoms, and you go in carriages pulled by tame dragons. And there are so many people, it doesn't matter what you look like. You cannot ever be lonely. There is always someone to play with. And food is served to you at a great table, whenever you want it, and you don't have to hunt it.

- Those were the stories she told?

- They were.

- It's funny, the dreams people dream.

- Yea. But for a long time I did dream of it with her. I practiced my skills. I wanted to protect her. I wanted to be in the place she spoke of. Then I grew impatient. I could not wait any longer for a land that seemed only a dream.

- Then did you find a clan that would take you in?

- I was very careful. I searched and watched for a year, or more. I found a clan not so violent—the New Lion Clan—who left offerings to the beasts, and did not kill them. I came in the morning, for they're less fearful then, more curious.

- And what happened?

- Five warriors beat me, and then I could not get up again.

- That was how they greeted you? And this is the less violent clan?

- Yea, but it felt good, to fight with other men at last. They did not kill me. They only laughed. They fought me for sport.

- My God. And then?

- The lord of that clan said he would not kill me, for I fought bravely, but I must leave and never show my face there again. And I had an idea then, from being desperate. I remembered that most clansmen feared to hunt in the forests. I told him, I will kill a spotted stag for you; then let me stay. And he laughed, for he did not believe me—but he agreed, because he thought if I survived the forest and did such a thing, it must mean I wasn't so cursed, after all, and would not bring harm to them.

- Is it difficult, to kill a spotted stag?

- Nae, not for me. But I never killed one, before that time.

- Why not?

- They were beautiful.

- Why, Rufus. Only because of that?

- Perhaps because I am so ugly.

- Oh, Rufus.

==

- Rufus, you are beautiful. You are a poet inside. Only you hide it so well.

- Nae, I am not a poet. But to hunt—it is like searching for an answer that is never found—that is the only poetry I know. The hunting.

- And the clanspeople never killed those deer?

- Nae, for long ago, those deer lived in the moors—they made the moors as they are, bare of forest and open to the wind. But they were so mild and gentle, and men killed so many of them—the stags for trophies, the does for their pelts—that all who remained ran into the forests at last, where the beasts guard them now. There is so little prey left to go round now, and the beasts will not share. It is the reason the beasts hate us—for we took the abundance of the earth from them. We have only the woolies now, those creatures some of our people brought with them from another place.

- But you killed a stag?

- Yea.

- You must truly be an excellent hunter.

- I am that. And nothing else.

- So what happened when you brought it back to the clan?

- They made me do a woman's work, butchering and cooking it. They made me watch while they ate it.

- Ah, Rufus!

- Nae, but it was a test. I knew it.

- Did you pass it?

- Yea.

- And?

- They took me in.

- So you lived with them? You were one of them, then?

- I thought so. I lived with them for three years.

- Did you love them?

- I don't know. I had no friends, not real ones. I drank with them, warred with them, slept among them. But they did not trust me. I was too quiet.

- Too quiet?

- Barbarians are loud. It makes them feel safe. Did you ever sing to yourself when you were a child, when you were walking in the dark?

- Yes. I did. If I returned from some chore that took me out late at night...

- Yea. My sister, too. She learned it from her kin. They all sing in the dark—they have songs that protect them—and they are always making noise. It makes them feel brave. But I could not be loud that way. I had lived too long on my own, learning how to be silent.

- Yes, I understand. It is hard to change what you've learned to be, even for something you desperately want.

- That is so, Queen Ella.

- And so what happened, after those three years?

- A man nearly killed me. It was over a woman. But I got away.

- Ah, there was a woman, then.

- Nae, not for me. Not for one such as me. But there was one who toyed with me one day, one that I thought would have me.

- Did she want you, this woman?

- She wanted something, I could see that. I used to watch the women, try to find one that seemed lonely. For most of the women are owned, in a clan, by the strongest men. Only a few men own all those women, and so they get lonely and forgotten sometimes, and the other men are lonely, too, who have no women of their own.

- What a horrible system. It makes no sense.

- Nae, and fights break out.

- So you found one who was lonely.

- Yea, and I came to her in the dark, when her man wasn't around. And she played with me until I could not think, and would do anything. But she was confused, see, for she wanted to satisfy her loneliness, but if she had a child by me, she feared her man would kill her. For the child might look like me.

- I see.

- And so she began to scream—her fear was more than her desire. By the time he came, though, I had gone. I ran and never came back.

==

==

- Where did you go?
- Back to my sister. I wanted to see her again, to know if she lived.
- And did she?
- Yea. But I killed her.
- Rufus!
- Not with my own hands, but she died because of me. I was a fool. I came to her window, called her with the call we used to call. Her man grabbed me and I shook him off. Then they welcomed me. They took me in.
- I don't understand.
- It was a trick. Three days later my father murdered her.
- My God. Rufus.
- For what she had done. Because they saw she had rescued me, those years ago.
- Oh Rufus, I am sorry. But why did you expose yourself like that?
- I could not take it anymore.
- Take what?
- The loneliness.

==

==

- I am sorry, Rufus. We will not talk of it anymore.
- I killed him, then. My father. And her lover too.
- My God. Are there no laws, among your people?
- The strongest wins. Every death is avenged. Those are the laws.
- But there was no one on your side.
- Nae. But the moors always took me in. They knew me. Nothing soft is there, all the grass is sharp, and the bushes shaped like a fire. But it's like my Rowana. It gives you nothing, no comfort, but once you've slept on its breast, you can never be without it. Nothing else can ever seem as real...
- Rufus, you are whispering so low, I cannot hear you.

==

- Rufus, are you awake still?

==

==

==

==

- Yea, my Rowana was like that.

- Mm... I fell asleep. I thought you were sleeping. Who is Rowana?

- Rowan, wife of Prince Leo.

- Wife? But Prince Leo... How could he have a wife?

- Yea, he does.

- But I have never heard of her.

- Nor has anyone, in these parts. But the Barbarians knew her.

- What became of her?

- I don't know, for I left her again. Three times I left her.

- Rufus, what is wrong? You are crying.

- Nae.

- But you are. Is she the woman who asked you for mercy? You must tell me.

- Yea, but she was only a girl then. No more than seven years old. Queen Mona ordered me to kill her. She was stepdaughter to Queen Mona, Rowan was.

- Queen Mona... The Barbarian wife of King William—cousin to Sol's mother. I remember, it was fifty years or more ago now. Something happened, didn't it? William was trying to gain power over the Barbarians, and so he actually lived there for many years, married to Mona. But he failed. He grew ill and died, I thought.

- They always fail. Even Leo will fail, in the end.

- Why do you say that?

- There is some old magic there, in that land. Rowan used to say, no man will ever be able to keep it. There is an old magic.

- What kind of magic? Does it have to do with the Dwarves?

- Yea. But it is female.

- What do you mean?

==

- Rufus?

- I don't know.

==

==

- Mona was barren, I heard. I never heard of any stepdaughter, or any other marriage.

- There was no other marriage. Rowan's mother is the Faerie Queen Rhiannon.

- Rufus...

- It is a long story.

- Tell me. Why did the queen order you to kill this girl?

- It was the mirror. A mirror does something to a woman.

- What do you mean?

- What happens to you, when you look in one?

- I don't know. I am used to them now. But I remember when I was young, I was afraid to look.

- Yea. And did you never wonder who invented the first mirror?

- I suppose I never heard. Though it was not long ago we first saw them... Perhaps twenty, thirty years ago. How strange!

- It came from Rhiannon, not long before that. She came from out of the dark wood and offered it to the Barbarian queen, Queen Mona, through her window, and Queen Mona took it. Then Rhiannon took William's heart, as payment.

- But did this mirror have some kind of magic, some power, that it was paid for so dearly?

- I don't know. But it seems to me...when a man feels a thing, he goes and acts upon it. But when a woman feels a thing, perhaps she may not. Mona was trapped and lonely. She could not act, but only turn the feeling inside. The mirror showed her herself, very beautiful. She looked in there... and she fell in.

- I suppose it is true that men cannot be driven mad by such things, for they are valued for other things than beauty. And with all their lives of danger and action, they have no time for looking inward that way.

- Yea.

- How do you know so much about her—this queen?

- I knew her.

- How?

- I was her servant. Her huntsman. After the things that happened to me, I offered myself for the job. They wanted a huntsman, for their others were all killed in the forest. No true huntsman of the clans would come to them. Only I would come, who was an outcast and wanted death anyway.

- And the child—you weren't going to carry out the order to kill her—were you?

- I don't know. I took her into the forest as Mona commanded me... Her hand in mine, she stumbled, she weighed nothing, like a piece of cloth floating behind me... She asked where we were going, I said I did not know. She knew I was honest and did not ask more. She trusted me.

- My God. What were you thinking?

- I thought nothing. I wasn't human anymore, not then. But she spoke to me again. She said, "Why are you afraid?" And that stopped me.

- Were you afraid?

- Yea. She was a strange child, with a sight. A sight that cannot see into a mirror, but only out and out, beyond...

- Rufus, when you have that haunted look in your eye, it frightens me a little.

- She fell to the ground and put her ear to the earth. I thought perhaps she listened to voices in there. Then she looked up, and she knew. She said, "Please don't kill me."

- Were you about to?

- I had my hand at my dagger. But I didn't know it, until she said that. And she did not beg, no. But it was as if the earth told her something. It was her first time being out there, in the wilds. Before, she was all her life in the castle or the convent. But the earth spoke to her, I know. Told her some terrible crime was to be committed, against the order of things. And she would be its victim.

- What did you do?

- I ran.

- You ran? You mean you left her there, in the forest?

- Yea, for I was not human then, not anymore. But something woke in me. I wept all night, in the moors alone. I knew then what I had lost. You asked when I became a man. It was then.

- And you did not return to find her, a child left alone in the wilderness?

- Yea, but she was gone by then.

- Oh! Why did you do it, Rufus? Was Queen Mona that frightful that you really meant to carry out her order?

- Nae, not frightful. But she had a power over me, before I became a man and broke free of her.

- What kind of power?

- I had only her, after my sister. But I hated her. She tortured me. It was all she thought about—her own beauty, and the effect it might have. She told me... She told me she would let me do things if I killed a dragon for her, or some other feat. I lay awake at night thinking of her, what she did to me. Stared at my wanting, made me come to her and touched me just enough to make me shake and then took her hand away—for I disgusted her.

==

- I have said too much. I forgot you are a lady, though we have spent these nights together.

- No, Rufus, it is not too much. I am no lady now.

- She was a wildwoman of the clans. Every man wanted her. She enchanted them all. But then she faded there and turned bitter. William stopped wanting her, for want of the Faerie Queen. The clans rejected her, for marrying him. She was alone in all the world, and it turned her to madness.

- But you must hate her terribly.

- Not now. I understand her.

- What happened, after you lost Rowan in the forest? You never found her?

- Not for ten years. I went to Sirenia then, like my sister wanted.

- After all that time? Why then?

- I became a man that day, that day Rowan spoke to me in the forest. I broke free of Queen Mona's power. I didn't want her anymore. I only wanted myself back, and to know I was good. I wanted to start again, somewhere else, and be better.

- Did the queen let you go?

- I never came to her again. I killed a fawn and sent her the heart by messenger, told her it was Rowan's.

- Did she really want Rowan's heart?

- She was Barbarian-born. For a Barbarian, to eat an enemy's heart is to claim their power.

- My God.

==

- So that's when you came to Sirenia. I suppose you didn't find the world of love and acceptance your sister dreamed of.

- Nae, but it was better than where I came from, in its way.

- Did our people treat you better than your own did?

- They did not wish to kill me.

- Yes, I suppose that's an improvement.

- It is the same everywhere, how people look at me. In Sirenia, everyone looks the same—at least it took me a while, to tell you apart. I looked even more different there, and that made them stare. But I wasn't the only strange one in Sirenia. I learned where the others lived, in those darkest, wettest places.

- The ones with Hummingbird ancestry, you mean, or—or...

- Yea. All of those.

==

==

- Yet you learned our language, and befriended a prince! It is amazing, when you think of it.

- It was only natural, living there all those years, for me to learn your language. I came to the king and asked if he needed a huntsman. He didn't, but he posted me as a guard, along the Golden River where the Barbarians used to raid. I don't know why he trusted me, but he did.

- And was it lonely?

- I did not like it much. Nothing ever happened. Some nights I walked into the city, though it was a long way, for I wanted to feel a part of things. I paid for women. I made a few wary friends, outcasts like me. Then, after a while, people began to pay me for other things, and I didn't have to work as a guard anymore.

- For your detective skills?

- You could call it that. I'm a hunter, and nothing more. But I learned to hunt in the city. I learned to hunt the things people lost. Or the children they lost, or people they loved or wanted.

- What makes you so good at it, do you think?

- I don't know. I am used to being alone and watching, and listening. I was always on the outside of things, trying to figure out the way of people.

- It is true. You can become almost invisible.

- It was from hunting dragons, that I learned to hunt anywhere.

- What do you mean?

- When you hunt a dragon, you learn the patterns. You come to understand.

- Understand what?

- Understand... I don't know. The place you are in.

- How?

==

- Try to tell me. If I were to hunt a dragon, where would I begin?

- You would walk a long time, until you were lost. You would follow what was beautiful. And then... The things begin to look like other things. All the twisted little saplings look like frozen fires, ready to spring to life. The big trees bend and crouch. Everything begins to look like something else, until everything is everything. For I think—maybe—that trees have grown to look like animals, on purpose, for they share a language, and all are mirrors for each other.

- Mirrors...

- Yea, and... Well, you speak of poetry. When you have wandered a long time and are lost, soon the forest begins to grow a kind of poetry, the way it surrounds you. You look for the poetry, the patterns the ferns make on the ground, the tree trunks leaning in to make tunnels.... You follow it, and it's always moving. When everything changes like that, and becomes nearer, and becomes more and more itself... Then you know you are nearing the dragons. You are nearing where they are, I mean. But they are not always there. The forest will change shape tomorrow, or when the light changes later in the day. The forest comes together around them as they pass through it, and you see it then, if you are there—you see it how it really is.

   - How what really is?

   - The world.

   - But there are no dragons in the city.

   - Perhaps there are.

   ==

   ==

   - How did Prince Leo kill so many dragons, then? If they are so hard to find, and if you need such a sensitive soul as yours to find them. You told us that once, years ago, he killed one for every clan! That's how he won them over. Is it true?

   - I was gone from the Northlands then, but it's what I heard.

   - How did he do it, then? How could it be?

   - I don't know. But once I wondered it aloud, with Rowan. And she turned to me as if I should know and said, "The Dwarves helped him do it." But I don't know what she meant by it, for she never explained things, once she said them. It was rare she spoke at all. Yet I believed her, for Leo claimed the same thing.

   - You're going to tell me that part of the story, aren't you? How you met Rowan again, and fell in love with her?

   ==

   - Rufus?

   - I never stayed up all night long before, just talking.

   - I have. Sol and I used to do that, when we were young.

   ==

   - Sleep seemed so unimportant back then. It was all wild feeling and... and wonder.

   - I know.

   - Anyway, I remember when you left Sirenia. You never told anyone. You just didn't show up for a while, and then we found out you were gone. It took us a while to realize, since they said you hardly ever came to the feasts anyway, you were so mysterious. But Sol finally summoned you. He said it was about time he gave a feast in your honor, to thank you officially for finding me and bringing me to him. But that's when we found out you were gone for good. Sol said you would never have refused his summons.

- It is true. Prince Solon—King Solon, I mean—was good to me. He showed me respect. I would always do as he asked. He did not need to pay me.

- He did respect you, very much. He envied your free life. You fascinated him.

- I hope he would not mind it, what we've done together these nights.

==

- Would he mind it, Ella?

- I don't know, Rufus, to tell the truth.

- Was he faithful to you?

- No, Rufus, he was not.

==

==

- Did it hurt you?

- It used to, once. Then it didn't anymore. Or not as terribly, anyway.

==

- So you have not said why you left us.

- Ah, it was only... I woke one morning and felt afraid. I had never felt afraid, before that. But I thought, if I stay here much longer, I will disappear.

- What do you mean?

- I don't know. Only that is what I thought.

==

==

- What do your people believe happens to you when you die, Rufus?

- Ah, we go to a land of endless summer, of course. Food in plenty that is always falling into your hands. Flowers the size of a man, and nothing hunts you. Warm and safe, with a warm soft sea all around—not the hard, cruel sea that comes sharp against our rocks. A land where you make love and sing all day long, where women are plentiful and full of longing and enough for every man.

- That's funny. Aren't the Barbarians too tough to dream of such a luxurious afterlife?

- But they do anyway. It's in their stories. And when your priests talked of the place called Heaven, they thought it was that.

- Oh! They never described our Heaven so luxuriously, with so much pleasure for the senses. It sounds more like what I've heard of the South Forest, actually, the way you describe it.

- Ah? I do not know. I have never been there.

- Nor I.

==

- You've never told me why you can't return to your homeland again, now. Why Prince Leo wants to kill you. But now I see, it's because of the woman, isn't it?

==

- Rufus?

- Yea.

- Well, what happened? You returned to the Northlands, and then?

- I bought a horse, and I rode there alone. When I came there, Ella—when I saw those ridges like the backs of dragons, those grey, hungry greens—I wept again. Two times in my life I have wept. Once, when Rowan gave me my manhood back. Once, when I returned to my homeland.

- It is strange that you ever left it.

- Yea, but I had to. Now it was different for me, see. I'd grown older, and could return now. I was twenty-five years old, and I thought, "The worst has already befallen me." I did not expect love or friendship or happiness, but I did not think anything could hurt me again. I thought that here I would find peace, and I said to myself that no woman could ever hold my heart the way these lands could.

- But weren't you loathe to be so alone again?

- Yea, a little. So I went back to the castle, for I heard tell that Queen Mona and her king had fallen, and a new warlord ran the place. I thought of asking there for a job, like I did before.

- What happened?

- I came upon the castle... I remember it. I saw perhaps three hundred Barbarian men—more than I ever saw before in one place—outside the walls. They were soldiers. They were training.

- My God. That was the beginning.

- Yea. It was strange to see them there, in the mists. It seemed to me they didn't belong.

- But they were Barbarians.

- Yea, but in a strange shape. Standing all in rows, one behind the other. I never saw such order there, in the Northern wilds. It didn't seem right, somehow. But I went on, and asked for the lord who ruled there. I thought a man who ordered his armies so coldly would not care if I was ugly. And I was right. They took my arms from me and led me to the Hall, which looked all different, hung around with weapons and no pictures, and I thought a Barbarian must rule here. But the man who greeted me had fair, Sirenian hair. There was no welcome in his eyes.

Yet he sat me at his supper table, and fed me, though I could not eat for everyone stared at me so—in a way I could not read. Not like Barbarians normally stare, with their fierceness clear upon their faces. These Barbarians who trained with him were different. And he asked me why I came, if I wished to join his army. And I knew for certain then that I did not. I did not wish to be owned like that. But I asked if he needed a huntsman. He thought awhile and stared at me, and I stared at him right back. Then he told me I spoke differently, as if I were foreign. I told him I was a Barbarian, but had lived in Sirenia these ten years. Then he stared even longer. Then he told me we would speak in private, after the supper.

- Could you tell, then, how terrible he was?
- I did not like him.
- Did he like you?
- I do not think he liked anyone. But he trusted me. He said I did not seem like much of a talker.
- Well, that is true enough! Why did he wish to talk to you in private?
- He had an errand for me. He asked if I could navigate the forests. I told him I lived there alone for almost all my first fifteen years. He told me if I satisfied him in the secret errand he gave me, he would hire me as huntsman. If I betrayed the secret, he gave me many threats of the pain I would receive from him.
- What was the errand?
- He told me that all fifty of his prize horses had broke free, and I must find them and return them. I told him it was likely many would be dead. He said he knew that. So I agreed. I tracked his horses. That was easy enough. But while I was tracking them—I was in the forest, and trying to avoid the beautiful places, trying to keep focused and away from the dragons. But one place drew me. It was a place I remembered, though I wished not to. The place I'd left Rowan, those years ago.
- Yes?
- She was far more silent, more stealthy, than anything I ever hunted before or since, so I would not have seen her, even being so close—were it not for the creatures.
- The creatures?
- I found the trail of two spotted deer, which seemed strange, for they are always in herds. And I heard so many birds, more than I ever heard before in one place, and many kinds. Six or seven willowets, a flock of scarlet doves, and many little creatures which ran away when I entered the clearing.

- And you saw her? Rowan was there, where you'd left her?

- I saw a lioness, resting by the waterfall. This was near the little rivers of the high north, beyond the Source, where the Dwarves are said to live beneath the stones. There was a waterfall, coming down from those plateaus and into the forest. It was one of the beautiful places. She lay there with her head raised like a queen and her eyes on me, as if she'd watched me coming forever—one of those black forest lions of the Northern Primeval, with fur as sleek as skin. When I entered the clearing, she rose up and roared. It was a sound so big, it blacked out my mind, and it was like I returned to my own birth and knew nothing. But the deer stood still and did not flee. The roar was meant for me, not for them. They were at peace with her.

- And—what happened? Did you run?

- Nae. For it was Rowan. And I knew her.

- How? How did you know?

- I cannot explain, Ella. It was like I saw two things at once. I saw the lioness standing and roaring, and the death in her mouth. At the same time, I saw within or behind her—as through a veil, or a dream—a maiden with bright, bare eyes full of winter light, and hair as black as the lion's, but with a tender heat inside it. I could feel that warmth as if I touched it. She was weeping into the waterfall. Seventeen years old. She is half a Faerie. She has not aged since.

- Did she see you?

- Not at first. She was weeping into the waterfall. She was calling into the sound of it. She was calling for the Dwarves. Pleading with them to take her back. She had a strange way of speaking. Her words all broken, like stones rolling through water, but I could understand them. She spoke the Barbarian language, see, but there was that other language in it, too—the Dwarven language.

- But she was also a lion—at the same time?

- She was so many things. She could change her shape all the time— and especially in the wilderness, free of the castle, she could be anything and everything at once.

- And weren't you frightened?

- Nae. Because all at once I knew her. I knew I had always loved her. I did not mind, whatever she could do to me. I knew then that I belonged to her, and to nothing else, whatever happened. She was my reason for being—she had made me a man.

- So you didn't run.

- Nae, but I did leave, slowly. Not because of the lion's roar but because of the maiden's face, when she turned and saw me. She looked at me as an animal looks—she froze as the deer freeze, without knowing they are beautiful. You could see she did not think of her body at all, or know the kind of wanting I felt. She was like a part of some great motion, the motion of the river and the earth, and I was not a part of that. And as soon as she looked at me, I knew I interrupted her in something sacred. She did not want me there. And so I went.

- It's strange what we call beauty. How we define it. What is it, after all?

- I have often wondered that. Jade, her son, once told me that we find beautiful the thing that reflects what is inside us. I liked to hear that, for I thought—sometimes I thought, maybe—that I loved Rowan because there is some beauty inside me, though you cannot see it.

- I can see it, Rufus.

==

==

- But that is why she could not love me. She had no ugliness inside her.

- I do not think it is so simple as that, Rufus.

- Nae, you are right. There were other reasons, too. She could not love anyone. I came too late for that.

==

- So I continued to hunt the horses, and I gathered them in the moors and roped them together, and I led them back to the castle of Prince Leo. All the horses that were left alive. Twenty of them. The sun was setting. I was leading them across the moors, and after a while, I could sense that we were followed. We were hunted.

- Was it—Was it Rowan, in her lion form?

- I don't know what form. I could only feel her, sense her—but not see her. Ella...never before had I walked with someone on the moors. Never before had I felt a presence that went where I went. And though I did not know for what reason she hunted me, and I knew if anything she might come to kill me, I cannot describe this feeling of joy. This place so beloved to me, to share it with another—who loved it, too, who knew it... I walked on and on, like in a dream, and sometimes I felt that we spoke together, or as if the moors were speaking for us. It was wonderful, to be hunted over the stones and heather that way, and to feel the horses moving all around us, going with us, white ones and red ones and black ones—Leo's most beautiful horses. The first time I met Rowan, when she asked me for mercy, I became a man. The second time... The second time, when she hunted me on the moors, I grew a soul.

- Oh. I believe you.

- By the time I could see the castle above me, beneath a lake of silver clouds, I felt her so close. So close that the wind was her breath, and I turned and turned around, and I felt a hunger worse than I had ever felt for a woman, in all my body and soul, and I could not bear it. All the hunger of my life had led me to this moment. At last I was dizzy, and I stopped and lost my breath, and she was standing there. The terrible path was before us, the outer ramparts, the soldiers who could already see her from the dark towers. And I knew somehow, before she said anything, that I had failed her again.

- She spoke to you? She was a woman then?

- She said, "I will go with them now. He will not hurt them, if I go to him." And I understood all at once—ah, I understood that she was Leo's! That she was Leo's captive. That somehow I had been tricked—I had been told I was sent to capture horses, but truly, I was sent to capture her. And I had done it. I had served his plan.

- What do you mean?

- I asked her what she meant—for Leo would never hurt his prize horses. And she said yes, that he would do it. He would do it if she disobeyed him or tried to escape. I told her no, I told her he must be lying to her. She didn't believe me. She was their protector, see. And she was the one who had set them free, so that she, too, could be free—without consequence.

- But why, Rufus? Why would you obey Leo in anything, even to hunt his horses? Even if you didn't know about Rowan being his wife?

- I don't know. I am stupid. I was desperate, and I told her I hadn't meant it, that I was sorry, that I would help her escape now. But she looked at me... And she looked down at my hands! I knew then that she remembered me. She remembered the dagger in my hands, and that I would have killed her once! Also I knew that she was like me. She could not think beyond this. She could not think of some other life, some other way. She could not free herself, not then. She went with the horses. Yet she went bravely. She went for love of those creatures.

- And she didn't trust you.

- Nae, and I did not trust myself. I could not feel confident that way, to take her somewhere else. I did not think she would wish to go with me. There was a kind of terror all around her. The soldiers had come down, and they took her by the arms, they took her away.

==

==

- And then what did you do, Rufus?

- I became Prince Leo's huntsman. He wanted to keep me, for the way I looked like a Dwarf. He was trying to convince his people that he had an influence with the Dwarves, who were the old gods of the land.

- And did you see her again?

- Yea, but it is another story. You must sleep, for tomorrow you are a queen again.

==

==

- Rufus?

- Yea.

- Was she weak, or was she strong, do you think?

- Rowan? She was both. She was the hunter and the hunted. She was both, to me. She was everything.

- But not to Leo. He did not see her strength, I think.

- Nae.

- She escaped him in the end, didn't she?

- She did.

==

==

- Do you love me, Rufus, in a way?

- Yea. Rowan is my wild queen. You are my queen of the hearth.

- I think I am too soft to win against him.

- Leo fears the softness, more than anything. He fears he'll sink. There is an emptiness Rowan left him with. He's afraid.

- And you? Did she leave you, too, with emptiness?

- Yea. But I live there gladly.

Ella

When I first heard news of the Sickness as something other than a minor scourge of the swampy ghettos, my first thought was not of your welfare, my people. I clasped Sol's hand under the table. My first thought was of losing him—of losing anything I loved, anything I had never deserved.

The royal family was speaking of priests that night, whose job was to humble the kings and queens who—in the old world, before the Savior came to us—used to be divine. The priests were saying now that the Sickness came as punishment, that the brothels must be closed, that the masses must be brought into the old cathedral for cleansing. That it must be given to them to decide what steps should be taken—for this was a case to be decided not by sovereigns, but by God.

"I thought the role of priests was to preserve the Word of the Savior through the teachings of His apostles," the king was grumbling, "and that's all—just pass on the Word."

"Surely the Savior's teachings are relevant outside the chapel," put in Narsa. "They are not just words we repeat. They are lessons we live by. And we are going to need them now, for a darkness is coming." Alden nodded at her with a respect that touched me. He was kind to his wife, whether or not he had married her for love. He laid his spoon down.

"Of course," he said, "but I think what my father means is that although the Word of the Savior must influence our every decision, it is not the priests themselves who should make civic decisions."

"This is a medical concern," agreed Sol just to say something, speaking with sumptuous ease around the food in his mouth, and I could see his mind idling half in and half out of the conversation. *Aren't you afraid?* I was thinking. We were happy then. Sol had been faithful to me for some time. It seemed that fatherhood had brought some sense of responsibility into his conscience after all—something I used to hope for and then gave up hoping for. I took my children to watch him in every tournament. I still hungered for him, and he for me. The queen was looking sour. The king stopped eating and placed his elbows on the table, flexed his fingers, worked his tongue around his mouth.

Sol said, "Once, long ago, let's say our people spoke directly with the Savior, and He spoke to us. Now such a thing is almost forbidden. The priests stand between us and Him. But the whole point of the Savior was to connect us with God on a personal level!"

No one answered. Sol looked up. "Wasn't it? Wasn't that the point?" Kiera smiled across the table at him.

After a while, the king nodded. Like Sol, he was more interested in complaining about the priests than addressing the disturbing news of disease. "It's all well and nice that the Savior paid us a visit," he said, "but here's the news, my friends: the world is just the same as it ever was. People are still corrupt, and the priests appointed to manage the corruption are the most corrupt of all. They enrich themselves with funds given for charity; they make decisions based on favoritism and their elitist power structure—"

"They condone violence and prejudice," Alden murmured.

"It's rather like falling in love," continued the king, and I could see now that he was drunker than Alden, on this night. Alden was mostly alright. "You meet a lovely other, you praise his or her perfection, you get married and determine that everything will now be happily ever after, and then it isn't, and you end up hating each other."

"Are you saying, Sir, that our faith in the Savior is like a failed marriage?" asked Narsa, looking at this point too horrified to continue eating.

The king shook his head and avoided the question. "Nothing has changed. Men are barbaric, women are whores, and everyone wants to step on someone else's head to get a better view of someone else going down."

"But that will all be over soon," said the queen, speaking at last, now that she had quietly finished eating (she never rushed). Her hands were in her lap, her face still. "What you speak of is the reason for the Savior's coming, after all. He is coming again to wipe this corruption from the earth, and those of us with our faces turned toward Him shall ascend with Him to the Kingdom of God."

"Mother," said Sol, the only one in the family who ever seemed to contradict her, and I knew he did it just to be contrary, "this is some sickness festering in the slums. This isn't the apocalypse. This isn't the final judgment. I know where you get these ideas—those hysterical cults who think they speak in tongues and faint in ecstasy over supposed divine communication only they can hear. They're everywhere these days."

"Not everyone who speaks in tongues is a fraud," said Narsa, trembling with anger. "God communicates to those who are willing to listen. Only two hundred years since our dear Savior died for us, and already we have gone so far astray! You are too cool in your complacency, Prince Sol. You live a life of luxury here in Sirenia, and you forget our ancestors who brought us here were willing to suffer any torture or death for their faith—so absolute was their experience of that divine connection, they martyred themselves for it! Think how He will judge us, when He comes."

I held Sol's hand beneath the table, but in the enjoyment of his argument, he slipped it from me.

"And what kind of life do you live?" he asked Narsa, leaning back, enjoying her discomfort. "Not one of luxury, I gather? Are we to assume you undergo secret deprivations in private... Alden?" He glanced at his brother, who scowled, but lightly.

"The question in all of our hearts is, will we ever see our Savior again?" said Alden. "And it frightens us, to see how much we've lost touch with the Savior's true message. It saddens us to see the world falling apart all over again. Deep down we fear that we will never feel His presence again the way we did once, long ago, and that's why we are becoming belligerent about our beliefs."

"We?" said the king ominously, but he was eating again.

"We impose our religion on the Hums, for example, because—"

"We need the South Forest," said the king, waving his hand carelessly. "That's why we *impose* our beliefs—to get them to be civilized and work with us. We need the timber for building—it lasts better in the swamps than the timber in the North Forest, which serves as a barrier between us and the Barbarians anyway."

"I'm not speaking of timber," said Alden.

"Well maybe you should. Something more practical than—"

"So what's your theory then?" said Sol, staring now at Alden.

"It's the way we live," said Alden. "The luxury, the noise and fastness and carelessness of the City—We must let the priests tell us what to do, because we don't have time to think on it ourselves."

"Speak for yourself," said the king. "You sound like them. The priests. *We're all sinners and must repent.*"

"No, of course not; the point is love. He loved us, and loves us still, and because of it, we are inspired to love each other."

"Except we're not," said Sol.

"No," said Alden. "Because we've lost the place inside ourselves in which to receive Him. Look." He pushed his plate away and began to speak with his hands, his eyes brightening. "Have you ever seen something so beautiful—a certain sunset, or a wild thing you'd never seen before—so beautiful that you didn't know what to do? Almost as if you didn't have a place inside yourself to hold such beauty, to understand it, to digest it. And all you could think was, 'I must tell so-and-so later... I must tell someone about how beautiful this was.' Already you are thinking how to describe it in words, thinking about how you will remember it later, because you have no way to take it in right now. It's too much." He looked around eagerly, but no one responded.

"It's because only our souls can receive such beauty," he continued. "And when we are shut off from our souls, through the noisy actions of our daily lives, we can no longer access them when we need them. We have forgotten that our souls are the vessels in which to receive Him. The only thing we can do is sell Him to someone else. Like the Hums. Or whomever. And we don't do it lovingly, either, because we can't really feel His love anymore."

The truth was, with every day that went by, I admired Alden more and more. He would be a good king. He might even be the kind of king they spoke of in legend, who could re-make the world with righteousness. I hadn't really thought, before, about the plight of the Hums, but I thought about it now, since Alden brought it up, and I knew his motivations were always noble.

It was Kiera who broke the silence. We all looked at her in surprise. "Do *you* believe He'll be reborn, though?" she asked Alden, with touching little-sister respect. "Like they say?"

Alden sat back, relinquishing his quest for any response to his theory, and smiled at her. "I don't know, but I don't think we should sit around and wait for Him, or for the apocalypse either. We must live as if He is alive right now. Because He is."

"Maybe He'll resurrect somewhere else by accident," said Sol. "Like the South Forest, or Zara. Wouldn't that be a joke?"

Alden ignored the jest in his brother's voice. "Well, after all," he said thoughtfully, "we don't know that it will be here in Sirenia. No one has said that it would be. Only that it would be here on this continent, which really is larger than we've ever explored."

Sol, who had finished eating, leaned back and hooked his elbows languorously over the spokes of his chair. "What about you, sister?" he said, grinning. "What are your opinions on all this?" For a moment,

I wished, just a little, that he might have asked me. Didn't he want to know my opinions, the opinions of his wife? Or did he think that the opinions of a commoner could not match the education level of the royal table? But I was ashamed, for really I did not wish for him to ask me—no. It was true that I would have nothing to say. I hardly knew what I thought.

Kiera swallowed and kept eating, unruffled. I was struck more than ever, when I watched her at the table, by how adorably she straddled childhood and adulthood. She tended to speak passionately with her cherubic lips still churning open around her food, both wise and ill-mannered at once. She was both poised and naked, careful and careless. You couldn't look away from her. "What do you mean?" she said. "About what, specifically?"

"Well, about the priests, about..." Sol leaned forward, took a loose breath, drawled with a jovial wave of his hand. "About how we relate to the Savior in modern times—all those lovely things that Alden was saying."

Kiera nodded. "I think they're lovely," she said.

"And is that all?"

"Let me think on it," she said. "I don't like being put on the spot."

Sol laughed, but there was tenderness in his laugh. "Fair enough."

"The point of all this," said the king suddenly, "if we could return to the matter at hand—"

"But Father," interrupted Sol, "it is so late at night to be returning to matters at hand."

"—is that we must separate, somehow, what the priests control and what we control. They cannot very well have a say in every damned thing."

"But that is actually part of the problem," said Alden. "More and more, they are instilling in us the separation of our spirits from the rest of our beings. In their system, they represent the spirit—"

"While we, the monarchy, represent the body. Very well," said Sol, bracing his clasped hands behind his head and leaning back again. He grinned at me—the first time he'd looked at me during the conversation. "Then I will happily take the part of the body. I, Prince Solon Cygnini," he deepened his voice to lend it a stiff, mock gravity, "shall undertake to play the role of the sinful, corporeal form, while the holy priests shall play the role of the spirit. Yes, I accept gladly! Someone has to do it, after all. Let the play begin!"

Kiera giggled. Sol narrowed his eyes at her. "You, on the other hand..."

"I don't know about the Virgin Bride, though," said Kiera suddenly. "That's what I have to say."

"What?" said Narsa.

"I mean, was She really a virgin?"

"I don't know," said Sol. "But you're going to be, sister."

Kiera sighed with dramatic exasperation. "Oh, stop. I'm just saying, it's still debated—even among the priests, to some degree," she said. "It's still an open question, exactly what Her role was—"

"Yes, but it's not you who should be asking that question," said Alden.

"*Everything* is debated," said Sol. "That's what's so ridiculous. The priests act like only they know the true word of our Savior, but the truth is, they completely disagree among themselves about what He said or did or anything. No wonder we don't trust them."

"I trust—" Narsa began.

"It's all horseshit," said the king.

"My lord," said the queen, and her voice held power, though she restrained it.

"Woman is sinful," continued the king. "Woman, to be more exact, is *sin*. Some say the Savior's Bride was His temptress, sent to test Him, and not his Bride at all." (It was customary, then, always to use the word "Bride," when speaking of the Savior's wife, as if to honor the sacred ceremony of marriage while negating the long years they spent together fulfilling that promise—it is something I have wondered about since.) "I say He could not have had such a bride. No woman is so pure as to stay chaste throughout a marriage and then take her own life out of respect for her husband when he dies. As they say She did." He spat each word, laughing without humor.

"You only say these things to be horrible," said the queen calmly.

"Those aren't the only possible histories," said Alden reasonably. "They could have just had a normal marriage, with normal relations, and been faithful to each other."

"Hmph," said the king. "Well, it's a pressing question, and it will become more so, for women these days are gaining power, wouldn't you say, Princess Ella?"

Mortified by his sudden address, and the eyes that turned toward me, I froze. Fortunately, the conversation quickly retreated from me, like a wave, before I had time to answer. They hadn't really wanted to know my thoughts. It was only a sort of joke, to pretend to ask me.

"Personally, I don't believe a woman can be that pure," the king concluded.

"I am pure," said the queen. She was not defensive. She displayed no emotion at all. She was calm, as if she knew herself without a doubt to be right. But everyone at the table tensed—I could feel it.

The king said nothing. He scowled. I sensed he'd been momentarily beaten, not at the level of argument, but at the level of his heart.

"Although," added the queen, "I would not kill myself if you died. As queen, it would be irresponsible of me, of course. For the Savior and His Bride, it was a different situation."

As Sol and I ascended to our rooms—or rather to my room—that night, we stopped at a window between stairways to gaze at a starkly delineated crescent moon in a clear night sky. The breeze hovered under the archway and pressed strands of my hair to my lips. Sol held my hand.

"My parents don't sleep together," he said.

"How do you know?"

"Everyone knows," he sighed. "She says it's a mutual agreement they came to after Kiera was born: a chaste marriage, in honor of the Savior and his Bride." Another sigh. "He says it's because he refuses to sleep with her, to punish her for executing one of his mistresses, a long while back."

I squeezed his hand, surprised and frightened and I don't know what else. I looked at that moon, razor-sharp. "That's terrible," I said. I didn't even know what I meant. Which part was the more terrible.

He squeezed my hand back. "Do you think so, Ella?" he said low, almost whispering. "We'll never be like them, will we?"

I shook my head with vehemence. "Of course not," I said. And then, "Sol?"

"What is it?"

"Do you think it could come here, to us? The Sickness they're talking of?"

He didn't look frightened, but he thought about his answer for a moment longer than I liked, and then answered, as I had, "Of course not."

♛   ♛   ♛   ♛   ♛

In the city they were calling it the Poor Man's Fever or the Poor Man's Curse. It was common then for sickness to settle like a constant fog among the poorest of you, for you were left to build your floating huts in the lowest, marshiest channels, where the water hardly moved, and sewage festered, and floors rotted and walls molded. Without access to burial grounds, and lacking funds for such, you lay your dead directly into the bogs, which seemed to devour them—but there was disagreement as to how fully they disintegrated there, and you lived in the stench of ghosts. Things lingered there, perhaps, that should not have lingered.

The rest of us hardly turned our heads, at first. Yes, we were that cold-hearted. Eventually, the king sent soldiers into those districts to keep the peace, but did nothing to investigate the cause of the deaths. I suspect that deep down he believed those areas ought to be thinned out a bit anyway, however that thinning came about. One of the reasons he didn't take the Sickness seriously, I think, was that the priests did. They were all raving back then—*He is coming for us, take stock of your souls.* Such talk made the king irritable.

But I was waiting for it, long before it was the common talk of the palace. The first time I heard of such darkness, and the way it moved—the way it surprised people, families, whole communities, with death—I felt certain it moved with some hidden intelligence. I believed the priests. I believed the queen. If ever God decided to reach out and take from me what I had taken unto myself by sinful magic, this Sickness, I thought, would be His hand.

I remember the day Alden told his father of a "witch" who had been burned alive in her home, to appease the dark forces who were causing the Sickness. I was nursing my younger son beneath the willows, watching Anna and Jonah catch frogs in the pond, and I tried not to listen. Jonah was always gentlest in Anna's presence. When they played together, they moved almost as one being. Anna, only two years old, watched over Jonah like an angel, and he trusted her utterly. Normally he was a brooding child, prone to sudden fits of wailing I could not understand, but Anna could often quiet him with her little kisses and whispers. Jonah was barely a year old then, and of course today he denies any memory of her, but I think she took a piece of him with her. That day he watched her to see how she held her hands in the water. She gave him her soaring smile. Then she chanted a little "fairy spell" over the frog, maybe to transform it into something else—I never knew, because I stopped her halfway through, leaping up and crying, "Anna! No! We do not cast 'spells'! It is an offense against our Savior." She burst into tears immediately, and I held her, but I could not speak the apology that burned in my breast, because I saw Narsa watching me coldly, and I knew I hadn't been able to ignore Alden's conversation with the king after all.

Landowners came to lay out appeals and disputes over property rights because so many had died. Widows came to argue claims. Lords came to beg assistance for their villages whose members were turning lawless in the wake of a madness that seemed to overtake infected people in the last hours of their illness; or they came to beg revenge for the death of their children. The most commonly blamed were not the witches but the Wyes, whose wealthy ascension over the past few years in Zara had already drawn much attention, and whose city was suspiciously free of the disease. Had they set it upon us?

Alden agonized over the mistakes he felt we'd made. We hadn't done enough to alleviate the famine last year. We hadn't addressed sufficiently the crowding in the poor districts; we had procrastinated the re-channeling of those waters. We hadn't done enough to form better alliances with the Wyes so that they might share their medicine with us. At last the king charged our best doctors to determine the cause of the illness and even offered a high reward for any Wye doctor to come and assist us with his expertise. But none came.

Kiera repeated, at dinner, things she had heard, and she was upset. I remember her saying that whole families would sometimes die in a day. She said that grown men who seemed healthy in the morning could be dead by evening. People were saying you could get sick if you looked upon one who had died of it. They were saying you could get sick if you had wronged someone who died of it. They were saying you could get sick by smelling a rotting corpse, and that the only way to survive was to carry flowers against your nose all day long—and all the gardens had been raped and decimated by desperate flower-pickers. They called it the Torment, for the way it drove people mad, first through a succession of physical attacks—itching and searing, random pain—and then by infecting their minds, ruining their speech, obliterating all memory of their loved ones, wracking them with suspicion. Some people got well again, but most died, and you could never tell who would recover and who would not—for it did not favor the young or the old or the weak or the strong. Sick people scratched themselves so badly, in their torment, that some began to call it the Bloody Madness. They stopped calling it the Poor Man's Curse, and simply called it the Curse.

The priests (who were also dying) said that God was clearing the land, making way. Many of you really believed this was the apocalypse so long forecasted. You ached to believe it. There is always great suffering before a time of rebirth, you said; when we are in crisis, when we fall so deeply into despair that we lose all orientation, then we are alone with God; then He is beside us, and there is nothing left but Him. Believing this, many more people than ever before began to collapse in the streets in religious ecstasy.

But it wasn't always religious ecstasy that caused you to do this. It was the Sickness itself.

I remember the servants found a peasant family hiding with the cows in the circular enclosure at the base of the silo. God knows how they found their way in, but it must have been difficult, for they were pretty badly scraped up, and one of the children had broken his arm climbing down from the wall. They said they thought they would be safe in the royal palace. They said they knew that God would never touch us here, for we were His chosen ones. I guess they hoped to hide here and somehow survive, as if somehow we might never find them. They had lost their minds from fear. We felt sorry sending them back out into the streets, even though they received no punishment and we mended the child's arm. We thought we were casting them out of paradise. We were wrong.

I should have known the end had come when Kiera stopped laughing. Balls and other events were temporarily put on hold, but Kiera didn't mind; she didn't feel like dancing. Whenever I wasn't with my children, she was with them, huddling over them, as if she sensed even more than I did the danger we were in. She and Anna became inseparable. The king and Alden moved about with stormy brows and did not speak to us. The queen spoke to the people from a boat near the shore to reassure them. But there was a pile of rotting bodies just outside the market place, and even if there had been room to bury them all, everyone was afraid to. The rats were eating them.

I spent every morning and evening in prayer. But I couldn't feel it. I felt like a liar, and there was panic in every word I spoke. My children grew afraid of me.

When Narsa begged Alden not to go out and help the dying, he refused to heed her. But when I begged Sol, he stayed. To this day, I don't know whether it was his weakness or mine that kept him. But he wasn't meant to be strong like that. My Sol was never meant to be king. It was Alden whose soul was a hero's, whose destiny as king was foretold not only by his birth but by his selfless love for his people—and for this very reason we could never have him as king after all. This, I would learn, is how the world is made.

I knew he was right to go, but I had never seen Narsa weep before. I had never before felt sorry for her, as I did then, and still do.

Kiera had to fight her entire family for the privilege of helping her people. Even I tried to dissuade her, and Alden for a time refused to take her with him. Her father forbade her to leave the house and threatened to lock her in a tower if she disobeyed him. She said, "Mama, they are dying alone! When they get sick, they are abandoned, and they die in agony and alone, without even their families beside them! And no one to bury them, or give them their last rites! It is too much, Mama. It is too much."

In the end, it was Solon who defended her longing.

"You may lock her up," he told his father, "but I will free her." And he rebuked Alden for demeaning her with his protectiveness. "A person must be free," he said. "That is all that matters. A caged, protected life with no risk, no adventure, no inspiration for the soul is no life at all. Sometimes we must risk our lives in order to have a life worth living."

Alden and I were both surprised. "But I would not expect this of you, Sol," protested Alden. "If anything, you protect her more fiercely than anyone. To travel about in the city and engage more with the people is one thing. She can do that once this is all over, if that is her desire. But how could you allow her to take a risk like *this*?"

"It is not mine to allow or disallow," snapped Sol, turning from Alden, and I knew he was just as afraid for her as Alden was.

That half a moon when Kiera was leaving the palace every morning to tend to the sick, the dying, and the bereaved among her people was the only time in her life when she was truly happy. I know this from the little time I knew her before, and because Solon confirmed it years later with his own perceptions. I know it because she so often came home weeping. That was when she finally learned how. She wept for her people, but I think she wept also with relief. She had found a use for herself, a purpose through which to give the gift of her dazzling presence to the world—not by dancing for beaux or flirting from within the gilded cage of a carriage, but in a way that dearly mattered to her. I am sure that even the dying were cheered by the sight of Kiera's smile, and that the sickest child would be soothed by the kiss of her lips upon its brow. If she feared for herself, she never showed it. She seemed bouyed by her own sense of purpose, as if she believed that in acting for a purpose of utter good, she would be protected by God. I think perhaps I believed that, too.

I consoled myself for my comparative selfishness, thinking, *She does not have children she must protect.* But that is not the truth. For she would have protected my children as if they were her own. She thought of all the world's children.

I remember watching her alight from her boat one morning from my tower window, with Anna in my arms. I heard doors banging, murmured cries, and a storm of fabric against stone as the family rushed down to greet her (for she had been missing overnight, and some feared she would never return), and though she apparently came without Alden, my first reaction was one of relief. She lifted her skirts with her usual neatness to step onto the dock, laid her little gloved hand in the one held out to her, and bowed her silky head with grace, her hair simmering in wild white sunlight. She floated into the inner hallways and disappeared. I kissed Anna's head, turning to go down, but Anna—who had been watching Kiera's arrival with me—looked up at me with a quizzical concern in her eyes.

"Ghost?" she said.

What I thought then, I do not know. What she said made no sense, and I could not reason why she said it. It was a word she knew, a word she perhaps tried out at random, as children will do, or perhaps associated with the eerily white shining of Kiera's hair in that moment's sunlight. But before I knew it, I was running down the winding stairs, erupting through archway after archway, all the while gripping Anna in my arms. I did not even think to put her down, and she did not cry out, but held fast to me as I ran. I pressed her to me as if she were my last hope of rebirth, my only salvation, my only angel, my one and only antidote of joy against the graveyard of my past which I was forever, forever escaping and which forever pursued me. I pressed her to me and would not let her go, because she was my first child of this new life; she was my little girl; she was my second chance at innocence, at childhood, at love. And forever I wonder, if I had not held her so tightly in my fear, if I had set her down in the nursery with her brothers that morning, instead of carrying her down with me to greet Kiera, would she have lived?

For I don't know how the sickness spread. No one ever knew. But I know it infected not only the mind but also the heart. It affected every feeling—physical and emotional—that makes a person what they are. Anna was all heart, and so was Kiera, and their hearts were entwined. And if anything could have passed from one person to another that would spread that awful death, that death they called the Curse, I think it was the look upon the face of one so cursed. It was that look in Kiera's eyes, when Anna and I saw her.

She still held her body tall with dignity, and yet there was a rigidity to that dignity which I had never seen before, and her face was grey. Her eyes were cold chambers that had forgotten the light. I don't know how any child could survive looking into those eyes. Tears had made engravings through the dust upon her cheeks, so that she looked like a statue.

"Alden is dead," she said. Sol rushed up to her—for he had entered just behind me—and she fell like a little tree into his arms.

Narsa instantaneously lost all trace of the woman I had known her to be—a woman I would never see again. She tore at Kiera's dress and hung upon her arms, screaming and blaming and begging Kiera to tell her why she had abandoned him, and where—*where is he, or damn you to Hell*—until the king wrenched her from his daughter's helpless form and held her screeching in the crook of his not-too-gentle arm. Even in his age, even in his drinking, the king remained physically rugged; it seemed nothing could diminish his lusty strength, even the weariness of his own soul, and in the end the Curse never touched him.

"They said they would keep him for us," murmured Kiera earnestly, beneath Narsa's screams, and I could barely hear her, for I had not moved from my frozen position. "They will keep him, until we come back for him."

"Who, darling?" said Sol, tightening his hold in order to lift her face closer to his own. "Who will keep him?"

"The kind merchant," she said. "I am sorry, Sol, I was so tired. So tired and they said I should get home now, and then come back later..."

Sol looked up at me through the forms of his parents, who also leaned over her. Kiera was delirious. Alden was dead. We would never find his body. I would have done anything to soothe the horror in Sol's eyes. I felt that somehow he expected me to—needed me to. He depended on me for comfort. Yet what could I do?

Narsa ran from the palace, then, screaming for a boat. On her way out, she scooped up her son in her arms, for he was standing, sobbing, near the doorway, having gone out to watch Kiera's boat come in. He loved boats—loved being on the water or near the water for any reason. That's the only thing I remember about him.

The king turned away from his family then, stiffened, and then amassed himself like a dark cloud and swept away in ominous silence; and then he drank, and then drank some more, and as Kiera continued to sicken, he bore down upon every servant, high or low, with unbridled fury.

The queen sat by Kiera's bedside as she tossed in her fits of pain and delusion, at one moment tearing her mother's robes as she begged—"please, please make it end, Mother"—and in another moment drawing back from any one of us, accusing us of playing some trick on her, or being demonic copies of our real selves. The queen's face was like a diamond, never loosening, but her tears fell so fast and hard, they dampened Kiera's quilts, and her eyes never left Kiera's face, and for all her hardness of pose, she seemed not to be aware of anyone else's presence; she seemed hardly to know where she was; and before Kiera was dead, she, too, had sickened.

Sol sat equally helpless by Kiera's side. When I asked him to help me move her, or fetch fresh cloths, or request some broth, he did everything he was told: he did it in a stupor. The look of bewilderment and disbelief that had overcome him when she first fell into his arms never left him. Behind us, Anna hovered in silent compassion, staring at her beloved aunt from the doorway for I don't know how long, before Sol discovered her there, crouching with fatigue, and whisked her away to a nursemaid. That last look on her face, the last look I ever saw, was a look of fear.

While Sol was out of the room, Kiera grasped my hand and turned to me in a moment of clarity. "Ella," she said, in her old, sweet voice, "it is like I told you. We have everything but we have nothing. It is all a dream and a lie. Beneath it is only darkness. Even love..." She shook her head, her face contorting again, but her voice was still calm and forgiving. "It is all a lie."

And I could not even protest or reassure her, before she closed her eyes again, for her words echoed all my own deepest fears, and upon hearing them uttered by someone as cherished and sinless as Kiera, I had not the wisdom or strength to deny them.

Kiera was barely more than a child when she died. She died a maiden, a virgin, more desired than any woman in the kingdom; she died still wondering what romantic love might feel like, and never had the chance to find out if any man could give her the joy and wonder that she gave simply by existing. I did not see her draw her last breath, for by evening I was ill. For me it began with a lightness in my head, a taste of insupportable bitterness in my mouth, and a shocking weariness that swept through my bones as if they were decaying inside me, and it began after the High Priest came to us, standing like inevitable doom in the light of Kiera's doorway.

"I have come," he said, low and strangely breathless, "to inform your Majesties that I have determined the cause of this curse upon the royal house. I think you already know it in your hearts, but it is my duty, as you have charged me to protect your souls, to proclaim it openly."

Sol stood up, ready for I know not what, a look of battle upon his face. But the priest looked at the queen, whose head remained bowed over Kiera's. "Long have I foreseen the dangers of your younger son's marriage to a common woman of mysterious past whose girlhood was spent—according to my sources—largely on the streets. A woman whose previous history of sin is still unknown. A woman whose own mother—"

"Enough!" shouted Sol, and I clutched the bedside to arrest my dizziness, as I realized I had left my body during this speech and was only just now returning. I knew now. I knew that my children's need for me and my fear of infecting them wasn't my only reason for avoiding the samaritan path Kiera and Alden had chosen. I feared that even if I went out among the people to do good, I would not be a force of good. I would be part of the Curse: perhaps I had even caused it.

But Sol *shouted* at the priest—I had never heard him shout so. "Away with your stupidity, it is you who sin! For in our time of grieving, you seek to deny us even the comfort of those who are left to us!"

The priest sighed. "My good Prince Solon, I have seen how this woman deludes your senses and poisons you against God's ways—"

"Go!" came the roar of the king behind him, and he was bodily thrown backward by a mighty hand. But while he sputtered and stumbled, I watched the king's posture deflate almost immediately with the weariness of sorrow. "Go," he repeated, turning from the priest in disgust. "I have done with you and your sickly ways. I do not know what God looks like, but I do not see Him in you. Go and be grateful that banishment is your only punishment for attempting to dishonor my family. Know that you shall not see my face again and live."

When he re-entered the room, I bowed my head in shame, but no one was looking at me; they were looking at Kiera. I was shaking so hard I thought I would come apart. Kiera opened her eyes and looked at me, and for a few seconds the old teasing light danced there—I don't know how much she had understood, but she seemed almost herself in this moment, and seemed almost to laugh, with me, at the silly old priest, as if she would mock him with me later, when we might stand again upon the bridge with my children and gaze over the moonlit water. I listened to the king's footsteps recede behind me. It had been the only time I ever heard him speak of God as if He existed. And it was the first time I knew for sure that these were my family now, and that I could never be cast out from them.

I am glad I never got to see Alden in his final hours. Kiera was younger than me, and though her last hours of madness were torture to us all, they could never sully the essential purity of who she was for me—she was only someone good attacked by an evil that infected her from within. But Alden was something else for me—my ideal of all that was dignified and poised and wise in royalty. He was the all-knowing guide, the dream of future paradise. I needed to remember him that way. To this day, that memory helps to guide my actions and decisions. I don't know what it would have done to me, had I been forced to witness him descending into madness and decay, as Kiera did. Even imagining it, I could hardly forgive him his mortality.

Some of you know and remember what it was like, to be Cursed. How you lost yourselves in every nightmare you'd ever dreamed. How repetitive sounds, like raindrops on the roof, seemed to lacerate your flesh and slam the last drops of sanity from your mind; how certain scents, for no reason, arose from where they should not—the scent of roasting meat from the latrine, for example—and made you vomit and cry. How your loved ones seemed only to mock you with the seeming care of their attentions, while it seemed to you that they were themselves the cause of these sounds and scents—that they were in fact creating them remotely, by magic, only for the purpose of toying with you. How everyone joined forces to haunt you, living and dead. How you suspected, as Kiera said, that everything good you had ever believed in was a lie.

I thought the queen was my old stepmother, and I wept and wept, telling her how sorry I was for my deception—my foolish attempt at escape, my sinful pretending to this other, better life I had been living. Only Sol appeared to me as himself, neither cruel nor mocking. But I kept begging him to tell me if he were a ghost, for I felt certain that the Savior would take him from me in punishment, that he would sicken, that he had already sickened, that he had left me—and I could never believe him when he denied it. I saw a sorrow in his eyes so crushing, so unfamiliar to me in that place, that in my maddened state I could not interpret it in any other way than to assume he was a dead man—only returned briefly to say goodbye. I knew the Savior was coming. Everyone had said so. I knew He would take my beloved, my prince, away to a Heaven as beautiful as he was, and leave me alone.

I dreamed that the sin of magic I had made beneath a waterfall in the dim recesses of the wild River Golden was a living entity that flew into the air, something like my idea of the dragons in childhood stories—snake-like, yet winged. It flew away to the top of the world. I dreamed the Urodel turned to mud, and then blood. I dreamed that dragons made the rivers flow, and they could make them flow in any form, and all this time we had assumed rivers must run water—but they could run anything. They could run death instead of life. And it was my fault. I pleaded with the Savior to take me instead of my daughter, instead of my children, instead of my family. But He never answered me. Instead, I felt myself pummeled beneath the waterfall until, thrashing for air, I was suddenly stilled to calm by the hand of my mother, whom I could not see, clasping mine underwater. When she did this, I knew for the first time since the night I first prayed for entrance to the ball that I wanted to live. I, Ella Cygnini, whether I deserved it or not, wanted life. And as with that first prayer, prayed hopelessly over a grave, I learned to my surprise that when I wanted something, no matter how selfish I might judge myself later, I was stronger than I knew.

When my fever broke, the queen was still alive. But when word came that she wished to see me, I did not even lift my head. I was curled up in my bed, my whole body bent to the shape of Anna's as I held her corpse in my arms. I did not know where Sol was, and I did not care; I did not feel I deserved him. I thought, *I have done this*. What better proof that I was the cause of the Curse, than that I myself—and my beloved prince, whom I had made dark magic to claim against all odds—were the only ones who survived it? And how cleverly I had been punished. The dearest gift ever given to me, now taken away again, and I didn't even see her go.

When the servant came the second time, some long time later it seemed, to tell me the queen absolutely commanded my presence and would not be denied, I lifted my head and considered the girl from the faraway dreamland of my grief. She seemed some oddity to me, something out of place in my world, as if from another country. "It does not matter," I said senselessly.

"You must come," the girl repeated. She was simple and stubborn and without compassion, but when I thought of her later, I admired her for stolidly continuing with her duty day after day in this household of death, knowing that she, too, at any moment, like half the rest of the household, could sicken. "The queen commands it. No one can refuse the queen."

I was holding my daughter, thinking, *I will never leave you alone again.* But the servant said, "She is the queen. You must go." And even in my delirium, I remembered what that queen had taught me, about how to carry the crown. I must do my duty. It was the least I could do. Did I draw some final wisp of pleasure from holding my child's body in my arms?—then yes, I must relinquish even that. I did not deserve it.

I laid Anna on the bed and stood up. "No one touches her," I said, in a severe, certain voice I didn't recognize. Then I went to the queen in her own chamber, a place I had never before stood. The king sat beside her, his face in shadow, but when she saw me she brushed him away. "Go," she said. "I will speak to this woman alone."

The queen's bed was decked in heavy red brocade, and her dressing table was of gold and glass, and all the floor and the walls and even the ceiling were carpeted with velvet and tapestries, which seemed to billow in the wavering light of the candles as if in some imaginary wind. I did not pay much attention to my surroundings. The only thing I could think was how she had called me a "woman" for the first time.

"Come here," said the queen from her bed. "Periodically I seem to lose my mind, and I must speak to you before the next time I do."

I sat upon the edge of her bed, looking down upon her. I felt no fear. What had I to fear?

"I am glad to see you are well again," she said with business-like calm. "My son and daughter are dead, and soon I will join them. I know about Anna. Your other children are well?"

I nodded. As far as I knew, yes. Though life had never seemed less certain. When I first woke, I'd screamed for Sol as best I could, in my weakness. I didn't know he was attending the death of our child. When he came to me, I grabbed him by the shirt, by the arms, by the hair. "You're alive," I'd croaked, "you're alive?"

"Yes," he'd said, shaking his head, "I'm alive." I'll always remember how he said it. As if it didn't matter.

I took her hand. "Queen Anna," I murmured, losing my voice the moment I found it.

"What?" she snapped. "Speak up. I am dying."

"Do you think the Savior will come now?" I heard myself ask her. I asked as if she were my own mother, as if I were a child and she were all I had to save me from the senseless chaos of the future, the crushing question of life.

But the queen, ever stoic in her devotion, ever the most graceful example of faith, the one who had quietly asserted for so long, without defensiveness against the king's or anyone's mockery, that surely the Savior was coming and that God's salvation was utter and real, never answered me. Whether it was the question I asked which caused it, or only a sad coincidence, I will never know, but she immediately lost herself in one of the "periodic" bouts of madness she had warned me of. Her eyes rolled backward into her head as if yanked by some demon behind her, and she arched her back with a wail and began to writhe and scratch so mightily at her sores—which I only now perceived in the darkness—that several servants I had not seen came running from the corners of the room to hold her down and bathe her face with cool water. During that time, she frothed and sweated, and the sounds she made were so unlike her, I believe it may have been these which caused me to weep later, when I returned to my room and broke down for the first time, knowing I cried for more than just my daughter and Kiera and Alden. I cried for the collapsing of the world.

When she finally recovered herself and refocused her eyes upon me, I had no time to ask my question again, even if I could have recovered myself enough to ask it. For she spoke to me with sudden urgency, as if her imminent death had become more obvious to her and left her no time for idle talk. And the words she spoke were perhaps the most frightening I had ever heard in my life.

"You will be queen," she said.

Fortunately, I had some time to digest the shock of this obvious truth, for the queen seemed to struggle with her next words—whether from fatigue or from delicacy, I do not know. She did not seem to notice the look on my face. "Solon..." she began finally, and then stopped. She reached toward my hand, then, and for a moment I was astonished to think she would take mine in hers, but she did not. She seized up again and began to choke and writhe, more quietly than before, and with enough mental clarity to wave her hands impatiently at the servants as they came rushing back, indicating that they should remain where they were. But it was a long time before her suffering subsided enough for her to speak again.

"When he is king," she said finally, and much more faintly now, "he will need your help."

I nodded mechanically.

"He is not meant to be king," she said. "But he will be, never the less. I will tell you a story before I go, Princess Ella." There was coughing then, and intermittently throughout. "Many years ago... I don't know how many—fifteen? Twenty? Perhaps more. My husband had an affair with my dearest lady in waiting." I must have drawn in my breath, for she made a weak, brushing movement with her hand above the bed, as if she could sweep me clean of unnecessary emotion by simply passing her royal fingers through the air. "Oh, don't look so surprised," she rasped. "He is only a man after all, and anyway it was not the first time. But she was closer to me than any of the others. She was descended from the Barbarian people, but so beautiful that a Cygnini man from my cousin's reign there had kidnapped her and taken her back with him. My husband's affair with her went on for years before I discovered it. And she was the only one I knew of who birthed a son. A bastard, but still a danger to the throne, and already ten years old."

Now she watched me very closely. Next to the bed, one of the candles flickered out. I heard footsteps running outside, but they passed on.

"When I discovered it," said the queen, "I had her killed."

I did not move. It did not matter. I knew she could read all my thoughts, just as she always had. I realized for the first time that for all I knew, she may have heard my ravings when I was sick and mad. She might know more about me now than I knew of myself. And yet she was dying, and I had nothing to fear. Only this moment mattered.

"I did not hate her," she continued. "None of this has anything to do with how we feel. We do what we must to maintain our power. I would have killed the son, but to kill a child is too great a sin, so I banished him into the Northern Forest and warned him never to return, under pain of death. I don't imagine he survived."

I looked down. "You're saying I ought to have—" I began, thinking of Leyla.

"I do not say you ought to have done anything!" The queen attempted to raise her voice, but only succeeded in triggering another coughing fit. "A queen does not dwell on past mistakes," she continued when she was done. "A queen does not *make* mistakes. I tell you this story only because I am dying, and you will be queen. And you must understand what is necessary in order to maintain your place. No one will help you to maintain it. At the first sign of weakness, all the world will seek to knock you from it. You must prove it to the people, and you must prove it to the court. You must prove it to Solon."

I looked at her. *I do not even want it,* I thought.

"And you must prove it to yourself," she added.

♕   ♕   ♕   ♕   ♕

Yet in the days that followed, I did not worry much about being queen.

It is selfish to mourn the death of one child when you have two healthy sons left, and it was nothing short of a miracle that my sons both lived. Almost everyone else in the kingdom lost more than I did. And yet I was never able to love any of my children the way I loved Anna.

When she died, I believed I knew without a doubt that my sin had killed her. I felt that my sin was responsible for the death of those I loved—for only the purest and the best of the Cygnini family had died, and how could they be at fault for it?—and no matter that they defended me, no matter that they never suspected me, I did not deserve their love. I had managed to forget the witchcraft I had practiced under the waterfall long ago. But now I remembered it with full force, and knew I had been living in denial in order to enjoy the luxuries of this fine life. Yes, Sol was still alive, he had not been taken from me—but at what cost? The life we'd known lay in ruin, and the fact that I remained alive, healthy and forever separated from the people who had loved me most angelically, was a worse punishment than death.

I prepared my daughter for burial but I could not release her from my arms. I could not give her over to any priest or any person who sought to bless or take her from me. I could gaze for hours into her face, and pretend she was sleeping. I could hover my fingers just near enough to hers to imagine that if I touched her hand, it would be warm and cling to mine. I neglected my sons. I do not know what Sol was doing all this time, for he only came once to the room where I'd locked myself away with her, and he came in a fury.

"Sol, doesn't she look—" I had begun when he opened the door, glancing up at him almost with gratitude, remembering suddenly that he was the only person in the whole world who might, at that moment, understand with me what really mattered—but he interrupted me in a tone of tattered agony, averting his face—

"Take her away, Ella!" he roared. "What is wrong with you? She must be buried."

I looked back at her.

"She is *dead,* Ella."

"But she is here with me," I said. "And I don't want to let her go. Not yet. This is all the time I have left with her."

Sol turned away and moved to leave me. I hated him then. "Ah, God," he muttered, scraping his hand upon the door in a strange clumsiness as he opened it, "I cannot stand it. It isn't her."

♛   ♛   ♛   ♛   ♛

In those first days of grief, I began to feel that Anna had never belonged to me, just as I never really belonged to this family. I belonged to the people, to the peasants, to the dirty, forgotten streets I had come from—and Anna, with her boundless compassion and fervent heart, who inspired the best in everyone who had come in contact with her—also belonged to you. She was my gift to you. Returning her to you felt to me like returning a gift from God that I had stolen.

As far as I know, no one saw me leave the palace with her body. I did not tell Sol. Why should he care? *He told me to take her away,* I told myself. *He does not want her.*

I thought that by removing myself from that palace, I removed the sin that was cursing it. I walked all day, preparing to release her, and preparing to die. For I felt sure that the Sickness would finally claim me, if I walked through it like this, the way Kiera and Alden had done. I did not understand that the Curse was finally fading now, nor know that the Savior had already examined me during my time of fever, and found me wanting. I had more yet to learn. I was not ready to come home. To die then was merely another selfish wish of mine.

The streets were at once desolate and full of madness. Fearful eyes haunted windows of darkness. Fires burned at every corner, until the heat was sometimes unbearable, and still they did not cover the stench. Occasionally a scream streaked across my path or above me; or a hysterical person, whether in agony or fear I could not tell, came rushing toward me as if in a comedy of ridiculous motion—I averted my eyes. Starving children in the alleys turned a game of tag into a theatre of death, with every child tagged pretending to fall into contortions. "The Curse, the Curse!" they cried, making horrid faces. I did not blame them. We thought the world was ending. We thought we would all be dead within days.

Yet without realizing it, I discovered something precious on this day that would support the heaviness of my path in years to come. On this day, I discovered that the social hierarchy which had oppressed my spirit for so long, making me tremble each day for the uncertainty of my performance within it and the insecurity of my height on its ladder of respect, was an illusion. On this day, I saw something of what humans are made of, and I saw that nobles and peasants are made of the same: terror in the face of the unknown; a fierce clinging to the reality we thought we knew; disbelief in discovering what happens to a body when God dismantles so easily that which He has built. Whatever people tried to tell me hereafter, about who was higher and who was lower, who played the game right and who played it wrong, I knew that at any time, the rules could change, and it is not we who change them. After this day, I was no longer afraid.

I followed the stench willingly, until I came to the great pile of bodies, but when I arrived I could not place Anna there. It was too much, just to be there. The way they were thrown there—their faces! Oh God—as if no one loved them! I sat in the corner of the square with my whole body curled around the stiff body of my child, and sobbed. I cried until the sun went down. I waited to die. But nothing happened, except that I lifted my head to find a small circle of people around me—not close—but close enough to watch me. You whispered. Your faces did not betray your intent, if you had any. Your clothes were dark, whether rich or poor I could not tell. I had been nauseous from the stench, but now I was not. It was because I had vomited on the ground. I saw that now.

You recognized me: Princess Ella. I know, because one old man came near me, his eyes giant upon their bony shelves, his thin white beard just brushing my feet as he knelt. You did not even know yet, any of you, who among our royal family was still alive.

"Did the fever take your little girl, Princess?" the man asked kindly.

I nodded. "I thought to bring her here," I said. "I thought I would..." I could not say it. I lifted her a little.

"Princess," he said gently. "You are upset. With respect, Princess—you don't want to leave your daughter here. You will bury her with honor, at the royal palace, of course."

"No," I said. "I have brought her here. She would want to be with her people. She would want to be—" I was crying and could not go on.

The old man stood. He looked back at the bodies, and then at me. He was thinking. How could he be so calm? "If you would like, Princess," he said at last, "I will take her for you."

I nodded at once, and the old man reached for her, but I could not seem to loosen my hold on her body. I looked down at her. I had not seen until now how disfigured she was, how her face was swollen and turning black. I gasped. What had happened? What was this? Where was my girl, my child?

"Come now," said the man. "She is no longer here, you know. The Curse has taken her body, you see, but her holy spirit has gone elsewhere. She has returned to the Savior. She is safe."

I remember, my people. I shall always remember. How you took the form of this dear man. "She is not here, Princess," you assured me again. I found my hands had loosened now, and gently you lifted her from my arms. I saw my hands rise up after her, as if animated by some other spirit. I seemed to reach for her, but you were walking away. I thought I would go after her, but I did not. I closed my eyes and felt her heart against mine.

What happened to me after that, I do not know. The next thing I remember, near dawn, I was walking along a tributary of the river I did not know. I could not see the palace. I wondered if perhaps I was dead. The swans were floating beside me, and their wakes made soft arrows in the water. The river was only water after all, still—not mud, not blood. The swans did not seem bothered at all—none of their family had been taken by the Curse. I could not see what moved them. They moved with gravity, but without effort. I followed along beside them, and found Narsa under a bridge.

She was crouching in the shadows, on a jut of stone just large enough for her body and no more. She did not see me. She was reaching out to the swans as they passed. I thought perhaps that she wanted to feed them something, but I could not see.

It seemed I woke from some dream, then, at the moment I saw Narsa lost in hers. It was as if I came to my senses because I knew that I could wake up, and suddenly I appreciated that ability, because Narsa no longer had it. I came down as close as I could to her and called to her, leaning over the water. She did not respond at first, and I was afraid she might have forgotten her name. But finally she did turn, and she looked at me a while, as if trying to place me.

"Where is your little boy, Narsa?" I asked urgently, because I feared that in her maddened state she might have left him somewhere. But at this she shook her head, and as she turned and reached out to the swans again, weeping out loud as they passed further into the distance, I knew. It was the same with her as it was with me and Anna. She'd brought him with her in order to keep him, and by doing so lost him. Perhaps she had given his body to the river.

"He is gone," I acknowledged out loud, to myself or to her I don't know. Until now, there had been suffering all around me, far worse than mine, but I could not feel it. I could feel this. I saw something I had never thought to see: Narsa broken. And the irony is that she saved me that day, even though I was never able to return the favor.

She would not come to me on her own, but when I reached her, she accepted my hand. I found our way back to the palace, and we took the boat home.

Sol waited for us at the dock, his face disfigured with worry. It panicked me, and I reached out my hand to him as the boat came in, crying, "Is it the boys?"

He shook his head. "No, they are well."

"Then what?"

He lifted me into his arms, ignoring Narsa. I began to shake. I had forgotten what his body felt like against mine, as if it had been a lifetime ago that I had known him, that he had been my husband, that we had felt passion for one another. I couldn't believe, still, that he was alive, that I could have this, still. When he pushed me back to look at my face, I wished he would keep holding me instead. I did not want that searching look. I only wanted to rest in him.

"Where did you go?" he demanded. "I thought—I don't know what I thought—I thought I would never see you again. Where did you go?"

"I'm sorry," I said, seeing the pain in his eyes. I saw that he really did need me. I saw that he would not be able to live without me.

"I've lost everything—I cannot lose you," he said impatiently. "Where is Anna?" And when he asked it, he sighed and pursed his lips and touched my cheek, and I knew that even amidst his deeper grief, he felt sympathy for me because he knew what she'd meant to me, and that touched me so much I felt guilty for what I had to say.

"I... I buried her in the city, in a place special to me, from my—from my childhood," I lied in a rush. I had a feeling he would never know. He would never see the city as it was right now. He would hear of it, and he or the king would send out those who could take care of the mess, once things had calmed down, but he would never really understand what I had seen, or that no one, now, could be buried.

♕   ♕   ♕   ♕   ♕

The next several moons were lost moons. I cannot say that much leadership came out of the royal household during that time. To direct the disposal of the dead was all we could manage—and we managed it, I admit, in the simplest way possible. You know how it went. The alleys of marsh where no one goes, no one builds, no one boats—anymore. And when those were full—the way our loved ones smelled when they were burning.

Yes. We royal ones were lucky with our graves, I know. The king spent most of his time beside them, in that place in the palace courtyard which is designated for our ancestors. Another priest succeeded the one he had cast out, though the former's expulsion was never forgotten by those loyal to him, and I'll wager it is haunting me still. This next priest didn't last long in our household either, but though he always seemed to me worn and uninspired, as if the plague had beaten his spirit from him, I remained grateful to him for overseeing the funerals of our loved ones. He said the usual words about rejoicing—how the Savior had chosen to take these good people into His arms—and I did not feel blessed, and I did not feel like rejoicing, and I hated all his words, but I was grateful to him anyway, in the end, for providing one simple ritual that felt like the way things used to be.

Some sense of order was necessary for those who lived on here. The servants often came to me with empty hands and blank faces, unclear about their roles and duties in a household where many of those they had served were dead, and the events their work had once revolved around were no more held. They seemed as unaccustomed to idleness as I had been when I'd first arrived here—and as frightened by it. What was idleness, but a collapse of all the structures that kept one from falling into that black hole Kiera spoke of? No one wanted to be alone. The servants seemed to value my industriousness, my plainness of demeanor, and my soft manner more than they had before. For now these things were needed. Now servants came to me for instruction. I was grateful to give it to them, just as they were grateful to serve; we all needed to do something. The issue of my pride no longer mattered to me. There was no longer anyone to impress, or whose favor I needed to win.

My youngest still woke often in the night, and when he did, both of us were restless. Instead of sitting up with him, I would pace around the palace, bouncing him as I circled the Hall, for it was winter then and too cold at night to go out on the balconies. No one stood guard. We had slackened our attention to such things. The Hall was empty, and I paced it so that I could remember those who had died, those of whom its emptiness seemed to speak. I stared at the glass hanging thrones, glowing just barely in the moonlight, losing myself until my baby whimpered again, and I must bounce him and walk, round and round. One morning I woke up in ashes, sleeping with him upon the cold hearth.

I don't know if you have ever noticed how the Great Hall is marked on each side by a sacred gateway. To the North, the thrones; to the East, the chapel; to the South, the doorway to the world; to the West, the hearth.

When I woke in cinders that morning, I felt an unexpected comfort in the familiar humility of desolation, the black soot along the side of my arm and face, like the dust of a sorrow so old, it did not even belong to me. It felt like what I deserved, and it brought me peace. Yet I held my child in my arms, just stirring now and whimpering again, and I must light the fire again for him. When I stirred the ashes, one coal glowed, and I gathered a little wood and started the flames leaping. And I remembered, for the first time, my duty as fire-keeper in the house of my father as something important. In my childhood it had seemed like just another task, one more thing I would be beaten or punished for if I forgot it. Yet I'd woken every morning in those cinders, and my first and last task of every day was to nurture this essential flame that kept my family warm.

Years later, some of you still know me as the Queen of the Hearth. I began that morning, and never stopped, for as long as I lived in that palace. I was the one who lit the fire in the morning, and I was the one who lit the candles in our upper windows each night to let you know we watched over you. I always tended the fire myself. I cannot explain to you why. I could never let the job go, even after. I kept it going for me, for my children, for my family, for you—for who we are, for whatever spirit makes our kingdom a kingdom.

♛   ♛   ♛   ♛   ♛

Five months after the day I left Anna in the city, the king died of grief. The queen had said she would never take her own life, if he were to die before her—that her role as queen was different from that of the Savior's Bride, that she had a responsibility to her people. But it was different for the king. Perhaps he did not really care for God. There were times in the past when I'd thought he did not really care for anything, least of all the queen. But it wasn't true. When she died, the emptiness inside him revealed itself in his face. We could hear it in his looming silence, which echoed every word we spoke. Without her, he ceased almost instantly to be king. His death seemed only an afterthought. There was nothing left of him, by then.

I'd never noticed, before, how soft the surface of glass felt against the palms of the hands. The double glass seats swung a little, heavily, when we sat upon them, but I never felt that, because by the time I sat, Sol was always there already, on his side of it, his weight holding the whole thing steady. I remember feeling surprised at the submissive silence of such beauty. The way it cupped us without protest, digesting the light just as before, scattering helpless rainbows upon the floor: I felt the cool clarity that shaped the queen, and the sorrow in everything, most of all a throne.

Lemara

the sorrow of the Roses

Once, long ago, when I was a little girl, I saw a Hummingbird woman who was raped by a band of Sirenian men. The elders were leading her deep into the Forest for the beginning of her long healing. They stopped at my Nuba palace and asked me to bless her, for I was a child then, with a child's innocent power of renewal, and I would also be Priestess one day. I don't remember what I said or did, but I remember the look in that woman's eyes. I saw that what I did meant nothing to her. I saw that where her life had been inside her, there was nothing now. Once she was a girl, too, and once a woman, who craved beauty, ate beauty like food. Now she could not even see beauty. She looked at me and did not understand what I had to do with her.

And you tell me these—these bodies in the doorsteps—these are my people? All my people look like her now.

We enter now what remains of the Forest, its edges drowned in Roses. The very Roses that protected me in my sleep now devour my sacred Forests, weakened by so many years of timbering. A thing is beautiful until it is all you can see. Then it is no longer beautiful.

For the first time in my life, I know this. A truth my elders never told me.

The Wye guide closes the carriage so that we will not be wounded by the thorns that thrash it as we pass inside. The road narrows. He is taking me to see the new Priestess.

They want to join forces with us, Micah told me. If I am to believe the word of this emissary. He has seen the Sirenian soldiers in our streets, the made-up taxes they collect, their increasing demands for space at our ports. He knows something of the pressure we are under. His prince thinks we will join him in challenging the Sirenians, perhaps, out of desperation.

And will you? I said.

I don't know. I don't know this prince. I don't know whether he considers us weak, for no one knows the way we train in secret. Perhaps he plots to win our allegiance so that like the Sirenians, he can overtake us easily in the end. I won't know until I meet him.

And you invite him.

I do not invite him. But this man tells me, he will come. Prince Leo of the Barbarians, they call him.

Do you know, King Micah, what they have done to my people?

Do you know what the Sirenians have done to mine? They blamed us for sickness, for drought, for anything at all, and they murdered our children.

Why tell me? Why tell me anything? I wasn't invited to this meeting, because my presence—my voice, my feelings—shame you—

Because I cannot trust you to keep calm, Lemara—

So don't pretend you come to me for my opinion. You have your Prophets for that. So?

They are divided. They say a great battle is coming. They say we will lose either way, whichever choice we make. And yet we will survive, as surely as God survives all things: we must trust in our God and not be afraid.

Trust in your god then. I will not stay, in a place that invites Barbarians. I will not speak more, to a man who welcomes them to his dead-tree table.

I return to the South Forest undressed, free-moving, wrapped in garlands and Grass bands and Air, nothing more. Let the Wye guide who drives the carriage wiggle uncomfortably with his offended Wye sensibilities and his stifled Wye lust; I do not care. I want my home to recognize me when I enter it.

But I do not recognize my home.

We must come during the dry season, for they told me the mud is too dangerous during the wet. It could slide in great avalanches and overcome us. But what can you mean? I asked. Our mud is not danger; it is the stuff of life. Our flesh is made from it.

Deforestation, they said. Nothing holds the earth now—it blows away with the wind, washes with the rain. Dust rises from the ground, instead of mist. Sick people alone on doorsteps. No one makes any ceremony. Symbols of the Sirenian savior hang in the doorways.

"To ward off the 'Dark Faerie'," the guide tells me.

Roads tell people where to go. They walk bent. They rest and stare. They beg. Children run and play, sounding almost the same as children have always sounded. But not quite.

"All that you see is now under the jurisdiction of the Duke of the Southern Kingdom, or so the Sirenians call the man who rules here," the guide tells me. "In treaty after treaty, we have ceded our rights to this land, in exchange for freedom in Zara. Our army is skilled, but the Sirenian army is much larger. We can only hope to win through negotiation—if there is any hope at all."

But you are not winning.

I thought Micah would try to stop me. Instead he offered me a guide. I did not even know such a thing could be offered. I had never thought to ask.

Did you think I was keeping you prisoner? Is it romantic to you, to hold forever to that fantasy, Priestess Lemara? No—it is right that you should see what is happening there. Go. But Uriah stays here, he said.

Why?

I was angry. Always he must level his will against mine, just for the sake of doing it. He doesn't want Uri to learn where his mother comes from, I thought bitterly.

But he said then, *I keep Uriah, so that I know you will return.*

With sorrow in his voice?

I was taken by land, not by Sea the way the Wyes used to travel to the South Forest, long ago. Now they use the Bridge which they have built, over the River Golden, up past the Ho Volcano. The Bridge which first carried me into Zara, leaving my childhood and all my past behind me.

Both Wyes and Sirenians use this Bridge to come into the South Forest and do what they will. When we reached the foot of it, my driver argued for a long time with the Sirenian soldiers there, who told him he must pay a toll now to cross. *Our people built this Bridge,* he told them in his fury (a quiet fury, like Micah's), *which we have been generous enough to allow you to use. The Queen of Zara, Priestess of the South Forest, crosses here. Let us pass.*

The Volcano rose behind us, misty red with memory and foreboding, and the River filled my mind with her complicated sound. And the Wye driver looked at me, no doubt awaiting my imperious command, but I said nothing, for what do I care for their exchanges of money? I would get home if I wished it, one way or another. I was busy listening to the River, to the changes in her story. I closed my eyes to hear better, and so that I wouldn't have to see yet what lay beyond her. Something thickened her. Something slowed her like sorrow—the sludge of Earth that fell into her, lost from uprooted Trees, not where it belonged. *I am no longer beautiful,* she moaned. *The Salamanders have left me.*

I told the guide to leave me once I knew where I was. But I don't think I am going to know where I am. Even in the Forest, I do not recognize anything. The Roses don't smell the way I remember them when I woke. They smell sweet like the perfume of Sirenian women. They bind my senses. A person could hardly walk along the Earth, for all the thorns.

When I was Priestess, my people wandered with the seasons. They had no houses; they slept in the Trees that beckoned them along the way. But the new Priestess has a house, just like a Sirenian or a Wye. Even the Sirenians know where she lives. She lives there always, in a silly little tower.

"Leave me here," I tell the man.

"But Mistress, how will you survive here? Shall I not wait and make sure that the new Priestess welcomes you? And you cannot return alone. They will stop you again, at the Bridge."

"No," I say, descending from the carriage and kissing the Horses each on the cheek. "I will find a way."

"King Micah bade me stay with you. He told me you were only staying for a little while."

"He was wrong," I say.

He leaps down from the coach, still holding the Horse's reins. He is nimble, but already frightened, I can tell, by the unknown around him. "But Mistress, you are pregnant. King Micah worries for you."

"No, he does not," I say. "He already has a son, and that's all he wants. He has no need for the daughter I'm making in my womb." I slip into the undergrowth faster than he can think. While he calls after me, crashing and thrashing, I continue onward, until I am safely gone from him. I only hope he doesn't get lost. I can't be responsible for him.

Alone, I unwind the garlands from my body and loosen my hair. I do it slowly, to allow the Jungle mist to dress me instead. A young Violet Rain Tree has lurched out from the grasp of the Roses and flutters its lowest branches near my head. I toss my hair. All is not lost. I don't know where I am, but when I offer myself to the Jungle, she still feels me.

When asking for serious audience with the Priestess, one always appears naked. So I come to her. But the young men and women I see laughing and embracing around the base of the tower, just as young lovers have always hung about the Priestess, are clothed partially in Sirenian clothing, and do not see my coming for a long time. I think they are not really listening to the Forest. There is something wrong about them. Oh they are drooping like the ones in the dusty villages, but it is worse than that! Something gross, something lifeless in the way of their bodies, the way they hang upon each other with smoky eyes, their smiles vague and complacent, nothing delicious on their tongues. Oh they hang, they hang upon each other, and I see it now—I see the way the Wyes and the Sirenians see my people, lazy and greedy, creatures to be pitied! Oh Esha, oh Tiras... We are not this.

And I want, almost, to turn around, to run back to the carriage, but it is too late. The young people have seen me and are frowning with surprise at my nakedness. The Priestess has seen me from her pretty balcony and is calling down.

Why do you care if I return or not? I asked Micah. *You do not even love me, any more than I love you.*

Micah dropped his head into one hand. If he had held his face in both hands, I could have wept with him. But it was more painful, to see him hold it in only one. As if he were too tired even to feel sorrow. *Mara,* he said. *How can I talk to you?*

Talk to me, I said.

We are bound by marriage, Lemara, he said. *I am bound by a vow I made to my God, who knows better than I what is good for me and for my people, in honor of my ancestors' wishes. I will never break that vow. Instead, I will commit myself to it all my life. I will commit myself to whatever teachings this marriage brings, whether or not you do the same.*

And because I was so sorry for him—a little boy ruled by some tyrannical parent-god, whose every wish he must obey—I went to him and kissed him on the forehead. He did not move, but I could feel him feel it. I could feel his heart, when I leaned down to him, and I touched his arms with my hands. He recoiled from me, like he always does when I touch him there.

What is it? I cried at last. *How can you have wounds that never heal? I do not believe you. It isn't possible, not to heal from some battle years ago.*

He locked his eyes with mine, and I saw for the first time that with fury, I will never win. Not with him. *Because they are wounds that never heal. Magical wounds. And they are not from battle.*

What do you mean? What wounds?

Only a predator would watch me the way he watched me then, and yet with such bitterness—a bitterness unknown to Animal life.

Wounds sustained in the course of rescuing a princess.

I reached for him again, but was afraid to touch.

Yes, he said. *I know you were not a princess, and I know you didn't wish to be rescued, but never the less, that is what I did, and now we must live with the consequences, Lemara Wye.*

This? I asked, nodding toward those places I could never touch.

He made no motion. *The roses,* he said.

No flowers, but a Hummingbird sits near me, suddenly, in the Air. Suddenly buzzing around my hair, asking, asking. The first I have seen.

"Please come down," I say to the girl. "I wish to speak to you."

She kicks a little stone off her balcony, drops her eyes. Her face is painted, but carelessly, as if by a small child. She is very beautiful, but perhaps one of her fathers was Sirenian. "You can't command me," she says. "I am the Priestess."

"I am not commanding you. I am asking you."

All other faces are watching now. The breeze surrounds us. "Who are you?" she asks.

"Once I was also a Priestess of Hummingbirds. My name is Lemara."

And then everything changes. The Priestess goes all melty, loses her artificial pride. "Oh!" she cries, and slides fast down a vine she has hung for this purpose. She comes right to me, reaches for my hands. I hear them breathing fast behind her, for they remember the story. They have heard my name.

They touch me as they ask their questions; they nestle in; we sit and press our buttocks and thighs to the soft wet earth. They want to know what happened when I fell asleep. They want to know how the prince woke me, and what was he like. They want to know what life was like, so long ago. And it is not the lazy emptiness, the dreary flesh, the rudeness, that was gross to me, after all. It was something worse that disturbed me. It was the silence without the Humming. It was the way their eyes looked. It was knowing that behind all that lounging about, behind the peaceful deadness, they were starving. Beauty for them is like food their bodies can no longer digest.

When I said goodbye to Uri, he cried twice over. Once for losing his mama, and again because he wanted to go where I was going.

Where the La! he cried, for I had told him about the La-deer. *Hum,* he sobbed. *Hum.* I had told him about all the Animals and about sleeping in Flowers. I had told him about the Dancing in the night. I had told him about the palaces in the Trees. *I want,* he cried. *I want asleep in a Tee.*

I hushed him and told him the Cats would keep him safe while I was away. I told him to speak with the Moon, for the same Moon would watch over me and reflect his sweet face in Hers, so that I could see him. I told him my Ancestors would watch over him until I returned.

But I did not believe my own words the way I once did. I did not know if any of these things were as true as they once were.

As I left, I remembered the prophecy Micah's ancestors had made, that a child of his marriage to me would one day save his people from the Sirenians. And I realized, he is not keeping Uri so that I will return. For all his talk of marriage and sacred vows, all that means nothing to him, compared with the fate of his people. He only keeps Uri because he doesn't want to lose him, that is all. So that he can use him for the prophecy. I have no part in it.

I cannot love Uri the way I want to, because I will not be able to keep him. I will not be able to kiss his feathery head every morning, or listen to him as he wakes humming with the Cats in my room, who watch over him. Soon he will be Micah's to raise. It took me these few years to understand it fully—so terrible, so foreign, so unreal is this knowing. But I know it now. Women are only tools, in Zara, for the birthing of men.

Alone later in the Forest, I cannot find my way. What was close has opened, and what was open has grown in. Everything has changed.

When I'm weeping from hunger in the evening, a Hatta-Bird gives me one of her Eggs. It's one of the reasons I came back now, finally, to the Jungle. I am making a girl inside me, and I want to give the Ancestors a chance to be reborn through her, if they wish. To do this, I must eat all kinds of Plants, I must eat of this place. I eat Eggs, which only pregnant women eat—they are vessels of creation and make babies grow stronger.

I nest in a Tan-Tan Tree for the night, in the highest branches, to talk with the Moon. The Moon is telling me what I don't want to know, and I close my eyes quiet and listen. She is shining, like a sheet the Wye people might lay over their dead, over the mountain just there behind my left shoulder—and I know that mountain. That mountain is the Temple of Women, and it is the highest place. I know where I am, after all. But I cannot look at that place where I slept for one hundred years—all grown over now with Roses and forgotten.

Moon, beautiful, do not weep over there—but weep over me! For I am young again. Now the Jungle nourishes me, at last! I can feel the little girl inside me eating the good round Egg I ate for her. And the Owls are singing! The Moon takes Her flight over the Sky, falling silently in and out of clouds, dressed differently in each one. Back in Zara, there is no one to sing this story. Here, the night throbs! All the leaves go transparent around me. When I close my eyes, the passion of the insects beats with my heart, and I rest in the universe again. How can the new Priestess not feel it? Could it be that something the Sirenians offer is more powerful than this?

when the Barbarians came

It was during that time when the Earth lived without the love of the Sky, and the People were without the men who had left them, that the Barbarians came. The Earth felt dry and cold then, and the Air hung dim and still in between Her and the nothingness—the way I remember it hanging over my broken people the day Micah dragged me from the Roses and carried me over a bridge to nowhere. The God could not come to us as love, then, so He had to come as violence.

Who were the Barbarians? They were the anger of a man who has been denied woman all his life. They were the anger of a man who has been taken from his mother as a child and taught to hate her, as perhaps one day my son will be taught to hate me.

They came and tore down the Trees. They came and murdered the Animals. They came and took whatever they wanted, no matter the season. They came without Ancestors. And they raped our women and did to us unspeakable things.

We sent them away by magic, those of us who had not yet been violated, who still held our magic strong between our legs and could send it up in Fire. We worked together in the Temple of Women, we drew up the rage of the Ancestress from the center of the Earth. We came upon them by night and terrified them. We sent the River flooding after them, We made flame from the flint of the Caves and cast it after them, we made them gone.

But our people were broken. More of our women were wounded and bleeding than were still whole. It took a long, long time to heal them. So long that the Hummingbird men who remained—who were at first so full of gentleness and compassion—began to grow restless. They could not heal those women who were torn, for only other women, only the Elders, could heal them. The men felt useless. They were bitter in their uselessness, they were angry at themselves for they had never learned violence like the Barbarians, they had not been able to defend their women and they thought that they should. They could not sit still and be helpless now. They were angry. They were lonely for the women, who did not want them anymore, who could no longer be lovers because they were torn. They were frustrated, they were shamed, and no one was left to comfort them and touch them. And so many of them left. They sought a new kingdom far away, beyond Zara, and never came back.

The ones who remained were humbled. They submitted themselves to the binding of their hair. They were sorry for what the Barbarian men had done, and they understood now what all of us understood: that something exists within men which is dangerous and must be handled with care. It was necessary now to say what had once been obvious: that men must respect women, that any violence against woman would now result in Death, in surrender to the Jaguar. And the men bound their hair as an expression of their promise, to be unbound only by women in their own choosing. And we bound our love faster around them and around all of us, knowing that violence is a thing that happens in the absence of love.

During this time the Sky heard the wounded cries of His Beloved, the Earth who cried with Her women, and finally returned. He returned and loved Her with the Rains again, and She took Him in as if They had never been apart. But He could not feed Her as He once had, for now She fed Herself through Death, and this frightened Him. And He never stopped weeping for the sorrow of what had been done in His absence, so that His Rains now were also this weeping. And the Sun carried, every morning, the joy of the Sky Father's return, but the Moon, every evening, carried the sorrow of His forgetting.

without Jaguars

I have never been afraid before, in my own land, but now sometimes I am afraid. Sometimes I sleep in the tops of the Trees, and wrap my body in Moonlight for protection. I find enough food to survive, but not enough to ever be full. Many of the Fruit Trees are dead beneath the Roses. Only mature Nuba Trees bear nuts, and most of the Nuba Trees here are too young. I still don't know where I am.

One morning I find a few of my people gathered around an old shrine to the Faerie of the Deep Forest. They do not ask me to explain who I am, but welcome me as in the days of old. They are seven women, two men, all of them older than me and kind. They know the old way of speaking, with bodies and hands, the way Wind and Sea speak. They wind and unwind my hair, and do not ask me any questions. They share a feast of Beetles and Eggs with me, knowing I am pregnant, and it is the first time in a long time that I have felt joy.

"I do not understand the Roses," I tell them, as I hold their hands in a room of giant Nuba roots.

"No one understands the Roses," answers one of the women.

"But are they evil?"

"No," she says. "They are frustrated. They don't belong here. Like us, they no longer know their way."

"But why?"

"They come from another place," says another. "Here they do not belong. Foreign things that grow here, that do not understand their place here, become greedy and overtake everything. You know how it is here. This is a magical land. Anything that grows here will succeed—sometimes it will succeed too much. You must be careful what you wish for, because you can have anything, here in the South Forest."

I nod. I know this, of course. I made that mistake myself, and will regret it for the rest of my life.

"Poor Roses," says one of the men. "They do not mean to destroy everything. But they don't know what to do with such richness—just like our people don't know how to handle the richness of the Sirenians. These Roses are far from home."

And I think I understand. I feel sad for the Roses, who have become horrible and hated. I feel sorry for their clumsiness and awkwardness in a land they do not know. I know what it feels like, now, not to belong anywhere.

I sleep enfolded among my people and do not Dream. In the morning, we greet the Sun with shouts and roars, and then I go on without them. Without the Jaguars, who were all slaughtered by the Sirenians for their skins, the Air is thin; something feels upended in the Earth; the element of Fire is unhappy. When La-Deer pass through the shadows, they pass warily, not knowing where to train their senses, the way I feel in Zara surrounded by stunted Trees and hunted by nothing. The Jaguars fill up the Dream lands, angry, pacing. Even the Insects seem to stumble in their singing. They are missing the old rhythm of silence—the beat of the Jaguars' silent paws against the skin-drum of the Earth, that used to make the measure of their song.

The Roses scramble the places. But I follow scents I remember. In my Dreams, the Faeries never speak to me, but sometimes I taste with the tongues of Snakes as they taste where the heat of life has come and faded, and I follow that path. *Priestess of Hummingbirds,* they say. They know my name.

I follow the sound of falling water. Sliding on my belly, slip-swimming through descending pools, I follow Dragonflies to where the Water leaps and thunders out of the Earth. What laughter we laughed here! Here Awhee shared her first kiss with Mescol, and Tika first painted my inner thighs with mud that felt like fire. AlaNAmana could speak with the Water Snakes; she could rise from the Water and speak in their tongues and make us Dream. The elders used to call this place the Council of Waterfalls, where the many Waters meet to talk over their journeys, before continuing on, as one, to the Sea. I will look over the edge and see the Water shooting from below the Ferns, fanning larger and larger, free-falling into the cavern far below where it joins a circle of Waterfalls from many directions, where Tiras first shouted that he loved me.

I crawl to the edge, sink my breasts into the soft green. The Water's still coming, falling, following the same path, the same shape it has followed forever since the Earth first woke. But the other Waterfalls no longer join it—the soil has collapsed without the Trees to hold on, and has merged with the paths of the Water so that nothing else has any form at all now but only my Waterfall, the only one left—the Waterfall falling beneath my own body and only dying in a great thickened pool of lost Rivers, lost Rain, tired Earth spinning and settling, going nowhere.

I look but I cannot see. I die. I die again. The Council is dead. *I must see. Rhiannon, I must see clearly. Help me. I must understand.*

Around the pool below, the Wyes have built a wall, something protecting the now barren land from the flood of the River. And as far as I can see—what seems to me hills and hills of desert. I have come out again to the wasteland. Once, I could not believe this land was the land of Hummingbirds. But it is. I know because I know where I am now.

I see the new Priestess with her foolish name—Flower, a foolish Sirenian name for a Hummingbird girl—sitting on the wall. She dangles her feet, stuffing something soft in her mouth and chewing, her expression aloof, her friends draped around her.

I climb halfway down the cliffside and hide in the mist of the falls, watching them. I look for some sign that they are really my people. I think perhaps that I—Lemara— have died, after all. That a Jaguar is the true Priestess now, somewhere none of us can see.

The Sirenian men and women, careful to avoid the scent and touch of the stuffed, lounging Hummingbird bodies—disgusting to these people—stop and offer them Things.

Look, they tempt. *How beautiful.*

My brothers and sisters squabble over the offerings. Even the furs made from our very own Creatures, that they do not recognize. My people, who once shared everything as one people, who never owned one thing—not house nor clothing nor food nor Animal nor one an-other—and never needed to, you argue now over these things, things to cover up your bodies because you think they are more beautiful than you are.

We will give you these things, say the Sirenians, *if you let us watch the Dances tonight.*

When I jump from the Waterfall below, the Priestess and her friends babble in terror and jumble each other, falling into the Water and scrambling up onto the stone. For a moment, I was Jaguar. And when they saw me coming, they saw Death.

"Oh, Lemara," says Flower. "It's only you. Won't your prince miss you?" She is not teasing me. They truly believe I am so lucky, to be married to a king, to have all the pretty clothes I could want.

I open my mouth and speak in a roar. The Sirenians draw back, their women clutching their men.

"You defile the body of the Goddess," I tell Flower. "You are Priestess." I clutch her fist full of sweet bread and squeeze it. "Do not eat their food. Do not Dance for them."

"I am the Goddess," she hisses back at me, whipping her fist back and out of my grasp, stronger than I expected—for some hint of the old power is in her, after all. "To be Priestess is to be Goddess, don't you know that?"

Oh sweet girl, not anymore, I think.

"And we do what our bodies love—that's how we honor Her, don't you know that?"

Oh, not anymore. As she brings the soft bread to her mouth. *Now you can no longer trust your body. Now your desires betray you. Now the priests can come to you and tell you not to trust your body, for it's no longer yours. Now how easy it is, when you're stuffed full of emptiness that does not nourish you, when you cannot feel your own self, to forsake Her.*

"She comes from the old ways," Flower is telling the frightened Sirenian women, as I slip away. "Can you believe it," she giggles, to entertain them, "when a baby was chosen to be Priestess, they used to leave her out in the Jungle for the Jaguar to test her! And if she wasn't accepted by the Jaguar, the Jaguar would eat her! That's what *Dark Faerie* really means! Did you know that?"

Oh, little Flower, not anymore. And oh, but no one ever Dreamed you. How alone you are! And none of you know how to speak without words, anymore. I listen for your inner speaking and hear only an angry buzzing, like a Bee trapped in a room. But maybe it's my fault, too. Maybe I have begun to forget.

For neither was I ever chosen by the Jaguar. My mother denied me that ceremony. And for that I was cursed, forever.

Still, what can I do? The Moon will be coming, and I have work to do in the tops of the last Nuba trees. Who else but I can do it?

between two worlds

When I hear the Ocean Faerie calling to me, I follow her across the desert to the shore. I hear the Seabirds wailing at the soft Sea Edge, loud in a way they can never be loud in civilized Zara, yet our Sea is gentler here, at peace with our shaggy, petaled coast. I follow the shore with the desert to my left, a thin line of nervous trees touching my fingertips as I creep and climb, keeping to the rocks that divide me from what I can no longer bear to see. I cross Welcome Beach as the Sun falls on the third day, and stop to sing. Then I follow the rise to the place where the Earth empties down into Water, through leaf-furred openings of Stone. And oh, such Stone—such a clean, sheer grey like a Gull's wing, but also swirling, as if it were sand the tide only just carved this morning, and remember, Esha, how long and long we traced such shapes with our fingers, searched out their replicas in our hair, our own Sea-sticky curves? A Wind I know circles me, as I gaze into the womb-place of the Sea, the Cave I entered as a virgin, where I wove my young body into Water among the beautiful boys and girls of the Ocean. I do not ask myself where they are now. It hurts too much.

I just sweep my legs between my braced arms, dip my feet into the hole, and drop. Somewhere in the middle of the Air I seem to feel Esha's cool hands softening my fall, like breaking through a nest of feathers. I spear the still, black Water many person-lengths below, fall deeper where beneath the stillness Water surges cold and turns in slow confusion, where the River Golden has entered the round space and lost its way briefly before it will burst suddenly and finally, like a waking, into the Sea beyond. In here the Water bounces me back up like a baby and cradles me in its thick bed. The opening above lets the Sun touch me, but the current keeps pushing me gently into darkness.

With my hands upon my pregnant belly, I fall asleep upon my Water-bed, and the Faerie of Ocean folds her arms around me and rests her hands on mine. We Dream like that, until finally, she speaks to me again.

She tells me that my people are dying.

She tells me the Sirenian people are so sick, their Sickness is spreading through all the world. It is coming now into the bodies of my people, who were made empty by the Emptiness of the Sirenians, and now hunger after everything the Sirenians have—even their Sickness. They eat the bread of the Sirenians and breathe their breath. They enter into their city and offer themselves as slaves. And now they are Sick like the Sirenians. No one can save them, for it is a Sickness of the spirit.

My people are stuck, says the Faerie of Ocean. They do not move and flow through the Forest with the seasons, but they live in little huts in the dust, and the Sickness finds them there and kills them. They cannot escape it. They are Sick in great numbers—I have never seen, nor have my Ancestors ever seen, a Sickness of such power, but I will see it now, says the Faerie of Ocean, because the people do not move, they eat food without nourishment, they starve for beauty, they forget the medicines of the Forest community.

The Sickness comes to awaken them, says the Faerie of Ocean. The Sickness causes madness among the Sirenians, but for the Hummingbird People, it will bring on the Dreaming. They will Dream in ways they have forgotten how to Dream. They will remember. But they will not know their own remembering, for they have no Elders to guide them, and they will die in their Dreaming, and the Dreams will be forgotten.

I say, *I am their Priestess. I will stay and guide them.*

And she says, *You are their Priestess, but you cannot guide them now. You must care for the daughter in your womb. You must walk away from Death now, and go where you are safe.*

But I am their Priestess.

She says, *It does not matter now. They cannot recognize you. Not now. The tide comes and goes. It is time to go. Recede.*

I wake in sorrow, but my mind is smooth, and the Water is all around me, pushing me ever and ever onward. I dive beneath it and swim through the underwater tunnel into a Waterfall that lands me in the Sea—the only way out, which only the Water and the ancient Hummingbird People know.

As I climb through the Forest between the Cave and Zara, a Forest I have never traveled and do not know, a Forest so thick that no Wye-man has ever traversed it, guided only by the directionless throb of the Sea beside me, the Dreams wind me tighter and tighter inside my belly, so that I am sick in there, and whether it is the pregnancy or the Sickness coming for me, after all, I do not know. I cannot remember when last I ate food, and sometimes I fear this girl-baby will leave me, as did the last one, for lack of nourishment and hope, but instead she seems to hunker down like a Spider and only waits. *Go home,* she says, or says the Dream, but I don't know where home is. Sometimes I Dream I am walking, and wake to find myself lying still, as if I exist in two realities that have nothing to do with one another. The last image I remember—the spires of the Wye-palace thrusting like soldiers into the Sky, but then they're only mountains and I fall.

In the end, Tiras carries me. I know it is him. The way his hand sweeps hot over my hair, engulfs my head in tenderness. The muscles in his belly, his heart singing against my ribs, his tears of relief on my face. *Of course I would find you,* he says. *I will never forget you. Never.*

I wish he would take me away with him, to any world at all. But he returns me to the palace Wye, to my own bed there. *I am watching over you,* he tells me, *but you will not know. You must live on here. I cannot be with you, as we were before. I can only love you, without hope.*

I will never be home

When I'm well enough to stand up from my bed, I go in search of my son. I search the kitchens, the gardens, the favorite balconies of every Cat he knows. All the women love him, but today none can remember where she saw him last. I'm beginning to panic when I find him at last, in the Temple Hall, where the warriors are practicing.

At first I remain in the doorway and do not show myself. When I see Micah's big hands cupped over my boy's tiny shoulders, I feel love and fury, both almost too much to bear. Micah is sitting on a stone bench, bending forward with Uri between his knees, and Uri leans into him, staring open-mouthed at what he sees. I am staring, too. I cannot help it.

The warriors fill the room with their motion. I have never seen them train before. I have never seen them. At first it chokes me to watch such violence—even when they do not touch each other, such violence in the way of their motion—as each movement is a pounce, a dart, a killing blow. A breath cinched tight, closed, zeroing in to an echoing silence. I see why Uri cannot look away. It dawns on me strangely that what I see is a Dance. *This* is their Dancing. A killing Dance. A Dance where everyone Dances the same—they are not free, they are not themselves, they express nothing. Yet in that prison of their trained shapes, they gather and speak with their bodies such awesome power, it mesmerizes me. They move in unison—elbow jab, flicking fist, high kick, leap, spin, crouch and catch. Then they pair off and begin to fight. Sometimes with curved knives or long sticks. I cannot always tell where the attack ends and the defense begins.

For a moment, I Dream I stride into the room, shocking everyone with my wild body, unbathed and half-clad, my womanness and my unpredictable everything—stopping time. But I'm not doing that. Tired from my journey, I sit down on the stair and wait. Waiting is something I know how to do now, something I have to do, something I brought back with me in a Jaguar's breath, or maybe just the teaching of the Cats who've slept beside me for so long now.

"Lemara," says Micah when at last he comes out. The men are still training. Uriah runs into my arms and I bow my head. To weep silently— this, too, is something I have learned, though I haven't meant to. "Are you well?" My husband holds out his hand, but I stand on my own.

I look at him. Now that I've been to the South Forest again, the effort of speaking his language exhausts me.

"Lemara—do you realize I was searching for you, for almost two months? Your guide told me you disappeared into the Jungle the moment you arrived, with no word—nothing."

I close my eyes and feel the pump of the warriors' feet, that precision, that cold exactness, as perfectly controlled as the turning of the constellations from season to season that makes Time. That merciless rhythm. There was a blackness, there, in that room—as black as our Jaguars, as black as the hole of Dreaming where the future comes from. The boys where I come from do not fight, and they let the women lead them. Shulao joked, Kar Danced aloof and elegant. Tiras held me sweetly, surrendered to the helplessness of knowing he must wait. But Mescol— sometimes I saw something in him. Rebellious, with his angry brows. Bored with women sometimes and running alone, or with another boy, stalking Animals as if he would know their secrets.

Outside my closed eyes, I hear Micah sigh. "Come," he says low. "Come with me now."

And though I hate to be ordered about like a Wye woman, I want him, suddenly, so badly that I let him lead me by the hand wherever he will take me. He is not Rain. He is a Volcano that rumbles beneath me, threatening.

He leads me upon the winding stairs, around to the outer pathways again, through the Sea-wind and Sea-sound. We leave Uri in my room with the Cats and go on. When Micah first touches my throat, my spine, the curve of my buttock, I shiver. I close my eyes, releasing myself in little streams, then torrents. I am so delicate. Some piece of me was returned to me when I visited the South Forest, but something in me was also broken and can never be repaired. I found Tiras but could not keep him. I found people who held me in the Mist, but I did not really want them. I was frightened, because I could not feel their touch. All these years, I've held in my heart this secret assurance—that I could always return to the South Forest, if all this became too much. But now I have done it, and it did not save me.

Yet I want, and want! In wanting I am alive. Oh just this once, I will forget about past and future. I will be one thing, one moment, one life, the way I was long ago before all this happened to me.

His breath in my ear.

Our erotic nature is sacred to us, I told him once, *and that is why we are so free with it. You judge me for my freedom, but as the Goddess it is my sacred purpose.*

It is sacred to us, too, he told me, after a long moment of silence. *And that is why we protect it within the sacred vessel of marriage. That is why we do not spill it everywhere; that is why it must be controlled.*

It's all over in a moment. He held it back for so long, he overflows now and is done. I open my eyes again, and the past and the future come over me, threatening to kill me, and behind them: the thing I have been begging Rhiannon to know. The Dream I Dreamed for a hundred years—always, I almost, almost remember. Tiras is there, inside that Dream. I know he is.

I remember the Waterfall, how it falls to nothing now, how the Rivers who once held council together had bled into mud and died. What will the River Golden tell the Sea, when she arrives without their songs?

I don't know

"I want to speak with the Queen of Sirenia," I tell Micah. I stand at the window of his study-room full of scrolls, which overlooks not the Sea but the city.

I feel him shaking his head behind me, though I don't look.

"I want to speak to her as a woman, to make her understand what she's done."

"What has been done," he says softly, "cannot be undone. You know that."

"Don't you think I know? I have seen—" I cry these words out loud, angry, but when I whirl to face him I see the compassion in his eyes, and it shocks me.

"It won't matter, Lemara," he says with so much gentleness, I have to sit down, for the pain of it. My little girl moves in my belly. "If only you knew how many times I have met with those people. They'll give you smooth words, but none of it matters."

"I don't care. I'll feel better, just seeing her. I'll hate her less, if I can look into her eyes."

"Not now, Lemara. Their people are beset by plague, and they won't be able to hear you. It's chaos there. And you're vulnerable, you're pregnant. I'm not forbidding you—but please wait. I have more hope for the future king, anyway. The son, Alden. I can tell he wants to work with us more as equals, but fears to contradict his father."

I don't answer him. We still haven't spoken of those wounds, the wounds of the Roses. I think we will never speak of them. I know now, how not to touch him. I only watch him, and he watches me. I understand his thoughts sometimes as if he were a part of me, as if we were blood-related, as if our bodies twined together every night so tightly that our hearts recognize each others' rhythm, even though they don't. It comes and goes, this understanding, like a shape made of Butterflies, and I never ask for it. It must be the threads that bind us from love-making. He is the only man I have ever made love with, in this world. When you make love to another, you are bound to him all your life. Not in the way the Wyes teach, where you cannot love another, but his feelings are in you, just the same, whether you want them or not.

"I know I need your help," I admit to him at last. "I know you are trying to help my people. I know."

But perhaps a Wye-man doesn't know what to do with a heart so open. He leans forward eagerly when I say these words—I can feel his mind pouncing, and I draw back. I remember again that he has spoken with Barbarians, that he has invited them to this place.

"The highest priority right now," he begins lecturing, "is to hold back the plague. It is at our doorstep. Yet while thousands die in Sirenia, only one has died here. We battle it effectively because our medicine is more advanced and because we understand the source of it and because, frankly, our city and all the systems of our living are much cleaner than Sirenia's. Our cats keep the rats under control. We have fewer people, and have taken pains to keep it that way. Such conditions would also benefit your people, Lemara. I am perfectly willing to teach them our medicine, our waste systems, our hygiene—"

"We do not believe in your medicine!" I cry, standing and pacing again. "You do not understand everything. You do not understand our Sickness."

Never once, in all his "helping," has he visited my land or my people. Only the one time, the time he stole me away. What is he afraid of?

"What, then? What are your people doing to stop the plague that is beginning to kill them, Lemara?"

Nothing. I am doing nothing. I have only memory. When someone in the community grew ill, it was a teaching. We thanked that person for bearing the lesson, experiencing the pain which belonged to all of us. We surrounded that person day and night as she spoke out her Sickness. We Dreamed with her and for her. We felt what she felt, and each of us transformed it with the special, individual Dance that was our own. When she became well again, it was for all of us; when she healed, it was all of our healing. For a body is not a broken bowl to be glued back together. It is our language. And to walk into Death, if it must be done, is also a Dance done in ecstasy—for that person carries with her into the Other World our answer to the Faeries' message.

But I saw the Sick people in my homeland. They sat on their doorsteps, all alone. They sat in their doorways and died, sometimes not even mourned. When the Faeries send such a message, that takes so many lives, it is a great message. But no one of my people can any more hear it. I think of Flower. *My people fear Death now. And so they are trapped forever, like the pale people, between worlds.*

Sometimes I wonder if they must all, every one of them, be returned to the worlds from which we come, the Earth World of Ancestors, the Sky World of Dreams, in order to remember who they are. Perhaps Death has come to my people to invite them home. And will I remain without them, here in Zara, all alone?

"And the Barbarian prince?" I ask, not answering his question. "Has he come?"

"Not yet."

"And you will join with him, when he does?"

"I don't know."

"I don't want killing."

"Lemara, do you realize that if we agree to help Prince Leo's army, we'll have leverage to protect your people? We can demand that once he's in power, your people will be left alone, your forests never again plundered, your people left in peace."

"No. I don't believe it. This is not the way."

"What other way? We have not enough might to stop the Sirenians now, not without Leo. If you would rule beside me, then rule your people. Suggest a plan, Priestess Lemara!"

But a Priestess does not rule. What does it mean, a *plan*? I was born of my Ancestors, and they were born from theirs. The Rains came every year forever, and the Sun reared up and made the morning, and the Sun slept and made the night, and the Moon was a white tunnel into Dreams. This was Life, and we traveled the circle of it. There was no counting of years. There was no future that would come and be different. I just want to start the wheel turning again. I want my people to start moving again.

But I know. I know Micah is trying to help me. From the open window I watch the people with their horses and carts in the paths winding through the hills below. Their flowers are tinier, tamer, and fewer; their faces more closed, their voices quieter; they hold themselves more carefully and do not Dance; and yet there is peace in them. I see that now. It is not emptiness, after all. They are content. Their smiles are real, and hold light.

For whom are the tears that pass over my face? I think today, they are for my mama. I think of the pressure she must have felt then, the decisions she needed to make which she could not make right and which even now I cannot make. How to undo what was already beginning to be done. How to stop *Time*—a thing brought to us by the Sirenians that we never knew before, by which one thing changed to another and could never go back to how it was. My mama was foolish, making some agreement with a Wye-man. She was foolish, denying the Dark Faerie Her rite. But they were so hard, the choices she had to make. They were not choices that had ever come to us before.

I remember the Dream

I remember, now, that I Dreamed a Dream for a hundred years. Perhaps all this time I have been Dreaming it still.

I Dream I arrive in the South Forest just after Sunset. My people have sung the Sun to His rest without me. I can see Esha and AlaNAmana and Tikka and all my friends, and my mother, singing and weeping, but they cannot see me. I go on alone into the twilit Dream, and Rhiannon holds my hand, and I know I am going to die.

A deep drumming follows us, pounding upon the soles of our feet through the shell of the world, and it is my Ancestors that drum my path. A web of Faerie music weaves the Air: I can hear it in my mouth and in my heart, and it is made of high, stretched threads, both living and dead, like hair. We pass into a forest of Violet Rain Trees, and each one is lit from within. I know these Trees, for I've walked this path before, but I never saw them shining. We come to the cliffs where the Council of Waterfalls meets, and look down. Rhiannon's hand in mine is so tight, I want to wake up—I want to come away, I am afraid. I cannot see Her face. Her skin looks like Tree bark and Her body is gnarled, but She stands strong and easy, Her white hair so long it gets lost in the Water.

I see that the many joining Waterfalls which I have known all my life form a crystal palace in the center which I have never seen. The walls of this palace are always moving, because they are made of Water. Rhiannon leads me down a long Moss stairway through curtain after curtain of Mist, some warm and some cold, until we reach the place at the bottom where the Waterfalls collide in foam, and the foam makes a soft, undulating bed inside the moving palace, upon which languorous River Faeries hold court with Dragonflies and sing white melodies. Rhiannon twines her hands with theirs, and they rise up in fountains and follow us.

Then we climbed up the other side through the dark curtains, and the Moon is rising at the top, and still Rhiannon leads me by the hand. I hear the silence of the River Faeries following behind me, and this comforts me, for they have the kindness of Water, which makes everything easier. But the Moon is a virgin, and when I look at Her, I see my own face, frozen, and look away again in terror. My body is the blackness.

In the Meadow on the Green Hill, we become very small, so that we can be the size of the Meadow Faeries in their grass-beamed castles of Spider silk, with their feather plumes and hallways of Wind. The Meadow Faeries are always laughing. They run beside us, and when we grow big again, they ride in our hair.

We go on and on into the night. Maybe I will die because I have betrayed my people by offering up our Dances as if they were for sale—a crime never committed before. Or maybe I will die for some other reason, ordained by my Ancestors. I only know that Rhiannon is taking me to my execution. And I know it will hurt beyond anything I have known.

We pass through the dripping Flower Palace where the Young Forest Faeries join us, and through the Palace of mud and tears, where Marsh Faeries silently comb the Egrets' tails. As we move through the many places, Rhiannon the Dark Faerie shines brighter and brighter, until I can hardly look upon Her, and everybody's colors are more vivid in the reflection of Her light. At last we come to Rhiannon's palace, at the center of the world.

It is made from every kind of light. The roof is made of Sunlight, and the floor of Moonlight. The archways are made of reflections, which we pass through and through. When I look through the windows as we pass them, I can see the darkness of the midnight. Rhiannon is weaving a giant web around us. She is the Spider. At the center of the web sits a dark person with bowed head, so dark that all the colors are swallowed inside him, and he is so still, I do not know if he is real, but I cannot take my eyes from him. When She has finished weaving the circle, and all the Faeries from all the places that make the world are crouching and flickering at the end of every thread, Rhiannon stands behind this dark magnetic man in the center and says to me,

"This is your executioner, Lemara. Come."

And it's you. It's you, Tiras.

But you don't recognize me. "He does not know you," says Rhiannon. "He will not know you until you submit yourself to his sword. You must do it willingly, or it cannot be done."

I stand trembling before you, and you stare right through me with the cold nothingness that we feel in the grey Air before morning, when we wait for the Sun to rise and wonder if He ever will. I do not trust Rhiannon.

"What if I do not submit?" I say.

"Then you will live forever, and always be alone."

I kneel down before you. You are also kneeling, with a sword lain across your lap. I look at your beautiful, fish-smooth hands and realize with surprise that you can grasp it, that you will, and a tremor goes right through me.

"Tiras," I whisper. "Don't you know me?" For I think our love will not submit to violence—our people are never violent. Our love is only love, and never destruction. With our love we shall live forever, and not be alone.

But the words you speak back to me are not human words. They seem made of Water, and I don't understand them. You look into my eyes, but your eyes are the universe, filled with stars and Violet Rain Trees and Waterfalls. I begin to cry, I reach out to touch your chest. But your skin burns me, so that I pull back in pain. Now I see in your chest a great, smoky wound, behind where your heart should be. I see you flinch, and I know it burns you, too, and I feel so sorry. I cannot understand it, but I know this smoky wound is the cause of your strange language, your inability to form human words. I wonder how you came here, into the Faerie World, to be with me. I cannot figure out the answer to this question, for in the Dreamlands there is no cause and result, no reason and answer, and it is very hard to figure things with one's mind. But I sense that you have also sacrificed yourself in a terrible way and made a great effort of love to be here with me. And so I know I will submit to you: I will let you kill me.

"What must I do?" I ask Rhiannon.

"You must open your heart," said Rhiannon. "And you must never close it, never, not even when the pain is so great you cannot bear it."

Then She gives us a cup, made of some unknown creature's skull, from which to drink. I drink first, and then hand the cup to you, and you drink, too—we drink blood. I have never tasted blood before, and I taste the horror of *it now, like the taste of dense grey metal in the Earth which should never, ever be bared. Yet I know also that it gives me the strength to do what I have to do.*

All the Faeries tighten the threads of the great web, stretching my arms wide apart, splitting open my chest. And in the darkness that opens there, I know such fear that all my mind is erased, my body turns to fire, and I scream. You plunge in the sword. The pain is so great, I forget who I am. I lose all my words. I go back to the beginning of all things, before anything thought or spoke or moved. I can hear all the Faeries sighing for the beauty of what I do, and what you do to me, because they can never feel what we feel. The only way I can ease the pain just barely is to open myself wider. So I do. I open, and open, until I turn inside out, until the pain becomes no longer pain but a quiet, soaring flight over empty skies. You are screaming with me, my love. I can feel you inside me.

And this is the first ritual. The Ritual of Sacrifice.

Mina

I've decided to stay.

Because the Ghost People feel so unafraid, their fearlessness calms me. They aren't afraid of loss; they aren't afraid of anything, least of all death. They have weathered sickness before, and they ask nothing, only to love quietly from the sanctuary of their meditations, disturbing their world as little as possible.

And because I cannot go without Nicolai, who will not go, who cannot go—because of the fear he will not name, that if he ever leaves this place, he will fall at last, irrevocably, into its forgetting.

And because of what he doesn't know—and if he knew, he would hold me here even by force, if necessary, but I don't tell him, because I'm afraid to give him hope. I'm pregnant. Despite all my foolish dreams of witches in towers, I'm pregnant, after all. And then what if in the stress of travel, I lost my child? How could I live with myself then?

And most of all because I have become so rooted here, it makes me nauseous to think of travel. Not only because of the sickness and death that await me. It is something less definite than that. I feel I will lose something of myself, if I leave this place. I was braver back then, when I was only sixteen and rode all the way across the world on the back of a wolf. I did not think about the fragility of life. I did not even think about being alive. I did not even know that I was young.

After all, surely Nicolai was right when he said, if they want to escape the Sickness, they know how to find me. If I went to them now, I'd only endanger myself. Why wouldn't they come, when they already know the way? Perhaps they are already coming. Who knows but I might actually pass them by accident on my way to Sirenia, if I went there looking for them, and never know it? And if they came here, they would be safe forever. They would adjust, eventually, to the way of life here. Or I hope that they would. The longing is so great, it is better not to write of it. But if they were all here with me, we could raise our children together, we could grow old together, and I could be with Father when he dies, in this place where once he sought his fortune and found mine instead...

They wouldn't be the first to arrive. We've not received many refugees so far, but enough to make us all wonder what the future holds. They've come in a couple of waves, I think twenty-two altogether—groups of people that didn't know each other when they left, shabbily patched-together, pale-faced huddles of panic and despair. Even if they did not bring the Sickness itself, their darkness—this new kind of darkness—infects my heart. We believe whoever would have carried the Sickness must have died en route—for it kills too quickly to survive the difficult passage. Sirenia is collapsing, say the ones who made it here. The buildings still stand; the river still flows; the cattle still pour over the hillsides, but the people are disintegrating from the inside. I greet every new arrival, selfishly, with the names of my loved ones on my lips—*have you any news of them?*

I don't know if Amos was really the first to invent that special compass he used to navigate Sleeping Lake, but whoever made it—or perhaps many did—it is more advanced than anything that came before it, and more commonly used. Every passage made across the Lake makes it easier for the next traveler, as maps are drawn and shared. So although the journey is still arduous, it is made more often now. We do the best to care for them, of course, when they arrive. They stay in our houses, share our food. They have absolutely no means of surviving here on their own. I wonder at the desperation that caused them to brave such a journey, not knowing what they would find. No one here speaks their language, except for me.

They're homesick and scared. They do a lot of praying. Nicolai heard that they've been congregating sometimes at the castle ruin. They've seen some kind of vision there, related to their Savior. I think it makes some of the Ghost People uneasy, but we leave them to whatever comforts them.

But what happens once they recover from their trauma, and the Sickness fades from Sirenia at last? Will they return home? I think we all expect that. And yet what of the riches they have seen here? What of the stories they will tell back home, of this new ease of travel to this unprotected, undeveloped, unruled, and—to their eyes—unowned land? My heart tells me the refugees are the beginning of some larger question we will have to answer, sooner or later, as a people.

It's true that I write now to convince myself of my decision, to calm myself, because all I can think of are my dear ones in Sirenia, and will they live or die. But little one within me, whoever you are, whoever you will become—I will stay. I will stay on as queen, whatever that means. I will stay for this family, here.

early autumn

I thought I would write here, to relieve myself of unwept tears, since I cannot weep to Nicolai—I cannot ever tell him. And yet I find no comfort in the page. I have sat here so long, pen hovering in my hand, and darkness falls at last, like a cloak the day has wearied of holding up. I must return or Nicolai will worry—and I've already worried him too much, with my mysterious sickness, a sickness I hid in the woods and would not tell him why.

I'll only say briefly, then, that while I bled, the pain was so great, I swooned into some dream. I was lying right here, in these leaves, where just now I buried the last remains to keep them from the crows. And I dreamed someone held me in her arms. Dark arms, dark as the bottom of the sea must be dark, as if a shadow embraced me—but this shadow felt hot. A woman into whom I sunk so deeply, she seemed limitless, as if she were all women, descended from every woman since the first woman who birthed the world, and descending from her into undying future. She whispered comfort, not only with her mouth against my ear but with her hands upon my throbbing belly, with words I recognized though they were not my language, as if she spoke Wye but in a form of song. She moved against me like a lover, so that my body learned how to move through the pain, how to give birth to it, how to release it, as if my body knew things I had never known, from a knowing older than I was. She turned my pain to fury. She roared while I cried, fountained while I wept, and I seemed to feel my babe emerge from her—as if in some other, shadow version of my life, my child was born alive, not dead, and would live on without me in the arms of a woman much stronger than I.

next day

Everything happens at once. I'm still recovering, so that Linny noticed my paleness when I opened the door and asked me if I was well. She gave me a letter—a letter from Queen Ella, of Sirenia.

As the only one who can read Sirenian, or really read well at all, I read the letter aloud to them. It informed us, in the gentle, polite hand of a woman, a wife, a mother, that the writer wished to make friendly contact with the people here. That the plague was at last receding from Sirenia, leaving barely half of its inhabitants alive. That following the death of most of their family, the writer and her husband, Solon Cygnini, had ascended to the throne. That she was well aware of the increasing pilgrimages of her people to our land, in pursuit of the visions seen here, and wished only to assure us that their intentions were peaceful, and to ask, out of respect for us, if her subjects were interacting with us in the friendly, fair manner she would wish them to.

The letter was addressed to "the king and queen of the Ghost Kingdom," with an apology for not being acquainted with our names. It was brief, but there were things in it that moved me—innocent though I am— to trust her intentions. The careful lettering, as if she had refused to let a scribe write the letter for her, and as if she still struggled with literacy—as one who was raised poor and neglected surely might. And then there was her mention of her daughter's death, for which there seemed no reason, other than to show that she opened her heart to us.

The three of us looked at each other afterward for some time, without saying anything, in surprise.

"She assumes we are a people," I murmured at last. "She assumes we have a king."

"You must reply to her," said Linny, hardly noticing my words, I thought.

"Yes," said Nicolai. "As queen."

"Well of course," I said. "I am the only one who could reply in Sirenian."

"As queen," said Nicolai again. "They must hear from us as a people, in order to respect us. And it's better coming from you, queen to queen."

Queen to queen. I stared at Linny. I wondered if she was thinking what I was thinking. That I was preparing to reply, as queen, on behalf of a people who didn't even call themselves a people. Whose refusal of all organization, all progress, all claim on unified life in this world was so adamant, they could not even be called together for a purpose such as this, to agree together on a response to a message from another country. How could I speak for them?

"People here trust you, Mina," she said, with a quietness I didn't normally see in her laughing, active, curious eyes. "Because your heart isn't burdened, like ours are, by the past. Your perspective is unclouded. You've never even seen a unicorn. You can speak from a clear mind."

"What have unicorns to do with it?" I said, frightened.

"Unicorns have to do with everything," she said, and she surprised me, because no one here speaks of them, ever.

Lying beside Nicolai last night, I asked him again what he thought. I could feel him turn to look at me for a long time. I didn't look back, for I felt afraid somehow, and besides we can hardly see each other in our hut at night. But there was something cold and beautiful in his looking, like the floating of gulls over the sea.

"It makes sense," he murmured finally.

"What do you mean, it makes sense?"

"It's what drew me to you. Your pure heart."

"That's not what Linny said," I said, feeling irritable. "She didn't say my heart was pure. She just said—"

"But it is," said Nicolai. "You don't even realize it. That's how pure it is."

"It just threw me, that's all," I said. "About the unicorns. And... Nicolai, I don't understand anything. I live here, and I seem to pretend that I understand, but I don't. What are they? What is Rhiannon?"

"I don't understand, either," he said.

"We don't even know where she comes from—this witch that changed everything, that cursed you and made us what we are."

"Rhiannon? She comes from the Southern Primeval Forest."

"You know that? She told you?"

He didn't answer. Normally, I could never speak to Nicolai of such things, but something had shifted. The focus was on me. There was an anger in me I could not explain, an awkwardness that wrestled with my heart, from Linny's words. And I could feel Nicolai respecting that.

"And where is the South Forest?" I said. "Is it very far away? Some of your ancestors came from there."

"It's beyond Zara," he said. "They have some ancient connection with the South Forest—the Wyes."

"Do they know about Rhiannon there, do you think?"

"I don't know. Why all these questions, Queen Mina?"

I heard the sweetness in his voice, and his use of that title, at last, without any mockery or envy. And I also heard his uneasiness, that I should think of that place. As if he knew that Rhiannon had some hold on me. As if he knew I'd kept a secret from him, a secret of hope and blood and pain in the forest, only days ago. As if he knew what I was thinking just then, though of course he couldn't.

That I wish I could see that place, which I have never seen. That place where my own mother came from.

I forgot to mention that the vision the Sirenians have been seeing at the tower—the one that's inspired pilgrimages now, so that we've counted almost a hundred travelers from Sirenia since the beginning of the Sickness—is a vision not of the Savior Himself, but of the Holy Virgin that was His Bride.

mid-winter

Dear Queen Ella,

I apologize for the delay in answering your letter, and I pray for this letter's swift passage over mountain and swamp to make up for it. Not only are messengers from my country to yours less frequent than from yours to mine, but I was delayed in writing due to my own griefs. Not long after receiving your very kind and welcome greeting, I received news of my own family's death. I had a father, two sisters, and a nephew in Sirenia. All perished in the Great Sickness which also took yours.

I was raised a Sirenian like you, before I came here to marry King Nicolai of the Ghost People. My heart, already bound to Sirenia by childhood, by family, by blood, is bound even more tightly to that people—to your people, and inevitably to you—by our shared losses. I cannot adequately express to you the compassion I feel for the burden you carry now, as sovereigns and as a people, to repair not only the wounds of your own heart and family, but those of your kingdom.

I had two sisters I could not imagine ever dying. I could not imagine illness having anything to do with the fierce, cracking laugh of one and the rosiness of the other. The death of my father, who gave me nothing but tenderness since I was born and whom I never saw again since I came here, I will always regret. The people here have tried to teach me to be still and quiet with the first shock of grief I wake to each morning, when it feels as fresh all over again as in the first moment I heard the news. They teach me not to think, not to fear grief, not to escape into moaning and wailing. For the grief itself causes no violence, they say; only thinking what it means causes pain. I am not done grieving. I cannot bear to think how early their lives ended. Perhaps you feel this even more so, for your little girl. If I live on, I have to accept that their stories ended, and abandon them to live on into stories I can never tell them. I don't know if I'm ready for that. So I find my deepest comfort in simple experiences that have no story, like tending roses. *Though I am queen of this place, it is simple work that I do here—lifting and turning the damp weight of soil, slitting delicate bean pods that cling to my thumbs as the smooth beans in their nourishing, patterned wholeness clatter into a basket. These kinds of quiet tasks cocoon me. My good husband the king has held our lives in place while I have collapsed inside; I have been able to trust him thoughtlessly, and he has given me the silence I've needed. He picks up the work I have forgotten, and when the confusion of grief takes me out of my body, and I don't know where I am, he waits patiently for me to return. You have surely less space and time for grieving there, with all your busy responsibilities, than I do here. But I wish you comfort, Queen Ella, and perhaps a gentle garden in which to be still.*

I did not mean to tell all this, Queen Ella. If I had written back immediately, as I intended to, I am sure I would not have done so. But grief has deepened me and blurred the formal boundaries that once held me. I reread your letter and found a depth in it I had not found before. I hope you don't mind my saying that I feel a kinship with you. I have wondered about you since I first heard of you. I would love to meet you one day.

There is an elder here to whom I entrust my feelings, at times, and my doubts. During this time, I came to her needing a comfort so deep, I could not name it. She told me not to be afraid, for she can tell I am already comfortable with death—because I am comfortable with silence. I didn't understand at first what she meant, but I remembered that I was born of death. I mean my mother's death, when she birthed me. I had been living with death all my life. It's as if all the grieving I do is an echo of that first grief, which I was too young to feel. I feel that, when I am quiet with myself. And I think of you, Queen Ella, who also lost your mother, whoever she was, when you were young. Do you remember her? I don't know why it strikes me to tell you this, or why it came just now into my mind, but I think we must try to remember our mothers, with gratitude, in order to heal ourselves. Perhaps you will understand what I mean. I'm not sure that even I fully do.

Your concern for the wellbeing of our people, in their interactions with yours, is very much appreciated here. Thank you for asking. So far, all interactions have been peaceful on both sides, and we hope and believe that such will continue. I cannot do other than be plain with you, Queen Ella. We have no weapons here, no means of self-defense, no desire for any kind of fight. We live as humbly and peaceably as any people can, and all we ask of our visitors is that they do the same. That they respect our resources, take nothing but what they need to survive, and live gently on this land. As long as they continue to do this, we will continue to assist them in their survival here, when they come to worship or simply to live. This land is rough enough that they cannot very well survive here without our aid, which we gladly give. And I promise to communicate with you, dear and honored Queen who rules the country of my childhood, about any concerns or questions that may arise in future, from the interaction of our two peoples.

My husband Nicolai also sends his greetings and condolences to you and King Solon.

With respect,
Queen Mina Fox of the Ghost Kingdom

I felt ridiculous afterward, of course. Asked to respond in an official capacity to a missive from the queen of Sirenia, I'd written about shelling beans.

But I worry less about the wording of my letter than about the emptiness behind it. I wrote of my personal griefs, hoping to connect with her woman to woman, hoping to win her allegiance by shared vulnerability of heart, because I could not write of my people themselves. My people do not exist. They are merely ghosts of a people. They make no claim to anything. They defend nothing. They ask nothing. And yet it isn't true that there's nothing they are attached to, nothing that binds them together. I am certain they want this land respected. I am certain they wish for no one to ask anything more of it than the barest survival. And yet they will not come together and say so.

It's a quiet day, today. No neighbors have come by. Life continues on here after all, bean by bean, season by season, and sending a letter to the queen of Sirenia (by way of two adventurous young men who wanted to see that city for themselves) makes not the slightest ripple in it. I think everyone knows about the correspondence, but I can't be sure.

I watch Nicolai sitting outside on the wood-chopping stump, fingering his bow like he does some days, when he's in a brooding mood—as if it's an instrument he longs to play again, but I've learned never to speak of it, just as I never speak of that other, spiraling instrument that I threw once into the sea. I'm thinking about a story I know, and I don't know how I know it. I think it was whispered to me, on the lips of that woman who held me in a dream while I lost my baby. The creation story, perhaps, of her people. In the beginning, I remember—In the beginning, the world was not a world, she was not anything. But then the sky came down and inspired her, seduced her, threatened her, asked her, touched her—I'm not sure which. Before that, she had no color, no form, no definition. But then she did.

It was in meeting with that Other, that She was forced to become.

Ella

The first time I thought about the world beyond the palace, across the river—the first time I could think of you again, even a little, the way a sovereign should, was when my father came to beg of us.

When I sat down beside Sol on our throne that day, I saw before me a man I hardly recognized. I hadn't known or cared if he survived the plague, nor had I even thought of him for a long time. The dull planes of his face—blank, saggy spaces that expressed a temperament perhaps stupid, perhaps lazy, perhaps weak, perhaps merely lacking in human feeling altogether, I never knew—had once reflected my own loneliness back to me with such intensity, the way a mirror reflects sunlight so that it burns. But now they had roughened and filled in entirely with lines of suffering and agonized thought; his once heavy, opulent limbs were flabby and thin; his clothes were frayed and his hands shook constantly. I felt instantly sorry, and was hurt by Sol's unkind tone in speaking to him, even though I knew he only spoke that way in defense of me and what I had suffered.

"Merciful lord," my father groveled when Sol gave him leave to speak, "as you know, I am the natural father of your noble queen. I have watched proudly as my dear daughter rose in her splendor and found such good fortune as to be welcomed into the royal family, and never would I presume to request any special boon or station or even acknowledgement for reason of my relation to her. I have always made my own way in the world. But now I humbly beg you to consider..."

He spoke of a life unrecognizable, a family demolished. He spoke of lawless streets, neighborhoods, villages in which the poor took from the rich and no one could stop them, in which there were not even enough lords left to hold the lands, not enough soldiers to protect the borders, not enough workers to tend the fields. He spoke of enriched peasants buying land from destitute lords, merchants becoming nobility, anyone becoming anyone or marrying anyone and nothing to hold the order. He spoke of losing everything he had ever owned or been, and the reorganization of the world. He spoke of what we already knew, what we heard thirty times a day from every supplicant, and Sol was unimpressed.

"I do not ask for riches or handouts of any kind, Your Majesty. I ask only that I and my huntsmen, and the huntsmen of my two remaining brothers, be allowed to hunt small game in your royal forest. I know that at times in the past, this has been allowed, for certain—"

"There is no need to remind me what has been allowed in times past," snapped Sol.

"Yes, Your Majesty."

Sol glanced at me, and I nodded. "You may hunt in the royal forest once a month," he said, turning back to my father. "Small game only. I will alert the guards. And I remind you also, the forest extends many days' walk beyond the royal boundaries—that wilderness is open to any man, at any time."

My father faltered. "The Barbarians, your Majesty..." For although Barbarians had not raided us from that direction in many years, and the wall was no longer guarded, still many men feared them.

"It is open to any man," repeated Sol. "And many, in circumstances such as yours, are already trying their luck there."

My father paused, but not for long, and then bowed low again, his forehead nearly touching the ground. "Thank you, Your Majesty! Your generosity is highly spoken of, and not in vain, I see."

"Go," said Sol softly. He disliked compliments of that sort. They hurt him because he did not trust them, and because they were aimed at his heart, which was always sore.

Since the Death, I had not thought of myself as queen. I'd learned to manage, more or less, the massive daily clockwork of the kingdom inside the palace walls, whose workings Sol's mother had handled so gracefully that it seemed to flow on its own—though of course it was not quite so massive now. I kept my boys close to me and would not allow a nurse to tend them. I needed them as much as they needed me. I watched them tumble and grasp at life with such immediacy, thinking of neither past nor future, laughing when no adult could yet remember how. I allowed my broken heart to fill with gladness when they brought me mud gifts, animal discoveries, irrelevant questions. When I thought I had no will to rise in the morning, when I would have lain in bed trying to think out a reason, my boys woke me by force, with noise and with need. I listened hungrily to Jonah's imaginary conversations with his dead sister, willing myself to believe it was a real spirit he spoke to and heard, until Sol broke his faith one day, shouting *Who are you talking to?*—because Sol's grief was not like ours. (He would not have us speak of the dead. He would not have us mourn in his presence. He would not have anyone enter the rooms of the dead, which were closed off.) I read my children their stories. I taught them about the simplest facts of life which still seemed to be true: what a king was, what a knight was, how to address one's elders, how to hold a fork and spoon. I lost myself in motherhood.

Sol didn't have that luxury.

After this meeting with my father, the last supplicant of the day, he turned without looking at me toward the back exits, and I knew he sought Aurora and Aurora alone—for his evening ride. Unscheduled adventures in the countryside, of course, were no longer his lot. He had needed to become a king overnight, with no elders or family to guide him, except for various uncles who would rather undermine his authority than assist it. He must choose his council, instantaneously identifying friends and enemies. He must remake his city, make speeches of new hope, allocate funds among an entirely restructured society and aristocracy. He must do all of this while enduring a grief which, however painful my own loss, was incomparably more so. He moved with a hard, joyless stride I did not recognize. I think that even to him, his new form was still so new, so brittle, he felt instinctively that to compromise it would destroy him.

Nevertheless, I stopped him that day. It was the first time I had done so. I could not help it—my father's plea had moved me, against all my expectations. I had no anger left for that broken man, only pity. I feared Sol's impatience and irritation, to be interrupted in his path to the stables, but he was so unused to my voice at such a time, I saw at first only confusion in his eyes.

So I asked him—very humbly at first, and rightfully embarrassed for my ignorance—about the rules governing use of the royal forest. Were not others allowed to hunt there? Couldn't anyone hunt there, who had need enough? Surely we had more than enough to feed ourselves, and there was after all no other forest left in our kingdom—and no other way to access the Northern Forest except by crossing great rapids to the north and risking one's life?

Sol laughed gently at my question. "No, my love."

"But why?"

"Hunting is my only freedom, my only time away from all this. If the forest were filled with rabble, we would have no more free spaces. Our boys might not be safe when they begin their own hunting, with arrows flying everywhere. All the game would soon be gone."

"But surely things are not so black and white," I said. "Surely we could give a little."

"I do give a little," said Sol. "Did I not give way to your father?"

But not enough, I thought—what is small game once a month, to feed a family? Something hurt me, in the way my father had needed to beg us. I didn't want anyone to beg from me on their knees, and yet that was what people did, with kings and queens. And I remembered suddenly— and wished I did not—a conversation I'd heard between Kiera and her father long ago, in which Kiera had asked innocently why we could not take more of the lumber we needed from our own forests, and less from the Hums. It was too similar to the answer the king gave her then—this answer that Sol gave me now.

Perhaps it was then I began to wonder who this man was—this King Solon. He was not the man who had come to me in those first nights after the Death, who wept in my arms like a shipwrecked sailor (I had not seen that man again, not for some time now). He was one who could not afford uncertainty. I knew that much, from sitting beside him each day on the throne, in silence. I knew he made decisions about the allocation of resources and law-keepers, the choosing of stewards, the welfare of the poor and the rotting houses in the swamps, in an instant, impulsively, with little advice, just to demonstrate confidence. I knew he was not the prince who'd once defended the brilliant culture of the Wyes, for he sent his soldiers across their borders now without their permission; and I knew he was not that high-minded, curious friend to all people, who defended the weak and questioned every man from every walk of life with respect—for these people were a burden to him now. If he concerned himself deeply with anything, it was with keeping the priests in what he felt to be their rightful place, only because they challenged his authority daily, and after the desolation of the Sickness, their words had a hold on you that his or mine never could. Still he chose the High Priest and solidified his title without consulting anyone, charging him with keeping other priests in check, and naming him and his attendant hierarchy of Sirenian priesthood the highest spiritual authority in the land. I knew he did that from fear. I knew he thought in terms of consolidating power, not in terms of alliance or communication.

Yet how could I argue any opinion of my own, even if I'd formed a clear one? He was king, and he had earned it. He could talk me down from my opinions in an instant, and made decisions so quickly it dizzied me. I could not imagine such responsibility. He had chided me once, with a hand in my hair, thinking he was teasing me and unaware of his own cruelty, saying, "It's a good thing you are not king, my Ella. You would gather together the entire populace and listen to every one of their voices before you made any decision. It would take a year for you to make a single command."

And yet I was queen. Sometimes, at least, I pretended to be. I pretended, perhaps, when I sat beside Sol on our twin thrones each day and listened, still dazed, as if I'd just woken yesterday from Anna's death. I pretended when I ran through the day's rulings in my mind afterward, and questioned them to myself alone. And I pretended when I wrote a letter to the "king and queen" of the Ghost People—personages I was nearly certain did not exist, ruling a people who were little more than a children's fairy tale to me. I acknowledged the meeting of our two peoples and asked how I could facilitate its peaceful development, as if I were in control of such things. The truth was that I wrote this letter to the Ghost Kingdom because there was no other kingdom on whose treatment I could opine. I could not speak up for the Hums. I could not question the treatment of the Wyes. I could not send out my official good will to the Barbarians, nor would I have thought to, at that time. The Ghost People were the only ones that Sol did not think of, for they seemed too few and far away to him even to be real. Writing to them, I could pretend to be the queen I would wish to be, with that sense of honor.

But my daily thoughts were selfish. I ached bodily for the comfort of Sol's family, their living presence in this world. I wanted the queen I still thought of as the true queen to summon me in the morning, reprimand me and set me straight. I wanted to hear Kiera's sweet conversation like animated birdsong, and her breath as she slept by Anna's side. And I missed Sol. I missed my original charming knight, my seducing champion who climbed up the tower wall to creep in my window when he returned from adventures. We were so good together, as lovers and bedfellows, as children chasing each other down palace hallways, as prince and princess dancing or gazing with adoration across waving flags at tournament. But we were another thing altogether as king and queen.

I wish I could have spoken to you then, my people, about what mattered—but I had not yet learned to speak to you at all. It was so difficult, then, wasn't it, to hear the whispers of our Savior? They were drowned out by the screams of our loved ones, echoing in our empty houses, following us in our daily errands, as we passed again and again the burial swamps in the city and the fields where bodies were burned among the farms, until their covered ashes became features of our landscape, and the sedge and the vetch grew over them, and the birds picked through them for seeds and briar berries, but their songs could not cheer us. Would the Savior come to us at last on the heels of the Sickness, just when our despair seemed unbearable? Or had He already come, and those of us foolish enough to mourn had somehow missed Him? Had all those innocent ones who passed away before our eyes actually risen up with Him into the Kingdom of God? Was their suffering an illusion, merely a final trial of humility before being saved? Were the best ones taken on purpose by God, in His profound love for them? Or was this a fake apocalypse, brought about by evil? Was the real apocalypse still to come? I remembered how the Queen had writhed in madness when I asked her, on her deathbed. I liked to think He did come to her at that moment, and that she burned in the intensity of His divine touch, knowing that she would soon be released unto Him. But we who were left behind never knew such terror, such fire of agony; nor did we know bliss. We were left alone in our beds, waking to another cold morning.

Our new High Priest made suffering sound like the most blessed of undertakings: the more we suffered, the more our loved ones had suffered, the more we emulated the Savior who died in suffering—and the more precious we became in His eyes. We tried to draw meaning from that—or from anything. I don't mean to speak disparagingly of the priests who tried, some of them earnestly I am sure, to comfort you, or of the sustenance you drew from them during those trying times. To think that a perfect end was coming, when everything would come clear, and the good be clearly divided from the evil, and all the little daily agonies be revealed as but a crescendo of drumbeats toward the one great explosion of truth and salvation, where the Savior's appearance would be that much more ecstasy, that much more relief, because of the desperation of our need—this was the greatest temptation of our time.

But no one ever spoke aloud the fear that I am certain bound us: the fear that there was no meaning in the Sickness at all. That the apocalypse never came and never would. That we would sacrifice our ideals of salvation on the altar of Death, and then continue on. That life would just continue on. And that we had not arrived anywhere, but merely stumbled on through a wasteland among ghosts that half-nourished and half-destroyed us, and that the people we'd once idolized, terrified lest we should lose them, were still with us, but not the same.

♛　♛　♛　♛　♛

Sol still came to me, perhaps once a month, for comfort. I was the only one who saw his softness, his weakness, and like any woman, I treasured these secret gifts my man entrusted to me alone. But I did not understand yet the shame that was a necessary side effect of this vulnerability, and how it pulled him inexorably away from me, even as he leaned deeper into my arms. And as much as I comforted him, there was never anyone to comfort me.

I was queen. I thought sometimes of my mother, and the forbidden magic she had given me. All I had asked for was to go to a ball and dance in a pretty dress along with the other pretty girls. I never could have imagined all of this. I thought often of the Savior's Bride, who was spoken of more and more by pilgrims who claimed to have seen Her in the Ghost Kingdom. Though in Her image I found only chastity and servitude, qualities which did little to guide me in my present station, I needed to think of Her because I needed to understand how to love and be loved by the Savior. How to bind Him to me.

I wasn't conscious of that then, my people. How I'd lost my sense of the Savior, in Sol, and now was searching for Him with ceaseless desperation.

I think the day I stopped Sol, the day he turned my father away, I relived the loss of my father, when he chose not to defend me as a little girl. Seeing him that day broke my heart all over again. And that same sense of loss crippled me when Sol, later that same year, took Loren from me. Loren, once my husband's favored knight, had become over time my closest confidant. His little poems no longer frightened me—I knew them as expressions of kindness and no more. I sought Loren out for confession, for I found he understood both Sol's heart and mine, and could comfort me in my loneliness. And I could not understand Sol's suspicion of him at last, since it was he who had once explained Loren's chaste chivalry to me, when we were (it seemed to me) so much younger, a long time ago. But Loren was not chosen to be even one of Sol's men, when Sol solidified his position as king. And Sol refused to justify his decision to me, or to admit that jealousy played a part in it, but I knew. He asked me never to speak with Loren privately again.

I mention this now because it was after rereading Loren's first poem to me, one day—and feeling those words fall so softly on my heart now, with that pure, unselfish devotion that was Loren's special gift to give and that I was now, at last, sadly grateful to have received—that I decided to visit the new cathedral. I couldn't have understood the connection, then, between these two acts, but I understand it now.

Work on the cathedral had not begun again since the Sickness, because so many of the artists and masons had died, and we were hard-pressed to replace such talent. I had not visited the structure—if you could call it a structure—even once since work had ceased, partly because nothing reminded me so utterly of the plague's desolation, or of God's seeming abandonment, as the thought of those silent, forgotten arch frames, those uneven walls like a ruin, dust twirling lazily in the sunlight where once chisels and stone had rung together with joyful energy and voices had called direction back and forth as if guided by God's own intelligence. Also I hardly went out of the palace at all in those days, as you may well remember. I was heavily pregnant at that time and would soon go into my confinement again, which was a relief to me—to be forgiven all responsibility for a little while, and to have only one, simple purpose: the birth of another prince.

I entered those half-formed chambers alone, my servants waiting in the carriage as I requested. If anything, the silence that remained beneath the skeleton framing, in a partially mortared alcove that might one day (when all this was past and forgotten, I thought) be a confessional or a cubicle of prayer, seemed to echo more clearly than ever the presence of Him whose love I sought. Overcome by a new guilt, the guilt of being untrue, all this time, to the structure we had intended for God's honor, I sat on the ground like a child, resting my belly in my arms and closing my eyes to try to feel His presence. The last thing I remember, before I fell asleep, was fingering the letter I'd received in reply from Queen Mina of the Ghost Kingdom, which I carried always in my cloak. Its reference to my mother frightened me, and I didn't know what to do with it. Sol knew about my correspondence with that people, and it meant nothing to him, and yet that letter still felt like a forbidden secret, hidden against my body day by day. I had not really expected it. I had not really expected that my words would reach anyone, or that someone far away would believe I was queen.

In my sleep I seemed to hear singing, the kind of fervent, supplicating, thrilling song our souls might have sung long ago when faith was easier, the kind of singing that blends disparate voices of longing into a harmony of hope, a kind of singing I had never known—the song of women with intentions joined as one. I didn't let it wake me all the way up. It was too soothing, too much of a relief, to hear it, as if someone wept so that I didn't have to, and I could finally rest. Yet when I did wake, I woke knowing this truth before me: all the world wept the same sorrows that I did. A nun knelt upon one knee before me, her fingertips upon my wrist.

"Your Majesty?" She half-knelt there, well-balanced and nimble like a boy, and yet with an old, imperturbable peasant's expression. I wish I could picture that face now, but there were no striking features that I can remember. Only a long, fluid kindness, like the Golden River where it bends so widely, over and over, through the farmlands, as if it had all the time in the world.

"Oh," I said, passing a hand over my face. "Forgive me." And I struggled to rise, but found myself, as usual in this condition, more ungainly than I remembered.

"Hush," she said, with what could have seemed brazen familiarity, but was instead so gentle. "Take your time. I will not rise before you do." I stared at her as she motioned to the other nuns, who stood behind her waiting in the most delicate, unobtrusive manner, to go on without her. And they went on without her, to where I don't know. I don't think I was dreaming this. I think I really did wake to this woman before me. And I never really knew, in my confusion over the hierarchies of the world, if the members of our religious order stood above us or below us, as sovereigns, but in the face of this woman, I only know I felt—oh, not equal exactly, but something more than that. I felt her touch, that's all I can say. Like water.

"Are you well, My Lady?" she asked.

"Yes," I said. "Only the sun is very hot. I only meant to sit for a moment, and rest."

"Of course. Can I help?"

And she helped me to stand. She was quite strong, for a little woman.

"Did I hear you singing?" I asked her.

She nodded. "Oh yes."

"It is good that you come," I told her, taking her hand with impulsive gratitude. "It is good that God knows our intention for this place—knows that we keep it, I mean. And my dear sister-in-law Narsa, is she well? Is she still with you?"

For this first order of nuns, formed only recently since the Sickness, had taken Narsa into their kind shelter, after Narsa had lost her mind. And my longing for the past was so great, in those days, I even missed her. I missed her as a part of Alden, and Alden's love, and Alden's steadiness and strength and the way he had held her together and made her whole. I hadn't realized that she, too, had been an essential part of his goodness.

The old nun nodded and patted my hand. "Of course," she said. "And have you found what you were looking for, in coming here today to the blessed cathedral, Your Majesty?"

"I—I don't know. I don't know what I was looking for."

"These are hard times," she said, not in the least flustered, unlike me. "We all commit the sin of doubt, sometimes."

"Have you yourself doubted?" I asked, shocked into tactlessness by her way of speaking.

I remember her smile glowed the way stone glows when the sun has filled it all day long. "I have overcome today's doubt by coming here."

"Is it true? Do you feel God's presence here, so strongly?"

"I do feel God's presence. But even when I cannot feel it clearly, I still come. I keep the faith. I show up for Him. We are responsible for our Savior's presence in this world, Your Majesty—we, ourselves. But you know that, of course."

I looked away. I felt the tears coming, and to be honest, I longed for them—a feeling of release inside my throat—as if I'd been waiting for them forever. "I miss Him so much," I heard myself say. To this day I don't know who I really meant.

The nun stood comfortably before me. I looked down at her bright old hands, folded together in loose union, as if she held peace inside them. "We Sirenians are experiencing a great loss now," she said in her unhurried way, as if receiving each word one by one. "But we know loss already, in our souls—we know it in a way no other people knows it. We knew the loss of our dear Savior, two hundred and fifty-three years ago, and that was the Great Loss. Forever our hearts are stained with those tears. Every loss after is only a humbling, a return. And our yearning for Him teaches us that all our yearning—all our yearning for what is lost and what is missing—is a yearning for God. It is a sacred yearning, a sacred grief that you must feel. You must not be afraid, dear Queen Ella."

I didn't say anything, but let the tears fall. They fell down my face and upon my own folded hands, and the touch of them upon my skin brought me the most exquisite relief, as if they were not my tears at all, but my own Savior's tears. Her tender use of that address, by which no one else ever called me, touched me to the core. For I remembered that there was someone higher than king and queen, someone even more responsible than we, who could call even "Queen Ella" by an endearment like that, as if she were a child. That someone was not the nun, of course, but God.

She leaned in toward me, as if imparting a secret. "The king and queen must never lose faith," she whispered.

"No!" I cried. "Of course not."

"Not even in the privacy of your own rooms," she said. "Never, not even in your heart."

I sat down suddenly on the stone wall near me.

"Your Majesty," she said. "You must be tired. Shall I help you to your carriage?"

I shook my head. The sun felt like such a burden upon me, beating down. I wanted to confess everything, but could not. I had not known until this moment that my selfishness as queen, my avoidance of my people, my inward turning into motherhood and deafness to your tears, was still nothing more than guilt—and that feeling was the most selfish of all. "Oh Sister, do the sins of kings and queens curse all of their people? If someone in our family had sinned, could all of this—all this loss—be our fault, somehow?" I looked up at her. I still carried this question, after all this time. It kept me from tasting my food. It kept me from taking joy in the new child that grew in my belly. It kept me from being able to imagine the future.

"I cannot answer that," she said, instinctively crouching down again so that she did not stand higher than I.

"Can't you?" I tried to dry my face and looked in the direction of my carriage, where my servants had waited diligently for far too long. I felt sorry. I heard your voices in the street, ever rising and falling, and felt overwhelmed by every moment of every day of the whole life that stretched before me, and sorry forever.

At last the nun sat down beside me. "Your Majesty," she said. "You do not need to confess to me the burden of your past sins. But perhaps you sin right now, in this moment."

"What—why?"

"Forgive me, but I refer to the sin of pride, when you assume that your sins alone could destroy an entire people. I refer to the sin of arrogance, in thinking you can choose whether or not you deserve the gifts God has given you, and in thinking you can understand why they were given."

I looked at her, I don't know how long. She was the only person, besides the queen before me, who had ever named my darkness out loud. How could she know?

"What is your name?" I asked her, and she told me. But I cannot tell it to you, for I feel certain she would wish it kept quiet. Everything those women did, I know, they did without recognition, faceless, for God. I never saw her again. I knew where the convent was. I could have gone there for comfort. But I never did. I understood, after this conversation, the necessity of sacrificing every crutch that had upheld me. My childishness. My need. My guilt.

"Do you know what sin means?" she asked me as she walked me back to the carriage.

"Something that opposes God's will?"

"No. For God is love. To sin is to deny His love. Some people are saying that the Savior saved us from our sins by dying. But that is not quite right, Your Majesty. The Savior saved us from our sins by loving us. Our job is to carry on His love."

"And you—how do you do this? How do you carry it on?"

"We go among the poor, Your Majesty. We give alms. We give comfort. Anyone who comes to us for solace, for shelter, we give it."

I looked at her, this little woman with her earnest words, who had sent the other nuns away so that she could hear my sorrows in private. I believed her. "And Narsa, too?" I asked. "Narsa does this?"

"Yes, Your Majesty."

"And it is healing for her?"

"Yes."

"And do we—does my husband the king give you money to distribute, and comforts to distribute, among those who need them?"

Maybe she hesitated, but only just barely. "Yes, Your Majesty, King Sol gives what he can."

"What he can?" What could she mean? But I stopped myself. If I couldn't make Sol explain himself to me, how could I ask it of her? Still, the sorrow in her eyes—was it sorrow, or did I imagine it?—hurt me. "Sister." I stopped before my servants, or anyone, could hear me. I leaned into the archway for support. One day, this arch would be our entrance to God. "Do they speak of me? The people? How do they speak of me, their queen?"

This time she didn't hesitate. "Your Majesty, they remember how you brought your little girl, how you gave her to them, to be burned with their dead."

I shuddered. "Yes?" But there was no tone in my voice, no breath.

"They miss you, they never see you. But they remember how you gave them your little girl, and so they know."

"They know what?"

"That you love them, Your Majesty."

♕   ♕   ♕   ♕   ♕

Dear Queen Mina,

I thank you for your gracious response to my letter.

It is true that these times ask much of us, as sovereigns, as queens. One day soon, after I recover from my next childbirth, perhaps you and I will speak of these things in person. I intend a pilgrimage myself, to visit the Holy Virgin where She has appeared at the shrine in your country. I would join some of my people in this quest, for the sake of all our healing. I would reconnect, by Her guidance, with our Savior and His plan for me. I would ask Her forgiveness. I would release, there, whatever is left for me to sacrifice, so that I might give myself more wholly to my country.

In hope,
Queen Ella of Sirenia

Lemara

the spinning wheel

It must be the sound of women's laughter that pulls me up the tower stairs, where I press to the half-closed door. How rare to hear such laughter in Zara! Something has excited these women, old voices and young, and they huddle around it—some thing—and now I hear it, the real sound beneath the laughter. The Hum.

They open the door to me. "Lady Queen, see this magic just brought to us! It is called a Spinning Wheel. From across the sea! A gift from the island Mellea, and it spins wool into thread."

Oh Rhiannon. The Hum. How fast it whirs me back into the Dream. The rhythm so fast and yet slows me right to stillness, whirring as Hummingbird wings whir and blur, pausing Time in Air, both moving and frozen, the way the River Golden is always the same and always moving. Deep down in that center I am in my heart always running—running away forever along the beach and then into the Jungle, scattering the leaves of the Gala Trees which are already the color Gold but I had forgotten (I forgot everything, when I saw that color Rhiannon wove for me), flying barefoot in the way that I could fly when I was a girl, my eyes in my feet. My lover, it must be, who waits for me, and yet more than him—some great ceremony which will take us in, which will answer us and which we will answer—and I am coming, coming up the hill—

"Queen Lemara, what is wrong? She looks faint—"

"It's her time, call the midwife—"

And I wake to a wheel that is turning, upwelling within, spinning the life of my daughter into being, and I don't know who carried me to this room or why these women kneel around me with expressions of fear upon their faces. I remember their shock when I birthed Uriah, how they stood back in awe just to see me control my own contractions to slip him into my own hands with ease. I remember how for Wye and Sirenian women, childbirth is agony, they have forgotten their muscles, it happens like some violent accident—and no one blessed me the way they should, and Uriah was born with an airy, fragile spirit that has only survived by the protection of Cats. How I wish now for those quiet, furred, intent companions—they are better midwives than these. "Get me up," I say impatiently. "Help me to the Sea."

"Queen Lemara," the midwife tries to gentle me, as if I don't know what I say. "Lie down and rest. The baby is coming, but there is some trouble. Do not strain yourself, or you may lose blood."

"Help me to the Sea," I hiss.

For I can hear the Sea's heartbeat, all the way from here, wherever we are, and only the wash of those timeless waves will soothe the tension of the wheel ever spinning within me. *Rhiannon.* She seems to sing my name, like a warning.

They guide me down, stair after stair, and colors blur but my other senses pulse stronger with every step, with every pulse of my womb—the sickening meat smell, the smothering bread smell, the deathly-fresh Sea smell now bursting cold over my skin. I feel my feet smacking sand, cutting on stone, I hear the song from the waves. Some wild, weary, hungry song I know—and I think it is the song of my daughter, coming to meet me.

Shouts and pleadings, urgent whispers, even a man's voice in the distance, I ignore them all, cast away the gentle arms that seek to restrain me, nothing can restrain me, who is more powerful than a woman giving birth? All the strength of Creation is in me, as I squat over the incoming tide with the waves anchoring my feet in their cold, cold, splendid grasp. But Roses, Roses—they tangle me fiercer than ladies' arms, they tangle me in pain in Dreams forgotten, they strangle my womb even as I fight to be reborn, to begin again in this world, *let me live.* I fall to my knees, the Sea swarming low, tingling at the backs of my thighs, puffing behind my ears, and I Dream I am running over the crest of a hill into so much light, into a young breath of Mist that touches me without sticking, a world I have never known, where the Air is alive. I hear the singing of all the beings who live and love and hunger in the Sea, and I'm surrounded by white Horses with spirals of light spinning like the thread from the Spinning Wheel from the center of their eyes up into the knowing Sky. They snuff around me, shaking their manes with curiosity and joy, smelling of spices and wine. And within the circling river of these Sky Horses, a woman is moving, too, a woman of fiery hair, hair the color of the Sun's goodbye. Oh, that fire which keeps the Sky Horses from touching her but draws them ever to her, that Fire which can warm or burn a world! She is the Other Priestess! The Priestess of the Other World, the one who is taken by the Jaguar, accepted by Rhiannon and crossed over. The one I have never seen. The babe laid out in the Forest is either spared, to lead as Priestess in this world, or taken by the Jaguar to lead as shadow in the Other. Both are necessary. I know it's her, because she smells like a predator. I wrap my arms around her, and the Sky Horses pass behind me so close that they touch me—a slide of fast cloud—and light bursts from my womb. I hold to her. I hold to her strength like a column of Tree rising up inside me, strength to continue on, on, into this life after all. *It is you who will live,* she whispers. *You are forgiven.* And my daughter falls forth to the Earth.

But something is wrong. I collapse into the seething waves, watching Micah who has rushed forth, Micah who lifts and bends over her, praying. The midwife slapping her tiny body, lightly, calling out—but she doesn't know my daughter's name. The voice of the Sea gone quiet. Too quiet.

Ruya, I whisper, for that is her name. But she doesn't whisper back.

"Dear God, give her breath, give her breath," my husband is praying, my daughter's face darkening, my own heart frozen as I see him bow his head, the weight of his faith heavy on his shoulders, his earnest pleading, his tears for our daughter who lies breathless as the Moon emerges suddenly from a bed of clouds where She's been sleeping and my anger erupts at last.

How dare you, you pretending god! You who would give or withhold mercy from my husband who prays for my daughter's life! Who demands the death of Animals! I do not even know you. What do you know of the questions a woman faces, trembling between Dream and waking, upon entering this world? Give her back!

And I wrest my baby back from their arms and rise up strong on my watery legs, and I am Priestess of Hummingbirds spinning within myself, spinning a power that can always be recalled by any woman in service of her child, no matter how deeply it has been lost. I whir on Hummingbird wings into her center, feel the horror of her doubt, and call my Ancestors behind me, call the Death Priestess, Queen of the Ghost Realm of Sky Horses, Mina Fox—*We speak to you, spirit of Ruya, daughter of a Priestess, you are right to hesitate at the entrance of the world, asking what kind of woman you will be, Wye or Hum or ghost of the past, and where you are and why, your people in ruins and your mother living nowhere, but I call you now, I call you Ruya to life, and I promise you that for you I will survive. I will watch over you. Live.*

I press my mouth to hers, and breathe my life into her. And she takes it in, and breathes it out screaming into the sad, salt Air of this new world.

matters of state

"Mara."

"Hm."

"I am sorry, but I must speak to you."

Speak to me, I don't mind. What should I mind? I draw a circle around the little eye of her belly button with my finger. Her skin—ah, all day I have been trying to name such a color! Like the shadow in the throat of an Iris, yet her palms and her soles buttered brown—and her eyelids damp and blushed over the hidden light of her giant, wondrous eyes. Already there is some clever quirk, some bend at the edges of her lips, some laughter that will unfold her heart. We Dream together every day, Ruya and I. On her ninth day, she Dreamed of a great Mare, restless in her stall. I did not know Horses, where I came from, but now I think of them in the stables of Zara, slaves to men, a secret force that might someday break free.

"What are you doing?" asks Micah.

I turn to him with the laughter of my daughter in my eyes. "What? Do you think I cast some spell?" I tease him. I think, *How can he anger me now? I have her.*

He scrutinizes me for a long moment, and I feel sorry for him that he has not this joy to heal him. I can barely read his expression, he is so far away, and the effort tires me, so I turn back to Rue. "It is nothing to laugh at," he mutters. "The women whisper of what you did. There may come a time when you must publicly refute these rumors."

"What rumors?" But I remember how I raised my head in joy when Rue first cried out, and how the faces of the midwives reflected only fear.

"The Prophets say you called upon false gods. That you are dangerous. I have defended you, but—"

"I gave my child life. I am her mother."

He keeps his voice gentle, but I hear the effort it takes him. "I am glad—I am overjoyed—that she lives. But this magic—my people call it arrogance, to raise yourself above God in this way."

"Oh Micah, there is no above or below, for me, for my people, for us. There is no humbling, no begging, no bowing down. We do not pray to Goddess and God. We become them."

His face recoils, his upper lip wrinkling. "And this is not arrogance?"

"No," I say, feeling only compassion. The time a woman first spends with her infant—this must be the loneliest time of a man's life. "This is surrender, Micah."

He doesn't answer, and I give Rue my smile again. She's looking up at me, searching for reassurance. I see her search me all the time, to make sure—to make sure I will keep my promise. *I am here.* I remember the way the Mare paced in her Dream, back and forth, not yet furious to be free—but she would be, I could feel that. She would be soon. We Hummingbird People have no family names like the Sirenians, for we are all of us family. We are not called like Micah Wye, or Uriah Wye son of Micah, for we do not need a name to tell us apart from other peoples—we are the original people, we are the People. But we have each of us a shadow name, a name that hangs onto our Human-called name like a tail, an instinctual name, a name that roots us in. This is the name of our Animal partner. A Priestess' shadow name is always Hummingbird. I am Lemara Hummingbird.

And my daughter is Ruya Mare, of the Unicorns. Mina Fox gave this name to her, in our shared Dream. But this, only Rue and I know.

"Mara, are you listening? I'm trying to tell you something."

I look at him. This man. The king of Zara.

"You know I have agreed to ally with Prince Leo, we have spoken of this—"

"Yes, yes, we have spoken. Do not speak of Barbarians here, now. You have made your will known—now leave me, if that's all you can speak—"

"No, that is not all." He takes a breath and I clutch Rue tighter, not knowing why. "Lemara, I must tell you this now. Prince Leo will be paying us a visit soon, in the service of our planned alliance. He will bring his wife and son. Mara, to form an alliance with another kingdom is a heavy thing. We must make some offering, to demonstrate our sincerity. Something to symbolize our promise to each other."

I watch him, waiting, like a Cat.

"This is what I am coming to. Both sides must make an offering. We must seal the alliance in some way."

I wait.

"This is often done through marriage."

Almost, I begin to laugh, for I do not understand what he means, and it is funny to me, but then suddenly I remember his words—*He will bring his wife and son.*

"No." My voice is quiet. It does not need to rage, because my life is mine now. And I will fight to the death. Never. Now I know, yes, now I know why I am alive.

"Mara, please understand, you can still raise her as you wish. I have sacrificed much to give you that. But when it comes to the future of our kingdom, our children do not belong to us; we do not even belong to ourselves."

I shake my head, amazed. I know this could never happen. I am only amazed. "She is your own daughter. What is a promise worth to you?"

"Mara, I just told you, you are free to—"

"To raise her until you take her from me. Do you think it a game for me, to be a mother, to raise my child? For no reason? For no love? Do you know, Micah, that I, too, am alive? That your daughter, also, is alive and shall love?"

"Mara, you must understand, this is necessary. If they break their promises to us, if they are anything but kind and respectful to us and our family, if we see any reason that Ruya might come to harm in their hands, then the marriage will be forfeit."

"You." I grab his face in my hand, and I can barely speak for fury. It isn't the Barbarians I fear. I gave my child life, and by the same magic I will protect her. What I fear, what makes me lose my grip again as he pulls away, is knowing that I can be so hurt—not by some monster prince who led monsters of violence down upon us long ago, some Barbarian prince—but by this man. This man who swore to honor me as his bride, who swore to protect my people, who swore to sanctify the life of my only daughter, my only hope, to my care. "You will do this?" I ask him, my voice hoarse. *This is your last chance, Micah. You will never know me, after this. You will never witness magic, never again. You will live in dust.*

Micah retracts his face gently from my grasp, his eyebrows tense, concerned, unyielding. "Yes, Lemara. I am telling you, I must."

"When?"

"The bond will be cemented now, when Leo comes. The boy is only two years old, Uriah's age. When they are of age—"

"And you think my will in this matters not at all. Am I not your queen?"

"I don't know," he says, angry now in that way he gets—angry like a man never gets with a woman in the South Forest. "I don't know what you are, Lemara. I don't know who you are, or who you stand for. You think only of your own needs. If I knew you could take into account the needs of the people, of both our peoples, and consider them more highly than your own, I would discuss matters of state with you, and we would make decisions together."

"Matters of state? Matters of state?"

"You are hysterical."

Rue is sobbing.

"This is my daughter's heart you speak of! It is not a matter of state!"

"I'm sorry, Mara, I know she is beloved to you, but the personal desires of one person's heart, no matter how beloved, are not to be prioritized—"

"I know nothing of prioritizing! The love of a Priestess is the will of the Goddess. Where it leads her is the future of her people. *That is what is.*" I only notice, now, the wailing of my voice, now that it quiets again. I close my eyes, willing myself not to be sick. I knew this would happen. I knew I would be betrayed. Didn't I always know? But if I do not have a voice, I have silence. If my words cannot be heard, then I will survive by denying him my touch, my presence, everything I am. I crouch backward, encasing Rue in my arms, waiting in the silence of the Cats until he stops speaking, until he stops trying, until he sighs and turns away, and I hear his footsteps receding stair after stair, away.

I Dream

I Dream I wake with you, Tiras, on the banks of the River Golden, in a place I do not know, in the cold misty hour before dawn, and we are just barely alive.

Rhiannon reaches a Silver arm from the rapids and hands us the bone cup, and bids us drink. And we drink, and raise ourselves up, and are revived. For it is tears that we drink, this time.

The River rushes by us, sleek and free, and makes us very still. I hear an Owl calling, a low, reaching, skeletal song, and from the hot lava center of my body I lift a golden Seashell filled with light. I lift it high, and we both gaze at it, recognizing it, and we gasp together in relief and disbelief and joy, and you, Tiras, begin to crawl toward me, licking your lips, and when I see you reach for it, I hold it away from you, laughing. Then your face softens with devotion, and your eyes make me an animal promise. And you grin and leap up, and with that careless sweetness in your swinging arms and that predator zeal in your fast, hard legs, you jump and snatch, but I run away.

You chase me. I burst through thicket after thicket of Flowers, feeling your fingertips brush my hair and arms and buttocks in your grasping, and I feel so ticklish with fear and excitement, I stumble often, and your arms flicker upon me ever more sweetly, and you bite at me, laughing and begging. We run like this. I stumble through the River, and you catch me there, reaching around my body for the shell which I hold above my head and behind me and under me, our naked skin kissing and sweating, your lips passing my ear, and me wiggling all around and between your parts, so that I can keep you from reaching this sacred thing while feeling your wonderful urgency all upon me. I slip away again. But I know that you will catch me. I giggle all over with anticipation, my flesh leaking its hot gel of desire as I run, because I know you will catch me, and I am waiting and waiting, and I love your wanting, and my waiting.

I run through a forest that deepens and darkens, and I don't notice the deepening and darkening, but it tangles me further and further, so that in my giggling anticipation, I trip and roll among its ropy arms, until you come upon me all wrapped and caught in a net of Vines. You stop and rear over me, seeing me caught like this and knowing you will win; your breath comes wild and deadly, and I am afraid, but my desire tears me open like the threads that opened my heart to your sword. The Faeries are singing. You are no longer smiling, for your desire has overcome you so completely, you have lost everything; you can no longer think, you have no free will, you think you will die of it and you hate me for it.

So you fall upon me like the Jaguar, only without the Jaguar's love, and the shell falls from my hands and is crushed all to pieces beneath us as you trap me beneath you, and you spear me in my other heart, the one between my legs where Flowers grow, and you thrust with all the weight and all the hatred of your male soul, but I love you more than ever, and I give all my tenderness in taking you, for I know the pain you feel—I know how with every thrust, you give up everything. I know because I feel you: we are together, Tiras, and we win and lose together.

When you are empty I kiss you and soothe you, and you suck at my breast, loving me again and belonging to me forever, and we sleep. We Dream the other lifetimes we have lived together, but I will forget them later. When I wake, you are still sleeping, and I begin to kiss your breast where the smoky wound is, for I want to know what it is; I want to know your secret, as you now know mine. I feel that your breath comes from here, and it labors and creaks, and I want to know why. But you wake, roaring in fright, and in a flapping of wings and a thumping of hooves and a tearing of claws, you are gone from me.

Still the Sun has not returned, though the time feels so long. I wander alone in search of you. You are a little white Stag disappearing in a moon-wash of fear through the heaviest, oldest vines that drag upon the whispering Earth, and I become a Jaguar, tiptoeing through the Tree limbs high above you, watching you stop and turn and wonder, learning your every move, every hesitation in your twitching ears and flanks, and then I fall upon you.

But you slip out from under my giant black paws. So I follow you into still valleys and along all the Deer paths of the Jungle, until finally I hear you whisper, and I know you are a tiny Moth flying near me. So I become a Bat, sending signals to find you. I fly in a long, uneven flapping of webbed fingers, through the tunnels of the Trees, and I listen to the shape of you, so tiny and powder-perfect, throbbing toward the Moonlight. I follow you out to the Forest edge, and into the Wind that tosses us so hard, we cannot direct ourselves, and we are torn apart from each other. I cry and cry for you, seeking you in the Wind, until I become so weary with crying that I fall into the Sea. You are a Rainbow Fish and I am a Dolphin, aching and sensitive between the press of the waves, my mouth hard and toothy, and I slice the depths for you, but you rise up again, laughing in your freedom, a little boy who refuses to come home, and you change, and change, and change.

When you are a Mosquito, I become a Dragonfly, and chase you in slow horizontal arcs at the edges of the world. When you are a Monkey, I became an Owl floating behind you, a shadow of silent light. When you are a Poison Frog, I became a Python, tasting your slippery passage, undoing my mouth to take you in whole. But I never find you, for every time I think I've almost reached you, you change into something else without my knowing, so that I only chase the memory of what I thought you were.

He is testing you, says Rhiannon from the Wind. He wants you to recognize him. But every time you change form, he is frightened.

But he changes, too! I say. And it isn't fair.

Then Rhiannon laughs Her rude, Raven laugh.

When I'm too tired to go on, I become myself again and return to the River Golden, but it's nothing but a dry, empty channel now. I make a nest in the dead Riverbed, from dead Ferns and the feathers of rotted Birds, and I sit and wait for you, and all is silent.

And when you come to me, you are a yapping, wild Dog, vicious and angry, and you creep around and around me, yipping and keening, like a wild Dog who wants the food at a gathering of Barbarian humans who cook meat by Fire, but is too frightened of the Fire to come closer. And you don't recognize me, though you're drawn to me and don't know why, and though I speak to you and try so hard to coax you with my gentle words, your cries are so hateful and lonely, I begin to doubt that I recognize you at all. Now it is time to call the Sun, and there is nothing else I can do.

The Sun is rising now, and we are both Human again, but we sit apart from each other as if in different worlds. And we are hollow and starving and weary to the bone. And Rhiannon tells us we must hold a ceremony of mourning for the sacred shell that we broke, when you took me in the Vines. But all we know how to do is to take the shards in our hands and eat them. We sit here all alone on either side of the empty River, not looking at each other, hateful and hurting, grinding the shards of shell between our teeth as the Sun grips and strains at the edge of the world, swallowing them without Water, and they tear our throats as they go down.

And this is the second ritual of the Dream I Dreamed for a hundred years, oh Beloved. The Ritual of Forgetting.

Rowan
(the son)

thirteen years from now

My dearest Rue,

Only my first day without you, and already it echoes—still beautiful, as every day in Zara is beautiful, but lacking in some dimension. It is too serious here without you. Everything just as it is, and that's all.

The South Forest pulls your mother more, instead of less, as the years go by. And this time she has you with her on the journey. She is fulfilling her dream. And though you are promised to me in marriage, and I to you, my heart knows differently. She said she would return with you in less than a moon, but I don't believe her.

I have decided to write you letters, even though I can't send them, to bridge the pain of missing you, and maybe when you return, you can write me a letter in reply. I hate to go against your mother in any way, who is the closest I've ever had to a real mother of my own, yet I cannot help but encourage you in learning to write. I have seen you learn anything you set your heart to, Rue.

Speaking of mothers, yesterday before we said goodbye, you said something about mine that hurt me. We had never spoken of my mother before. I know you don't understand. You are only thirteen years old, and even if you were older and wiser, you would still struggle to understand a life lived so far away from yours, in a land so foreign to the graceful ways of Zara. Yet still I wish to explain it to you, in the hopes that you might try. I can never say these things in spoken words. I cannot place my deepest thoughts into your mind the way your mother's people could once speak together in silent telepathy. Only the written word has ever allowed me to speak truly what I know and feel.

You seem to have some romantic idea of my mother, because she is half-faerie. You said that maybe I never understood her. And you are right—for no one did, and no one ever will—but to think that you could understand anything about her motivations, never even having laid eyes on her, is very foolish, Rue, and you know it. Sometimes I think you say certain things only to vex me, but I know it means you care about me somehow—even if caring for me means you want to hurt me—unlike my mother who hurt me over and over without meaning to, because she never thought of me at all.

I think my father hoped that by breeding with a faerie woman, he would produce a son with the best features of both worlds: the fierce fighter instinct of a mortal man and the invincible, supernatural power of the faerie world. Instead, I ended up with the hopeless romanticism that is humankind's greatest weakness, and the delicate physique, eerie intuition, and uncanny memory of faerie. I remember things that no regular boy could remember: my birth, for example, and the first time I ever saw you, when you were only an infant and I only two years old.

People say my mother was pregnant again once or twice after I came into the world, but lost the babies before they were born; I do not believe it. I think she terminated those pregnancies by some violent magic, after discovering that being a mother was nothing but pain and displeasure to her. I came into this world unloved by any person and with the sorrow of an old man in my every breath—which, in the first year of my life, came labored and weak. I knew that my parents hated one another, only my father expressed his hatred by seeking to dominate and devour my mother, while my mother expressed hers by disappearing. Passing through her body to enter this world was like passing through an abandoned hallway of shattered glass. It almost killed me. There is nothing human inside that woman. She is not capable of love. Though my parents hate each other, they have never realized how alike they are. If you think (as surely your mother has taught you) that Prince Leo is stubborn, cold, and unyielding, I tell you, Princess Rowan was too.

One of my earliest memories is the beating of my mother by my father. I did not see it happen, but I knew what violence was happening when I heard the sounds she made. Though my nurse was kind, I think, she was overworked (nurturing an infant was not a task highly prioritized by anyone in that castle), and had little time for me. Accustomed to long hours on my own, I learned to send the feelers of my mind into other rooms of the castle, as I lay in the cage of my crib, so that I could make a map inside my head—not a visual map, but a map of feelings. I knew that my father was hurting my mother in a room nearby, and because I was made of their flesh, the violence of one upon the other hurt me also. I wept and tossed and tried to climb from the crib, though where I meant to go I do not know. An infant does not experience anger, perhaps, but sometimes a kind of outrage when basic needs are not met. I felt that outrage when I heard my mother's cry. At first I felt it for her sake, because my father was hurting her. But as the cries went on, I felt it also against her. What outraged me was that her cries were not human. They did not resist or beg or express any compassion even for herself. They were the ragged, bewildered, terrified cries of an animal whose only instinct is self-preservation. I could not bear their absolute helplessness. I was one year old, and they set inside me a fear deeper than reason which I have never been able to shake. When I heard them, I could picture the vacant expression of her eyes.

To explain—my mother was beaten at that time because she had run away from my father. She had tried to escape, but Rufus James returned her to him (though he loved her, but he was slow in his thinking and did not always make the best choices). And though I know she had every reason to wish for escape, it never occurred to her to take me with her. I was her son, Rue. I, too, lived at the mercy of a monster. Unlike her, I truly was helpless. But when she ran away—as she would do again one day, and just as selfishly—she ran away without me. Without even thinking of me, and without looking back.

Rufus would never believe me that I remember this. He would not admit that it happened. But I remember her beaten, half-blackened face rising up above my crib that night, like a nightmare. I remember how her wounds sprouted fur, how her fingers turned to daggers, how she reached for me. There was no hatred in her eyes—there was just nothing. Sometimes I do not believe my mother thought anything at all. She was not made of thoughts. But I was a problem for her—I kept her from disappearing, I was her child, I made her real. It was Rufus who stopped her. He had torn up the stairs, limped wildly through the halls, beaten down the door when he heard her screaming. But he came too late to protect her. Instead, he was able to save me from her raging claws.

Rufus, the only person I know who ever loved my mother, shared the deepest considerations of his heart with me, and though I was very young, I listened, for I loved him. Before they ran away together, Rufus raised me until I was seven years old, for my father was disappointed in me from the first, and turned his attention to his stronger, bastard sons. He gave me over to Rufus to make a man of me, respecting Rufus' brute abilities without recognizing the sensitive soul hidden behind them, not realizing that Rufus would unleash upon me all the tenderness he had kept pent up since the death of his sister long before. Instead of trying to stamp out my poetic tendencies, Rufus admired and encouraged them, for though he was raised in a world that would not believe he had a soul, he was always seeking some way to remind himself that he was more than a beast—that his sister, in risking and losing her life for him, had not died in vain. It was easy for me to see the goodness in him. But my heart was hardened forever against the woman he loved, my mother. When he spoke of her, I heard only the pain in his voice, and saw only the selfish way she used him. He used to lament of his longing for her, wondering aloud why it was that she seemed sometimes to yearn toward him also—or at least to accept his attentions. Was it because he reminded her in some way of the Dwarves, who had raised her and whom she seemed to remember with a kind of longing? Was it because he was kind to animals, whom she felt to be her kin? Was it because he offered her her only chance of escape? He did not want her to go with him only because she felt she had no choices. He wanted her to go with him because she truly loved him. But this was an impossible dream.

You talk of freedom—and my mother's need for it. But you have a mother and father and brother who love you dearly. I have no one. I do not mean to sound hard, but I think it is an easy luxury, for someone like you, to speak of—or long for—something called "freedom."

I know what you would say. You would say she had been hurt so badly, as a child. She had been abandoned to the wilderness and left to die; she had been raised by some kind of primitive beast-men whose care of her we cannot imagine; she had been mistreated by the husband who claimed her by force. If she never came to know herself, never came to love herself, never looked in a mirror, never believed she had a self at all, can she possibly be called selfish? I tell you yes. She can. In fact more selfish than you or I could ever be. Because listen to me, Rue—I, too, know what it is like to be treated cruelly. I know what it is like to be unloved. Yet still, I am capable of love. I have enough sense of self to feel my own wounds, and in this feeling lies the ability that makes me human—the ability to feel the wounds of others.

For this reason, I don't resent Rufus for leaving me, for falling under her spell. I know what it's like to love someone so hopelessly that your mind begins to be warped by it. Sometimes I think I knew from the first moment I saw you, as an infant in your mother's arms, that you would one day break my heart. I know that no matter what promises have been made concerning us, no matter what destiny is planned for us, no matter how you tease me and lift your skirts in the waves alongside me as we splash through our childhoods arm in arm, I do not have you. When you are old enough to long for touch as blushingly and painfully as I long for it, I will not be the one whose touch you seek. And in the coldest corners of my heart, I am still the sad old man I was when I was born, and I know that I wait in vain. Over the years, while your beauty unfolds, my limbs will stiffen. My voice will whither with swallowed-back kisses. My lips will turn to stone.

I have said much more than I meant to, now. Perhaps I will not give you this letter after all, my Rue. The truth is, some piece of my mother's misery is in me, and one day I shall die of it.

Whatever happens, whatever sorrow befalls me, I will always be grateful for the kindness your family has shown me. I will always be grateful for the mere existence of your kingdom, which at this time, by some miracle, calls itself my home. If at some future time I am not so fortunate, I will still remember those two encircling dolphins in the Wye coat of arms with joy. You take it for granted, having lived here all your life. But I did not know that people could dream and build an interconnected palace of a city that mirrors and expands upon the natural beauty of the land—the mountain peaks, the crystal waves. I did not know they could, instead of fighting for the most of everything in a starving, miserly world, limit themselves sensibly in order to live like civilized beings in a land with few resources, irrigate the land with forethought, restrain their lust in order to make just enough children to form a society but not enough to exhaust the earth. I did not know they could be more than their animal instincts; that they can, in fact, live and strive freely in the highest aspects of humanness—philosophy, spirituality, medicine, intelligent discourse, cultural collaboration and exploration, mutual caring for each other and for the creatures that depend on them. I did not know there was a city in which not only could I pursue poetry as a vocation, but that vocation would also be one of the most revered and respected. I did not know that a people could work together for justice, in a land where there is no need for prisons, because everyone forms the laws together, and those laws serve everyone, and no one would ever want to do anything that earns the disapproval of the community which gives them life. I did not know that men could be respected as men not for their violent dominion, but for their responsibility and self-restraint as warriors, their sense of duty to comrades and friends, the power of their minds. I did not know that women could be what women are here: angels of mercy, intuition, compassion, and mystery who unassumingly inspire art.

I still fear your father, but only because he is better and wiser than I can ever be. He is a warrior in a way I will never be—and not only because he is physically a better fighter, but because he does not succumb to dark yearnings or self-pity or an old man's sorrow, as I do. He is humble to his sacred duty and nothing else. When my only vision of royalty was my father, I had no respect for kings. But I know now that what proves the power and effectiveness of a king is not his charm, not the legend of his personality, not the accumulation of his wealth, and not even how much the people love him—but the health of the kingdom itself. The beauty of this kingdom is a reflection of his rule and the rule of all his ancestors. The people obey him not because they have to, for he has no army that belongs to him, but rather because they respect him, and he facilitates their living. He is their servant as well as their master. They know there is no luxury to being a king—not here in Zara—and there is no outsized power he must fight others to hold.

And yet despite all this, those far Northern places are somehow in my blood. You know this, and you knew it when your eyes first met mine, and I believe it is the reason you trusted me. You know my uncertainty, and I know yours. Our parents think they know us, but we see what they don't wish to see. We live out the questions our mothers refused to answer, by closing their hearts to love. And the question, Rue—the question I, son of a monster, and you, daughter of a priestess, live without choice, without their permission or their knowledge—is the same. The same loneliness.

I have no words for it. No words but for poetry, and that is a snaking way of getting at anything, but it is all I have. I cannot answer the question. I can only speak my soul, and hope you will come to meet me. This poem I give you here, I formed recently, based on some incoherent notes I kept after Rufus and my mother abandoned me to the moors. You remember the hollow-eyed, silent creature I was when I first came to you. The style is different from what you've heard in Zara, but you must realize that in the place I come from, there were no civilized structures, no rules for art, no art at all.

Perhaps this poem is about my mother. Yes, of course. I know it is. Everything is about her. That's what's so terrible about her, why she terrifies me all my life. She is everywhere, in everything—as desperately as I wish to, I cannot deny her beauty, and even in her nothingness, she hunts me still.

But I wrote it for you. I write them all for you, in the hopes that you will learn to read them and that I might see that true creature, that unknown creature that is you and you alone, whoever you are and will be, passing suddenly behind impenetrable dark eyes, watching, fighting, rising, becoming.

Who you are, I don't know any more than you do. But I see you, Rue. I see you—more than your mother's daughter.

Your always friend,
Jade

Only

The words in this poem have no effect.
Not even so much as whiskey
after a long walk, seeing only birds.

I tried to imagine
thronging market squares
like you have there, here
in this land of peak and shadow, not knowing
that no land like this
could yield a city like that.
It wouldn't.

Beside me, the land buckles, sighs, rolls over, falls off,
without warning into mountains so old they are sunk
in green sea valleys
through which they bite and rise, in casual silence,
into blind, majestic faces,
like our ancestors, through cloaks of fog and by desolate water, reaching
for this place, no place
these shores, disappearing
this wind only
is all they found.
And yet.

Though it is strange to speak of land
that moves,
it does. It turns
so suddenly that though you stand at the top,
a whole people might live just there around the corner

and you never see them—
so fast
does the ever-turning land secret them
away.

An echo only, this seeming movement, of chaos in frozen tumult?
Or do these leering pinnacles shrink and swell in the sun, or do their
shadows liquify them, or do they actually press me up, and up into sky
    which clogs with mist at midday, this sky
    which is always with you, which you cannot forget like you can in
other places—
    a sky so
    active, then, at sunset, with clouds racing faster than anything on
earth and more monstrous
    passing over my eyes like dreams over the eyes of a sleeper—Beauty
    to distract us
    from ceaseless loss, this wind.

No army will ever attack this shifting shore.
No one will ever find us, and rivers, these rivers everywhere falling
so hard they break living bodies to pieces, off the grey teeth of sea cliffs
at the edges
    of the world where our ancestors came scrabbling,
    arriving,
    by fragments of luck
    and desperation
    during some sea serpent's afternoon nap.

The grasses will never ever
ever
be still, yet
this song is death's song, these last, soft bushes
brittle as bird bones, and yet the stone, the shadow,
    that clump of fur shivering on a blade, and everything, everything
    is alive now
    and then.
Harpies, lions, grizzlies, dragons—the land breathes and thinks.
It does not love us.
There are places we never go.

And there goes Rufus, rotating in and out with his lopsided gait and
thus passing between, in a way other men cannot, surviving only because
the forest does not recognize him
as human
and there stands my father, far above the lonely closeness of forests,
above the damp decay, thinking he sees all the moors' breadth, this
would-be king,
who will never attain dominion over this land
which can neither make an army
nor receive one.

And yet.
Ceaseless hunger.
All the stillness ever-moving
And all the vastness is detail, upon detail, in which we always lose.
I move by inches, on my belly, around
the membrane of this silver, dangerous
pool, with my heart leaning over
the umber lichen and the yellow, gorgeous, flowered webs.
And yet.
I cannot look away.
Everything
is here.

And I know this poem—
how there is no organization to the wind
as it goes, and jumps upon me.
Yet I must follow
these words it ever swallows,
only to follow
something,
only
to chisel tomorrow apart from yesterday, and *only*
to pretend life apart from death, and *only*
to keep
from madness,
my love.
My love, they ever bind me—
these only ropes of wind.

Mina

spring equinox, year 5 in the Ghost Kingdom

Already it feels like a rich, good year for our people, with healthy crops everywhere, mild weather, and several healthy births. The mountain goat population is returning, and the land looks newly lush. The children have begun fishing in the sea, and the adults seem to accept this taking of life, perhaps because we need it so badly—we all look a little starved most of the time. (Someone brought back a couple of chickens from Sirenia once to give us eggs, but the predators got them before we could form a sizable flock.) My meditations anchor me more deeply than ever. I believe they are the secret to surviving in this place with so little. I like to rest my mind, sometimes, in the thought of the unicorns. I feel about them the way I feel about the stars. I do not need to come any closer to their reality, and yet the wonder of them makes life meaningful.

I was just telling Nicolai something I realized that has helped me tremendously (he does the meditation more often now, especially when I encourage him to do it with me). I used to always be waiting for my thoughts to completely settle, but they never do—even five years into my practice. But I realized my whole being is more at peace. When I sit, I feel I could sit forever. There is a freedom in sitting, now, almost as if something is opened right away—a kind of flying. And I realized that this peace is happening below the level of thought. It is foolish of me to think about my thinking or to wait, with my mind, for my mind to stop. I will never be able to put it into words; my mind will never be able to know it. But I know, with some other I, with some other kind of knowing, that it is there.

Just as I know that Nicolai, my husband, is king—and I, then, am also queen. Even if only in symbol. Even if we don't fully know what it means.

Last autumn I began visiting every member of my community, methodically, to ask the same questions—something that had never been done before, I think, by any of us. I did it with caution, I was honest about what I did. *The Sirenians are here,* I said. *And the Sirenians are coming, and will keep coming. What are we going to do?* Because some of them are staying. Some of the priests, with their preachings and their laws, are staying. Some of them are leaving and taking unicorn horns with them. Are we afraid to admit this to ourselves? Are we afraid to ask ourselves if it matters? Some of them are hunting. Some of them are taking advantage of our generosity, which has no spoken bounds. Is it true that we refuse all organization and law, or do we live by laws which we refuse to name?

Most people agreed with me. We need to know what we stand for, I said—at least in the face of the Sirenians. And we need someone to stand for us, at least in semblance. We need to show the presence of a king and queen. Who can these be? They don't need to be us. But they need to be present. They need to be seen.

Of Nicolai, of course, they would have been suspicious—if he had come with such words. Of me they were not, but they spoke openly of their fears. The specter of their own downfall rose up again in their memories: the temptations of civilization and power were all too clear. Two families refused to work with me. They refused gently, but they refused. I started to carry people's objections back and forth between houses until I grew exhausted, and then Nicolai and I lay awake one night talking, until we figured out what to do. We need to hold a council, I told them—I can no longer be the sole bearer of your communications. Come together at last. Nicolai and I will facilitate so that everyone gets heard, but we will never offer a single opinion. We will not lead. We will only record what is said.

And then of course there were those who refused this plan also. And with Nicolai behind me, I did the hardest thing yet. I confronted them.

"You say you refuse all organization," I said. "You refuse to attend a meeting. So on the day this people meets, you refuse to be part of this people. So whatever we decide, you have no part in it, you cannot agree or disagree, it has nothing to do with you. That is your choice."

In the end, everybody came.

Council questions included: How shall we treat the newcomers? Shall we feed and assist them when they find themselves in trouble here? Shall we allow them to take the riches here? If we create rules for the treatment of this land, how can we possibly enforce them?

The following agreements were made—the first agreements ever formally written by the Ghost People, in my hand:

1) Nicolai and I will call ourselves the king and queen, in order to give ourselves an air of authority, and will make a point of finding and greeting all newcomers that we hear of. Nicolai will stand as king, with the clout of a man's presence—a presence he can make quite large when he wishes it. As a former Sirenian, I will translate their language and smooth our relations. We will all work to sew "royal" garments which, though they can't compare to the garments of Sirenian royalty, will hopefully look more impressive than the rags we're accustomed to. And yes, this does, ironically, require journeys to Sirenia and the selling of our own forbidden jewels—the very ones we worry will inspire Sirenian greed. And since we have no castle, we tell the travelers we come from an ancient palace in the heart of the forest, guarded by old magic, since they're already afraid of the magic here (several Sirenians have been lost at sea for mysterious reasons, and sometimes mischievous Ghost children play jokes on the travelers at night, playing on their fear of spirits). No one wishes to venture too far into the forest, anyway—there are no riches here.

2) We will not fight to keep any jewels or other riches, which are anyway not ours to keep. The Ghost People do not believe in attachment to such things, and besides there is no way for us to defend them. Fighting is utterly contrary to the nature and belief system of the Ghost People, even if we had the means for it.

3) No more horns will be taken, because enough offense has already been done to the unicorns, and it is the least we can do to prevent them from ever being dishonored again. In secret, we threw all of the remaining horns in the entire kingdom (with the exception of those affixed still to the castle ruin, which no one has been able to move) into the sea.

4) If any other family or persons arrive who wish to make their home here, we will welcome them if their intentions are honorable and humble. In these conditions, no one can survive here without the support of the community.

Every one of the fears expressed in this Council haunts me. That even now, discussing such rules, we have begun to argue. That conflict over sacred land will infect our children's hearts, turning them aggressive. That the first time we sell our jewels for fancy clothing, that will be the seed of greed that never stops growing, that makes it easier for us to convince ourselves that we need another thing, and another, to prove our worth to the world. That we could make laws against such accumulation of wealth, but then we would have laws and control, and someone would need to keep those laws and that control, and then we would have government and corruption, and so on to the bitter end everyone (except for me, I know) remembers.

And yet. We could find no other way. In the end, the Council was done well. Everyone's voices were heard. Nicolai and I said nothing. The people decided unanimously that we did well in this role, that we should be named—in name only, for the sake of confronting the Sirenians, and with no actual power over anyone here—king and queen. Only to pretend. Only as a kind of game that we play with the world—never with attachment.

It is enough for Nicolai—at least for now. It is more than he ever had. A sense of responsibility, for the sake of ones he cares for. A sense that his life is necessary, that he plays a special role, that others look to him for protection. I no longer miss the beast in him as I did before—child that I was. Both of us are witness, now, to the power in his humanity. How much clearer his sense of himself, when he can list with firm decision the rules his people command. How much more articulate, when the people stand behind his words. How much more grace in his civilized bearing, when strangers call him King. How much braver his touch, when he touches me now—how much more present he is to me, in his love-making, when he sees himself a man in my eyes, a man with a country, with borders, with precious things to defend and a way of life that has been entrusted to him. He touches me with pride, with joyful tenderness—he finds me again, and I find my way down, again, from the dark, howling tower of my memory, into his loving arms. *It's been hard for you sometimes,* he said. *I have not been there for you, in my sorrow. I am here now.*

And we have conceived a child.

autumn

Should I not have said it? Should I not have written it, at the end of my last entry—as if casually, denying to myself that the whole entry was nothing compared to that, the whole entry was about that, it was all that mattered. No, not all, and yet... Oh it is foolish, to think this way. As if Rhiannon curses me. As if there is any such thing.

I felt so sure of it, I even told Nicolai this time. And so now his grief, too, I must bear.

Autumn is unbinding this reality again, with its sudden, forceful sunlight dismissing the fog, its random rains, its rainbows and mermaid songs and aches of the body destroying what we knew just when we knew it. Nicolai isn't well. Is it the grief that's overcoming him? If only I hadn't told him. If only I hadn't given him hope. I think his spirit, with all he's been through, is more fragile than mine.

The symptoms seemed subtle at first, and at first we paid little mind to them. He tires more easily and sometimes loses his appetite. At first I thought these were symptoms of depression, but there are others as well. A persistent soreness has developed in his joints, to the point where some days he finds it difficult even to walk. He gets headaches. His digestion is finicky and sometimes, even if he can bring himself to work or eat, he can't abide my touch, for he says his nerves are ringing, and his stomach is in knots, and he doesn't know himself.

It isn't the feelings that harm us, say the Ghost People; it's our mind's attachment to those feelings. It's the tendency of my mind to whirl into future fears and dire predictions, connections with past losses. I remember years ago, after that first day Nicolai, as a man, left me in the castle while he went hunting—how I waited for him to return in the evening, fearing that a love so ecstatic could not be kept, that I would lose him. But then suddenly there he was, rising up against the stars, coming homeward to me—and how blessed I felt!

May I always be so blessed, that Nicolai returns to me each evening, alive and well.

Rhee taught me a meditation to help another person in his suffering. It has to do with destroying self-love, transferring all love to the other in the form of compassion. To do this, I must take on Nicolai's suffering—breathing in his pain, and breathing out my own health, love, and wholeness, into him. And I thought I loved Nicolai with my whole heart. But I must be more selfish than I knew, because I struggle with this practice more than any other. I feel overcome sometimes by Nicolai's fear and despair, so much so that I can hardly breathe at all.

Something I have realized lately—so subtle it is never spoken, but I think it is true: though I tend to focus on the couples who do have children, because I envy them so, many couples do not. I shocked myself a little, to remember suddenly that in Sirenia, such a thing would be unheard of. Everyone had children, unless they were barren. Children are the continuation of life. They are the most fundamental assumption of life's existence. And yet here in the Ghost Kingdom, there is no such assumption. The Ghost People love children for what they are, and yet I am not sure that as a people, they really want to continue on. They want to be at peace. I wonder sometimes if the Ghost People are moving more and more, like monks, into a preferred state of celibacy. Do they look silvery, their hair shimmering into the palest, most fragile mist even in sunlight, because once they were touched by Unicorns, or because they are, in fact, disappearing now? Births are still celebrated, of course. How could they not be? And yet. They do not fear death. They do not really want anything for themselves.

early winter

The tide of Sirenian pilgrims slows to a trickle as winter comes on, but this moon we received three visitors from another country—explorers from Zara, my mother's homeland to the west. They had been curious, they told us, to know if anyone still lived here, and what was the nature of our people, and how do we relate to the Sirenians who "invade" us. In contrast to the Ghost way of asking nothing, holding to nothing, regulating nothing, the Wyes hold to their land with unparalleled fierceness, as the very symbol of their people's survival. And from what they told us, they regulate every aspect of their lives with such precision, there is no act of life that does not follow some law, and no law that was not passed down to them from on high by their god himself.

Most interestingly, they told us of their king and queen: the queen is a Hummingbird woman, a priestess of her people, who is rumored to know ancient magics and secrets of the forest from which she arrived. In thinking of what we know of Rhiannon, of where she comes from, and of the curse she laid upon Nicolai which may still, for all we know, linger in some form, it occurred to us that this priestess-queen might know some help for his illness. She might understand a kind of darkness we do not. And though I'm a little less fearful for Nicolai now because we've learned that many others here have experienced similar symptoms (perhaps it's a sickness in the water or something carried slowly through the elements, which affects people in different ways over years, once paralyzing a child but for other people disappearing completely, at least for a time)—and survive, for this same reason we feel it would be useful for all our people, not only Nicolai, to find a cure. Nicolai seems stable for now—he will need more rest, the people tell us, and cannot carry the same work load he is accustomed to, but he is stable enough that I can leave him for a time, I think, without fear.

And so I journey to Zara in a few days time, with those three explorers who have happily offered to take me back with them in their boat, and then return me safely home again (boating is second-nature to those people, a daily activity, of little more account than walking).

Anxiety keeps me awake each night, and it's not only the prospect of leaving this place and community which have bound themselves to me as my only home, my very sense of self, and not only the prospect of floating upon that mass of water I have never even touched, giving myself over to its unknown powers for an unknown number of days— no, it's also, I don't know, something else that's wrong with me. I don't know why it's so difficult for me to recover from my simple losses. I don't recognize myself, sometimes, in the moods that take me. I find myself wearied by simple tasks, irritated by things that break. At night in the woods, I think of the Dark Faerie—not even with the fury or hatred I expected to feel, for the idea that she might have cursed me, but instead with a childish longing, as if she offered a kind of comfort I cannot give myself. *Come to me at the Solstice,* she told me once, *and I'll answer any question.* I never have.

My people trust me, with all the gentle, elusive, wild-animal trust that is theirs to give. The explorers told me so. Your people speak of you highly, they told me. They say you are what you say you are, that you have come here from another place but with no selfish motives, that you serve your community with a good heart and an earnest practice of the meditations, whose intention is to help us release all personal desire. The Wye men, though their culture sounds so strict and ordered, so foreign from our own, felt themselves very much aligned with this intention and understood it instantly when it was explained to them. It's for this reason, partly, that I in turn trust them—to bring me home safely again. I just hope I deserve the trust that is given to me.

winter solstice

Dear Queen Ella,

Have you ever traveled to the city of Zara? I write to you en route home from there, passing close along the swampy, arching coast between that country and my own. I never knew the way was so easy—easier than the passage to Sirenia, and yet no one travels it. I think of the prejudice I grew up with in Sirenia, regarding the Wyes, how I tended instinctually to avoid mentioning my mother's ancestry. I wish you and your king could see that place, if you haven't, for I think you would be amazed by its neatness and loveliness and well-mannered kindness, and wonder that our peoples do not all mingle more freely and learn from one another. When you and I meet at last, I suppose that will be a beginning.

I don't know if you've ever traveled upon the sea. I was frightened at first, but we've kept to its edges, and the waters were calm in those two days it took to arrive. All the time I looked out across the sun-crackling field of its surface, its limitless colors and shifting patterns, and imagined I were brave enough to sail free upon it, to where I don't know. And everywhere I walked in Zara, I was thinking of those patterns—I seemed to see the triangle panes of wavelets in designs of glass, and the creative, ever-breaking, ever-forming structure of the sea in the grace of every carving and poem and vessel—the kind of structure you see at the surface of unfathomable depths, indescribable because the artwork itself is only an echo of the truth you feel inside it. I speak like this because I have seen beauty in Zara unlike anything I have ever known, made by human hands. I did not know such things were possible. There is a library there, filled with all the collected knowledge of humankind. The king and queen live in a palace so intentionally beautiful and yet so humbly interwoven with their city, you cannot see where it begins or ends, for in courtyard after courtyard, garden after garden, it extends its arms to its people, feeds its people, welcomes its people as part of its working whole.

Everywhere we walked, I thought of my mother, wondered who she came from, wondered where she played and schooled and wandered as a child. I never knew her lineage, and so could not ask the Wyes to recall her. My father, in his sorrow, never spoke of her—we could not speak of her—and my sisters only told me she was good and kind, they hardly remembered her. Do you remember yours? I think I asked you, in my last letter, and you didn't answer. Perhaps I shouldn't have.

The shyly cordial fishermen who greeted us at the shore set me up for the night in the cottage of a family who tended one of these gardens (where these people stood in any kind of hierarchy was a question I couldn't find words for, nor do I think they would have understood it), and they welcomed us warmly. The king and queen couldn't see me until the next day, though they sent their apologies, for they happened just then to be entertaining visitors from another land—which land, I never knew. Surely not yours, or they would have said? Perhaps one of the island peoples I know they trade with for some of the wondrous goods we used to see in Sirenian markets.

The next day I was treated to a small (by your standards, but large by mine), elegant feast, in which every dish was spiced in some manner I had never tasted before. The king greeted me standing, without a throne, without any trace of hurry or surprise, with the gentlest of courtly bows and the most intent and earnest listening to all I had to say. He seemed grateful for the friendly overture and acutely sensitive to the effort and courage my voyage had required of me. The queen—

first new moon after winter solstice

The queen of Sirenia arrives in the next pilgrimage, this coming spring, and what will she think of this queen of Ghosts, haunted by so many shadows, not least of all herself? How will she find our king?

I started a letter to Queen Ella while on the journey home, but in the middle of trying to come up with a discreet way of describing Queen Lemara, I became distracted by the songs of mermaids. Or at least, that's how I remember it. I didn't expect their voices in the dead of winter. And I didn't expect to feel afraid, least of all then—when I could already see the rocky coast below our castle ruin in the blush of sunset, the rocks all slicked with golden light. The song was beautiful at first, though it sounded like crying—it wasn't the sort of crying that weighs one down with sorrow. It was more like the songs knights used to write for Princess Kiera in Sirenia. Then it was like a felt darkness that spilled upon me and stained my flesh, and then it was like the sound of my name, seductively hopeful, with a gasp inside it, and a rushing release like a sudden downpour. I begged the men to row faster, worrying for Nicolai. I sat down on the floor of the boat to steady myself, reaching out to cool my hands in the water. I had never really felt it before. So cold, yes, but also so soft and so reckless, like loose hair, weighing nothing and yet full of substance. It was not like the water of creeks or rivers. It was not going somewhere. But it had an older knowing, the kind of knowing you feel in dreams, that you cannot remember when you wake.

I closed my eyes and all at once, everything I had experienced with Queen Lemara came flooding back into me, as if I couldn't bear to let myself feel it until now—and I still couldn't bear it, but the song made me feel it, and I had no choice. At least that's what I tell myself now. That's what I tell myself here, in this journal, which has known me since I was a child. Queen Lemara was that very woman who has held me in dream after dream, beginning with the dream I dreamed while bleeding out the hopes of my future in the dark of the forest, that night I lost my first baby. When I saw her in the flesh, I think I would have run, but she knew me at once.

The night I arrived in Zara, I woke before dawn to the sound of an owl crying. I didn't know that's what it was, but I knew it reminded me of mermaid song. When I stepped outside under the stars (feeling I could never sleep, now that I had woken), I found that it drew me not in the direction of the sea, but into the flowering shrubs that outlined the garden. In Zara, there is no true wilderness—all the predators have been driven away, the land tamed, every plant tended by human hands. But the scent of those blossoms was its own kind of wildness, a scent that moved me everywhere and turned my skin to waves. Perhaps I heard, in that stuttering echo, some familiar suffering I could not ignore. I pressed through the snap and thrust of branches until I knew I had startled the crying thing, for its cry flew up in a panicked, fountaining tumult of little, breathless hoots, and then I grasped it, amazed—a struggling handful of wings, sharp and soft all at once, no bigger than a rabbit but grossly powerful with fear. In my shock, I dropped it, but then saw it lope along the ground, not flying, struggling in vain to reorganize one wing, and I knew it was hurt. So I picked it up and enclosed it against my chest, and not knowing what else to do, moved in the direction where I thought the royal chambers lay.

As I walked, I stumbled often, not watching where I stepped, but I learned to hold the little creature against myself, to cup my hands over each side of it in such a way that it could not struggle too much and wound itself further. What had happened, I wondered—a cat, perhaps? For I'd seen several of them watching me when I'd first entered the garden. I moved joltingly, like a startled sleepwalker, spoke sharply to someone I did not know, and came finally, somehow—rumpled in the dress I had slept in, with a clutch of feathers between my breasts—before the king of Wyes, who even in the dead of night greeted me with a politeness and respect so reminiscent of my own manners toward strangers, I felt I knew him at once. He did not seem to take it ill that I woke him in the night with an injured bird, nor wonder why I would do such a thing. I asked him, foolishly, and as an excuse for my behavior, if perhaps the owl were a royal bird—for in Sirenia I know ladies sometimes keep doves, and lords keep falcons, and perhaps to keep owls in a scented night garden was some custom here. He told me no, but not to worry—that his wife would be able to help me, surely. She was good with creatures.

This is how I came to meet Queen Lemara in my waking life, though it never felt all that different from a dream. I ascended many flights of stairs to arrive at her bedroom door. Opening it, she looked first to the bird, for the bird was wounded, not I—and I understood immediately that for Lemara, animals are not less important than people.

"Ah, here she is," she murmured, and reached out her hands with such confidence, I was surprised into releasing my grip, and watched with wonder as the owl hopped onto her wrist, folded its wings, and went silent, looking back and forth between Lemara and me.

"A pet of yours?" I asked.

She looked at me with concern. I had never seen her face before, so forcefully curved, so meaningful in its emotion. She seemed to hold the wind in her cheeks, the sunrise in her eyes, and some sacred word in the lush tension of her lips. "I do not keep pets," she said with vehemence, and then she narrowed her eyes into mine. "Mina Fox," she said, and I swear she held the words in her mouth as if she could feel them there, sticky. "My dark sister." Then she reached out and ran the backs of her fingers from my chin down my neck and right over my heart—and I did not even think to resist her.

What happened then? We did speak of medicines, and of my husband, while the owl perched at the inside corner of her windy balcony and looked at the cats that lay everywhere, and the cats looked back at it, and all seemed at ease with each other, as if all of these animals knew each other as something other than the animals they seemed. Queen Lemara refused to think of any help for Nicolai (whether or not she actually had knowledge or medicines to share, I never ascertained for sure), at first harshly—saying she was priestess of her own people, and had nothing to do with the sicknesses of mine—and then more kindly, but still firmly, once I informed her that Nicolai was in fact partly descended from hers. Speak to the plants and animals of your own kingdom, she told me—don't you know that the medicines grow where the sickness grows? Why do you come seeking wisdom from some other healer, with some foreign medicines, in some other place? And why do you come asking for help for your husband, when you are the one who wants medicine?

"What do you mean?"

"What is wrong?" she said sharply. "Where does it hurt?"

"Nowhere," I said. "But I am barren." I said it without thinking, as if my heart recognized her question before I did, and when I said it I began to cry. I wanted to speak of the way I had dreamed her, but was afraid. Yet I thought immediately, childishly, selfishly, ridiculously, that she would help me—perhaps that's what brought the tears. But she did not.

What happened? A strange terror upon her balcony, where she led me, where she held me between her two hands of swarming fire, her hands upon my waist and they made my thighs ache. A sudden, dream-like fear of moonlight, which to the Ghost People symbolizes trickery, romantic illusion, danger, but now it flooded us like a real substance, bled the world dry of color the way dreams do, but made Lemara all the more brilliant as if she drank the milk of the sky and was nourished, and she pressed upon it with her magnificent, glowing flesh and said, "We cross here. Here in the moon we cross over, and we will not return."

The owl watching us with eyes like golden worlds. It is harder for me to bear the memory of her hands, easier to remember our shadows, their tangled, sickening interplay beneath us, rising up on the white clay walls like human ivy. I was pointing to the place in my shadow where my womb would be. I was saying, there's nothing there. The moonlight isn't real—it's just a reflection of the real light. I'm barren.

She knelt and touched my shadow, and it made me convulse, ugly, in places Nicolai could not touch. "Nothing is where life begins," she said.

I felt something like a knife between my legs, but it was part of my own body, like a desire so sharp and violent, it would hurt me if I moved. Thick with feeling, awkward, I turned to the side so that my shadow thinned, hoping to disappear. I cannot tell what's real, I wept. But she kissed me—I do not deny it, nor the salamander slide of her lips nor the quick of her tongue and where it reached me—and I could feel my own reality in her mouth, fresh and sharp like a star. "We aren't here to tell what's real," she hissed. "We are here to cross through a veil." And she opened the moonlight and parted it, and I wept as she did so, as if she parted my own flesh. She said, "Hush now. The Moon is Dreaming up the Sun. It is very important. You think the Sun bursts forth all on His own in the morning? No! A woman pushes Him out."

I felt the sea pounding closer, as if the moon were an island we sunk upon. I felt her stirring, within me, the waters of grief I didn't know I kept, grief she felt just the same—the grief of losing family, losing place, losing the world of childhood and the knowledge of ancestors, the memory of what we were. Losing her beloved, who was a wild thing, a mystery of hot breath and tireless running and soul-seizing eyes, who loved her with a clear, wanting love—but that was long ago, and now she has only a husband, a man of muttered words and distractions who, thinking he knows her in his mind, never feels her. She stirred me deeper and deeper in, the moon pooling around her touch, and it is true what the Ghost People say, that to feel is to suffer, and I wanted her. She breathed her breath into my womb, her lips at my entrance, her tongue unbinding my mind so that I thought I could never reclaim it, and said, "It isn't to be satisfied. It isn't to be transcended. It's to transform you. Go find what it is made of, and make it."

I remembered it all too soon, too fast, as I sunk down into the boat and my body turned to swamp, my thoughts to moonlight and memories Lemara—as two bone-white, webbed hands burst out of the water and offered me, in their open palms, the unicorn-horn instrument which Nicolai had made me toss into the waves four years ago. I reached for it without a second thought. Then I was thrashing in the sea.

The boat had capsized but not, I think, by the suddenness of my motion. It was the mermaids that did it—and I'll always believe that, no matter what Rhee ever tells me about rainbows and illusion, no matter that the Wye men, of course, saw no such thing. In this drowning that seemed not to end and yet was somehow delicious as it filled me, I could feel their tails flicking beneath me, their hair winding around my neck as their hands explored me with questions from the frothing, quickening sea. *What is it like inside—where the legs separate so? As much as he feared us, does he fear you more? For we live in the ocean, but the ocean lives in you.*

I woke tangled on the stones, my hair salty and matted against my lips. My shirt was wet, my nipples bruised; my trousers (which I wear at home in the Ghost Kingdom, for ease of work, and had changed back into as soon as we left Zara) were sopping with the sea. I could not look at the men as they helped me to my feet, exclaiming. This was that grey time before evening, when the colors have drowned themselves in the sea and the moon is rising, but it still looks pale and insubstantial, not yet casting any light.

Queen Ella, I lost that letter, my third letter to you, in the chaos of the sea. It will never find you, but perhaps it will haunt me the way everything haunts me. Perhaps it will return to me the way the horn returned to me in the hands of mermaids after I'd tried to lose it long ago, in a different form, with different, awful words, asking of you, Queen of Day, have you touched yourself truly? Have you ever touched yourself pretending it was mermaids, pretending it was whatever you needed—and have you needed it, as I did that night, excusing myself from the men who'd rowed me almost to shore, laying myself down in the mucky bottom of the abandoned tower where Sirenians see the Holy Virgin? Digging out the root of my desire with the hard, determined work of my own fingers, rubbing it smooth into a new substance I had never known before—did you know that this could be done, Queen Ella, or that a woman could do it? Do our peoples know—do they really know—what is in us?

In every mermaid face, I saw Lemara. Her skin like a musical tone. Her tail lashing between my legs. Her hands supporting my waist, so I wouldn't drown.

Afterward I lay still, alone, and readied myself to stand and make the long journey home through the night. I did not feel tired. Without look- ing, I could hear the hollow yawn of the sea, muffled by the safer, warmer sounds of skittering rodents or insects across pebbles, glass, hardened dead leaves, and I could feel the lands I loved all around me—the wide waving valley and the silver mountains that edge Sleeping Lake, the steep white hillsides of birch and the wind-brushed etchings of cedar and stunted, rock-rooted pine. There is something honest about that place, the ruin where no one of my people ever goes now, in which everything is broken, and at the same time kind, the way roses grow over the ruins and soften them with their colorful cascades. They smelled sweet like youth, like infant skin. When the wind blew, wayward petals skipped across my arms and legs. But I wished I lay in sunlight, when songbirds would be perching on those eerie, leaning towers of unicorn horns, just talking about their day, unperturbed by symbolism or history, guilt or regret. I didn't know what had made me so anxious before I left on this journey, but whatever I had feared, I knew it had come to pass.

I opened my eyes because I had to, and I was alone, smelling the life-death smell of the sea all over me, and my husband had ceased touching me like that a hundred years ago, and Rhiannon stood over me now. And I don't know what happened—was it the changing pace of the wind, or the sudden closing of the final blue horizon of twilight into blackness, or a rustle beneath fallen stones?—but I knew suddenly and with certainty that Rhiannon was real, as real as the moon. She was no illusion. I had called her here.

"Thank you," she said, "for rescuing my daughter."

I had no idea what she meant.

"But I won't answer your question, dear one, because you don't really want to know."

"Know what?" I managed, sitting up and wiping the tears off my face before I even realized I'd been crying.

"What a unicorn is. It's not what you think. Go home."

She was gone. I got up. I walked home. I walked half the night, across that silver lake of meadow, under the dying moon, into the lightless forest, and I've never been so afraid in all my life. Every other moment, I felt some cloudy something, like a net of spider thread, like an evanescent tail, brush my face. I seemed to see and hear with the supernatural senses of an owl, and yet I felt broken as that little owl had been broken, and moved hindered, helpless, never as quickly as I wished to. I thought I heard screaming. I thought I saw the eye of some animal, neither predator nor prey, eyeing me from the side of its face—I thought I saw forms of beauty blurred at the edges, paling into air, wailing like a woman touched before she was ready, who did not know she could lose herself that way. There were unicorns everywhere, that I could not see, and they hunted me, and they were not beautiful. I understood as if for the first time why the Ghost People never speak of them, and why they fear them even though they won't admit it, and also why Nicolai fears the beast. They were not ethereal, not made of light. They had shadows. Not shadows that fall upon the ground, but shadows that blinded me, when I tried to look at them. But I wasn't trying to look at them, no. I was trying to keep my look away. I knew that if I saw them, I would never get home, not ever again.

Now I'm here at last in the candlelight, watching Nicolai sleep, and its all breathless dreams and dust. Here are the familiar things, the names of people I know who came to offer whatever medicines they knew, and comfort, the welcome of friendly, concerned faces, the normal calls of owls in the forest I know, who cannot be spoken to by human beings, who have their own world apart from ours. And I'm sorry. I'm sorry, Nicolai, as I hold your hand beneath the candle, and my heart beats steady again, like the better heart I know, and I listen to your sometimes labored breathing and cry for you and what you suffered in my absence.

And I'm not meaning to think of it, but maybe because I'm so terrified of losing you, more than of any other thing, I'm thinking of the way you said goodbye to me, the evening you left me at the outskirts of Sirenia long ago, after you carried me home on your wolf-back because you loved me. Where we stood, I could see the little farms in the distance, and a winding road that would smooth out soon enough, beset by houses and people. You, beast, could go no further then, and I hesitated. I had not told you that I might never return to you. But in that moment I hesitated, you looked at me and growled. Before I could think, before I could run—and yet when I think back, I think there must have been time for me to escape, had I really wished to—you circled me and leaped, throwing me to the ground. And you were over me like a wave, all hair and breath, pinning me as the air slammed out of me.

Do you remember? The ground was mossy there, and it took me in sweetly. I seemed to feel it singing about my head. I seemed to feel the forest weeping. The melody of waterfalls we'd passed in our journey down the mountainsides came back to me now, like a dream I suddenly made sense of. I did not feel afraid. Everything was strange and stilled. You, the wolf, looked into my eyes, and your eyes were human. You opened your mouth wide, your tongue hooked and elastic, as if you would swallow me. I closed my eyes and waited. Everything I had planned, everything I thought I wanted, disappeared. I felt the weight of your heart, the huge chamber of your howling chest above my body, your tail swiping the soles of my feet, and I lost control of my face and became a fool. I felt your breath erupting against my neck. Very slowly, so slowly that without realizing it, I arched my whole body in suspense, you took the edge of my gown between your teeth. I heard the rip, slow and awful and wonderful, like the creak of deadly things in the night. I felt the serrated edge of your tongue. You tested me, opening your jaws wide, embracing each part of me with breath and restraint, brushing me with your teeth more lightly than rain, while each part of me flushed painfully with blood. I surrendered then to anything you could ask of me—anything—though you asked nothing, only that I would trust you.

Dear Nicolai, I have the horn still, that the mermaids gave back to me, wrapped up and hidden beneath our bed. I don't know what it's for. I don't know how I can bear to keep it secret from you, and yet I don't know how I can bear to toss it ever again into the sea. I only know I returned home without medicine, to find you sicker than you've ever been, cared for by others without my comfort, and that when I remember the wind upon the waves, and the songs echoing so much more vividly in their cups and slants (as if I knew finally what they meant), and the answering wonder of Zara's beauty like a healing in itself, and the ecstasy of Mara's merciless touch, and the holiness of that emptiness it left inside me, I realize that my reasons for going away were entirely selfish after all, no matter what I told you.

Lemara

When my son Uri feels me nervous or upset, he asks me to tell him again about the South Forest. He knows that to speak, in our Dancing language, of these things soothes me. Sometimes I've heard him telling my stories over again to the Cats, who always listen politely.

"Tell me the Animals," he says to me in the terrace garden above the courtyard, where we watch for Leo's coming. Because Micah is not here, he speaks with his whole body.

"La," he says, pressing my hands.

"Yes," I say, "the La-Deer, very small and all white, like Sea foam. And the Jaguars. Do you remember about the Jaguars?"

Uri grins, making his body like a Jaguar that slinks through the shadows. "And?" he says.

"There are Crocodiles, and Bats, and little Wildcats..."

"Cats—like ours?"

"Yes, only bigger and fiercer. And there are Fireflies, that glow all night." Even children who've been civilized like Uri, who have hardly seen any wild Animals in their lives, love Animals and want to know them. It is because they are still part Animal. But I know that soon, Micah will take this, too, from him.

"Is Fire? A Firefly?"

"Yes, a Firefly is made of Fire."

"How?"

"They are magic."

Uri moves his hands up and down in the Air, thinking. "War there?" he asks.

"No, there are no warriors. We do not fight, in the South Forest."

"Why?"

"We believe it is wrong, to kill people."

"You have this?" He raises his hands in the air like a fountain, but I understand.

"Do I have a palace?" We speak like this, as if I in fact live in this other world, as if it exists. As if by telling it, I keep it alive. "No, there are no palaces, and no houses, and no buildings at all. We do not need them, there. We sleep in nests we make in the Trees, like the Hummingbirds, or under the roots of the big Trees. We do not stay in one place. We are always moving."

"What you eat?"

"We eat many things—Nuba nuts and many fruits, and Mushrooms and Bugs..."

"Yum."

"Yes, yum. And we do not have to use forks and spoons. We eat with our hands. A Hummingbird boy would think you were rude, to eat with your fork and spoon, not touching your food!"

A slow smile. "You have a bed? A shoe?"

"We don't have anything. We don't own anything, in the South Forest. We don't need to."

"Why?"

"Because we have everything, there."

"You cry, Mama?"

"I always cry when I speak of the South Forest, Uriah."

"Why?"

"Because I miss it."

Soon Uri loses interest, lost in his own imaginings, and then he drops to the ground and begins to play on his own, collecting differently feeling things from the littered Earth—a petal, a fibrous tissue of underbark, a crinkled Lichen, a polished stone—and arranging them. Probably he is building a little South Forest. He ignores us, and so Rue and I let him be. Though he can grow fierce about some things he wants, and does not like me to leave him, in common moments like this he has a kind of easy detachment which reminds me of Micah—only he is sensual in a way that Micah could never be.

I love my son, but I am happy to secret myself away beneath a bower with only Rue, who is mine to keep and love for always. The question I whisper into her ear now, and every morning, is the same one I whispered once to Uri. *What do you remember, little one? Show me what I do not see.* In the South Forest, we know that in the places where one element merges into another, that is where the portals may be. Where the Wind moves the light through the screen of the leaves, that is Tree translating Sun. Where the little creek makes a shape of great beauty between the banks of clay, that is Earth translating Water. In such translations, Faeries may appear. And a Priestess should be able to move through such portals at will, in living body, when invited. But I have never been so invited, and it is because, the elders told me, my Mama did not invite Rhiannon to my birth, and so the way was forever closed to me—except, of course, sometimes in Dreaming. Babies have just come from the Other Worlds, and so they can pass easily. All the time I watch Rue watching things I cannot see, the way Cats do.

But when Leo comes, though he passes below us into the courtyard where I have told Micah I refuse to join him, she wraps her arms around my neck and hides her face, squeezing me with great force, and begins to tremble with eyes wide open.

"Rue! He cannot see us. Don't be afraid. I have you. But we must look. We must see what he is. Uri, stay close."

The way Leo moves—it's so different from Micah's striding, gliding pace: I never really saw Micah's movement before, how like a Cat's it is, and also how like the warriors that Danced that awful Dance in the Temple room. Where they meet in the center of the courtyard, neither bow, nor move a single hand. When Micah speaks, his voice sounds so low, as comfortable as the stones that make the walls of the palace around him, that I cannot hear him. But I hear every word Leo says. He speaks to Micah in Sirenian, the language of our common enemy, the only language we all share in common.

And while they stand there in boots on the tiled path, and I am crouching barefoot with my daughter in my arms among the little Trees above them, I understand things about the reality I am part of now that I did not understand before. When my mama told me that in other lands, men ruled and women suffered, I used to imagine that kings looked like this. It is the way I thought Micah looked, when I first saw him, because I expected that. And yet he doesn't. His face is not hard in that simple way that Leo's is hard. His eyes are not empty and at once cunning, the way Leo's are empty and cunning. His body is not made of fists, nor his feet spread so wide apart, nor his sweat so sour as Leo's is. And his voice does not growl, as Leo's does, as he mentions to Micah, "My wife. Rowan. She's somewhere—don't mind her. She disappears at times, but she won't go far. I have her pretty well tamed, but she is Faerie—still doesn't know how to speak to other humans." He says the words proudly, as if Rowan is a Thing he has made, something awful that no one else would be able to control, and when he names her as Faerie I gasp, and he looks up, and I shrink back further into the Tree. I was wrong to tell Rue he couldn't sense us. His senses are as sharp as mine.

Does he see us? Whether he does or not, his look tells me that whatever made the noise he just heard is prey to him, and if he made only the slightest effort, he'd feel sure of catching it. As if he knows a woman lurks here, watching him, and makes a note inside his mind about a game he'd like to play later. I understand that he has raped his wife, not once but many times. I understand for the first time what evil is. I understand how the world I grew up in really is gone, and maybe forever. I understand what the Sirenians really mean when they speak of owning. They mean what Leo means when he speaks of his wife. And I understand from the first that Leo's ultimate intention is not to ally himself with us or share ideas with us or fight a common enemy with us or make friends. His intention is to own us. He intends to own everything. There is nothing which will escape this ownership. This wanting comes up from an emptiness in the depths of a person, from a feeling of loss so deep, not sound nor warmth nor any light can travel out of it. Far deeper than my loss—which once seemed to me the deepest of losses.

Micah speaks something, and then Leo glances behind him and roars a word I do not understand. A toddler trots out from the arched garden entrance, and then slows as he nears Leo, not with disobedience or with fear, but as if the space between him and this violent man is so thick with fog, he has no hope of ever crossing it. I understand that the word Leo spoke is the name of his son. "Jade," I remember, is also the name of a stone we do not have here, one which the Sirenians have mined in the Northlands. Micah bends slightly and offers the boy his hand. This is the moment when many toddlers want to shrink with shyness into their parents' legs, but Jade has nowhere safe to shrink to, so he just shrinks—and lifts his little hands into the Air before him, curled, paused, unsure. The sad confusion of that gesture makes me cry out with compassion, and I know I will never be able to blame him for whatever plans these men make.

Leo turns again at my sound, and this time I jump down from the Tree and descend halfway down the steps. Cupping Rue in one arm, I reach for Jade with my other palm open. "Come," I say to him, smiling. He looks at me, his thin little body rigid and his mouth open, as if he's never seen so much color in his life. His eyes are heavily lidded like those of an old man. "Come to me," I say to him, not bothering to speak Sirenian, for I am sure he can understand. "I will show you beauty, while these men talk. You love beauty, don't you?" He's looking now at Rue, like one who is used to ceaseless hunger, but cannot be moved by it.

"Your queen?" says Leo.

"Queen Lemara," Micah says.

"Go on," says Leo to his son, and Jade, as if released from a spell, moves, but not directly toward me. He comes in an arching path, half-floating, unsure. The two men walk away together, and I sit down and call Uri to me. He's been watching all of us but without any special fascination. He looks down at his little objects, deciding whether or not to come.

Up until this moment, the boy Jade seemed blank inside, but now I see he was only very skillfully hiding. Released from his father's gaze, he steps toward Rue, who has ceased trembling and looks back at him, patient, warm in my arm, with an unaccustomed stillness in her gaze. He takes her hand in his, and she waits, as if she's been expecting him. He looks into her eyes. He turns her hand over and touches his fingertips to her palm with a reverence that feels almost like empathy.

"What a loving boy you are!" I exclaim to him in my language, touching his shoulder.

He looks up at me finally, and without making a single sound, and with a look so old and worn it sends chills all over my shoulders and breasts, begins to weep.

Rowan

Queen Mina Fox, queen of the Sky Horses, the Jaguar's other chosen daughter, Queen of the Other World, brings Rowan to me in the middle of the night—two nights after Leo's arrival. Rowan's husband hasn't found her, and he is going to leave in the morning with or without her, and though he claimed to be certain of her return, I've seen him clench his jaw every time he says her name.

In the morning I find the kings meeting in the Council Hall, with the other men at Council (but not the Prophets because the Prophets are always alone and never come to meetings). Listening at the door, I hear them speaking of Queen Mina's visit, and the return of those scouts who visited the Ghost Kingdom pretending to be explorers but really seeking to discover if the Ghost People could be allies against Sirenia, and if they were armed. Disappointed on both counts, the men turn now to other plans, with no words for the magic of Queen Mina herself. With no words about this woman who is made of ivory and Fire but with the heart of a Tree, hollow inside, an instrument of life-breath made from the oldest, strongest wood, the dead wood, the emptiness where worlds begin. Somewhere across the Water in a land of Ghosts, my people and Micah's people have fallen in love and live in peace. I do not understand it, but I know it now and cannot un-know it. My children, after all, are born of that miracle, that crossing of worlds.

"Lemara," Micah starts when I walk through the entrance, swallowing back whatever he would to say to me for interrupting the men's meeting where I'm not allowed—for perhaps, like Leo, he wishes not to reveal that his wife moves freely outside his control. That I have not spoken to him except by absolute necessity for over a year, not since he swore to take my daughter from me. "What is it?"

"Rowan is with me," I say, looking not at him but at Leo. I mean to speak only to Leo, but I cannot speak Sirenian well, so Micah must translate. "Prince Leo, she and I must hold our own meetings now, in our own privacy, in our own time."

Micah translates, probably changing the words to some kind of politeness for the comfort of his new ally. But even so, Leo stands. He makes no expressions with that rough-cut, deadly face, but it changes colors with every mood. When he speaks now, it darkens as if the blood will seep from his skin. I turn to go, but Micah calls out to me.

"Lemara," he says, and I can hear the sympathy in his voice—for me or for Rowan, I do not know. He has never stopped speaking to me with the same calm gentleness, in all the time I have refused him. I don't know if it is an act of love or an act of denial. A gesture of loyalty, or a refusal to acknowledge my silence. "Prince Leo says that there are consequences for her disobedience—if she doesn't leave with him when he wishes. He says she knows what these consequences are. I'm trying to calm him, to tell him he's welcome here and must surely be pleased to feast and enjoy himself further with his new allies, after all—"

"When Rowan and I are done together," I interrupt, "she will be able to stop these consequences. She will remember—" I shake my head. I can't explain, even to Micah whom I trust, after all, more than this enemy, even in the language we almost share. "It doesn't matter," I say. "She will stay with me now, because she wishes it."

Micah looks at me. He doesn't ask to meet her. He doesn't protest. I remember the day of our wedding, when I insisted I would go and sing to the Sun in His falling, and he only asked me, *When will you return?*

"How long?" he asks me now, looking into my eyes.

"As long as it takes," I tell him.

a Jaguar hunts me!

Uri will play alongside anyone who lets him be, who doesn't try to direct him. And Jade is perceptive and asks nothing; he sits gently by Uri, watching to see what is required of him. While they play in the garden with quiet intent, I return to my room and close the door behind me, something I have never done. I have never before seen the use of this thing called privacy.

I left Rue in Rowan's care, a responsibility I thought might bind her fluttering, terrified heart for a few moments while I left to tell the men. Now when I close the door behind me, Rue is sitting up with the Cats, and holds out her arms to me. The Owl that Mina brought is gone, but I feel her near. Lifting Rue, I glance out the balcony door and see a brush of black hair in the breeze. She's turned back human.

I sit by a window nearby, and don't look, don't say anything. I don't look at her even when she comes to the doorway, even when she begins to waft by fits and starts around the room, reaching her fingers to thing after thing without ever touching them, the way a Cat sniffs the boundaries and objects of a new space, always aware that you are there and yet never looking directly at you. I don't care what the men are talking about. I don't care if they arrange for the rebuilding or destruction of this entire city. I only want to be here, waiting for Rowan. I remember the feeling of living in the Jungle, where always we were hunted. The feeling of Jaguars all around us, smelling us, prickling our skin with their hunger. Our heartbeats echoing in the caves of their mouths—we heard them. The wild question of what Rowan will do, what she will say, what she is, flushes inside me like a fresh, free night when I walked in the fog, all the cries of the invisible creatures ringing around me, all my senses jubilant—and she is nourishment and relief, and waking, waking, waking into the circle again.

She doesn't know. But she isn't afraid of me. She follows the corners of the walls. She reminds me of myself, when I first came. A deadly sadness hovers over her shoulders, waiting for her to weaken. She can feel it, and hesitates.

"You don't have to be here," I tell her. "If you want, you can run out right now and never come back. I won't say a word, because I have often thought of doing that myself."

She says nothing, but still the hot, fresh glowing in my chest, still the thoughtless Forest springing forth from the damp life of my body, as if I remember at last what I am for. I listen to her breath—Leo or Micah would not be able to hear it, but I can—tiny and sharp and secret and quick. I listen for her thoughts, for I know she will be like me, able to speak without words. Yet I cannot hear them. I feel if I could only be nearer to her, perhaps I could taste them.

Rue is clawing me, so I loosen my Wye-woman dress and give her my breast. She suckles with quiet dedication, not like Uri who used to stop again and again, whining, as if he could bear neither hunger nor fullness. Rowan turns to me, and her eyes are embers; though the room is bright, they are brighter. There is a tremble where her chin meets her throat. Though she is pale, she emanates a thousand delicate darknesses, intensifying everything near her like wetness on a stone. I cannot read her look.

She watches me the whole time I nurse Rue, and never looks away, and soon her dark red lips part. When Rue falls asleep, I go and lay her down among the Cats. Then I return to the window. Rowan has moved a little closer to the wall.

"Come and sit beside me," I say. I feel she is in terrible danger, all the time. Or she herself is the danger. I can't say which.

She follows her fingers, following the angles of the room, all the way back around to where I sit. The light is on her. There is a tension in her slowness, as if she will at any moment break into wild running—or simply break. Her dress is too big for her, and she moves inside of it, a trapped Wind. With each step she lifts her beauty against the sorrow, her arms the bones of Birds. Now she is beside me, hot and cold at once, leaning into me, her eyes in mine, and I reach up and take down her hair—it falls around her face like the Forest around the Moon, it flows toward me like the River Golden, like the River Golden which flows from the dark North of our terror but also from our source—oh, they are where we come from, and we are where they are always, always going. Rhiannon comes from there, from where the Barbarians come from, longing for us. And Rowan breathes in deep, and out, and her breath smells like the morning Air smells after River Faeries have passed through it, as if she has never eaten anything—or no, no, but oh Rhiannon, it smells also like blood. Without taking her eyes from mine, she fingers the folds of my dress where they lie beside me on the wood, and though she does not touch me, I can feel the rhythm of her touch by the way the cloth pulls and sticks.

I look and look, drinking her eyes, but there is nothing in them—and then there is something, behind the nothing—a question I try to understand but now she's seizing at my dress in handfuls, never touching me or moving, only clutching at the material that hangs in loose ribbons between my breasts where I let it out for Rue and ruffles between my open thighs—and I can feel the cloth pulling and sliding, pressing into me where she pulls it hard, and the clumsy, childish, meaningless urgency of her stretching, poking fingers as they grip and release, and the heat of her hand so close to my skin, and I close my eyes and kiss her—her lips vibrate like the wings of Bees—her shoulders freeze and hunch, leaning, leaning into me—then a little cry, a Mouse ended in talons, and a nothing-blankness and she's gone.

But no, still here. Just across the room. I grip my own dress the way she did. I want to scream out. How lost I feel here, with no one hunting me. How anxious I am used to feeling, all the time, because there is no danger and yet I do not trust the safety, for it is not real. For all of time, humans have lived in the middle of the chain of life—until the Wyes and Sirenians, with their weapons and their walled cities, suddenly leaped to the top of it. Nothing hunts us here, and yet we are afraid, all the time. No wonder the Wyes must believe in this punishing, above-human god, just to imagine that there is something, someone, who could destroy us into Earth again, as in the days of old! And at last, at last, heaving, clawed, feeling still Rowan's fingernails in the seams of my clothing, not knowing if she will come upon me again or be gone forever, I feel Death like a womb once more surrounding me, as the Jungle surrounded me, as the Jaguars surrounded me with their mouths leading directly to the Other World from which we came—at last.

When I am calm enough to open my eyes, she is sitting among the Cats with Rue on the floor. She watches Rue's sleeping form with a look I cannot read. Rue opens her tiny palm in her sleep, and Rowan lays her white hand inside it, her face twisting. Then she draws back fast with a snort, like a Horse, and her look brightens.

"Strong," she murmurs, surprised. I come down before her on my knees. The Cats are all around her, Purring, looking up into her eyes. They lie down on her lap and along her hips. She is crying, I can tell, though there are no tears. I am about to ask her something, something about Rue—what does she see?—but she touches now the nose of one of the Cats.

"This one was your friend before," she tells me.

"Before what?"

"Kar," says Rowan.

I sit up fast. "Kar?" I laugh with joy. Why did I never think of it? That my friends would reincarnate among my Cats, to be with me again? The elders used to say, we hardly ever recognize the reincarnation of a loved one from a previous life. We are too attached to how they used to be, and so cannot see them truly. And Tiras... Oh, Tiras...

"And his sister," says Rowan. "Ama."

"Ama? AlaNAmana? That is her? And the others?"

"No others," says Rowan. "Kar protects the children. Ama stays here to be safe with you." She shakes her head hard. "A bad death," she whispers.

"What happened to her?" I whisper back. Did the Sirenians do something to her? But Rowan doesn't answer.

"Do they know me?" I want to know.

"They don't remember the life before," says Rowan. "Only they know they want to be with you, so that is why they came here, to this life."

I touch them—Kar, AlaNAmana whom I will call Ama now. Kar the Cat has always been lazy and aloof, like the light-footed boy once was, but pure-hearted, more loyal to Uriah than any of them. They are here to protect my children. I have always known that.

Rowan can understand the unspoken languages, just as I thought she could. She can listen, and she knows. She can speak without words, like the Hummingbird People, only she doesn't. She doesn't speak that way, in the intuitive way of the body, for her body has been ripped from its knowing. And so it seems as if she isn't here.

"Rowan," I say, taking her hand. "I am going to free you."

I Dream the Rains come, Tiras, while we sit in despair on either side of the dry River. When Rhiannon hands me the cup of bone, the Rains fill it right up, and I drink.

The Rains keep filling and filling the white cup, and I look into the pool made there, and the pool widens and deepens in the Earth before me, and I lean over on my hands and knees, looking into it, calling your name. Tiras. For I know you are here, somehow, inside the Water. But I am so afraid to reach in, because of all the pain I felt, all the times I failed to find you, and because of the darkness I can't see through in those depths.

The new light of the Sun illuminates the surface of the Water, like a live skin. I cannot see you—only my own reflection.

And all this time, I thought I was very beautiful, and I thought you desired me and loved me and I was your Priestess. But I am all alone now without you, and I have chased you and waited for you, and only lost you again, and the place where the Sun and the Water meets is so clear, I can see my face as plainly as if I were another person looking back at me, and I am not beautiful after all. No, not at all, for I look small and uneven and stupid now, my skin with dry places and damp places, my hair matted and worn, my eyes weak and my mouth big in its hunger. No, I do not like myself at all!—and I am all alone.

But now I see that the reflection in the Water is crying, and when I see the tears moving over her cheeks, and how they get caught in the corners of her mouth where once she was laughing, I feel so much tenderness for her, I am sorry. However ugly she is, I cannot leave her alone! So I reach out to the Water after all, where before I was afraid, and I trace the deep hues of her face, golden like the Sun and black like the Night. The Water feels soft, and so I lean in and kiss her right on the mouth, and then my lips pass through the Water and it is you I am kissing!

Then you rise up out of the pool, still kissing me, and we laugh and embrace, and I can understand you now, for you cry out in words, "I knew you were out there! I knew! But I was so afraid, to reach through the Water!" For what happened to you was the same. You, too, could see only your own reflection, until you were able to touch your own heart. And I show you where I looked in the Water, and how I could not find you, and you take me under the Water, also, and show me where you looked up at me. We are amazed.

Now we know everything. We know that the skin that covers our bones is like the membrane of Water where the Sun reflects us, and when we look at each other, we see only ourselves, but when we touch each other with compassion, we discover each other, and ourselves in each other, and each other in ourselves, and deeper and deeper we go like that—and so we want to touch each other now, now. But first we have to undress each other.

We thought that we were already naked. But now we find ourselves bound by weavings of Roses, like second skins we did not know we were wearing, that we cannot remember putting on. Only I can unbind you, and only you can unbind me. We use the wisdom we have learned in all our animal forms together. We use our teeth and our fins, our paws and our whiskers, to discover and unbind each other. We speak in touch. And sometimes your language is the language of flight, and sometimes mine is the liquid language of swimming; sometimes you bark, and sometimes I purr—but this time we understand each other. And all this makes our flesh tremble with such passion that we transform again, into Creatures we have never yet imagined.

Oh, Tiras, embrace me fully now, for now I kiss your heart to soothe and forgive you, and without demand, and now you enter me on purpose, and to honor me. The Sun rises, and you are the Sun. I am the Jungle, you melt me, you fill every place with light. You are the Rains, and I am the Earth turning to mud and movement, and the more you fill me, the more I soften, and the more I can contain. You are the ancient stones of the Seabed, whose shape remembers

*my swirling waves from the beginning of the world, even earlier than pain, and
I am the beginning of life, cradled in your arms.*
    This is the Ritual of Remembering.

    but I wake in tears

    Micah is telling me something. Rue murmurs in her sleep. The Sun
is hot today, in the Garden, and I want to close my eyes, but Micah speaks
to me sometimes, the way he does, knowing I will not respond, wanting
me to understand anyway—still believing, in his sad heart, that I will
become the queen he desires. He is telling me about Prince Leo, how he
must ally with him but mistrusts his ways of war, how he, Micah, must
proceed with caution. His own men, he is saying, the Wye men of Zara,
become warriors here when they are men, mature enough to understand
what they do. They are trained in a conscious way. If they kill, they know
why; if they die, they know why. They honor their adversary. *We are sacred
partners,* he says, *with our opponent warriors.*
    Sacred partners, I think. But I am not thinking of what he says.
    I am thinking, *if a girl could be made of Silver.* If a girl... could be a girl
forever, and never a woman. Made not of Hummingbirds, but of Ravens
and Doves. The cold hopelessness before dawn.
    Rowan left me with only one glance back, as unreadable as her first.
No kisses, no tears, no answers, but she said, "I have to go with him, Mara.
I have to go. But one day soon, I promise, I will not have to anymore."
    I would not have understood this, but Ama explained it to me. *She
was born of bitterness, raised by the cold gods of the Sky World. She was not
given anything human. The only human who ever held her hand abandoned
her to death at seven years old. When you touch her, she cannot feel it. She sees
you through glass.*
    We spent three days together, while Leo and Micah talked and feasted.
We forgot our children, for a little while. There are no wild places in Zara,
but out beyond the Sheep, the Wind tells tales. She led me into the fields
of Barley and Wheat, and I feared the horror she would find there—when
she knelt among the hissing fronds out in the long, crumbled swaths of
naked Earth, she touched the ground and drew back suddenly.
    "You feel what they have done to Her," I said, stroking her back, but
she bent low, slunk against the soil like a Snake, opened her lips to its dry
skin, listened with her mouth.
    "No," she whispered, and I could feel her lips as they moved upon the
Earth, as if they moved upon my own breast. "They can Dance this way.

They weave their Dream into Her. It is a loving that they do. But it could kill Her too. That is how the men do—when they love they make danger, they kill as they love."

I laid my hand on hers and felt the Earth through her. I felt how the Earth accepted this song, after all—the song of the Wheat and the Barley, the crops that people open Her up to grow. How She was gentle with the work of Her sons. "Agriculture"—the Wyes do it kindly, perhaps. And yet, every time a man enters a woman he breaks her—there is no other way.

Under the bridge where the Creatures tiptoe at night, we smeared Moonlight over each other's hills and ridges, our valleys and swamps, our hidden glens flowering. My body lashed and beat against hers, a sea, an open heart, the way I remember being helpless long, long ago. She was Faerie, the memory of my people moving lost through all my Dreams, unable to cross over into this life. Yet I touched her; yet my body—untouched for so long—died and woke, died and woke. My skin darkened with drinking her. And she, white upon white, only reflected me, her eyes always strange.

A Priestess becomes a Priestess because someone needs her to be. Someone needs her beauty, her love, her light. In Rowan's endless staring, her hushed body, her silent, empty call, she needed me. I was the only one who could hear that call, which was a scream, and continued even in her sleep.

Among my people, rape is always punishable by death. It has hardly ever happened between our own people, and never that I can remember, and yet it exists in our consciousness. It is the worst defilement. In our tradition, the rapist is bound to a Tree where the Jaguar will come and take him, so She can take him back into Death and remake him in a better way.

Leo will not be bound, he will not be received by the Jaguar and taught in the darkness what is sacred. He will live, he will make war, he will defile us. But someday, I think, things will come round. Can the violence of a man be sacred, as Micah says? I do not think so; I have never seen it.

I became a Priestess again to heal Rowan of her wound, because no one else could do it but me. To do this, I must stop touching her, though I boiled in her presence the way Esha used to boil secretly, steadily, in mine. I must gather that fire, to breathe life back into her.

I brought Rowan down to the Sea, in the center of the daytime, at the fullness of the mother-Moon. Everywhere I asked Rowan to go, she came willingly. She trusted me.

I asked her to choose a place that felt safe. She looked at me a long time, and then she looked out into the pale, disappearing horizon, and I knew she looked at Death. "No," I said, "a place in this life." Whereupon she dropped right where she was, on the sand, and bent her head.

But I did the healing. I passed my hands across her body without ever touching her, my longing became a portal, and I made the portal in the shape of Rowan's wholeness. When I called my Ancestors, they came through me easily. When I called every Faerie, each came willingly. When I called Rhiannon, I called in silence. Some knowing bade me not to speak Her name aloud in Rowan's presence. But I felt Her come, and there was no anger or vengeance, only a wave of the Sea. I felt Her darkness fill my flesh. Through me She flooded Rowan clean, burned her to ash, buried her in earth, and blew the dust away again, so I could re-make her.

When such violence comes to a person, they are remade in a bad way. A person should be made like a Hummingbird—beautiful and designed for love. At least my people are made that way, and perhaps others are made differently, but still they must fit the shape of love. When Rowan had violence sewn through her, it deformed her spirit, and that is why Rhiannon blew Her destructive breath through me, to undo the old weaving. If this false weaving is not undone, the person will attract violence to her again and again, and with each new violence, the weaving is strengthened, so that one day it will be too late for anyone—even a Priestess—to undo it. This is what Rhiannon taught me, as She blazed through me to return Rowan to darkness and gave me the fury with which to steal her away from the hands of the brutal, blood-demanding gods, returning her to the womb of the Goddess. For Rhiannon is the great weaver and undoer. She wove my fate when I made my choice at the base of the Nuba tree. And that night with Rowan, She un-wove the fate of one who never was able to make choices.

Then I had to remake her out of love. Rowan did not understand it, but she let me. The Cats had told her to trust me, so she did. She let me remove her clothes and bathe her in the Sea. She let me press my hands to the Air around her body, every corner and crevice, until the heat between my hands and her skin was a thick honey of protection.

But was it enough? In the South Forest, a woman who is raped remains under the protection of the Elders for so long—as long as it takes to make her whole again. She lives among women who are free and remember how to be free, remember how to be Woman. But I only healed Rowan for one day. And when I asked her to stand and say the word of power, she would not stand, and she would not speak. Perhaps she was not ready, yet, to be healed. Instead she lifted a handful of sand to her mouth and pressed her lips to it. She took the drops of Sea on her fingers and spread them over her cheeks, as if she would pretend the feel of tears.

"Do you feel it now?" I whispered to her. "Do you feel how he cannot touch you again?"

She didn't answer for a long time. Her throat clenched so still, I thought she wasn't breathing. She was looking far out into the Sea. It could be the Sea healed her after all, and nothing to do with me. "I see it," she said at last, in the voice of a Snake, and I thought I heard anger in the sound—I hoped I did, but maybe I imagined it.

"See what?"

"I see that he is lying. He cannot kill the Horses. He is weak."

I remembered how she'd laid her hand in Rue's—my little girl who Dreams of a Mare, a Mare who will break free one day. I came before Rowan and blocked the sight of the Sea with my own face, my own eyes. *Be here,* I told her with my eyes. *Live.* I saw the wild herds running there, in her eyes which, unlike her frozen body, raged.

She is gone since this morning. I insist on going barefoot, my feet hungering against the ground. The Air laps my skin like Cats' tongues. I can smell the milk in my breasts, the Sunlight on the dust of the path she walked, down from the first arches of the palace; I can hear the Trees, each leaf scratching the other, as if all the world is made flesh, and the Birds calling so hard and beautiful, they are trying to tear up the Sky.

Death opens a door into two worlds, the Below and Above. Below us, the Ancestors in the Earth, where our bodies transform into food to give life. Above us, a Dream palace of possibility, where the future is made. Not everyone can Dream there. They say it is cold, so cold that everything shines. They say the Wind there speaks a complex language. They say it is covered in cold, white glass, so beautiful it hurts mortal eyes. They say it is the stillness of a Hummingbird in flight, the silence inside the throb of Rain-season insects, when they call so hard they deafen you into Dreams.

The Cats told me that Rowan is from that place. Where the Dragons rule. Dragons are born female these days, they said. Only Leo doesn't know that yet.

After the healing, Rowan was shivering so hard, I held her in my arms. But I thought that the healing had worked at least a little, because Bees covered us where we lay. They hovered upon our necks, our faces, our hips, wading in the hairs of our bare skin like children in a field.

"Lemara?" she asked me, speaking for the first time in so long, not sure if that was my name.

"Yes," I said, and she repeated my name, a few times over. I was holding her, in the cave where I like to curl away from the Wind, and she faced away from me, out toward the Dream-beat of the waves, and I did not know if her eyes were open or closed, but I think they were open. I almost never saw them close.

"What you did," she said, "it was like what the Dwarves did."

"Who were the Dwarves?" I said.

"They took care of me and gave me their gifts," she said. "They were seven. Red. Orange. Yellow. Green. Blue. Indigo. Violet."

I clasped her hand. I didn't know what she meant, but I felt the Humming joy enclosing us, the old magic. "There were seven Faeries, too," I told her, "who blessed me, and gave me their gifts."

Slowly, as if unsure that she could do it, she squeezed my hand, and her body went limp, as if some skeleton of pain had dissolved from it at last. "But I cannot find them," she whispered. "Who told that story?"

"I know," I said, seeking to comfort her. "The old world is broken, and we cannot find our way back. But we still have the gifts."

"It is not enough," said Rowan.

Holding her was like holding Water. I put my lips to the back of her neck and drank. I wanted her the way the Hummingbird wants the flower. It is not the simple lust of one Hummingbird for another. It is the deep longing for flowers—Red, Blue, Indigo, Yellow. It is the source of life I wanted, that makes the Hummingbird what it is.

And no.

What is left to us—it is not enough.

I am still Priestess. I can still make a healing. But can I heal my people, alone? No, it is not possible. It is not possible to act alone. She left me in an empty world. She left me closer to Tiras than I have ever been, and yet never so alone. I hear him in the breathing waves, I smell him in the thirsty Earth, I feel his mouth when I open my mouth to drink Water. He is everywhere. And I remember everything. I remember the Dream. I have been Dreaming it ever since, just as I have always been hearing the sound of the Sea, just as I have always known the reason for that smoky wound in Tiras' chest—he died for me. When he learned he had lost me to the hundred-year sleep, he drowned himself in the River Golden, so that we could marry after all, in all the rituals of marriage, in a Dream we would Dream together for a hundred years.

Rowan came to me like a waking, washing over me, leaving me in ruin. I watch Micah speaking to me, and I cannot focus on his words, because this isn't the real marriage. This isn't even the real life. *This* is the dream. I know this. These people are not my people. Even this self is not my real self. I came from somewhere, where I made sense and had my place. Where I was seen and known by the one who loved me. Where everywhere I went, I was recognized as Beloved.

King Micah holds his hands steady, gripping his knees as he speaks, and I can sense the wounds now beneath his sleeves, the wounds along his arms and across his chest and over his heart, from Roses that scar him and hurt his pride, that will never heal, he says—but he doesn't know that his own tears, if he ever wept them, would heal them instantly. After all this time, I am not angry anymore. He never asked to see Rowan. But one time, he did see her. She and I were walking, at last, up from the Sea, our hands clasped, and I thought—I don't know why—that we would be together forever now, and this would save me. And I saw Micah see us together, and a look of wonder I had never seen before in his eyes. I saw that he was a little boy once, long ago. An answering wonder rose up in me—did he, too, love once, with that kind of love I knew for Tiras? Before he met me, before he, too, was forced into this marriage by forces greater than his own feeling or will, through endless tangles of invading Roses? Maybe this isn't his real life, either. But he couldn't remember. If there was a Dream he Dreamed, too, he couldn't remember it. He looked away. He was walking alone, like always, his face shrouded in invisible thought.

"Micah," I say now, laying my hand on his. He's so startled by my voice, by my touch after this long year of my absence, his mouth falls limp into silence. "I will go now and speak to the Queen of Sirenia."

"What?" His face washes clean, that way it did when he found me on the beach in the beginning, when we first kissed and he lost all his knowing in my arms.

"Before you start this war. Before you do whatever you will do. I will go and speak to her. Micah, I am sorry. I cannot live any longer in this world. There are things I have lost—and I need to know. I need to know what they have done to the world I knew. Where they have taken it, where it has gone."

He stares at me, and his confusion is like pain, and I am sorry, yes I am sorry, because I recognize it. I do, Micah. "Where it has gone?" he repeats. "Lemara—it hasn't gone somewhere. It's just gone."

"No," I tell him, with patience. "Nothing disappears. It only changes. They have changed it into some other form." I know he doesn't understand this. His people leave behind a word for each thing done and undone in this life, as if to make it permanent. But must the Sun write a record of His passing on stone, before sinking into colored bliss? No, for He will rise again, and everyone knows it. It is the same with each of us. We Hums used to pass the stories from mouth to mouth, like kisses, and that was all we needed to leave behind—a hum in the Air—because we knew when we died, we would only become another. "They have our magic somewhere," I tell Micah, "in their city, in their world. I will find it. I will begin by asking her."

"Lemara." I see my name leaving his mouth, the breath it leaves with—and even this is loss, even this is heartbreak. The first heartbreak, that sent them out of the Jungle in search of a way to live forever. "Do what you have to do. I will never convince you. I don't even understand you. But I tell you, Queen Ella isn't the one who makes decisions there."

"No," I say. "I understand that now." The woman is not the one with the power here, not anywhere in this new world. But she is the one who holds its secret. She is the reason for the violence. She is the wound.

Ella

I remember we had just made love for the first time in more days than we could count, the time he overtook me with that gaze I remembered from the old days, that heady mix of awed and urgent adoration, and told me that before Kiera died, he had left my bedside to visit her, and she had been herself again for a few moments.

This was the first time Sol had spoken to me about any of his family members' deaths, and what those lonely hours were like for him. He told me Kiera had asked about each of our children, and were they still alive. She had squeezed his hands and wrung them, bruised them, in her agony for Anna, but with eyes dry. Then she had begged him always to take care of me, to be good to me, for my heart was fragile, she said. *You must never hurt her,* she said. *You must not go with other girls anymore, you must promise me.* He told me all this, clenching my hair gently in his fists. It broke his heart to have fallen in the eyes of his sister; it broke his heart to know she was right. I know he wanted to keep that promise; I know he meant to.

But I knew which girls he would choose, even before he did. I saw the breathless way they looked at him—handsome and hot-blooded as ever in those years after the Death, with the new streak of melancholic tension darkening his expressive face and pulling at women's inner tides even more treacherously, and he was king now, after all, little less than a god in their eyes—and the way they whispered to each other and then pulled quickly apart when I passed. I saw the long lashes and graceful necks of the Hum-born women, who were rumored by all men to have a special internal musculature that could bring a man to climax such as he'd never felt before—without their bodies even moving. I saw the way his glance followed certain bustles and dropped below certain faces, the vague, distracted shadow crossing his eyes, the little smile and his tongue sweeping the inside of his lip in that way he did at tournament when he knew he was going to win. He sat on the throne always doubting but never speaking his doubt, with no one to guide him, not even God, all boyish freedom forbidden to him now. Alden and his father had lost themselves in drink, to survive the pressure, but Sol didn't drink. Sometimes I wished he did.

For better or for worse, I knew my Sol better than anyone ever would. I loved him so hard—I was bound so fast to him, my heart a flimsy thing tied to a branch in the Urodel, sometimes floating in sunny bliss, sometimes hurled along rapids, forced to surrender to the beating of rocks, the undertow of whirlpools, the grating of the silt and the splashing of animals, never free and never at peace. And yet I did not wish to be free, for to be free was to drown, and as long as I could hold to his warm body and follow the path of his heart, I told myself I could bear any pain. For he did not bare his thoughts to anyone as he did to me; he did not reveal his weaknesses, his terrors, his childishness, his hopelessness, to anyone but me. For this reason, he belonged to me. And for this reason, he could never be faithful to me, for with me he could not be a god—or so he thought.

He felt guilt for what he did with them, I know, but the lower he sank in his own eyes, the more he needed them. He could not bear anger or accusation from me. If ever I should criticize him or attempt to hold him to his promises, then I would lose him for some time after.

So I kept silent, and kept what I could of him.

You remember how it was then, my people. We all had to do the best we could, during that dark, strange time.

♛   ♛   ♛   ♛   ♛

All my life as queen, I never lost the girlish impulse, whenever visitors arrived from a foreign place, to run to a tower window, to assess their character by their approach, to wonder at their strangeness and what surprises might unfold from it—simply to be an innocent princess with the freedom to look down, to be entertained by the drama without playing any part in it. When Queen Lemara arrived, I felt like that—they told me that she came to the riverbank in a delicately engraved Wye carriage, curtained entirely by indigo fabrics, unseen by any of the populace; that she whispered with her horses and demanded a royal barge to carry them to the palace shore, unwilling to entrust them to our men; that she refused the hands held out to help her from the boat as she leapt to the steps from the water, and that she didn't look up at the height of the towers, as commoners do, when she walked in—but all I could do, of course, was sit down beside Sol on our throne, as if I poured myself into the mold of some regal, graven image, and helplessly wait.

I saw her enormous eyes first, their searing whites and depthless pupils arresting us in her vision before she even crested the top stair, and then her breasts, bulbous and brazen in their beaded coverings which swayed and stretched their shell-lined strands to wind around her back and up her neck and drip from her piles of rippling, impenetrably black hair. Her belly, bare, seemed to spiral as she walked, as if her purpose came from there, and her skirt made of overlapping wrappings of Wye fabrics mingled cloudy, underwater shades of violet and maroon to highlight the moving rainbows of her secretive darkness the way moonlight highlights the unreal. When she set down the naked baby she held on her hip and stood up in all her sleek splendor, I saw Sol's desire all over her—but it cascaded from her like water, and meant nothing to her. I felt the sudden stillness in his heart, beside me. He didn't twitch a muscle, but I swear he heated so fast and hard, I felt it in the gently swaying glass.

"Welcome, Queen of Wyes," he said. "What can we do for you?" He spoke in hoarse Wye, which royal children learn throughout their schooling but which I still barely understood, and thereafter I hardly knew what the two of them said. The child crawled to me and reached unsteadily to grasp the hem of my silk dress, and fearing that she would fall backward, I stepped down to lift her. Glancing at Queen Lemara, who watched me all the time that Sol spoke to her, but did not seem alarmed by this gesture, I settled back into my throne with the child in my arms, bouncing her, inviting her to toy with my jewels. I bent my head to her easily smiling face, to hide my face from Lemara who pained me by her beauty and whom I could not understand, and to burrow into the familiar—though fragrant with unfamiliar herbs—melting bloom of baby scent, and to hide the tearfulness this caused me, missing my Anna. When at last I lifted my head to face the tension between my husband and this proud, stormy queen who seemed to dance even as she stood still, it was upon hearing her say *No*. She was refusing Sol something. I was pretty sure he had invited her to rest herself, to dine with us, to spend a night here at least, and refresh herself before discussing business—something to that effect. When she spoke, her lips changed and curled with such unabashed sensuality, I could not help but turn and look at Sol's, which hung open with fascination, and did not close, no matter her words.

"She..." He began, explaining to me, leaning on the arm rest between us and inclining his head toward mine but never taking his gaze from her, "She is angry, this Queen of Wyes. She says..." He sighed, bouncing one knee with impatience. "She says we have made magic there, in the South Forest where she's from, and she wants us to undo it."

"Magic?"

"Yes, that's what she says."

He said something else to her, and she answered in words that were firm and insistent and rhythmic and also somehow like birds. I never saw someone speak with her body the way she did, not with the little thrusts and gestures that some people make haltingly for emphasis, but as if the words she spoke were only the brightly colored tips of flames that began and continued, moving indefinitely, in her spine.

"What magic?" I asked, feeling afraid.

"Gold, god, words," she said to me in sharp, ragged Sirenian, and I heard her squeezing the letters in her cheeks as if they tasted sour to her, the wide breath in her vowels.

"She says we have taken things from her people, and she wants them back," Sol added. I didn't ask what things. She began to wander around the Hall, and with a kind of quiet, impudently sensual fury, tapped her palms upon what made it—the columns, the sculptures, the tapestries. She looked up at the pictures in the glass, pictures of our Savior, pictures of God. I watched her with horror, but Sol, I think, watched her indulgently, with an interested smile on his face, as if she were a child. Thinking she admired what she saw, he began to offer her gifts, for her people, for both her peoples.

She looked at me as if she didn't hear him, and didn't expect me to, either. It didn't occur to her, I think, that I would mind what he said any more than she did—strange as I know that sounds. She sauntered directly toward me, reached out to touch the glass where it arched between me and Sol, supporting our hands. I think she said the word "glass" in Wye. I didn't know then—I wouldn't learn for many years, for hardly anyone remembered—that our throne was made by Wye craftsmen long ago, out of sand from South Forest beaches.

"Queen Lemara—" Sol grabbed her insolent hand by the wrist, ostensibly to remove it, but I think she knew he did it partly just to touch her, and she slipped it from him—not yanking it back like one startled, but twisting her arm like a snake to undo his grip.

"Not yours," she said. Then she surged toward me, leapt with a soft, animal leap right onto the raised stone platform over which our throne hung, and, there being so little room for her to stand, leaned lightly into me, her legs anchored against mine, and grabbed hold of the chain that dangled me from on high. So shocked was I by this advance, my frantic mind could only assume she meant to snatch the child back from me, but she only bent her face to mine and spoke to me in a low, beautiful voice whose tone was a command—not the command of a queen but the command of a heart.

"You are queen. Mother. You love. My place, my people, mother of my life, dead. Dead. Rape. Your people come, kill." She jerked her head with every word, her chin jutting toward me, tears loosening and spilling from her eyes with such freedom, it astonished me. "You understand? You are mother, give life, care. But you kill us. You magic our soul away. You take everything. You take our know, our proud, our imagine, our sense, our dance. Everything you have—you steal. Where is it? This? Why?"

My people, I had never in all my life given more than a few thoughts to the Hummingbird People. I had hardly understood that they were real. "It—it wasn't me," I stammered in a whisper. Sol grabbed hold of her arm—he was standing—and pulled her down and back to the floor below me, at first with a hungry kind of tenderness, and then with the force of his body when he realized—I think—that she was much stronger than he'd expected.

"Queen Lemara," he reproached her, "you are in a civilized house. You will not intimidate my wife, the queen of this kingdom, or violate the sanctity of this throne. This is your only warning." Then he said it again, in Wye. But he remained standing, forgetting himself, leaning over her in a clumsy attitude of confusion, trembling with conflicting emotions I could both see and feel clearly, in my own shame. How could she accuse us of magic? She had it all.

"What do you want?" I cried out. "None of these things can be undone. These things were done by people before my time. What do you want now?"

She reached out and the girl, though surely not two years old, launched herself easily into the arms of her mother like a little grasshopper into an outstretched flower. The pain of separation between her flesh and mine (oh it is just different, the scent of a baby girl, not like a boy at all), the loss of confidence it left me with—the emptiness of all my losses—felt so brutal that for a moment I hated that woman. I hated the sultry way she swung her hip aside to support her daughter, the way my husband could not step away from her and the tension in his hands, to know that she would leave us now.

"You are prisoner?" she asked me softly, her face so strongly shaped with emotion, I ached with it.

"I am queen," I said.

She shook her head. "No," she said, her mouth hanging open in desolation, and she kept shaking her head, and began to walk backward. I didn't know why she had come here, my people. I didn't know why. Sol reached for her again, as if to guide her out, and she shook off his hands with a snarl, snapping her lips shut. But still she gave me her longing, wide eyes, and the tears that fell from them. They were for me. Neither of us could look away.

When the great doors closed behind her, I held my head and sobbed. When Sol touched me, I could not feel it. When he tried to soothe me, I could not hear him; when he asked me why, I could not answer him; and I did not care when his tone turned to bewildered irritation, or when he left me alone there in the echoing Hall, where those magnificent lights and shadows showered me always with the loneliness of God.

In the days after, I would see him thinking about her sometimes. I knew he was thinking of her when I saw the sea in his eyes, in the middle of supper, even though he never spoke of her, even though I had never, at that time, seen the sea. But when I asked him once what he'd thought of her, he scowled, and then laughed a muttering little laugh which was grotesque to me in its falsehood.

"They're all witches, those women."

That was all he said. And I did not say, *But you told me, long ago, that you don't believe in witches.* I didn't say it because I knew he didn't mean that kind of witch, the kind who made spells and loved and was hung for it. He meant the kind who didn't need him, the kind who might curse him. And I said nothing because I was angry with her—Lemara the Hummingbird Priestess—though I don't know if I knew that then, and I certainly didn't know why. And because I was careful around Sol in those days, avoiding all confrontation, saving up all his good will toward me for the one request I treasured most, the one I'd been gathering my courage for all this time.

♕   ♕   ♕   ♕   ♕

Dear Queen Mina,

How delighted I was to receive your gracious, welcoming letter several months ago. You think your role as queen there, managing a small population in a forgotten land, more modest than mine, but in truth I question my own decisions perhaps as much as you do. I feel I can be honest with you. Your kindness gives me confidence. How much we shall have to talk about, when we see each other at last.

When you were a child, a commoner like me, did you ever imagine the royal life? When I was a girl, I think it meant little more, to my imagination, than luxury and freedom of every kind. When I was a princess, I thought it meant proving myself, raising myself to a standard. When I first ascended to the throne, King Solon's relations seemed to believe I would prove my worthiness as queen by my ability to hold that station and not be knocked down from it.

There were times when every one of them seemed against me. They tried to influence my husband against me. He even received news, once, of a plot against my life. No one had ever been able to believe I deserved him, let alone the throne itself. None of this hurt me much by then, for I'd suffered it so much when I was princess, I was accustomed to it. But it took effort to maintain my place. Once I'd climbed to this dizzying mountain peak, I must at first use all my strength and concentration merely to remain here without being blown off by the wind. I had no energy left for studying the landscape around me or determining how to rule it.

I believe I have held my place partly by kindness. I know it sounds strange. I never learned to play the games they played. If someone was rude to me, or Sol reported that he spoke ill of me, I would tell him openly to his face what I'd heard, and say I was sorry he didn't want me to be queen. I caught plotters unaware, I suppose, by my very naiveté. I cannot stand to be hated, and so I responded to those who would hate me with the feeling I thought our Savior would recommend me to feel for them. After a recent experience in our great cathedral, whose construction, I am happy to announce, is underway again, I remembered also how much my people long for this same openness and forgiveness from me—and how much more they deserve it than some stuffy royal personage whose favor I worried about winning.

Ever since the plague, dear Mina, I have insisted upon tending, faithfully and on my own, the palace hearth. It is something I did as a child, in my own home—in fact it was my special job. That tending symbolizes, for me, all that I wish to be as queen. I wish to tend the hearth, the heart, of this kingdom, with all the love that the Savior would wish for us. I wish to know every one of my people intimately, and each one's needs and sufferings. Though I always feel a little stilted on the throne, even now, and must give way to Sol's final word, I wander the city almost daily now, seeking the conversation of my people. I am their listener, their compassion. I want to know what matters to them. Sometimes with patience, with soft words placed at the right times, with humble requests, I can convince Sol to let me decide things in their favor when he might otherwise not, because I've convinced him that such areas of life are part of a queen's domain and of lesser interest to him. (The rights of widows, for example—some of them. The schooling of girls. Not the rebuilding of swamps or the dumping of waste in tributaries, too complex with the opinions of too many factions, but the preservation of certain spaces of beauty, at least, and communal gardening for the poor.) Sometimes the act of listening, in itself, is enough to make people feel understood, enough for me to deepen my understanding. Sometimes I listen not to solve any problems, but only to know and be known by them. Only to know myself better through their eyes.

But when I see you, I hope we will speak of so many things. How to take into account the voices of a multitude and be just. How to make our voices as strong as men's. What duties are ours as queens, and how they differ from the duties of kings. King Solon is surrounded by his chosen council of trusted men, though he doesn't always ask for their advice. If only I could surround myself with a chosen council of wise women, and if only I could feel as certain as he does, of any decision I make.

I am only waiting until my new son is just a little older, dear Mina, to make this pilgrimage—probably within the year. I look forward to it with trepidation and yet with all the joy of my heart. I know you will understand.

Yours in expectation,
Queen Ella

Dear Queen Mina. I never sent that letter, nor did I write you again, for years.

Then you learned, perhaps, why they say (at least here in my land) that a woman's promises cannot be trusted. It is because most of the time, a woman isn't under her own command. She speaks, sometimes, as if she is—wooed into confidence by friendship, the liquid merging another woman invites into her heart—and forgets.

♛   ♛   ♛   ♛   ♛

I wrote all these letters, but had never spoken to Sol of my inwardly treasured dream. Though he knew and approved—in an offhand, unthinking way—of my correspondence with the Queen of the Ghost Kingdom, the feelings I penned in those letters (and the feelings I considered and savored and smiled over in hers) all felt to me as preciously secret as the fallow fields, the willow and the waterfall, the flowering witch's grave I had loved and tended as an escape from childhood torments long ago. To leave, even for a month, the palace which had saved me from my nowhere life, given me family, entombed and yet comforted me in my grief, welcomed me home each day and entrusted its hearth to me—yes, this terrified me—yet still. Still I dreamed a breezy, balming, ivory dream, born on a breath, a word, that day I had spoken to the nun and to God in the cathedral. I dreamed I would go down along the river with some few among you, my people, who were so devout, so sure of God and yet so full of yearning, as I was, to know not only Him but the Bride—what was Her strength, what was Her purpose, what upheld Her and what knowing could She lend us—that together we would support each other over unknown waterways and mountains, murmuring encouragement and secret questions to one another. I dreamed I was the queen who would go among you in shared faith, questing for the vision of the Virgin of God. Protected by you, encouraging you, learning ever more deeply of your passions and hopes and sorrows, I would pass with you through a lake of mist up into heavens, and be welcomed by a fellow queen, a queen who like me was finding her way, who like me was young and humble and earnest in her desire to do right by her duty, who could talk over everything with me at last, who already felt, by the way she spoke to me in her letters, like a friend.

But she wouldn't have understood. She would have been unable to comprehend my weakness. How long I waited, how long it took me to muster my courage—not for the journey itself but for the asking. How long it took me to formulate an argument he might respect, and to believe I could articulate it with confidence. *It will increase the people's trust in me, in us,* I would say. *It will bind them to us in spiritual solidarity, giving us influence more equal to that of the priests. It will give me knowledge of another country, one we might count as an ally. It will prove my spiritual worthiness to both the priests and the people.*

But I hardly began these arguments, because when I finally began to speak I realized what I had denied to myself—that every one of them touched on fears within Sol that only I could see, fears we were implicitly bound not to touch. The moment I broached my request, I already felt myself failing.

"Not now, Ella," he said at first, his head in my lap, where we sat on my bed one night long after the palace had gone silent. "Can't you see how tired I am?"

"But I have been waiting for so long to ask you, Sol. You are always tired, and I don't know when—"

"Yes, I am always tired! Every day I can just barely keep on top of the decisions and tasks that are heaped upon me. The only thing I have to look forward to are these few moments of rest."

"I just think..." I stopped, furious at my tears. He rolled over and looked up at me.

"You really mean this? You want to go on a pilgrimage? Ella. Really."

"Yes! Yes, I mean it."

"You imagine yourself journeying all that way alone—" He was laughing.

"Not alone. With my people."

He laughed again, closed his eyes. "With your people."

"What? What is it?"

He sat up and rubbed his eyes. He wasn't angry. He looked at me kindly, stroked my hair like a child's, even though it was I—always I—who comforted him. "Ella," he said, and I was grateful for the sudden change in his mood, his serious consideration, and yet at the same time the very flesh of my face, my body, seemed to collapse in despair, because from that same tone I already knew his answer. "The truth is, there is much suspicion about these pilgrimages, that they are a kind of cult, that they focus attention on some foreign idol in some foreign land."

"Idol? It is the Holy Virgin you speak of. And what suspicion? Among certain priests, you mean?"

He nodded slowly. "Yes..."

"But Sol, you don't care what they think, and theirs aren't the only opinions that matter." I was incredulous.

"Of course I don't care. But we must tread carefully these days, Ella. I cannot think on these lofty ideals of yours; I must think practically, politically." He shook his head, turned away from me—his gaze turned inward, and I lost it. "Those priests," he grumbled, his voice turning sour. "They'll fight me for the last, tiniest bone of the people's faith, because the truth is they know they are losing. They know their God isn't so convincing anymore. Because they know we've all lost trust in the Savior! Why should we believe in a God who abandoned us to—" He broke off, gesturing with his hand into the shadows of the room, as if the Great Death were beyond his capacity to name. "So they try to blame it on sin instead," he finished bitterly, "to distract us. They'll even blame it on you and me if they have to. Pilgrimages to visit a holy woman, even the Virgin Herself, threaten them— they worry over witchcraft, and Ella..." He sighed and looked back at me. "You must be careful. We must both be."

So that was it. "But Sol," I said, my voice very low because I knew now, there was no hope, but I could not help myself. "What do you mean by 'their' God? Isn't He your God also, even so?"

But he kissed my head as he stood, told me to get some sleep. We were done.

And I wasn't surprised. I had always known he would refuse me, though I hadn't understood all the reasons—I had felt it to be so, and I knew now that this was why I had waited so long, why I had written in letters again and again of my dream, so that I could imagine it real for myself, knowing all along that it couldn't be. But what left me reeling was the realization that you, Mina, would never understand this. You would never understand why I needed my king's permission to do what I would, as queen. It may sound strange but you must believe me that it surprised me, too, to realize that I needed it, and to compare myself with you, and to know that you wouldn't.

I hadn't realized—I only realize it now—that I write this long letter, this self-soothing confession, not only to my people but to my wished-for friend, my secret self. To my sister queen, the one who would have stood stronger than me. To the wise-woman who I learned, years later, and could sense even then from those letters, always stood equal to her husband and was respected by him from the first to the last. To the real woman who could have given me such better answers than visions of a chaste, subservient bride, had I traveled to the Ghost Kingdom then, when I wanted to, instead of years later, with my husband at my side. To the one who expected me, that year, to bring the greetings of peace be-tween two kingdoms which might have swelled our confidence in the face of all the conflicts of men, all the horrors and losses yet to come—that kind of harmony I dreamed of, listening to the songs in the cathedral, one day on my own, following my intuition there with your letter hidden in my cloak. To a woman, to a woman's soul.

To you, Mina.

Oh, and to realize that the Holy Virgin I longed for, the one whose unconditional grace would pour over me and over all the world and all my life so that the colors would shift into meaning and sense and every-thing, somehow, would come right—to realize that after all, She could not help me here. It wasn't that kind of woman who would give me the strength to stand up to my husband. You may not believe me, Mina, but up until this moment, I hadn't realized that I needed such strength, just as I hadn't realized that the Hummingbird People were actual people whose losses were real to them and whose suffering ruined them, led by a blazing priestess whose rage swirled up from some ancient source in the earth that I could not imagine ever being confident enough to feel—but only be devastated to witness.

Yet I did feel it, and I feel it still. When my husband left me alone in my room without hope, it was her I thought on, not him.

Lemara

She comes when all is lost

We stop for the night at the foot of the Ho Volcano—the foot of the Wye People's god, but to me it is the wound in the Earth, the wound where they were born as a people and lost to us forever. The place where we were broken apart. They call it the height from which their commands came down, down from the lonely god. I call it the womb of fire where they were swallowed up, where they lost their color, their darkness, their body-knowing.

I am not thinking of Queen Ella's pale trembling, her pathetic fear of me and of her husband and of everything. I am not thinking of her words, which were nothing, and came from nowhere, nor of the deadly doctrine in her glass window-pictures, of all the pieces of bodies of Trees and Sky-Horses and Birds and Alligators and life hammered into the lifeless building that encased her and yet still she didn't even know—still she couldn't remember what she and her people have done with the things they've stolen.

No, I am thinking of the two of them, woman and man, sitting together upon a single throne. That throne was wound and bound like frozen Water, by the grace of human hands, by some old magic they didn't understand. Glass, made of Fire melting Stone that has already been ground to dust for a thousand years by Water. They didn't know how it was made, or from what or from where. They sat upon it, together, not knowing how to be equal and speak as one, not knowing how to balance each other upon that holy seat, not knowing what it meant.

But neither do I. I have never even imagined such a thing. That elements could be so changed, and be so beautiful. That two could rule as one—woman and man—and side by side. Is this possible? I did not know I would be so angry. I could not see her face past that anger. It was all I could see. I know less than when I began, and all my anger is spent now, like worthless riches.

I only know I am not going to be able to turn back Time. I am not going to be able to unspin it. I am not going to be young again, or find Tiras waiting for me at the base of the Nuba Tree. I am not going home. I am not going to ever find my way home.

The Wye-men offer me, of course, the cushions of the carriage to sleep upon, but I sleep on the Earth. When the Sun descends, I feel the Wye-men's protection, standing guard around me. I know. I feel how I need that protection now, in this world.

Maybe sometime in the night, Rue wakes and crawls a little ways from me, reaching for a Horse's face, whispering to him in the dark. I don't stir. I can't bring myself to open my eyes, and I lie here with arms empty, Dreaming on, alone.

I Dream you are comforting me, as I weep in the River. Holding me in your arms. Don't you remember, Lemara? How can you weep? Don't you remember the Ritual of Sacrifice, how much we gave to each other? Don't you remember the Forgetting, so sweet now to remember, all the beautiful Creatures we became in our desire and our pain? Don't you remember how we found each other at last through the mirror of the Water? Drink, Beloved, drink!

And we drink, yes, we drink now overflowing nectar. We lick the sticky sweetness from each other's mouths. The Sun has risen and the morning is blooming all around us and inside us, and we are beautiful, beautiful, and the Jungle is singing.

We kiss as if we can never be filled. At last I have remembered the Dream I Dreamed for a hundred years, the Dream which lasted only one single night and one single day in the Faerie World. Rhiannon—I have been begging and begging Her to show me the way to you—and at last She leads the ritual, She leads our marriage ritual, we are together at last. The Jaguar is speaking, and the Hatta-Bird and the Dragonfly and the Crocodile, and we are meant to listen and follow their instructions about remembering the stories of the Wind and keeping the flame entrusted to us, but we cannot concentrate on what they're saying, we are so in love, so hungry for each other. At last, Tiras, at last.

Rhiannon says, Be careful. Do not cleave too tightly to one another.

But oh we laugh, squirming with delicious love. We smear up against each other, devouring each other, seeking to become one. We can never have enough of each other. We are all alone in the universe.

And seeing us thus, Rhiannon binds us as we are. Just as we press so tightly to one another, so tightly there is not the tiniest breath of Air left open between us, She binds us together with Spider silk so that we cannot pull apart.

And what now, Tiras? Wrapped so tightly, we cannot move. We cannot tease or caress. We sweat and itch. We desire each other so badly that our bellies cramp up and our thighs twitch, but though we are touching each other in every place, we cannot have each other, for there's no room to pull out and thrust in. We cannot reach and touch with our hands. And in our frustration, each of us squirms just to selfishly soothe our own small needs, because it is all we can do. Each of us push to get a little friction where we need it, but this only makes the other more desperate, by tickling places that need relief and cannot get it. In our desperation, we forget our love and our tenderness, we forget who we are. We tear at our bonds and we tear at each other. The pain is relief. We would do anything to free ourselves from stagnation. And finally, this tearing, too, even in our bleeding and our struggle, becomes exciting, and we find joy again, aroused by our wildness, freed by our own vicious, separate wills, surprised by each other's violence.

Now standing at last apart, we look upon each other like predators, with glittering eyes. And now with new space between us, we begin to Dance.

We Dance close enough together, and far enough apart, that the Air between us becomes like the membrane of Water, like the skin of the Earth where the Rain first touches and turns to magic. That space of Air becomes hot, hot, like the hot pulp of some fruit that stings your mouth with too much sweetness. Inside that hot space between us, where we do not touch yet but Dream of touch, where we are not one but two, moving in and out of union in a forever-ecstasy of wanting and fulfillment, reaching and loss, the world begins to begin.

Don't you remember this, Lemara? This is the Ritual of Creation. This is how we made the world anew—by coming apart.

I do remember

I do remember, Beloved. Keep going. Hold my hand. If I can find my way to the end of this Dream we Dreamed together, I will know what happened. I will know where you've gone, where to find you.

Now the Sun stands midway in the Sky between morning and night, between male and female, all the way at the top of the world, so let us drink wine now, from this cup of bone. Remember, Tiras? Wine is darker than Night, richer than soil; it bites like blood and soothes like Rain; it gives us pleasure and pain at once, and we accept both gladly.

Now we hold the still-full cup before us, and the Sun glows through it, and it is a Golden beacon that shows us the way. Holding hands, we rise up together *and follow the path before us, for we have faced each other long enough now, knowing each other, that we are ready to turn our faces forward to journey beside each other into the answers. We will find the beginning of the world. We will find the place where it is bound together, so that it can never be undone.*

We pass through all the queendoms and kingdoms of the world. Our hands are bound to one another, and in that bond we are invisible travelers, protected in our sacred joy. We pass among the pale, sun-haired people with their dreams that are only echoes of life. We pass among the Ghost People, the silver-skins who seek the light but do not recognize it within their own darkness. We walk in the gardens of the Wyes, that grew from blood and will bleed again. We know everything. We see the Hummingbird People making their world by magic and love, the Wyes making their world by the power of the word, the Sirenians making their world out of materials with their hands, the Barbarians making their world by breaking it to pieces, the Ghost People making their world out of Dreams. We know what the Dead know.

We hold each others' hands. We try not to let go. Once, traveling in the Sea, you turn cold and afraid, and a great black mass swims toward you, unknown, blurred, and frightens you—in its slippery passing I lose you. But I search for you and will never stop searching. I search until I feel you in my body; I feel you in the strands of the Sea; I follow your darkness. I find you floating in jetsom, curled up in the current, not rising, not sinking, and I take you in like a Whale, spit you out on the shore, let the Sun revive you.

And once, flying in the Sky, I am distracted by the lightness and all the Birds, all the Birds passing on into unknown future making Wind in my belly, and I drift apart from you without knowing it. I grab at clouds, I am falling, I call out for you in terror—but you come under me, you support me in feathers, and we fall together and I know we will survive.

We will always find each other. Come now, with me, to the end of the Dream. We climb over barren hills where everything has been destroyed. No roots hold the Earth together, and it turns to Wind. No shape of Trees holds the Air together, and the Wind turns to Ocean. No living thing drinks the Rain, and no person Dances for it, and the falling Water hurts the Earth like Fire. But we make a real Fire there, Tiras, to keep us warm: we make it out of nothing, having only our faith in each other to fuel it. We have no wine to drink, and the light has gone out, so we drink each others' saliva to stay alive. Though we know we will exhaust the very last of our energy, and have nothing to eat, we make love all night long to consecrate this place which has been desecrated. For our bodies are all we have. And when you give to me of your life fluid, and I give to you of mine, we somehow receive more than what we give, and we survive.

We wake nourished and renewed, and the land begins to itch again with blooming, and the Rivers are running.

We remember this. This, the Ritual of Forgiveness.

And though it seems a lifetime, though a hundred years pass in the waking world, our Dream lasts only one single night and one single day. Now the afternoon rounds finally toward evening, and the Sun pulses with nostalgia and tenderness, and we lean close to Him, though we cannot look at Him. Soon, soon I will know. I will Dream this Dream again. I will Dream it forever, until I find you.

Together we bend over our work, concentrating with such attention on what we are making together. Around us, above us, and below us, great strange hills are twisting and groaning, and a Wind of sorrow is blowing—I have never known such a Wind. The Air is cold, so that all our senses shine bright and hard, and our eyes tear. Hawks circle naked over our heads, and the Earth is drumming, and monsters are holding Council somewhere in beautiful groves I cannot see, and when I look up I can see the Snow forming high, high above. I know we are in the Sky World, the Opposite World, where the Dead go after hundreds of years to Dream a new future.

What are we weaving, Tiras? The Sun is curling up to sleep, He is floating downward, and soon we must sing Him to his resting place. Rhiannon is letting us play on Her giant spinning wheel. We are one in our intention, for we have done this before, whatever it is that we are doing. It is iridescent. More colors than I knew, in that other, fake world. Like the patterns of Hummingbird wings, as seen by other Hummingbirds—not the colors themselves, but what they become when they are moving, and what they do with the light. It is so important, what we weave. The answers are in it. I must remember what it means, when I wake. But I know already, I know I will forget. I know I will leave it behind. Oh Tiras, I do it every time.

Just when the Sun is leaving, just as the singing begins—a singing of such sorrow, oh Tiras, I do not think I can bear it (I would rather have the pain of your sword a hundred times than the sorrow I feel in this song that is dying with the Sun)—I realize you are gone.

I do not know when you left me. I was trying to pay such close attention. I was waiting, watching for the end. But it happens like this every time. You slip away when I'm not looking.

I remember you fingering the edges of the weaving, perhaps fearing I would not guard it well enough, that I would leave it behind. I remember you cutting open the smoky wound in your heart, and me drinking it at last—not blood but sweet water. I remember every Ritual that came before. But I don't remember your leaving.

I think at first that you will come back in a moment. For haven't we always returned to each other, and haven't we always rescued each other, and haven't we always been found? Out on the cliff alone, I sing the Sun into darkness, and I am very, very cold, Tiras, and the great iridescent weaving lies across my lap, stiff and still, and you do not come.

But at last, at the very end, just before the darkness, I hear you call my name. I stand up and listen. Yes. Urgently, across a great distance, too great for me to imagine, you call me. I begin to run into the Sky. I run through Air and Mist, Snow and Rain, breaking and bleeding through thorns and Roses, and just as I feel myself nearing you, just as I hear your voice so clear and sweet and true, close as a whisper, saying forever my name, I wake.

I woke to the Wye-man Micah, in his awful Wye-man armor, bending over me as if I had only been sleeping.

Tiras. Ever since Rhiannon took everything, I have been begging Her to show me the way home. And She gives me only this. This old bone cup. This memory of the Dream that once was my life. I lost you again. All because my mother didn't invite the Dark One to the ceremony of my birth, and that one cursed me forever.

No, Beloved, forgive yourself. No one ever invites the Dark One to the ceremony. No one ever makes that choice. Because the gift She brings will hurt, and no one wants that gift.

I cannot bear to open my eyes. His voice is so close, like dirt in my hair, like the weight of the Sun's first ray, like a Mosquito. I open my mouth, my palms. I see Rhiannon behind my eyes. Still holding out Her hand for me to follow Her into the Dream again, for the first Ritual of Sacrifice. Offering me the choice this time. Do I want to live or not? For he is here. Not hidden in the sounds and the scents of the world—but no, he *is* these things.

I remember. I remember how we made the world together, my Beloved and I, the Ritual of Creation. When we were too close together, She pulled us apart, and in that distance we made space for all the beauty of the world to be born. The Dance of our longing became the limbs of Animals and the roots of Trees, and the colors of our heat became the colors of the Flowers, and the song of our moaning was the song of the Insects and the Monkeys and the Sea. And all of these, our children, Rhiannon took from us and lifted away on the flights of their destinies like young Birds dropped upon the Wind. None of them belonged to us, and none of them we knew for more than a moment, when they moved in the shape between us and then peeled outward toward the Sun. Sometimes we have to walk apart from each other, Beloved, for a long time, but we're still going this way we know. It's still our love story, and the world is still made of it, every day. We walk apart for a time, but see this world—there must be beauty in it somewhere, beauty that we made. It is yours and mine. Somehow we must find each other through it.

No one invites Rhiannon to the ceremony by choice. But She comes, sooner or later. She comes by trickery, by temptation, by the longing for a thread of Silver or a thread of Gold. She comes when you've given up wishing for the thing life promised you. She comes back reminding you, instead, of what you promised.

I wake to the sound of the Urodel River, the other River, the River out of Sirenia that feeds my new husband's people. I wake to Rue's hands as she crawls over me, squirming like a little snail over my belly, with funny, poking hands. I grab her up, laughing, and she makes her wordless sounds of freedom.

And I don't know what to do. But this River, like the River I know, is going on. Though it travels through Sirenia and beneath the palace of the queen who cannot see me, nor can I see her, yet it comes from the same source as the River Golden, and the place it's going to is the same. I had to discover, in the beginning, that the only way off the prison of my balcony was through that dark room, through the palace itself—lest I only gaze out forever, watching over Water I could never touch. Just so, this River like all Rivers, purifying and changing through the Dream of the Swamp, sneaking beneath the Earth like a great Worm of life through all the unseen darkness where roots live and hold, rising up again in channeled streams to irrigate Wye crops and fountain in Wye gardens, winding its mystery past statues and scrolls and palaces and paintings of long-ago peoples, past the Temple and the balconies and through the bodies and lives of the modern people wishing for their lost god, through all their stories of paradise lost, and quenching at last the thirst of the Wye king with the Rose-wounds branching all up his arms to his heart and I forgive him—oh, Micah, I do forgive you—this River, like my very own River, must go on. It must go on through those wounds in all its secret ways, and that's the way. That's the only way we can live, Rue. On and on like the River through all this civilized life, without hope or despair, toward the remembering Sea.

About the Author

Mindi Meltz is the author of two previous novels, *Beauty* and *Lonely in the Heart of the World*. Originally from the coast of Maine, she lives in an off-grid home in the mountains of Western North Carolina with her husband, cats, and goats. She can be contacted through www.mindimeltz.com.